Jacob Rico

CHINK
in the
ARMOR

J.F. ARIAS

Published by

Inspirational Fiction

a division of VMI Publishers
Sisters, Oregon
www.vmipublishers.com
ISBN: 1-933204-23-0
Library of Congress Control Number: 2006929966

Author Contact: JacobRicoseries@msn.com
Printed in the United States of America

In memory of my beloved son and in honor to my
Lord and Savior Jesus Christ who holds him on His lap today.
JONATHAN JAMES ARIAS ESPARZA
Born: February 8, 1984—Ascended to Heaven: February 11, 1984

I extend my deepest gratitude to my wonderful wife,
confidant, lover (and often painful critic!).
Thank you for your prayers, moral support, awesome editing,
and of course, BOUNTIFUL patience.
Thanks go out also to my wonderful friends Peggy and Joyce
who reviewed my manuscript and offered such loving input.
May God's grace overflow in your lives.

AUTHOR'S NOTE: While the characters and events in this work are fictional, I have tried to convey God's mercy and grace in their lives as accurately as possible. Two main sources of inspiration were the books of Acts and Revelation. I pray that this work, as imperfect as it may be, lead (or at least encourage) each reader to examine their relationship with their Creator, come to the saving knowledge of Jesus Christ, and decide to accept the free gift of salvation.

In Christ, J.F. Arias

JACOB RICO had been to hell before, figuratively speaking; but even as his wife prayed for his life, Rico descended into hell…literally. The moment his heart stopped, a shadow on horseback approached. Extending a barely perceptible form of a hand, it reached into Rico's body and pulled fiercely on his soul.

Horror filled Rico's eyes as he peered back at his motionless body. As the horse rose up to the ceiling, Rico had time to see Joey below. He tried to yell at her as he realized that the paper she was waving at the surgeons was the duly notarized Do Not Resuscitate form he had given her only weeks before—too late for a change of mind.

Rico resisted to no avail as the horseman placed shackles on him and rudely jerked him through the hospital floor. They plunged into nothingness for a few seconds and then floated upwards. It wasn't dark like he expected, at least not yet. The horse suddenly broke into a fierce gallop as if racing time itself. Ahead, Rico spotted dark clouds surrounding a black smoking gate. Ear-piercing wails grew ever louder from beyond it. The full force of where he was and its significance finally struck Rico, now screaming for Joey and Jennifer.

The horseman ignored him. Darkness enveloped them. The horseman stopped at the gate and shrieked.

Barely had the double gates creaked open when the screams from within shook Rico with the force of their anguish. He peeked ahead to see flames rising from gigantic pits scattered farther than his eyes could see. Millions of condemned souls turned to see the newest resident. "Mercy!" they cried.

Just before Rico was yanked past the threshold, he noticed four shooting stars streaming toward him from above. He determined that they were angels when one came to a stop, revealed its form, and then struck and broke the chain with a brilliant two-edged sword.

The horseman shrieked with anger. In response, ten hideously ugly creatures arrived almost instantaneously. Rico shuddered. Anger and hatred distorted their faces; grotesque boils covered their bodies. He gasped at the sight of them.

"The man of flesh belongs to Satan," one creature screeched. Others echoed the same in spine-chilling hisses.

Three of the angels engaged the beings with their swords and with words from the Lord of Hosts. "It is not his appointed time, thus saith the Lord of Hosts," trumpeted the one spiriting Rico away.

The creatures hissed with a greater ferocity, spewing hellish spit. One flew by and grabbed Rico's bicep, digging deep with sharp, filthy talons. The angels would have none of that; one struck the creature with an expert swipe of his sword. The creature screamed in agony, evaporated into black smoke, and then reconstituted itself next to one of the flaming pits. The other creatures broke off the battle and flew through the gates, slamming them shut behind them.

The horseman walked alongside the angels for a time, then veered off back to Earth. At first the horse—or whatever it was—just plotted along, then after breaking into a trot the horse and rider vanished in a stream of black particles. Seconds later, it came by with yet another soul.

Rico saw this even as the angels turned toward a gleaming cloud surrounded by iridescent walls. Rico figured he was about to enter paradise, unlike that other soul. Then they stopped near the entrance, encircled him, and assumed defensive stances.

Rico conjured up the courage to speak. "Angels of the Lord Most High." Being an unbeliever, he hadn't a clue how those words could have formed and flowed out of his mouth. "Why don't we go in there before things come back?"

"Thou son of perdition," the tallest and largest angel said. "Knowest not that thy name is not yet written in the Lamb's Book of Life? Yet three hours has the I Am said that thou will remain in this the Third Heaven, then thou shall be returned to flesh until your breath ceases again."

Rico processed what the angel said. "Angels of the Lord Most High," he said, again puzzled, and even annoyed, by the ludicrous words. "What was beyond that double gate over there?"

"Son of the world, that is the gate to the pits of the Lake of Fire. A soul is placed in the pit according to the primary sin it served while yet flesh."

Rico shuddered again. "And...and I was going where?"

"Is it not enough to know that thou had prepared a bed there, having refused the offer of a place at the table of the Most High God?"

Rico had a thousand more questions, but God shut his mouth.

CHAPTER ONE

"THE DARK, handsome knight rode and tamed the wind, forever altering the fate of two men…intertwined destinies yet to unfold…today that knight seeks that which the Prince possesses."

"Uhhh, yes sir, but, again…whom may I say is calling, please?" the Prince's secretary said. She shook off the odd statement. "I don't recognize this number or voice."

"Sorry, thought you were Miriam," Jacob Rico said, feeling the fool for a moment. "I'm just calling about some cash. I haven't called in a while. You must be new. Tell him what I said…well, the knight part, not the money part."

"Sir, I don't know how you came by this number, but it is used only by family members of Prince Michael, so I'll…"

"Exactly, so please…"

"One moment…" The nervous, young secretary put Rico on hold to confer with her boss, who quickly filled her in. "Sir, you will hear a click when I transfer you. I'm sorry for the delay…Jacob."

"Quite all right mum, no harm done. Good day!"

"Well, well, *HAY-cub* old chap," the Prince said, painfully mispronouncing Rico's name. "I figured you would've croaked by now."

"Please, Michael, remember that for you its *JAY-cob*…in English please! You hurt my ears otherwise!"

"Can't be as bad as your attempts at humor, KBE Jacob Rico."

"This insult from a man who passed drama class only because of royal blood," Rico retorted. He remembered that Michael had said Miriam would be leaving. "I guess your new assistant knows who I am now?" The Prince had in fact breezed through an explanation that his friend on the phone was an honorary Knight of the British Empire.

Though Rico found it strange to have his name appended by KBE, a certain air of superiority came over him when he thought about the honor of such a truly rare distinction. One day he might mention it to his soon to be fiancée.

Maybe then she would tell him that she, on the other hand, was a full knight, holding the title of Dame Joey Black by virtue of having dual British and U.S. citizenship. More than likely, she wouldn't say anything, for the sake of modesty—and of course avoiding a bruised male ego. The Prince, who had nominated her name to Parliament, wrongly thought his friend Rico already knew.

Prince Michael owed his life to Rico, who literally dropped from the sky into the middle of a battle during the Iraqi War and saved the day.

The Prince, over the years, made every effort to show his appreciation and the two had grown close. But over time, Rico began calling less and less. He had yet to tell the Prince about the cancer he had been battling for some three years, which was the reason he had distanced himself from him and others he loved. Now another reason presented itself—one not as easy to comprehend as a private fight with cancer—a reason that could sever the relationship permanently.

"Yes, she is new on the job," the Prince replied, again in the precise English that grated on Rico's nerves. For now though, the short silence worried the Mexican-American knight. Maybe they had already grown too far apart.

"All right...*JAY-cob*, seeing as you now only ring me in a crisis, or to borrow money, which one is it today?"

As straightforward as always, Rico noted. He sighed with relief at the playful tone. He overheard the muffled voice of the Prince telling his assistant that the lords would just have to wait, that he had an important call to attend to. Even hearing that, Rico wondered why he couldn't seem to feel secure in this relationship—or any of his other male relationships for that matter.

"Prince Michael, I'm shocked! But it's the latter I'm afraid...I can tell you're busy. Maybe I should call later." Rico thought he really would call back; Prince Michael knew he wouldn't.

There was more dead air. "Well, I need about two-hundred-K," Rico finally said.

"No-can-do...only loan money to family. You understand."

"Right. When can you wire it old chap?"

"Be that as it may, I can only risk one-fifty."

"That's quite all right, one-fifty will have to do. And Michael, please keep it between us," Rico said.

"Jacob, you are not one given to secrecy and this isn't pocket change." The Prince paused and frowned at the other end. "Fill me in on what you're working on. If you haven't noticed, the economy is a disaster. You've paid back the twenty-K from your schooling, of which you didn't give me a clue of how you did, and the fifty-five-K for your security business investment, so I know you're good for it. But at least tell me roundabout what you're doing."

"Seriously, Michael, all I can say is that I'm assembling a team for a big tasking." Rico offered the hollow explanation without a trace of doubt that it would suffice, only because of his friend's character, not his own. The Prince didn't know Rico had closed up shop in San Diego.

It was a confidence borne from a strong bond of friendship—the kind forged from life and death situations. The bearded Latino and the clean cut Englishman made an odd couple that drew attention wherever they hung out, something they had done less frequently over the years. In the beginning, they had managed to stay current on each other's lives. Rico visited him in Europe two or three times a year after leaving the military. As for the Prince, the entourage that followed him made it difficult for him to reciprocate, though he did visit him four years prior in Sacramento on a quasi-official trip. However, the last three years, picking up a phone had been hard enough for Rico, never mind hopping around the globe.

It never occurred to either of them that they were two sad, lonely bachelors who needed to get a life. They were both workaholics; one running from the supposedly joyous life of royalty, expected excellence, and public prominence—the other from fear of rising above the average and gaining any kind of prominence of his own.

The Prince had had many lady friends who had wanted to be more—as one would expect —but none had proven to be of much substance. Rico had had only a couple of prospects prior to Joey, but they didn't work out. Or rather, he caused that to happen as each of the few relationships became too constricting. But recent developments and the incredible, more permanent, lady in his life were changing things for the better. However, Rico wouldn't be Rico if he didn't complicate matters to the point of possibly disintegrating a very good thing.

"Now old chap, I just have to ask. You won't be blowing things up…right?

The out of context question caught Rico off guard. "Uh, no sir, not if I can help it." *I don't think so.*

"Day trading?"

"Well…not with your money at least. Besides, I made a good eighty thou and…"

"And you've lost…?"

"Not more than around fifty of it," Rico mumbled. "But I'll recover it. My broker managed stocks are over the top anyways."

"You just make sure I get my money back before my accountant starts asking questions."

"Yes, Sir."

"Don't call me sir, I work for a living." He waited patiently for Rico to stop his guffawing laughter. "Same bank, same name and routing number?"

"Yep. By what time?"

"Noonish. See you old chap."

"Adios, hombre."

Rico hung up and looked in the mirror. *You? A knight? Without honor maybe. After he finds what some of his money went for…will he still want to see my face?*

A few seconds more of self-reflection was enough to sicken him; the mere thought of the blackness of his heart caused him to quickly close the door to his soul. He would thank God no one could see it, if he believed in make-believe. At that moment, he was quite content to keep the full blackness under wraps, even from himself.

…Rico quietly confirms that all sectors are secure before giving his principal—or client under protection—the green light. The renowned author, speaker, environmental guru, and now leading San Diego mayoral candidate strolls up to the front of the stage and waves enthusiastically.

The crowd goes into a waving, hand clapping frenzy. Rico fights the urge to frown at the brainless worshipping he sees. Instead, he fidgets as he mentally urges his client to get back behind the protective podium as per the agreed upon security protocol; she had been adamant about obeying the rules. Instead, she moves farther away.

A man, clearly not in the same jovial frenzy as the rest of the crowd—a dead give away of some ulterior motive for being there—casually approaches the stage. An intense stare signals an ominous intent. The only slightly concealed handgun confirms Rico's well-honed intuition. Unfortunately, Rico grows lead feet and freezes in place and none of his subordinates are heeding his commands to take the man down. Is it a conspiracy?

Rico watches in horror as his client careens backwards, rounds riddling her body, blood splattering onto his face as he tries to catch her, death visiting her before he could lay the former mayoral candidate gently on to the stage.

"It was not your fault that you couldn't respond," the doctor says. "It was the cancer in your brain…and it was a conspiracy. Oh, and you'll be dead by tomorrow."

Rico awoke to a sweat drenched pillow. The recurring nightmare, a continually morphing dream of an actual event of three years earlier, wasn't losing any of its punch. The nightmare changed each time, yet when it came to his response to the threat that had presented itself, there was a common thread; each and every time Rico appeared helpless, or inept, or both. In reality, he had saved the life of the prominent mayoral candidate, never mind that he draped himself over her because he spotted a gunman that existed only in his imagination. It just happened to coincide with the moment a real sniper had pressed the trigger on his rifle—a most fortunate confluence of events.

It was fortunate for everyone; San Diego *and* California would have gone into greater turmoil at losing the immensely popular candidate—a future gubernatorial shoo in—to an assassin. The growing lawlessness would have surely evolved into complete chaos. Amidst the hoopla and media frenzy about his presence of mind in the heroic act, only one soul knew the painful truth—he got lucky. Unfortunately, the brain cancer—unlike the parts in the dreams where he froze up—had substance outside the realm of nightmares.

Rico popped a comfort pill to force some real sleep. The prospects of a prime-of-life retirement always crept in after each new episode; but then again, the sunset could wait. It didn't matter that the promising gold-lined future was no more; things happen, he reasoned. He sensed that somehow something more important than even great wealth waited for him just over the horizon.

"Dang it … it's ten!" Rico had slept way past his intended waking time on another typical, perfect, San Diego, April morning. He hurried, stuffing things into his overnight bag. Rushing to the checkout desk he instinctively slowed down when he saw a patrol car at the front. He monitored the patrolman exiting the lobby and then approached the desk.

"That Department ought to change their uniform…black's kinda intimidating," Rico muttered to the clerk.

"To thieves, murderers…and terrorist types, I suppose," the surly, blonde-headed, giant ox of a desk clerk said, speaking in a faded New York accent. It sounded like any other New Yorker accent to Rico. He had worked with several New York state types while in the military, but had never really attended to the minor accent nuances. The man glared at all of the five-feet-eight, one hundred fifty-five and a half pounds of Rico, who wore a snug fitting, white silk T-shirt, loose jeans, leather sandals, and sported a full, almost raggedy beard and mustache. Rico's muscles weren't what they used to be, but he was still well-defined and proportioned, with six-pack abs to boot.

The clerk was unimpressed and wondered only about Rico's nationality.

Oops! I gotta keep my mouth shut, Rico thought. "Si, señor. Check out please!" he said, trying to sound businesslike and unsuspicious. The imposing, heavy-set, six-foot plus clerk would be a handful to tangle with if Rico spoke his mind. He didn't appreciate being looked over like a common criminal.

"Room number two-ten. Let's see…no additional charges besides the Internet connection fee of ten dollars. That'll be two hundred and twenty-five even."

"Keep the change," Rico said, handing over $250—a steep price for the dump he chose to stay in to avoid cameras (thanks to a recent emergence of paranoia that came and went.) He left with restrained haste, the clerk still glaring at him.

Rico climbed into his well-kept, classic yellow, F-250, 4x4, extended cab, pickup. He peeled out of the parking lot and quickly hopped onto I-5 east, leaving San Diego in the rearview mirror.

After some two hours of driving, he pulled off at a rest stop for a break. He religiously checked the trailer hitch connection and the tie-down straps securing his Honda ST 1300 motorcycle and Yamaha jet-ski. The rest of his earthly possessions were secure inside the truck camper and trailer, with some junk stuffed between the two recreational crafts. Being semi-retired had its advantages in getting to really use them, even though boredom and loneliness were too often companions. Most everyone else he associated with had a normal job; when they inquired he would claim he was semi-retired or between jobs.

At the I-5 and I-10 interchange, he took I-10 heading east. Exhausted, he considered an overnight stay in Tucson, but instead stopped at a Quick Mart. It was time for sunflower seeds and cola refills—his supposedly original trick for avoiding a deadly nap at the wheel. He popped a palm full of seeds in his mouth and off he went.

Benson, then minutes later Wilcox, Arizona came into view, and then just as quickly faded away, though Wilcox not so speedily—he never sped in Cochise, County. The cops were sticklers and one too many experiences signing tickets had made him leery of getting within five miles of the speed limit. It was a worthwhile trade-off getting to enjoy the beautiful rock formations near Dragoon Road as he neared the speed trap. Several elephant-sized, sedimentary rock boulders sat precariously, touching only inches of the rocks below them—overweight ballerinas balancing on disproportionately small toes, just one ground quiver away from toppling over.

The boulders also offered a plethora of faces for those with vivid imaginations; and Rico had a vivid one. Even if he talked someone through the face lines he was seeing, a normal person wouldn't see what he imagined.

Daydreaming helped him edge out the less than comforting thoughts that crept up and combat the monotony of the encroaching desert. He thought about all he had learned about the county's namesake, the Comanche War Chief, Cochise. A book he had read claimed that the Comanche named Ju was the actual chief of the Comanche tribe—a position mistakenly attributed to Cochise by many historians. Supposedly, Ju was likely the mastermind behind Cochise's strategic moves and great successes on the war path.

I wonder why it took so long for someone to find out the truth. Wonder what it was like traveling around here back then, he mused. *It must have been rough traveling through this country, especially for the women and kids. What makes you think you can go home again. Don't you remember that guy that said you can never go back home? And it wasn't really ever home, anyway. Didn't she sound like she wasn't all that interested the last times you talked?* Those last thoughts popped in before he could cut them off. He wondered if it would ever end.

Aggressively shaking his head, he managed to snap out of it. He popped more seeds in his mouth as he passed the exit sign for Lordsburg, New Mexico. He thought of zipping right through, but his bladder commanded otherwise. So, for the umpteenth time since San Diego, he pulled into a convenience store. With no time to waste, he grabbed a bag of black licorice to counter the saltiness of the seeds and refilled his cola cup.

Deming appeared next on the horizon. Excited about being close to home, he unconsciously overrode the cruise control with subtle, excitement-born pressure on the gas pedal. Much needed rest awaited him in Las Cruces. *If I had traveled this same route before eighteen forty…something.* Rico wasn't good with exact dates. *I would have been in Mexico the whole time.* Epiphanies of such seemingly odd sorts were frequent occurrences—very welcome compared with those other thoughts. Blurting strange things aloud drew puzzled looks or laughter, often both, from bystanders.

His truck would get a break before he did—at least for the short time it took to sign a welcome back ticket that would set him back $350—and only a measly twenty miles from the barn, or five minutes at the ninety-six miles per hour recorded on the laser gun. He had entered the dreaded Safety Corridor, stretches of interstate in New Mexico considered accident-prone areas—and where fines were kindly doubled.

Thirty minutes later, nearing 10 p.m., Rico took the Main Street exit and pulled into Las Cruces and the Ramada hotel parking lot. After checking in and unloading his stuff in the room, he headed for the hot tub, a local paper and a *USA Today* in hand.

"State to take over 50 percent of public schools; even the principals can't read and analyze!" read the *Desert Bulletin's* lead story. Another front page article declared, "The percentage of medically uninsured in the US stopped rising for first time in 20 years, though numbers are still dangerously high." Another read, "US poverty rate reaches 35 percent and is threatening to balloon. Low wage earners are still losing ground and administration critics point to NAFTA, CAFTA and GATT."

The *USA Today* offered no emotional joy ride either. "Congress Accuses Previous Administrations of Gross Negligence: Economic Damage from Waves of Retirements was Completely Avertable," the front page noted. "On the heels of excessive foreign capital control in the US, the wave of retirements broke the proverbial camel's back says a prominent economist and historian."

"All hell has broke lose in the US of A…again," he mumbled to himself as he read about riots and attacks. Mexico found itself in even direr straights and seemed to be on its last legs before collapsing into complete anarchy. *So much for securing our southern border*, he thought.

A pang of sorrow caught him by surprise. In his heart was a growing desire to trace his roots. He felt almost compelled to journey to Mexico to personally contact any living relatives of his natural parents. Now the possibility seemed improbable. Drug lords and other sorts ruled most of the country; complete governmental disintegration seemed inevitable; the acting government in denial of course. The pain soon turned to numbness—a common state of being.

Conspicuously absent was any news on France. Even before Mexico's decline, France began an invisible downward spiral when for years the government refused to heed the international community's call for reform in the protection and justice for young Muslim girls who were being raped. No one seemed to heed the personal, graphic depictions of atrocities of female victimization made by Samira Bellil in her 2002 book "Dans l'Enfer des Tournantes" or "Gang Rape Hell" in English.

On the heel of Bellil's death in 2003 of stomach cancer, an increasing disintegration of France's social structure started in the fall of 2005; nationwide rioting gripped the nation. It represented the European Union's first economic and social disaster. And, in fact, it had become more like an Arab state than anything else; and the strict enforcement of fundamental shiri law was taking hold.

There went Rico's planned return to Paris, too.

A glutton for punishment, he read on. Though things weren't totally bad everywhere, many of the wealthiest around the world were feeling the sting of the world's vacillating economy by way of kidnappings and threats. Joey, the woman he was in Cruces to *visit* would tell him that the Bible had laid out this scenario in text penned thousands of years before. Rico's take on the matter was that the filthy rich were getting what they deserved—just an extension of Darwin's natural order. It was simply the way things were; survival of the fittest…or most desperate maybe.

Rico awoke at 11:00 a.m. "Not again!" he yelled at himself, punching the pillow. He had forgotten to crack the window shades. He always asked for a room with a window facing east so he could wake up to the bright, rising sun, whenever he finally threw off the blankets of course. Alarm clocks were annoying and in his hands easily manipulated to a quiet state, sometimes permanently; wake up calls were an equally rude awakening to reality.

He sighed with relief after signing on to his bank and account. *Thanks old chap.* You threw in the extra fifty-K after all. Hope I don't mess up and leave you hanging. Rico's thoughts wandered off to what was coming. *OK Joey, now to convince you…just as soon as I convince myself.*

CHAPTER TWO

"SOUTH SOLANO," he read from his notes. *Oh yeah, over by NMSU and the deli place.* As usual, he chose the long route, ready to reminisce about old times and places. The place still looked about the same, though the town had grown exponentially. Every time Joey had mentioned that the town was growing too fast, he had chalked it up to exaggeration. In reality, up to three years before it had been growing as fast as the sage brush. Then the economy and water problems brought the growth to an abrupt halt.

Man it's grown, but…it still looks the same. Can I really come back to this place? Maybe I made a mistake? What's this in my gut? I did…I did make a mistake. I should just turn around and ask her to move over there. What made me think I could come home, back to what never was? This little piece of…oh, man. Maybe, just maybe…Joey…

"She's waiting for you," said a little voice smack in the middle of his countless thoughts.

Waves of competing memories and feelings, present and past, poured in again—hurt, warmth, even some giggles—all muddled together. He couldn't tell which were real, highly exaggerated, fantasy, or creative adaptations of the past.

After Rico's adoptive parents' deaths—which followed some ten years after his natural parents' deaths—he made firm plans to leave this sorrow-filled town. He had grown up in various foster homes, experiencing some really good and some really bad times. Somehow, he developed a knack for reading. He devoured books of every genre. Specially selected titles offered by a caring teacher gave him the insight with which to mentally construct what his natural parents *must* have been like.

Oddly enough, not only did reading serve as a great escape, but it proved a saving grace in helping Rico pass the GED exam on his first try. He had no choice but to take it after he was kicked out of high school in the tenth grade for having better things to do; excessive truancy was the official reason. The lack of effort at offering some guidance, counseling or alternative discipline let him know instantly where he stood in the administration's priority and value chart. This gave rise to his first out-and-out explosion of anger—and his first visit to court and jail for vandalism of the school grounds and misdemeanor assault of a vice-principal.

Out of the blue, Rico joined the military on his 17th birthday, forging his guardian's signature on the waiver. It was a complete surprise to those who knew him; Rico and military discipline were guaranteed to gel about as well as peanut butter and jalapeños, they joked. Nevertheless, he managed to grab a hefty bonus by signing up for the Air Force Security Forces. It was enough of a bonus that he sweet-talked a bank manager to accept it as a down payment and take a risk on him so he could buy his then brand-spanking, almost new, pick-up truck. The dealer threw in a camper shell in a moment of patriotism.

Finally, he had escaped the pueblito. Twenty years later, with not too much more in the way of material belongings, he was back. To what and for what he didn't know.

More than an hour past his intended arrival time, he drove in to a parking slot directly in front of the large window to JB Martial Arts Academy. Black-belts-to-be were all busy at work. Joey Black taught the disciplines of the legendary Bruce Lee to youngsters and other competitive types. Rico watched through the window. He recognized the techniques, being well-versed in the martial arts himself. Not that he was gung ho about pursuing belts and such. Navy Seal instructors had trained his Delta Force detachment on many specific, very effective neutralizing techniques. On these, he focused and mastered because they meant the difference between life and death in the field. Otherwise, he tended toward the lazy side in learning anything extra, bodybuilding notwithstanding.

On the other hand, what Joey taught to her second degree black belts and above he wouldn't recognize in the least—if he were to see them working out. For some reason she hadn't mentioned this other discipline to him, or more likely, he hadn't paid attention. Either way, she carried out that training more discreetly.

Whatever Joey did, she did to extremes, and in her former military career she had sought out the most effective means of self defense for combat environments. She became aware of a discipline called Krav Maga and unabashedly pursued a semi-retired Mossad agent to train her. The Mossad, the Israeli's intelligence department, developed the world renowned discipline for close quarter hand-to-hand, unarmed self-defense techniques for use mainly in combat and high security environments. Several moves were intended to be lethal. Joey caught on quickly and soon reached Level III B.

Joey only taught Krav Maga to hand-picked students who were also willing to take an oath to never use it in sport fighting or street fighting, except as a last resort. It was just as well, because the Bruce Lee forms had served them well enough to earn them first place in tournament after tournament.

Not wanting to interrupt the class, Rico climbed back into his truck to wait. After about an hour—around 2:30 p.m.—he woke up to loud tapping on the window. Joey woke him just in time; the interior temperature had reached nearly 130 degrees. The truck had run out of gas—thanks to Rico's propensity to test the lower limits of the red zone on the fuel gauge—and, of course, the air conditioner had shut off.

"Jacob, que fregados estas asiendo?" Joey exclaimed as she pulled him out, giving him a concerned hug, or was it a very affectionate one? Loosely translated, "What the heck are you doing?"

"I, I guess getting overheated…waiting for you. I mean…I, uh…didn't want to inter…" Rico said. He was trying to remember if he had ever felt Joey's love for him radiate as it did just then. He was moved, and a little surprised, because he had noticed less and less enthusiasm in her voice during their phone chats—or was it his own negativistic feelings?

The truth was Joey had all but given up hope in any long term relationship with Jacob Rico, especially with all the lavish attention she was receiving from a handsome, wealthy, and refreshingly uncomplicated businessman—a seminary-bound deacon at her church. She had wrestled intensely with her fleshly desires and the promising possibility of a well-off life along with the prospects of a ministry partner. And the spiritual unity promised a tranquil, God-fearing home, maybe with some miracle babies.

But the days of anguish, pondering how to tell Rico about her spiritual and romantic conflicts, had ended days before and given way to peace as God revealed His choice for her. Rico was her assignment—and cross to bear. The Holy Spirit guided her to Hosea, a book she had yet to read. "My ways are not your ways," God told her.

No kidding, she had thought. The concept of how God telling Hosea to marry a prostitute and telling her to marry Rico related was lost on her. If God was in it, she would make it, she knew…somehow. And besides, Rico still held her heart captive.

"Well, I'm kind of flattered anyway, but I know what you meant," Joey said in Spanish, her cheeks flushed, mostly from the sun.

"Joey, what's with the Spanish?" Rico said. *And…kind of flattered?* he thought with some concern. His thoughts weren't completely drowned out while Joey went on and on with small talk in Spanish. They meandered into the studio building arm in arm, she oblivious to the thoughts she had provoked. He forced himself to brush the insecure thinking aside and enjoy the new kind of affection Joey, short for Josephina Erin Ysleta, was showing. She had often complained about what her parents could have possibly been thinking by torturing her with such a name. Rico always had a good time riling her up about it; secretly, he too thought the name dorky. Regardless, she knew how to hug.

"That's a rude question," Joey said, a little put-off about the Spanish comment.

They stood in an elegant, but simple, eight-by-ten foot, greenhouse type of enclosed porch. Apparently, the woman had a green thumb. Another surprise. Joey held the inside lobby door to the dojo open for him.

"Well…last time we got into it about our heritage, you were negative about me calling you a Latina. You were all of an Irish gringa, remember?"

He cringed, waiting for a tart retort as he edged inside. Not that there was anything she could have said to ruin the sweet aroma of fresh-baked, cinnamon dipped buñuelos—a Mexican treat akin to Indian Fry Bread—nor the equally pungent scent of the freshly chopped, blazing-hot, Mesilla Valley-grown jalapeno peppers. His lady was going all out for him he thought and was glad he rated such efforts.

The truth was he had arrived two days ahead of schedule—truly an aberration—and she was actually preparing enchilada plates for a church fundraiser. He'd just have to pay like everyone else.

"Yes, I was going through…an identity crisis. And…I didn't like how you said it anyway," she said in a near whisper.

"Done Blondie?" Rico asked, still cringing and waiting for a rougher response.

"As a matter of fact…yes," she answered calmly, surprising even herself. *God's grace sure is incredible*, she thought. "Some people do make changes. It takes time to build castles you know. Rome wasn't built in a day."

Some people? What is she getting at, he thought. "Yes, that's true," Rico said. "But normally people only make changes because of a traumatic, life-shaking event…or two. So I've read."

There came his psychobabble.

He wondered how it was that the two military campaigns they had suffered through could not have accomplished that change—experiences, which by any sane standard of measure would qualify as mind shattering and traumatic. Though they didn't cross paths in Bosnia-Herzegovina, as they did later in Iraq, they nonetheless experienced the same anguish from what they saw and experienced—he a combatant and she, at that period in her life, a struggling investigative reporter documenting what the combatants inflicted on each other, and innocents, in the killing fields.

"I, I've changed, too," Rico said.

"Put silk on a goat and it's still a goat," she mumbled.

"I resemble part of that remark. I'm…a ram," he said, feigning injury.

"A ram? I see…Still a goat."

He considered upping the ante on this little game they frequently played. He could brag to her that he was called the Big Shrink back in San Diego. He had tons of stories to tell about numerous well-to-dos, including some celebrity types. On the word of an acquaintance, former Mr. Universe Ty Chandler, some big wigs had given Rico an opportunity to handle their security matters.

Of course, he'd leave out the fact that those who hired him fired him within a week because he told most of them that they suffered from post situational narcissism. A monthly psychology periodical related to security, which Rico read religiously, described the effects worship, adulation and plain gawking had on public personalities over time. PSN would develop over time and cause many formally thoughtful, sharing people to become "Love, Worship, and Serve Me" monstrosities.

To the amazement of his agents and staff, the majority of clients that fired him called to rehire him after reflecting on what he had said to them. It shook them that he had had the audacity to say it at the risk of losing a quite generous contract. Rico's hired guns and the clients' friends and family noticed amazing changes in those same clients. After news of his special skill made it around the Hollywood circuit, Rico had to turn down offers.

Of course, he didn't recognize that his outward expression of anger or righteous indignation at these clients had worked out by nothing less than a miracle. Never mind that a certain degree of PSN had sprouted in him. And did he ever call Chandler to thank him for the business, the one person that would likely offer him a Biblical mirror? No. Why would he hang with a man that spoke incessantly about Jesus Christ?

Either way, right now Joey had him. So he kept his mouth shut.

Was he just a well dressed goat? He grinned halfheartedly, his mind mulling over the thought all the while racing back to San Diego, Bosnia and other places. It wasn't as if he wasn't offering every ounce of resistance. Of course living in one world is complicated enough for most people; living in two, or more, can be difficult to manage.

Rico, too antsy to stand still even with a beauty in his arms, roamed about while Joey shadowed. He was sure she had a maid; the kitchen in her London flat never looked this tidy.

He strolled into the dojo training room, a very large converted living room with a natural pine polished wood floor. He looked around at the walls expecting to see plaques and her military decorations hanging all about. Instead, he noticed a plexi-glass partition subdividing the room. A small portion was dedicated to what seemed to be a mini museum, the other for violent punching and kicking. Rico wondered whether this was really a karate studio, or an art studio.

The wall was lined with sculptures of all kinds. Some looked like a beginner created them. He didn't say anything.

"I see you like variety. These various artists sure make nice contrasts. But I don't see what your collecting theme is."

"A single artist, actually. You just might get to meet her. And the different mediums *is* her theme."

Rico just nodded. It was very strange to him not to see her military medals or any other sort of memorabilia anywhere. For some reason the artist, whomever that was, had preeminence.

"Ah! Still the consummate wanderer, aren't you?" Joey said softly.

If that's not the pot calling the kettle black…! "Yea…as a matter of fact, I've been reading very disturbing things lately. Like…"

Joey wouldn't get a word in for a long time if she let him gain steam. "Wait, I'm sorry," she interrupted, putting a finger on his lips. "Before we discuss any serious issues, let's go finish our teas. Then, I'll tell you about my most recent life-altering event."

She drew him close as they walked and gave him a peck on the cheek.

"I came all the way from San Diego for *that*!" he bemoaned in mock heart-brokenness.

Joey smiled, and taking the cue kissed him squarely and firmly on the lips. Rico's ear-to-ear, little-boy grin told her that even after all this time she was looking at the same gentle-hearted, quirky, mercurial best friend she had learned to love. A bright red blush reappeared on her cheeks.

When they first met, she thought he was a good yarn spinner, like many other British and American military types she had interviewed or otherwise dealt with. After hearing him recount what he had survived to make their meeting possible, she would not hear it from his lips again. Joey, then still a reporter with only an American Hero story interest in him at the time, concluded he had gotten it off his chest once and for all. Very quickly, she could tell he wasn't a macho man like the others, at least in private conversation. She decided to take a risk and follow the unfamiliar, romantic tug in her heart. The story side of her interest didn't pan out as well.

And now, here they were. The sense of warmth Rico felt in Joey's embrace, and the way she pierced deep into his soul with a love he didn't think possible, blew him away. The reunion exceeded his wildest expectations. During the whole trip home, he had verbally talked himself into believing in a great welcome home; there was definitely no let down. The lukewarm, kind-of-nice-to-see-you reception he had subconsciously dreaded never materialized.

Several minutes passed before either soaring heart ventured to speak.

"We've got lots to talk over, Joey," he whispered, squeezing her hand.

"Yes, we do," she agreed. "But first, I have a surprise for you."

Joey's eyes grew wide and her smile broadened. She led Rico to the back of the studio, through a door to the left of the kitchen, and down a short flight of stairs to one of the few basements in all of New Mexico—in reality a former wine cellar. He let himself think for a second that he was going to get lucky again after some three years of involuntary celibacy. Remembering his physical state he nearly panicked; multiple ways to excuse himself raced through his mind.

Once downstairs, Joey opened one of two side-by-side doors that led to two separate spacious bedrooms. Rico noticed the neatness again—a trait that eluded him—and the rustic, Mexican-style furniture. The colors and decor offered a definitely feminine, warm feeling—a direct contrast to the rough and tough woman he remembered; she had changed.

For a second he wondered if that was Joey's big surprise. Then he noticed something hidden under the blankets on what he thought was her bed; a long lump hinted of a person underneath. Before Rico could hazard a guess, fingers appeared and the cover inched down the person's face. He was speechless. In front of him was a face the likes of which he had seen before in real life, and then in on-going waking nightmares…memories of real faces in Bosnia. Thoughts of romance vanished immediately.

The person was clearly a woman. Other than that, he pained to see beyond the hollow eyes and wrinkled and sagging skin that revealed the bone structure underneath. He made every effort to disguise the nauseating feeling that had instantly and uncontrollably welled up in his gut. Rico was about to blurt out an excuse to head back upstairs when Joey silenced him, putting a finger on his lips. It was too late. The stranger on the bed had heard them and covered up again.

"Joey, is that you, Sis?" the stranger asked before uncovering her face again.

Sis? Rico wondered.

Before Joey could respond, the woman forced her eyes open and shivered as she stared at Rico.

"Is he here for me? Did they find me?" she cried.

Quickly, Joey sat by her and cuddled her.

"It's OK, Michelle," Joey tenderly whispered in her ear. "This is that special man I've mentioned."

Immediately, Michelle gained control of her sobbing and grabbed the tissues Joey offered. After what seemed like a long time to Rico, Michelle said weakly, "So this is your knight in shining armor, Joey?"

Joey was caught by surprise. She thought that her sister had not comprehended the little things she had shared about Jacob…or anything else for that matter.

Joey and Jacob looked at each other with awkward, sheepish looks.

"He sure seems a little shorter then seven feet tall, Joey," Michelle added.

Joey quickly interjected, "Well, I…I never said he was seven feet tall, Michelle. But…yes, this is the person I've mentioned in passing once or twice."

"Michelle, this is Jacob."

"Jacob this is my…sister…Michelle."

"Sister?" was all Rico could say, holding his stomach. The face he was looking at had no resemblance to the roundish, freckled, and usually bubbly face of his girlfriend Joey. The inviting full lips were absent as well.

"Jacob," Michelle said slowly with a labored breath. "You are rather short for a knight."

Joey looked at Jacob for second and burst out laughing. She had expected some profound, serious comment. Rico's face softened.

Michelle's hint of wit and candor, and especially the bright, piercing blue eyes pointed to the two women sharing the same genes. They were identical twins in fact. Many weeks later, a carbon-copy of Joey would begin to emerge from the emaciated, near-skeleton now in front of them.

Rico resolved to look past her present appearance and peered deep into her eyes. He immediately determined that she was definitely in Joey's blood line.

Joey shared how she found the sister she didn't know she had. Michelle listened intently—though sometimes unable to will her eyelids open—because she hadn't heard the story of her adventure that landed her in New Mexico, wherever that happened to be. It was in the U.S. she was sure.

An ambassador friend of Joey's had been at a London hospital visiting a friend. To his surprise, he saw someone, whom he thought looked like Joey, in the psych ward hallway, being led by an orderly. Because of his diplomatic credentials, hospital officials told him everything they knew, which was basically nothing. She was another Jane Doe among many in the overloaded ward.

He asked them for permission to visit with her because he was sure he knew her. Clearly, this was not his friend Joey, but there was something telling about her; especially when she turned and stared right at him. There was no way it could be Joey, mostly because she wouldn't risk being caught in dreary London again; and why would she be in the psych ward? But there had to be a connection.

Joey caressed Michelle's hand as she continued whispering the story to Rico.

That's when Mark, Joey's friend and U.S. Ambassador to England, contacted her in Las Cruces; asking strange questions. To answer them Joey had to reach deep into her mind, shuffling past some still tender memories. She faintly remembered playing frequently with another child when she was little; just a close friend she was sure.

Mark decided to investigate the matter further anyway, his gut gnawing at him. It occurred to him that Joey didn't know why he was asking such probing questions; considering he was sure he knew every detail of her life, why had she seemed so uncomfortable?

According to hospital officials, Jane Doe was an escapee from a mental asylum. They would find out later that she had been at the asylum only six weeks. Some days after her escape from the asylum, they found her disoriented and half-starved in an alley. That's how she ended up in that hospital's psych ward.

Her medical records stated that during lucid moments she would insist that she was being pursued by Irish and English organized crime gunmen. Doctors considered her a probable schizophrenic and had yet to find relatives to claim her. They proceeded medicate her pending a scheduled transfer back to the asylum two days later.

Getting her out of that asylum would have been very complicated; and Mark worried that if her delusions weren't delusions, someone would see to it to make it impossible, one way or another.

The ambassador bent some rules and broke others to declare her a missing U.S. citizen. He convinced the doctors that he had contact with the sole surviving relative by providing a blood sample from Joey and a certified power of attorney for transport. By virtue of Mark's claim, a judge ordered the hospital to provide a blood sample from their patient, proving once again that navigating a large bureaucracy is easier with official credentials.

"Thank God it matched and they accepted the power of attorney," Joey chirped. "He had her out hours before the deadline."

The ambassador immediately took Michelle on a medivac flight to New York, just in case any discrepancies on a document were discovered. From New York, they flew to El Paso. Except for the medics on the flights, no one else had set eyes on her, and then only saw part of her face. Mark had made sure of this because some of the gibberish and apparent nonsense Michelle blurted out when coherent actually mirrored intelligence briefs on European Union organized crime activities he was privy to—information so sensitive that no one outside the British intelligence communities of M5 and M6, including the prime minister, knew about. A CIA link to a M5 mole kept him abreast of serious developments.

Strangely enough, the hospital officials never contacted the ambassador when a pair of interested persons, two Irishmen, seeking information about a patient fitting Michelle's description showed up two weeks later.

Rico found the recounting very interesting. Not sure of the substance of what Joey had just shared, Rico nonetheless was glad to hear this apparent twin would remain in hiding. He would definitely help keep things under wraps, though not for the most altruistic of reasons. The wicked thought came and went so quickly he didn't have time to feel guilty about conceiving such a thing; he envisioned using the situation to his advantage later.

"That's incredible, Joey," Rico finally interjected.

"Yep. I found my sis. And she's doing great. Michelle should be out and about in about four to five months. Thanks to two friends, one an RN and one a med student, who dove right in and helped me out."

Rico barely heard what Joey said. "Michelle," Rico said in a gentle tone, leaning close to but not looking directly at her, "...about that medication they gave you. Is it out of your system yet? Is there any lasting effect to your mind that you can tell?" He felt embarrassed the moment the words left his mouth.

"Jacob, what kind of question is that?" Joey chastised under her breath.

"No, no Joey. Don't be upset," Michelle said, weakly squeezing her hand. "The friend said…that there would probably be some after-effects from the drugs. But with a slow, quiet recovery period I would probably manage well." She labored to take in a deep breath and blinked slowly before continuing.

"And to answer Jacob's reasonable question, I would say that I have night-mares. But I think…" She narrowed her eyes as she thought about what she wanted to say, "…that most of what I dream about is based on reality. Somebody *was* following me. It was almost like they just wanted to scare me for some reason. Then I started getting faint recollections of nasty beatings and dingy places…images flash in front of me when I'm fully awake."

Joey and Jacob looked at each other and cringed; how well they could re-late.

"I think you two have a lot to talk about," Rico said. "If you don't mind, I'll go upstairs and watch some TV. I'll see you both in a bit." Rico kissed Joey on the forehead and turned to leave.

"Hey, how about me, Mr. Knight?" Michelle asked.

He hesitated slightly and then kissed her gently on her sunken cheek. His stomach didn't handle it well.

"She didn't exaggerate about your kind heart," Michelle added. "I have a sense about those things. And Joey had it right…about your looks, too."

"Oh, no…Michelle! Now his head's not gonna fit through the door!" Joey said.

That was the Joey that Rico remembered. As he went upstairs, he heard a mini spat between the two. Not finding a TV slightly annoyed him. *Who doesn't have a TV? She must be hurting for money*, he guessed.

Actually, she was in between sets. The old clunker had just been thrown out and she was waiting for a good deal on a new one. She was tight on money for sure, but only when it came to spending on material things for herself. Something *not* typical of the Joey he remembered.

Rico went outside and grabbed a soda from the refrigerator in his truck. After ten minutes, he felt uneasy about staying upstairs and reluctantly went back downstairs. Joey still looked a little embarrassed.

"It's time to go back to the motel," Rico announced.

"Why? You're gonna pass up this wonderful place for a hotel?" Joey said in Spanish.

"Well, I could do the Hispanic thing and camp out like family," he said, part question, part comment. "But I don't think you have enough room."

"Well, I hear Joey has a nice queen-size bed," Michelle offered without thinking.

"Michelle, hush up!" Joey turned rosy again looking at Rico.

"I see," Rico said, also in Spanish.

"What?" Michelle asked excitedly, though still groggy.

Joey and Jacob waved the question off. Rico wasn't necessarily ready to mention that Joey and he had not slept together in almost three years, and then it had been the one and only time. It was a strange coincidence back then when just days after Joey had visited and stayed through the night in his bed she had accepted Christ into her life. He was too busy the whole week to answer one particular message she had left on his machine—one where she mentioned her new faith, and her decision about a solely platonic relationship from then on...*if* he was still interested.

That was the same week he was told he had brain cancer. Since he was rather put off by the reason she was unilaterally changing their relationship so drastically—just when he had experienced the good life again—it made it easy to use the situation to cover up his health status. She never guessed during the years that followed in their long distance relationship that his cooler emotional state was actually to protect her. Why expose her to the devastation the cancer was expected to wreak? And the timing of being denied the pleasure of female company, in intimate ways, worked out strangely well.

"Never mind," Rico muttered. "A motel will work just fine."

"What! What's wrong with my sister, pal? She's not good enough for you?" an angered sister asked.

Joey and Rico laughed.

"No doubt in my mind any more...she's definitely a Black," Rico said. "Well, let's change the subject...please," Rico said. "I don't mind staying here at all...but...hey wait a minute! Michelle you understand Spanish, don't you?" Rico asked after realizing Joey and he had code switched and had been speaking Spanish.

Michelle nodded with her last ounce of energy and fell soundly asleep, a slight grin on her face.

Rico looked at Joey with some concern, thinking of checking Michelle's pulse. She motioned that her sister was fine.

"I do have to get my junk from the hotel," he said. Eager to avoid any more talk about the still tender topic Michelle had brought up, Rico started out the door. Joey grabbed his hand gently.

"Hon, may I tag along?"

Rico couldn't figure out what gave him goose bumps more: the fact that she wanted to be close again, or her making his standing crystal clear when she called him *hon*. He tried hiding his grin.

Before that moment Joey hadn't considered that he harbored any doubts about his standing.

CHAPTER THREE

AFTER PICKING up Rico's belongings at the hotel, the freshly reacquainted Rico and Joey drove to the I-10 rest stop overlooking Las Cruces. In earlier years, this had been the Crucens' version of Lover's Lane. Like many other teenagers of his era, Jacob Rico had some interesting, fond memories about the place.

Since then, the greatly improved lighting and frequent police patrols scared off lovers' plans for secret romantic rendezvous, but also the out of control drug crowd. Now it was of more interest to reminiscent middle-agers just wanting to view the city lights and check out the gigantic, welded scrap metal roadrunner sculpture that faced the valley below.

Right then Rico only had eyes for Joey. The view of the sprawling desert town and the awe inspiring Organ Mountains—part of the Rocky Mountains—as spectacular as they were for sure, just didn't hold a candle to her. And now there was this peculiar twinkle in her eyes he couldn't put a finger on. It was more than having discovered she had a twin sister, or that he had arrived; something more was involved.

He stared and stared at her as they strolled down the winding, rocky path to one of the benches. It didn't help his attempt to be charming and debonair when he stepped on a loose rock, lost his balance and rolled down off the edge of the path. Luckily, he didn't whack his head on one of the many rocks lining the sides of the arroyo, the Spanish language equivalent of a rushing water wash out. But the many whimpered expletives he let out gave account to the number of prickly pear needles that speared him as he tumbled down the hill.

Joey resisted laughing, successful only until it was clear her honey was for the most part all right. She caught her breath before yelling down, "Jacob, are you all right?"

The amount of cursing she heard confirmed he was not seriously injured.

She wondered how someone who abhorred foul language could blurt it out so easily.

"I'll be right back with the first aid kit. I know where you keep it." Fortunately, he had stuck his key chain onto her belt. Hurrying to the truck she quickly located the well-stocked kit under the passenger's seat.

Jacob, you're either a paramedic, prepared or paranoid. A defibrillator, survival kit, fire extinguisher, emergency radios, gee whiz! And this…a bag full of pre-paid cell phones? She hurried back to Rico fully intending to ask about them. He was already waiting at one of the table areas. She prepared the alcohol, cotton balls and tweezers, laying them on the table. She quickly forgot to ask about the phones.

"I just had an epiphany," Rico said as he climbed back up the hill. "Now I…"

"Epiphany? My, my, aren't we getting sophisticated in our old age," she teased.

"As I was *about* to say…" he grumbled. "Now I remember why I left the stinking desert. Everything sticks you in the bu…OUUUCH…behind." Rico rubbed where Joey had tweezed a piece of cactus shrapnel. "A teeny, weenie bit gentler, please. You're more of a pain than the pricks."

"And you were Special Forces? A baby like you?" Joey said, no hint of humor in her tone.

"Well, I wasn't really in the Special Forces, remember? I was attached to Delta Force, and happened to go on missions. But, I was tough back then. Remember? Even got a Purple Heart I'll have you know." Blabbing senselessly was a good distraction.

"For wha…don't tell me…for the splinter in your thigh after flying into the shepherd's shack?"

She really was a pain. Now she even made the improbable safe parachute landing he had pulled off that time in Iraq seem so humdrum—never mind that he fell from an aircraft thousands of feet high and was tossed about by sixty plus mile-per-hour winds. Why, again, did he like and love this woman?

As for Joey, she didn't remember seeing a scar on him the last time they went swimming—which was not long after his discharge from the military. The nasty shoulder scar left by the bullet from the San Diego civilian incident didn't count. At least she pretended that it didn't mean anything. When she had heard the news she had almost fallen apart with worry, but he didn't have to know.

"That time in Iraq must have been the first time out of the office for you, I bet," she said.

"It's in a private place…can't go there."

"Too bad! I'm done with your back. You can sit on the table then and enjoy the view," she said, pretending to put away the materials.

"OK … OUUUCH!" Rico yelped as the prickly souvenirs on his bottom announced their presence.

"OK, blasted, sadistic woman," Rico muttered in Spanish. He leaned on the table, holding himself up with his arms and yelping quietly.

Joey continued extracting prickles until she couldn't see any more. Fortunately for Rico, the cactus didn't yet have fruit; the tiny thistles on them were tougher to find and pull.

"Stop laughing, woman…it wasn't funny."

"Actually…" she said, tears trailing down her round, sparkling cheeks. "…it was *really* funny."

Rico murmured sheepishly, "OK, Joey, but not that funny."

Joey's laughter subsided. She looked at him for a split second and attempted an expression of sincere sympathy, but burst out laughing again. "Yes, it was!" She could hardly breathe.

Rico gave in and they both laughed, hugging and squeezing each other. As they chatted, Joey used up every single tissue in her purse. Still needing a wipe, she used Rico's T-shirt sleeve.

"That's a little weird, Joey. No quiero tus mocos mujer!" He calmly removed some remaining pricks from his arms.

Joey just nodded as she continued drying tears and snot.

"I do hope you plan to wash it for me," he added seriously.

Rico gingerly raised himself up to sit atop the concrete table as Joey snuggled closely on the seat below.

They sat quietly and admired the incredible view of the valley and high rising mountains.

Rico leaned over and peppered Joey with tender kisses on her lips and glowing cheeks. The wholeness he felt didn't stop the "what ifs" that began to assault him. *What if I hadn't left? Would I still be married now if I hadn't? Would I have children going to high school now? Would I at least have a couple of real friends?* Other such thoughts passed in a blur, and he felt disoriented. The truth was that he had many real friends that he kept at arm's length.

To Joey he appeared peacefully mesmerized by the green Rio Grande Valley and the majestic, purple shaded Organ Mountains towering above the horizon. The sun, partially blocked by clouds and dropping closer to the horizon behind them, lit the mountain face so perfectly that post cards could do the view no justice.

Joey was surprised by the vibrancy she felt as she viewed her adopted city from a newly altered perspective; she hugged the source, raising her arms above her head and wrapping her arms around his neck. Las Cruces, New Mexico, a dry speck of a city as far as any New Yorker, Angelino, or former Londoner like her would be concerned, but to her it was a peaceful, almost heavenly place.

Her interest about the town, located on a former inland sea and established around 1848, was first piqued by one of Rico's first letters years before, where he mentioned in passing his boyhood hometown. Having seen deserts of different sorts, she of course had conjured a very uninviting image at first. But Rico, being a part of the equation, added another dimension to it.

She broke the silence with a whisper in his ear, "Remember when I paid you a visit when you were here visiting too?"

"Yup. I clearly remember the standard, 'What in the hell is this dry, dead, dreary place' look on your face. Bet you thought I'd lied to you, huh?"

Joey didn't answer. Instead, she snuggled closer. "How's Michael?" she asked softly, not wanting to ruin the moment, but anxious to catch up on things.

"Michael?"

"*Prince* Michael, silly."

"Oh, *that* Michael." *What's bringing him to mind? Last time we visited him they bit at each other's heels the whole time?* Rico looked at her with suspicion. "We're getting rather informal aren't we?"

"Last time we talked he asked me to call him Michael. Is that okay?"

Say what? "He's never told me that…when was this? And I thought you two were like…well…like cats and dogs still."

"Naw, mended fences almost three years ago…paid him a visit even."

Rico eyed her with more intense suspicion. "Didn't mention that either. I'll have to chat with that man about certain things…soon."

"So anyway…when's the last time you talked to him," she said, anything to interrupt his gaze.

His heart skipped a beat. *If I tell her days ago, she'll ask what we talked about. If on the other hand I said a long time ago, and she talked to him soon, she would learn otherwise.*

"Um, two days ago actually."

"Oh, good! And you guys talked *about*…?"

There she went. Was she playing nosy reporter, or nosy girlfriend?

"Doing great, still single. Busy as usual. Didn't discuss much."

She smiled at hearing her only English friend was doing well. "It's been a while…think I'll call him, maybe this week," Joey murmured.

"Good…good," he said. *Just great!* he thought.

Some time passed before another word interrupted the caressing, gently squeezing, and reminiscing couple.

"Hey, handsome, give me a real taste of those lips," Joey said, breaking the silence again.

"Well, ok. *If I have to,*" Rico whined, but obliged.

"Um…uh…I…uh…think you ought to check up on your sister," he murmured reluctantly through the lip-lock.

"Uh, yeah…good idea," she said, regaining her composure. She had been sure that in three years she had grown beyond being overwhelmed by certain emotions, or least to be able to *manage* them better. Now she was face-to-face with the whole truth; reading and grasping intellectually is easy. On the other hand, the real world maturing process of being tested with *this* kind of fire, and still walking upright before God already hadn't proved quite as decisive; especially when the temptation was in the now and tightly wrapped in her arms, not tucked away many, many safe miles away. She offered a whispered prayer of repentance and thanks as she searched her purse for the cell phone.

Michelle answered the phone Joey had taped to the headboard by saying "answer" into it. She said she was doing fine.

Having had time to rebalance, Joey thought it wise to leave. "We best head back," she said in Spanish. Without hesitation, Rico nodded in agreement, making her give him a look.

"What?" he asked.

"Nothing." She walked on in a silent huff. *Am I so chunky now that I'm so unappealing to you,* she wondered.

What did…? Now I remember why I'm not married, Rico pondered, shaking his head and following in thin-ice-silence.

Fortunately, Joey had grown much in the forgiving department and soon warmed up to conversation again. Rico considered the night and day change and worried about a possible bipolar disorder, but he couldn't have missed it all this years.

Back at Joey's place he was quickly distracted. Rico rolled out his sleeping bag on the dojo floor where the two cuddled and talked, watching the passing traffic through the large unobstructed window—a help for the two to behave.

Rico asked about the girls who always answered the phone. They were in Albuquerque at a tournament. Joey talked non-stop from there sharing minute details about the girls—even after he had crashed out promptly at nine.

She felt comforted that they were actually of interest to him. At least one obstacle to a deeper relationship was set aside. He lay asleep on his back. Her head rested on his chest, eyes and mind wide awake. Softly, she began humming, then singing, an old-time Gaelic poem, Saint Patrick's Breastplate.

> I bind unto myself today
> The strong Name of the Trinity,
> By invocation of the same
> The Three in One and One in Three.

Finished with her anointed singing—she had just sung the long and difficult song from memory though she had sung it only once before—the love struck Joey listened intently to the rhythmic beat of Rico's heart. For over an hour she listened, absorbing the warmth of his being. Since they had not shared the same bed after that one confusing time, she didn't know that by now a nightmare should have had his heart racing. She felt only peace in him.

Very tired but happy, she rose to check on Michelle and then prayed *fervently* for help to stay downstairs and climb into her own bed.

CHAPTER FOUR

RICO TRIES not to fire his assault rifle by removing his finger off the trigger. It doesn't matter. The rifle has a life of its own and rounds fire on automatic mode. Children's wide-eyed faces stare at him in astonishment. Then they look down and, holding their stomachs, drop to the floor.

Sometime during the night another of Rico's increasingly frequent, cold-sweating, nightmares descended on him—the ones he had told Joey were long gone and moments before had seemingly been delayed only by the force of her melodic voice. Like David's harp did for King Saul.

He awoke and felt somewhat comforted by the reality that surrounded him in Joey's place. There was an unexplainable sereneness in the place; a strange sense of safety. It was as if he belonged there. Never in his whole life had he ever experienced this feeling. But it scared him. What if he disrupted Joey's seemingly wonderful life?

He went to the kitchen, drank some water and popped a sleeping pill. Ignoring his conscience that begged him to get help, he was soundly asleep minutes later. Two nightmares a night—now—meant nothing. Every vet went through this phase…didn't they?

"Hey, sleepy head," Joey said with what Rico thought was a chirpier-than-legal bounce. "Breakfast is waiting."

To her this counted as their twentieth time rising together, in the same room at least—no doubt Rico wasn't counting—and things seemed promising for many more, in a more intimate and official capacity, of course.

Never mind all that, he just wanted to sleep.

"Oh, woman, way too early. Besides, I don't eat breakfast," Rico answered in Spanish, covering his head to block the sun beams that bathed him as Joey pulled the blinds aside on the east facing window. East facing like he liked.

"Doesn't matter to me lazy bones, but when Rosangelica and Tina come through that door in about fifteen minutes, they're either gonna scream and call the cops, or attack you as an intruder," Joey said, also in Spanish.

"Yea, yea. Dejame dormir mujer. Como fregas!" (Let me sleep woman. How you annoy so.)

Let you sleep? Joey thought. *You think I'm annoying now? Just wait!* She waited until she heard snoring again. Secretly, she called Rosangelica on the cell phone and gave her instructions, then kept on cooking.

"Come on, Jacob. The eggs are getting cold. Rise and shine. Look, my students just drove up!"

Rico sat up groggily as the two students walked in. When he stood up they screamed, "Sensei, sensei a thug!" They rushed and leapt on him as instructed.

"Hey, what are you doing? Ouch! That hurts, stop! I'm not a thug!" Rico hollered as he ran downstairs into Michelle's room. He heard Joey and the two young black belts laughing loudly.

In a hoarse whisper, Michelle inquired about the racket.

"Just your bratty sister…and those kids, up to no good, that's all. Need anything?" he whispered, getting closer but trying not to look at her morbid face. He felt instantly guilty about it.

"Not right now, but I sure could use some conversation later," she begged.

"Sure. I have to run some errands first. Is two hours OK?"

"That'll be great, Jacob, thank you."

"Bye," he whispered as he saw her eyes droop. He tiptoed upstairs, snuck up on Joey and startled her. "Ha, paybacks!"

"Gee whiz! You need a cow bell, Jacob," she said, somewhat embarrassed and for the first time attempting to untangle herself from his grasp. At least she made it look good.

"Uhm," the girls said and softly coughed.

"Oh, Jacob these two angels are my students and friends. This is Tina."

Angels, my foot! Jacob thought, but kept it to himself, a well honed cordial smile on his face.

"Hello, Ms. Tina. My pleasure. You must be twelve or so."

"Fifteen next month," she said, with only half a smile.

Oops! He acknowledged her correction with a nod and smile.

"And this is Rosangelica. Another one of my black belt assistants," Joey continued.

"Ms. Rosangelica. You must be about twenty."

"Twenty-two, sir," she replied in as thickly accented English as three simple words can be. She eyed his reaction and gave Joey a look.

A puzzled Jacob also looked at Joey, who gave him an "I'm innocent" shrug. Who called anybody "Sir" nowadays?

"Girls, this is Jacob Rico," she interjected quickly.

As if they didn't know. But Rosangelica was more than slightly surprised about his presence now that she thought about it. Joey had alluded weeks before that she was about to break off the relationship. She almost created a disaster by remarking about it. Fortunately, wisdom prevailed, not to mention that she was rather intrigued at seeing the man in person; and if Joey didn't want him, well...

Rosangelica glued her eyes to his as he made small talk with them in Spanish. He didn't know whether Tina was also Spanish dominant. She wasn't, but she could maintain a general conversation.

Joey didn't miss Rosangelica's rapt attention to the man the young black belt had tried her best—in her mind—to keep at an emotional distance from. She didn't trust him to stick around.

"Como piensas," Rosangelica murmured to Tina, "Tiene esa mirada de enamorada, verdad?"

"Yes," Tina replied. "I think Joey has that I'm-in-love-look, too."

"Joey," Rico said, tapping Joey on the shoulder to divert her gaze from him. She turned red as the girls giggled and headed to the kitchen.

"These girls are rather lively, or should I say giggly? They're affectionate too. Even gave me a hug."

"They did?" she asked. She found that odd. Tina, in particular, rarely hugged adults, especially males.

"Did you by chance initiate the hugs?" she asked Rico.

"No. Wha...what kind of question is that?"

"Oh, nothing. Let's go join them for breakfast," she mumbled.

Rico trailed behind holding her hand. He let go when he noticed the girls looking at each other suspiciously, resisting another bout of the giggles.

"That older girl, Rosangelica, does she prefer Spanish? I don't want to insult her speaking my bad Spanish if she speaks English."

"She speaks only Spanish. Except for little phrases that get her what she wants, she stubbornly refuses to learn. Extremely bright, but, oh so stubborn." Joey ignored the face Rico made, a face she knew meant he knew someone else present who was likewise stubborn. "She plans on returning to Mexico and opening a dojo there," Joey whispered.

Joey, you ought to know how improbable that is, he thought.

"Girls, you're acting normal…but, strange," Joey said, speaking louder.

"Oh, just a case of the giggles, that's all," Rosangelica blurted in Spanish.

With a frown of suspicion Joey served Rico a plate.

"Thanks," he said. He had earlier noticed the abundance of fruits and nuts sitting atop Joey's kitchen counters, nicely arranged in bowls. The fridge overflowed with vegetables, berries and natural juices. Sniffing the nice looking omelet for the aroma of chorizo, Mexican style sausage, or at least bacon, and smelling none confirmed his worries; she had become a health nut of some sort…maybe even a vegetarian!

"Don't smell meat," he said to Joey.

"Yea, forgot to pick up some steak and ground beef yesterday," she answered. She couldn't figure out the grin on his face.

"So what's with all this?" He waved to the counter.

Tina piped in. "Oh, we follow the Maker's Diet. That's why we never get sick!"

"You mean Baker's…?"

"Never mind, I'll tell you about it some time. Just eat," Joey insisted, eyeing Tina through squinted eyes.

He happily obliged as he realized what "Maker" meant; he didn't need to venture there…today. Chewing with enthusiasm and a look of satisfaction on his face made the girls grin.

"So are we visiting or…" Rosangelica begin to ask. Joey stopped her mid sentence.

"Don't really know," Rico said flatly. *Tough cookie*, he thought.

And that was that. After that the group ate in what Joey thought was an eerily quiet atmosphere; though she had caused it. Irregardless, her unusually quiet chatterboxes were busy gawking back and forth at the two love birds. Mostly, they inspected the stranger—that wasn't such a stranger—joining them; most likely permanently, they each privately deduced.

Fifteen minutes later Rico looked at the clock. Excusing himself, he walked to the sink, and to the girls' surprise, proceeded to wash his plate.

"Wow, he's even trained!" Tina chirped.

"Hush, girl!" Joey chastised. "Get out there and get the mats ready. And don't forget that we have two people testing today," Joey added firmly.

"OK!" they said in unison, in the standard adolescent exasperated tone.

"Excuse me, sir, we have to wash our dishes," Rosangelica said.

Rico signaled with his hand for her to hand him the plate.

"Oh, thank you!" she said in Spanish.

Her acceptance surprised him. He expected the I-can-manage-myself-thank-you-very-much attitude that Joey had mentioned on occasion. On top of that, she also gave him another quick side hug.

"Thanks again," she said, and left. Tina did the same.

Joey had stopped chewing, awestruck by the girls' behavior. *How come he gets sugar and spice…and I get fussing, whining and rolling eyes? It's wrong…completely wrong!*

She exaggerated a little; about the rolling eyes at least.

"He's a keeper," Rosangelica murmured in Spanish in Joey's ear as she passed by. Tina did the same in English.

Rico looked at Joey's incredulous expression. "What?"

"I can't believe it. 'Oh, thank you sir!'" Joey mocked. "And they gave you another hug! They rarely give me a simple thank you. That isn't right. I don't know what's gotten into those two…and…I can't tell if I like it. Frankly, I feel a tad jealous…and slightly undervalued and unappreciated, thank you very much."

She was as surprised by her petulance as he was put off by it, though he also found it bemusing. He didn't have a clue that she had a reasonable complaint—though no more than any average loving, nuclear family. But then, he was clueless about much of the intimate things in family life…including hers.

"Joey, I don't know what you're mumbling about, but I have to go. Be back in about two hours. Don't forget to check on Michelle," he said, as if he really needed to remind her.

He gave her a peck on each cheek. "Forgot to mention…love those freckles in the New Mexico sun."

As he walked away she followed and admired—before catching herself—the firm behind that even his loose shorts couldn't conceal. She wondered if the girls had noticed her looking. She figured more than likely. At least they didn't embarrass her by mentioning it, right then at least. But she *would* hear about it.

"Don't forget clothes!" Joey reminded.

After a while, Joey heard him come out of the bathroom and turned to see him in an expensive, well-fitting Italian made sports coat and slacks. She still couldn't get used to how well he cleaned up, but he was going to have to work on the beard.

The girls gawked as he started toward the door.

"Muy guapo, señor." Rosangelica complimented him, suddenly losing her shyness. She thought he looked handsome.

Rico nodded courteously and grinned sheepishly.

"Para donde va, señor?"

He pretended not to understand. She glowered slightly and in thickly accented English asked, "Wear are jew go in?"

"Why thank you, about the guapo part. Voy a la librería," he said respectfully.

"Me permite ... May I go tuu?" she asked.

Joey and Tina stopped their stretching regimen to gawk at her.

"What? Can't a young lady go to the library?" she said to them in Spanish, not so playfully aghast at their reaction.

"No, no. That's quite all right. Go if he'll let you, but he'll be gone about two hours. Remember we have two youngsters testing in two and a half," Joey offered, also in Spanish.

Rico sensed something was up. He couldn't decipher it exactly; these *were* women after all. The female gender was complex he had long ago concluded and had determined to ignore it or be entertained.

"Bueno. But I can't wait for you to change into something else."

"No problema," Roseangelica said and quickly threw on a large T-shirt, the one she was already supposed to have had on over her workout crop top.

Joey's policy required girls wearing tight workout or otherwise revealing attire to have an oversized Tee handy to throw on when males arrived. Otherwise, they had to wear the hotter gee top the whole time. Rosangelica, and Tina more so, thought modesty an ancient concept, though each quietly complied. They thought boys should control and keep their eyes to themselves, no matter how much skin they might show.

"Bye girls, chat with you later, especially you girl." Rico pointed at Joey as he waved.

Joey watched Rico climb in his truck and resumed stretching. She felt a tinge of discomfort when she noticed the girls giving each other one of those in-the-know looks for a split second as Rosangelica backed out the door slowly, finally shutting the door.

Joey, the mother hen, rarely missed anything.

Rosangelica wondered what Joey's strange, concerned look meant as she crossed the studio window and awkwardly waved goodbye, stretching away.

"She seems so self-assured with...a man...all of a sudden," Joey commented to Tina, as more an interrogation than a rhetorical statement.

Tina nodded in agreement. "Do you think maybe she is beginning to believe in herself? Or could it be puppy love?" Tina said.

Ah, the faucet leaked, and so easily. Joey hadn't lost her touch. "If it's puppy love we're all in trouble, unless Jacob handles this deftly."

Joey squinted, watching the truck back up and drive off.

Tina, in turn, eyed Joey. Something told her to hold back mentioning that Rosangelica had made comments alluding to being in love, at *least* twice, at seeing Jacob's photo on the refrigerator—a younger, buff looking GI in a GQ pose, intended for Joey. "Just an old friend," Joey always said.

"Joey…sometimes…you can be soooo dorky. Now tell me…if you *please*… what would a *normal* person use instead of deftly? And don't you dare say…"

"Look it up!" they said at the same time.

"You should've been an English teacher…or some…other kind of terrorizing adult!"

Tina, acting frustrated, stood to supposedly get water. In reality, she stopped to look up the word from a tiny e-dictionary she kept concealed in a drawer. Her speed at looking up words was getting as fast and precise as her roundhouse kicks. Joey had a clue that she'd been using some resource in the kitchen, but couldn't find it.

"Oh, Mrs. Webster, would you like a glass of water?"

"Why, yes sweetie. Thanks," Joey said as Tina handed her a plastic cup with ice-cold water.

"Didn't I just handle that deftly, Ms. Joey?"

Joey spewed out some of the water, unable to resist giggling.

"Why, you surely did young lady," she said, smiling and wiping her chin.

"Thank you kindly, Ma'am!" Tina wore a big grin. "But I don't blame her, he's got quite a bod for an old man…in a nonsexual kind of way of course!" Tina added quickly.

Joey was at a loss for words, which was a very rare thing, as she wiped more water off her chin. She readied to spew out a motherly lecture on how today's girl teens were *way* too sexually aware. Way beyond healthy levels and experientially based rather than parent or educationally founded, she would surely add.

Fortunately for Tina, thoughts of what she had been like when she was near Tina's age—way, way back when—crossed her mind. She hadn't exactly been ignorant or discreet herself even though she could at least boast that she always stopped before going to the extreme. She would just have to guide this girl more directly than she had Rosangelica.

"You don't believe me do you? That I'm not like…attracted to him. He's old," Tina mumbled.

"Let's just say I'm a teeny-weenie-little bit wary of how much you know about yourself, as a girl I mean."

"Wary? What…oh, never mind!" Rolled eyes and crossed arms made the conversation final from her end.

"OK, girl, let's get serious. Our young Jedis are here," Joey said, her words not fitting her thoughtful expression.

"Sure," Tina acknowledged. Outside getting seriously flustered when having to discipline the two girls, Joey rarely showed anyone else her serious or uptight side. And actually, that's what Tina loved about her friend. Of course, *rarely*, was the operative word. A couple of uncooperative, high browed administrators and teachers had already felt the heat of her wrath when Tina had had problems, occasionally.

But when it came to karate, her lessons were loosely planned, often spontaneous and filled with practical jokes. Whether teaching karate was Joey's actual goal, or it was just something that happened along the way, Tina still couldn't figure out. But she had noticed that trophies and other more substantial victories happened to people—those who had otherwise failed in many aspects of life—who listened to or befriended her mentor, Joey. As painful as it was at times to tolerate her standards.

Joey's apprentices were mainly preteens and young adults, though there were a few adults who wanted to learn how to defend themselves. Police officers and other government officials also attended separate sessions weekly. Joey preferred working with the youngsters, who could take her jokes in stride. Of course, the income from the government types paid for the fun with the youngsters. And so did the ability to impact the lives of many of them—Tina, her recently promoted blackbelt assistant, being one of them, as painful as it was at times to muster up patience and understanding.

And Tina required much patience. She was fourteen when she came into Joey's life almost two years before. The young girl already had had a lifetime of disappointments. Her father had long ago faded out of the picture, as had the fathers of countless other children across the country. She also had a mother who tended to be overbearing and controlling, though not necessarily abusive. Unfortunately, she was also incarcerated for the umpteenth time. This promised a continuing sorrowful future—at least until she met Joey.

The product of Mexican and Vietnamese parents, Tina was a very cute girl who felt self-conscious about her slanted eyes. On top of that, she regularly looked in the mirror and lamented that most other girls her age were taller *and* almost fully developed; she was flat as a board. For those, and other reasons, she sought a sport to help her make friends and minimize her differences.

Soon she became a star volleyball and soccer player and was headed for a scholarship in either. And in her mind her academic aptitude would also open doors that her self-perceived lack of good looks wouldn't. Her future looked bright, but even then she wasn't a very happy person. She still hungered for a deeper connection with another soul; more than what she got in two-hour games and practices.

By happenstance, she met Joey at a karate tournament that her friend had invited her to. She was only there to be kind to her friend, but the experience changed her life. As she roamed around, she noticed that many of the instructors were rather intense. Then she spotted Joey and noticed something different about her. She watched closely. When she saw Joey demonstrate unusually calm behavior even when one of competitors lost badly, Tina thought maybe she had found the kind soul she had longed for.

In the next match, a national title bout for brand new black belts, Rosangelica was losing by a point with seconds left. Then she delivered a precise and forceful knockdown with a kick that gave her two points and the victory.

None of the five judges indicated anything out of the ordinary. But Joey went up to Rosangelica and held a discussion with her in Spanish. It was not in a loud voice, so Tina had to scoot close to hear the conversation. The cheering crowd made it hard to hear, but she could clearly see that it was some sort of argument. Hand gestures gave a clue about the topic.

The last words Joey said, with just a little edge to them, were, "Si acceptas el trofeo, busca otro instructor." (If you accept the trophy, find another instructor.)

What struck Tina was that Joey's face registered more hurt and concern than anger. Tina could decipher "otro" and "instructor" but didn't know the context—until Rosangelica stopped the presiding Grand Master from raising her hand to confirm the decision and awarding her the championship.

The crowd, already drawing silent, became eerily still. At first she tried to whisper to the lady, but the Grand Master directed her to announce it aloud to all the judges.

Rosangelica, a mixture of disappointment and shame on her face, spoke in Spanish. "I want this victory and trophy with all my heart, not only for me, but also for my friend, Ms. Joey. Only I can't accept it because I won, or more precisely, didn't win with honor."

Honor? What does that mean? Tina had wondered at the time.

"I don't deserve it because the last strike was illegal. I know the judges didn't see it, but a fact is a fact."

Tears still streaming, she began to smile, "To make my friend and confidant proud, and to safeguard my character and testimony the way she has shown me, I wish for my worthy opponent to receive the honor due him." With that she bowed to her opponent and indicated to the referee to raise his hand.

The poor guy didn't know what to smile about the most, the victory or the nice hug he received from his gorgeous opponent, tough and sweaty as she was.

Joey would later explain to the incessantly inquisitive Tina about the about the illegal move Rosangelica had used, and what testimony meant. The concept of honor proved much more difficult for her to grasp than the actual definition of the word, but learn it well she did. And with Joey's and Rosangelica's pains-taking guidance, she would grow in obedience, not out of fear, but for honor's sake.

Up to then Tina had never seen such love and sacrifice. Tears streamed down her cheeks as the other spectators broke into loud cheers and applause. One thing she knew instinctively was what character was; Tina determined in her mind to hook up with Joey and company.

She approached them and blurted out, "Miss…" she said, wiping her nose as Joey turned, "…will you be my teacher too?"

Flattered by the respect, Joey said, "I'm not sure I would be the one to get you a championship trophy. Maybe you should talk to…"

"But you don't understand…that girl there," Tina looked at Rosangelica. "She's a champion in a hundred ways. I would like your help to become like her…and you."

Tina looked down, waiting to be given some lame excuse about cost or space, or any other excuse for not having time to devote to her.

"Well…Sweetheart…" Joey paused, twiddling her fingers on her chin for effect.

Rosangelica thought it an annoyingly habitual bit of melodramatics, but it made Joey, Joey.

"…I have this very strong feeling that you are probably already there, being a champion I mean. But, if for some reason you want to hang around a couple of crazy people like us, you would be more than welcome," Joey continued.

"Miss, does that mean you'll teach me karate or not?" Tina caught her at-titude and covered her mouth. "I'm sorry…I, I just missed your answer," she said, almost crying again. She had been mentally replaying the list of excuses she had repeatedly heard throughout her life, and they had drowned out Joey's response.

"The answer is yes, but I have to ask you a question. Do you think you can get along with this girl here? She would be your actual instructor."

Tina looked at Rosangelica who was by then wearing a broad smile and making funny gestures. Tina didn't respond verbally, instead she stepped forward and squeezed Joey, at first tepidly, then forcefully.

Rosangelica joined in chirpily saying in Spanish, "Hey, how about me!"

Tina's tears and snot mixed together on Rosangelica's sweaty gee.

"Joey…who are we hugging?" Rosangelica asked.

"My name is Tina," she said, still sniffling, drawing a quaky breath.

The three laughed and walked to the entrance where Tina's ride waited. The woman who had given her a ride looked perplexed at seeing two strangers hugging her daughter's loner friend. The lady knew Tina had few, if any, adults in her life, much less friendly ones. She had doubted Tina was even capable of demonstrating affection.

"Do you know each other?" the friend's mother asked.

"We do now," Joey offered.

Everyone introduced each other. Tina gave her friend's parent Joey's business card. They discussed the possibilities for Tina. The lady was only a ride and referred Joey to her foster parents. This was the beginning of Tina's new *family*.

The two strangers enroute to the library sat quietly in Rico's truck. They turned onto Picacho Avenue off Solano Drive and a minute later into the parking lot across from the former Las Cruces Police Station. They said nothing to each other even as they walked into the library.

"I have something to take care of Rosangelica. So…" Rico finally said, speaking in Spanish.

"OK, I go to…reading sum bukes," she interrupted in broken English.

I thought Joey said she didn't like to speak English? "I'll be over there later." He pointed to the just completed cavernous computer lab marked by a large sign above the entrance. "But, I have to get a new card at the front office."

She nodded and smiled.

"Two hours," he reminded her in Spanish.

Minutes later Rico sat at a computer station, thanks to the twenty it took to sweet talk the occupant into offering it up so he wouldn't have to wait for the next open slot two hours later. For some reason he just wasn't as patient as he usually was. It would've been cheaper to use a coffee shop computer, or his own, but paranoia was already creeping in. Rico pulled his to-do list from his briefcase.

First things first, he thought. Once on the Internet he ran a search for real estate in Las Cruces. A particular realtor's site appealed to him so he clicked it. He started typing "business" in the web site's search box, but changed his mind. He remembered the flyer he had grabbed at a house across from Joey's studio. He had scoped it out and peeked through the windows. He found the listing on that realtor's web site.

Rico checked the zoning. The description read, "Dual use property. Prime location on Solano, three blocks to NMSU and University Dr.; about 4,000 sq. ft., including 2000 sq. ft. first floor; three bedrooms, two full baths and den upstairs; first floor has small reception area or foyer, small dining room, large kitchen, one large office/bedroom, and a very large formal dining/conference room or two offices. Lease, or lease to own, arrangement possible at $2,800 a month, first month rent due at signing plus a month deposit. Utilities separate. Viewing by appointment only."

Rico punched the numbers into his cell phone. The virtual reality walk-through offered a peek at exquisite old adobe walls and natural wood ceilings. The view from the full length upper deck outside the master bedroom was the clincher. It brought a smile to his face.

"Hello, Desert Realty, how may I direct your call?" a courteous voice answered.

"Yes, I'd like to know if that property on South Solano…the old mansion… is it still available?"

"Let me transfer you to the agent handling that property. Please hold."

"Hello, this is Sandra,"

"Hi, my name is Jacob Rico."

"How can I help you, Mr. Rico."

"I'm interested in the property on Solano, the two-story…mansion place." *That sounded smooth.*

"Right now, sir, that property is under contract."

"Are you obligated to lease to that client?" Rico asked crossing his fingers.

"There is a contingency in the hold agreement that allows overriding the hold. Let me double check. Yes, if another offer is tendered with a signed one-year lease, with at least two months lease payment, *and* it is tendered in cash or cashiers check within twenty-four hours of the offer. Still, the client does have first option to match those same terms."

"Pardon my ignorance. That means what?"

"If you make a much better offer to the owner, let's say right now, the client that made the first offer would be called and asked to match the offer."

"I would like to do that. So if I offered to make a six month lease payment up front they would have to match that also?" Rico said, salivating.

"That's correct, sir. Have you seen the property already? Your name doesn't ring a bell."

"No, I grabbed a flyer and did the virtual walk-through thing on the Internet."

"Good. But if they match your offer they get it."

"Well, if the owner is willing, I'll pay one year's rent at closing and enter into a purchase agreement tomorrow morning. What do you say ma'am?"

"That's a rather attractive offer...Jacob. Nevertheless, it would be up to the waiting client, sir. If you give me a number I'll call you with an answer in about two hours," she said.

"Don't call to this number, it's a pay phone...but, I don't recall the number I do want you to call. Well, if you will, please look up JB's Martial Arts Academy and leave a Yes or No answer for me. Wait, never mind, Sandra. I'll call you in two hours instead."

Jacob Rico, Mister Complicated.

"Yes sir, I'll wait for your call back. May I ask why at first you wanted me to call JB's Martial Arts Academy?"

"I just arrived in town and my friend is letting me stay there," he said, hoping he hadn't misspoken.

"Oh! Interesting...you must be *the* Jacob. Well, welcome back. Have a good day."

Interesting? The? What is that supposed to mean? "Uh, you too, bye."

Rico hung up. A strange thought came to mind, "What do you know about twins, finger prints, hair follicles, and DNA?

Scouring the web for forty minutes, all he conjured up was a severe headache. He'd have to do it another time; hopefully forget about it, actually. He swallowed a two-milligram morphine pill and closed his eyes. Less than ten minutes later, it worked its magic. He considered, for the umpteenth time, to go get the implant that would release precise dosages automatically and give near instantaneous relief; it was effective but just too creepy.

He headed downstairs to locate Rosangelica. He saw her right away as soon as he reached the first floor.

"Missster!" Rosangelica said in a loud whisper.

She was walking up toward him with a pile of books. Rico tried to get her to stop before crossing the sensors, but she didn't see his hand signals and kept approaching.

BEEP! BEEP! BEEP! The louder than necessary alarm sounded. Books went flying and scattered all over as Rosangelica panicked and reached to cover her ears.

He had expected a startle, but not exactly this bizarre reaction. Rico rushed over, kneeled down and tried to calm her down. One of the librarians rushed over and began to pick up the books as she whispered that everything was fine. Rico wrapped his arms around her to help her up.

"Mija, it's just a silly alarm. Why are you so scared?" he whispered into her ear in Spanish. He led her to the children's section, away from peering eyes.

She just murmured that she didn't know. They sat and he wiped tears from her cheeks. It wouldn't be until much later that they would both discover that sounds similar to the sensor alarm—wrecker trucks with backing up alarms—had been all around as she lay semiconscious inside the wreckage of her parents' car; the same one they were pulled from, already dead.

The librarian approached silently and laid the books on the table.

"Sir, do you know this young lady?" she asked.

"Ask her," he said a little perturbed, nodding toward his young companion.

"Mija, do you know this man?" the librarian asked in Spanish.

Rico had a tinge of fear when Rosangelica hesitated a moment; she could have taken the question literally. She grabbed Rico's hand and squeezed it as she nodded yes.

"I'm sorry sir, I just had to ask," she said, lips tight.

I read the papers too, lady, Rico thought. It was a scenario that repeated itself too many times for his liking whenever he was out and about with the two lovely girls.

"You think me a cry baby now?" Rosangelica said in Spanish through sniffles. "I'm so embarrassed. A blackbelt acting like an infant!"

"You should be," Rico said, also in Spanish, after some thought as to how to help with such an obviously handicapping fear.

"What? What kind of comment is that?" she said, cheeks flushing again.

Boy, she's a live wire! "Well, you forgot to do the dance!"

She stared at him, then said, "You're crazier than Joey let on."

"Don't believe everything she tells you." He wondered what her raised eyebrow and suspicious look meant. "Anyway, would you like me to show you? Or do you want to sneak out because you're so embarrassed?" he asked.

Rosangelica felt comforted by his new tone and compassionate look. She recalled that Joey had alluded to being drawn to him for something she couldn't quite quantify; Rosangelica was sure she now understood what Joey had meant. Of course, she wasn't going to show him so quickly that he was winning her over.

"You're mean, Mister," she said in English while shoving his chest with four fingers. "Joey didn't mention *that* about you."

Joey's been yapping again! "OUCH! That stung girl, I'm no tough guy, OK. No hitting, pushing, or whatever...just hugs...got it?" he whined only half jokingly as he rubbed his chest. To Rico she seemed glad to have some power over him. Just like a woman, he thought.

"Show me the dance then," a smiling Rosangelica whispered. Rico wiped one last tear from her high, pronounced, round cheeks. She took hold of his hand and rubbed her cheek with the back of it.

"I think Joey said the truth about everything else," she murmured, secretiveness in her tone and look.

He wondered how much of what Joey remembered of him was still true.

Rico made a mock disagreeing face and got up. He made a show of getting stretched for the dance. Rosangelica looked around and covered her face as another patron and her child passed by staring at Rico's antics.

"OK, let's go," he said, taking in deep breaths.

He got a book from her pile sitting on the table and frowned. He noticed the English title, "Little House on the Prairie." Rico was sure that the reading level was way beyond her. Smartly, he said nothing. Instead, he had her stand by a bookshelf. She grabbed a book to pretend to read. Standing about fifteen feet from the sensors, she watched, anticipating one of the zany antics she had heard about from Joey, believing very few of them could possibly be true.

Rico waved subtly and walked toward the exit with an exaggerated nonchalance. The librarians at the desk eyed him curiously. He passed the sensor and it blared again. After a few more steps he twirled around three times on his tip toes and announced quietly to everyone watching, "Oh my, I'm sorry, I do this all the time, please carry on, my apologies everybody."

With that he strutted back toward Rosangelica. She was beside herself and turned red as he turned around and proceeded to do it again. She hid behind the book and bookshelf.

"Please sir, stop that!" whispered a very agitated librarian.

Of course, the security guard was also on the way.

Rosangelica followed Rico back to the table trying to refrain from giggling aloud. She looked around to see who might be staring, then decided that checking out books to impress Rico would draw too much more attention. They hastily left empty handed. Rosangelica cringed as they passed through the sensors, one behind the other.

The two orphans were bonding quite nicely, as strange a way as it was.

Rico and Rosangelica arrived at the dojo just in time. Joey had just finished whole class instruction and everyone was on a rest break or stretching. Rico snuck in and waved as he continued on to the basement to chat with Michelle as promised.

Joey and Tina, without any effort at being subtle, closely eyed Rosangelica, who wore a distinct kind of radiance. Rosangelica ignored them and supervised her group of students as they went through their routines.

Downstairs, Rico and Michelle chatted in between her catnaps. She apologized incessantly about mumbling and rambling among other things. Rico grew more annoyed with each apology, but didn't mention it. He didn't like repetitive apologies, especially when there was no offense committed.

He got in some reading every minute Michelle gave him a break. He was browsing through a trade magazine, *Protective and Offensive Tactics Monthly* for equipment he might want to test. Even though he was a staff writer for it, he rarely read his own column, "Equipment Heaven and Hell." The title was his idea. As corny as he felt about it after the first appearance in a real magazine, a cult following developed within a few issues. He didn't find anything of interest in this issue, so he tossed it in the trash bin.

Minutes later Joey walked in. There was no smile on her face, more like a pout. She had tried all day to shrug off the conviction in her spirit about him staying in her home. It was perfectly right as far as the world was concerned, but she just couldn't escape the fact that God had a different design for her life, like for every other child of God. She just had to tell him…some way.

Rico was rather intrigued; she had to be ribbing. Needless to say, he drove to the hotel, again wondering what had broadsided him. *Boy, when did she get fanatical?*

Maybe one day he would come to understand Joey's uncompromising devotion to doing right, according to a Godly worldview of course.

CHAPTER FIVE

THE NEXT morning Rico stopped at the bank to buy the required cashier's checks. From there he headed to the realtor's office. He had received good news when he called the realtor the day before.

The standard small talk followed as Sandra led Rico to her office.

"So, Mr. Rico…Jacob…your plans still the same?"

"Yes, Sandra. I take it it'll take a while for the paperwork?"

"I trusted my instincts, considering your local connection, and got everything ready."

Local connection? "Thanks," Rico said.

"The figure I came up with is $65,000 for the year, half is thirty-two point five."

"That's a bundle," Rico whistled as he opened his briefcase. "Here's a cashier's check for thirty-two thousand and five hundred."

She had a very pretty smile, a big one.

"I need a key today," he said, a nervous grin on his own face.

"Yes. Now, let's exercise your signing hand," she offered and explained the multitude of e-forms.

He signed in a flurry of scribbles using the light pen, his hand quivering ever so slightly. He was, after all, actually committing to setting down roots; further thought could easily change things.

"Here are the keys, Mr. Jacob Rico. Enjoy your new place and welcome back."

There goes that welcome back again. "I…I…don't recall saying I was from here…did I?"

"No."

"Oh, good. I thought for a second my brain was going quicker than I planned."

Sandra laughed, thinking he was joking.

"So how did you know then?" He eyed the sly look, and rather beautiful cat-like eyes.

"You mean besides your credit report?" *And Joey mentioning you once or twice?*

"Oh, yea that makes sense. I didn't mean to sound paranoid…or whatever. Anyway, thanks. I'll see you around."

That was an odd encounter, he thought. Not at all unpleasant…just odd.

Rico drove back to the dojo. Though he was anxious to brag about his new place, the nauseating headache that had started at the realtor's office was a whopper. Hiding in the bathroom he pulled his pill bottle from his pocket, but it was empty. He made a flimsy excuse to escape downstairs to find his carry-all, where he kept his spares.

Joey thought his behavior bizarre, and more so when fifteen minutes later he hadn't returned. She snuck down to take a peek. He was slouched on the love seat in Michelle's room, snoring away.

An hour later, he bounced upstairs. The others were in the studio; he walked in from the kitchen, biting into an apple. He asked if anyone wanted to see his new place. At first, there was tension in the air—such as when one walks into a room where people have been going at each other, and they stop only because of an outsider's interruption. Apparently, there was some contention in the Black household. Rosangelica didn't look so radiant now.

"What's going on here? Joey, is something wrong?" Rico asked. He tried to be concerned, but the only thought on his mind was to show off his new office…and home. "Hello! Is anybody home? I guess not. I'd better go see my place by myself."

Making exaggerated movements as he edged toward the door didn't help things. Everyone rolled their eyes, except Rosangelica. Joey found that almost as annoying as the practical joke Jacob was probably pulling. His jokes were only zany and humorous when she was in the right mood.

Still, he was a guest, for now, and deserved some attention; so the three dutifully followed him outside and climbed into his truck.

"Gee whiz, you people move like molasses in the Artic."

Rico climbed into the truck and tapped on the steering wheel. The others just stared at him.

"You do realize you're acting like a teenager," Joey whispered icily with a demeanor to match. Rosangelica didn't seem to appreciate the comment, but kept quiet.

"Yup," Rico answered, making a dorky face.

Tina giggled. At least she was warming up.

Rico drove south on Solano Drive, then west on University to El Paseo. From there he made a right onto Idaho going back up to Solano, then headed south again toward the dojo. Joey almost screamed thinking he had just wasted her time with this little joy ride.

She was about to let out a few choice and unspiritual words as they neared her house, when Rico turned into another driveway—just in time. The driveway into the ten-vehicle parking lot belonged to a Santa Fe style, luxurious-looking, two-story building—a building Joey had always admired—a stone's throw away from the dojo. Now she knew Rico must have been jesting. He just never showed this kind of taste, or hadn't noticed. And then there was the issue of finances. She didn't think he had any.

"Jacob you're crazy. See girls, I told you about this!" Joey muttered, shaking her head in disbelief. "Okay, that was a tad funny. But, now can we get back to my non-fantasy place, please! We have real work to do."

She continued grumbling as Rico got out of the pickup and started toward the front porch, an elegant one in its simple pueblo style. Walking across the wood planks that composed the porch floor made that mysteriously appealing noise reminiscent of old Westerns. As much as she wanted to, she couldn't really stay angry about his fooling around; after all, it was the main trait that drew her to him. But then again, she was a different, more sensible person now; and she had serious responsibilities to meet.

Joey's jaw dropped when he actually opened the door and disappeared inside. The girls screamed with delight and rushed out of the truck, leaving the apparent sour puss behind—the one whose heart was now pounding with excitement and couldn't move.

"Is he staying? He is!" Joey kept repeating under her breath, altogether surprised by her girlish reaction.

Rico popped his head out the door and waved. She waved back, pretending to not be too interested. A slight hop in her step gave her away as Rico disappeared from the doorway again. Joey got there pronto. The girls' screaming and jumping resounded from upstairs.

Tina yelled loudly, "Hey, Jacob, I can see right into our dojo from here!"

Wearing a big grin, Joey moved closer to Rico, who was then doing the gameshow hostess thing as he led her around. She silently savored that Tina had said "our" dojo. So many things were falling into place—just as she had been promised.

"Mr. Rico, you weren't trying to get a view of my bedroom, were you?"

"Hey, I…"

Joey shut him up as she grabbed him around the neck and kissed him without reservation.

"Who's acting like a teenager now?" he mumbled between kisses.

"Yea," Tina said, both girls giggling again as they snuck back out of the room. Joey edged away from him.

"See what you've done!" Rico said. "Now they'll giggle all night—you mark my words, woman."

Besides each other, they also found warmth in the condition of the original wood beams found throughout the century old, Spanish style, adobe structure. The building was once called The Little Mansion, where a wealthy Don had lived. And it was every bit a fine place—with retrofitted necessaries of course. A large kiva-style fireplace in the corner of the spacious formal living room, which Rico said made for a suitable conference room, made Joey bubble over even more; if that was possible.

"Isn't this place…slightly beyond your means, Jacob?" Joey gently opined in Spanish.

Rico looked for a pattern to her language switch. He just nodded and shrugged. His thoughts were only on how perfectly his lady fit in the elegant place; especially in her embroidered, bright blue peasant blouse, never mind well-fitted jeans. Her blue eyes seemed to radiate light.

"That really answers everything Jacob. Thank you so much for alleviating my worry that you might be flat broke in months."

Rico's only answer was another passionate kiss at the front porch. While outside, they admired the various flowering plants in the gardens. There was just enough grass around the xeriscaped lawn where people could lounge on blankets. The mix of sweet aromas from a variety of rose breeds, Jasmine, and other flowers, plus the visual treat of fluttering butterflies and buzzing bees about made it a rare rich moment for him; the girls he had just met being mesmerized by butterflies landing on them, soothed his soul even more.

"I'm really gonna use this front porch and yard. Barbecues every Sunday and on Monday nights, and any other day there's a game. I'll even do it for baseball games…naw. Maybe…golf games…ah, a double naw."

"Excuse me, dreamer…," Joey interrupted as they started strolling to the dojo, "…but normal people do their barbecuing in the back yard."

"Well, that's…"

"Oops, never mind." She raised her hands up in mock surrender. "I forgot who I was talking about, or to…or whatever," she added, finishing in Spanish again. She was driving him crazy already.

He would be barbecuing in the front and side yards. He had harped and lamented in numerous letters about people being so closed off in their own worlds, not like in the days of old—the 1950's or so was what he had told her. And the ample-sized front porch and veranda would see extensive use if he had anything to say about it.

"Let me hear you say one time, one little, teeny-weeny time, that you hate my quirkiness!" Rico taunted.

"Well … if it wasn't for your *quirkiness*, fueras bien aburrido. (You'd be outright boring.)"

"Remember that, it'll serve you well…soon."

CHAPTER SIX

"**Wake up** sleepy head!" Joey said.

Rico, still snoring away, managed to ignore her only the first couple of times she rudely announced morning had arrived. Right then he noted an early rising pattern—and not an agreeable one. It was his first night in his new place, barren of furnishings as it was. Her mention in one letter years before that she rose at five thirty every day came to mind. He had thought she was exaggerating.

"Hey woman, just like yesterday, it's *still* too early," he grumbled.

Rico had given her a key and, of course, an offer of his bed, or sleeping bag as it was. He knew better than to ask such a thing. He was going to need some help—and lots of it. This one special lady deserved proper courting; if only he had some experience in that.

"Seven isn't too early."

He didn't stir.

"Come on!" she begged. "Let's take a train ride."

"A what?" he asked, wiping his eyes.

"The bullet train, remember? The newest leg just went operational two months ago!"

Bullet train? He had forgotten; it sounded like something just down her alley. "I've got an appointment at the dentist I'm looking forward to, so I need more rest."

"Oh, you lazy bum! I told you about it two years ago. So come on honey, por mi…tu carinosa amor. (for me…your affectionate love.)"

Rico got dressed—she wasn't playing fair—but he took his sweet time. Meanwhile, he tried to remember what Joey had mentioned regarding the train. A faint recollection of her taking the idea to some people came to mind. He had thought it was just talk; he was going to have to start listening better—and believing.

"Let's walk," she whispered, hugging him close.

"To?"

She just smiled and led the way. They strolled past the deli and walked across University Avenue onto the campus. Rico admired the well kept campus and the impressive architecture of some of the newer buildings. The university had grown much since his departure, way back when. He started feeling his age as teenage-looking students bustled about. Shrugging it off he took in everything as he and his companion walked hand-in-hand—love-struck youngsters in their own right.

Joey could not help but stare at him, looking fine with still plenty of swept back, curly black hair and sporting a grey blazer, red silk tee shirt, black slacks, and matching black running shoes.

Across from the business center was a building he hadn't seen, an imposing dormitory that definitely altered the skyline. Started in 2005, the building served as focal point for many students' activities and social gatherings and a focal point of university police patrols as well.

Minutes later, they neared the station. Extensive renovations had transformed the Pan Am Center into a regional architectural landmark—renamed Pan Am Central Station, the PACS. The neighboring, newly built Aggie Dome now hosted the university's athletic events.

They walked into the PACS. The high arching tinted glass sky dome lit up the place beautifully. It reminded him of Crystal Mall in Arlington, Virginia. Of course, the eateries catered to the Southwest taste buds, but the curio and gift shops offered all varieties of Americana. The majority of the commercial businesses were located on what used to be the pit area where the Aggie basketball and volleyball teams played. Midway up, another level had been carved for shops. The actual boarding gates were on the ground level.

He picked up a promotional flyer that read, "From a standstill, our monorail bullet train reaches cruising speed of up to 250 miles per hour at three-quarter mile. At a top speed of 300 miles per hour it is not as fast as Japan's bullet train—350 miles per hour—but, it is the world's only solar powered magnetic levitation train."

Actually, during two to three months of winter it ran off the grid for half of the day. Likewise, running at maximum speed required grid power supplementation.

Rico breezed through the pamphlet. It went on to tell about the three year old, all privately funded and operated enterprise. The idea had come from a private citizen who did not want to be named, and who recommended it to some key people in the government sector. They turned it down, but forwarded the idea to one CEO who just happened to be interested in the large transportation project. Reluctant at first, the severe energy crisis the previous decade, and with no relief in sight, tipped the scale.

"Yes, it was partly the potential for big bucks that drew my attention, but mostly the great vision it represented for our environment," the primary investor was quoted as saying.

"Sure! Sounds like baloney to me," Rico murmured as he read.

Rico stuffed the flyer in his back pocket as the announcement from the conductor instructed all to be seated. Fasten seatbelts lights went on and the two buckled up. Rico looked around, surprised at how full the cars were—almost at seventy percent capacity. The take-off sure was silky smooth, Rico thought, but not as fast as advertised. Then the train straightened out on the I-10 south bound leg. Within seconds, it was cruising at full speed, and the ride was still silky smooth.

The scenery hadn't changed much. Desert shrubbery still looked like desert shrubbery. Ocotillo, mesquite, sage, and that painful prickly pear lined both sides of the half-under-, half-above-ground rail tube. Two minutes later, it approached the Mesquite station, ten miles south of Las Cruces. It stopped in less than a quarter mile without causing heads to lurch forward. Two minutes later the cars were near eighty percent capacity. The take-off and reaching of top speed was quicker this time. There were three more two-minute stops at the La Mesa, Anthony and the Canutillo terminals. The cars were ninety percent full after Canutillo.

Joggers, walkers and bikers could be seen on the left and right sides of the railway on the concrete paved tracks shaded by the solar panels above. The same concrete barrier that shielded the track structure protected the people using the tracks from an errant vehicle.

Rico thought it ingenious. An all-purpose thoroughfare; people with brains live here, he mused.

He looked to his left. To the right of the Transmountain Pass gap was an attention getting, shiny new structure.

Joey saw him studying it. "Nice isn't it. It brought some high paying jobs into the region," she said.

"It's...?"

"That's the Homeland Security Joint Directorate for Intelligence and

Southern Border Management. The locals shortened it to J-DIN." She watched him show no response and figured it wasn't of interest.

Just great! he thought. *Langley types on my front lawn. So much for a few days notice.*

"They're probably still in chaos, moving in and unpacking. The core upper echelon is just now transferring in from Virginia. I'm sure they're thrilled about their trek to the desert. They get a nice, unobstructed view of the Rio Grande Valley though. They'll probably laugh at our idea of a river," Joey added, eyeing Rico's subtle grin.

She wondered what part of what she said he found amusing.

Not operational yet? Hmm. Another thought he kept private.

It was a picturesque structure to say the least; an extensive amount of bronze tinted windows, perched high up on the face of the Franklin Mountains (also part of the Rocky Mountains). It was partly dug into the rock face one hundred feet deep—forty of it inside rock. The secure operations room was in an even deeper cave in the rock, no doubt. The visible part of the structure was almost two football fields wide and three stories high.

The location was a brilliant choice, Rico noted, and easy to secure from any accidental, or planned, physical penetration. Yep, people were getting just a little too brainy in the sunny Southwest for his taste.

Joey had only a couple of minutes to be annoyed at his thoughtful frown, and romantic-ambiance killing silence. Her seedling ire was interrupted when, fifteen minutes and forty miles since leaving Las Cruces, the train pulled into the El Paso University Station.

The terminal was newer than the PACS, though likewise it shared its parking lot with the adjoining stadium. From there, shuttle buses took passengers on the five-minute trip to downtown El Paso and other central work places and commercial centers.

The love birds did the tourist thing for an hour, walking around downtown El Paso. Rico was ready to head straight home once they toured the Insights Museum and cultural center.

On the trip back to Las Cruces, Joey insisted on visiting the Space Port, located some thirty miles north of Las Cruces. Rico begged out. Joey agreed to let him off the hook if he would agree right then to join her on a flight into space in a few months. He only promised to leave the possibility open.

Ironically, the expensive tickets were courtesy of Joey's former romantic admirer—competition Rico still didn't know existed—who had fully expected to be the second part of the twosome, of course. She was still wondering how he took the news about Rico coming into town permanently, since he left on vacation without saying a word—very unlike him.

Back at Joey's, Rico managed to sneak in a two-hour nap. Joey was out and about nonstop. She was happy not to have him tagging along. He wouldn't understand all the things she did. She might fill him in later. The two quickly fell into a routine; he managing some writing, and lots of sleeping; she doing her thing. He was already feeling comfortable and thinking he just might fit in, until that evening.

Joey and the girls were in the room just off the practice room at Joey's place. It served double-duty as Rosangelica's bedroom and family TV room. A newly delivered 46-inch LCD television hung on the wall, courtesy of Rico. Roseangelica had a way with decorating Rico noticed; she had a very feminine, sophisticated touch. Stuffed animals peeked out from every nook and cranny. There didn't seem to be an affinity for a particular type of creature like most people who collected things seem to have.

Rico arrived during a set of marathon commercials and decided to join them. He edged over by Joey before realizing what they were watching—*The Greatest Story Ever Told*. As he sat down, the girls gave Joey a funny look, one Rico caught from the corner of his eye. He tried acting interested but soon was out cold.

He awoke later to hear an ongoing conversation among the ladies.

"Joey," Tina piped up. "Don't take this wrong or anything, because I am *trying* to understand…and maybe *believe*…but how do we know it wasn't a fake thing, or just a story?"

"That's a reasonable question, girl. The answer is prophesy, which is something stated before it happens. Hundreds of years before, it was said and written that it would happen. One place specifically is in Isaiah," Joey offered in a hush.

"But…that's still from the Bible, and we don't know if it is reliable…or is there information about Jesus coming back to life outside of the Bible?"

Joey was taken aback at the teen's analytical sophistication. "As a matter of fact, I asked that question of someone *years* before *I* believed. Someone gave me a book…I threw it on my shelf; I didn't read it until recently, in fact. You're really serious about an answer, girl?"

Tina nodded.

"You'll have to do some studying."

Tina nodded again, not so emphatically this time.

"At the library, find the works of the non-Christian Roman historian, Flosifus, related to the resurrection time frame and then some other writers. At a Christian book store, buy the book *Sherlock's Faith* by Frank Harber. I'll loan you *Evidence That Demands a Verdict* by Josh McDowell. That last book offers answers to the Bible's reliability and accuracy as a historical document. And Harber says there is no other document on the face of the earth with more copies of the original texts still in existence."

"But...why don't you just tell..." Tina stopped herself. "Oh, well. Where's the cash?"

Rico had been listening with his eyes closed. Once again, he wasn't prudent, speaking before thinking. "Joey, why in the world are you confusing these girls?"

Joey gave him a look he didn't see and it would have sufficed for any sensible person to tread carefully; but even if he had seen it...well.

"How's that, Jacob?" she said, slowly drawing out his name.

"You are talking to them as if the story, or...fable...is based on any facts... or reality."

He could have still made it unscathed out of the hole he was digging by heeding Joey's annoyed look, but he also missed Rosangelica's and Tina's glare and continued. "Do you guys talk about *Aladdin*...or *The Little Mermaid*...like that? Or about...."

"Mister..." Tina said. "You're challenging my intelligence. And if you plan to be around me, you'd better never talk to Joey like that again. Because I'll kic..."

"Tina!" Joey said, saying her name like only a mother can.

"Well, I'm not gonna stand still and watch the person I respect and love the most in the world be spoken to with such...such...lack of respect. He can go to..."

Taken aback at Tina's first verbalized feelings for her, Joey didn't know what to say. Even then she was about to cut Tina off with a verbal lashing when Rosangelica reached over and gently place a hand on Tina's shoulder.

Rico didn't miss the power of the connection between the two. Though a little late, he did catch a glimpse of Rosangelica's glare, and he quickly looked away.

She rose to her feet and left with Tina in tow.

Rico caught part of another barb when Tina said through gritted teeth as they walked away, "I thought Joey said he was bright?" Just as quickly, he heard Rosangelica give her a firm hush.

Joey rose to leave. She really didn't want to say anything, but stopped and turned. "We'll agree to *limit* our *religious* stuff around you, but you really, really, need to control your mouth about matters that *are* real and important to *us*."

Rico weighed what smacked him harder; the fact that she walked out without a gentle touch—like other times when she had been much angrier—or that once again he sat in another place, as comfy as it was, utterly alone.

Is there some easy trick, a pill, out there...somewhere...to help me break this nasty, lonely existence life has handed me?

CHAPTER SEVEN

SOME DAYS after the train ride—and the rude awakening the girls had given him—Rico and Joey snuck away for a stroll at Young Park.

The girls had already graciously forgiven Rico's conduct, so most of the tenseness when they interacted was gone. The fiery Tina took much more prodding than Rosangelica before agreeing to forgive. Vengeance was something she had more practice at; only now, through prayer and guidance, the child was slowly—agonizingly slow for Joey—learning not only to show mercy, but receive it.

Strolling on the sidewalk that circled the small, man-made pond, Rico was stuck as to how to broach the subject he needed to discuss with Joey. So he just dove right in, cannonball-like—no form, big splash.

"Joey, I have an obligation to something that's probably going to dramatically affect our relationship," Rico tossed out.

Young's Park in the early morning coolness, the leaves dancing on their branches, would normally sooth his soul. But right then he wasn't enjoying it much, waiting for Joey's response; he drew only silence.

"Joey it's a rather complex set of ..."

"If it means..." she began to say, looking at him with big blues that pierced into him like daggers, "...we can't be together permanently...then I would prefer that you just leave quietly into the sunset one day...whenever a whim hits...and just leave me a note...OK?" She swallowed hard and nervously bit her lower lip. "I can't believe you rented that place and are now considering bolting," she blurted. "Or maybe you've run into a...woman you knew before, or reconnected with, and...."

Her heart began to miss some beats as she imagined the courtship she longed for evaporate like a desert mirage. And there went the storybook wedding; her version at least, a small and intimate ceremony with just the girls. That *had* been her simple, wonderland script.

Another woman? Where did that come from? She can't mean Jennifer! Rico was too stunned to answer. But Jennifer wasn't around; not physically at least. Not to mention that there hadn't been anything *really* serious between them. And he had been quite candid about her. He wondered if, even worse, she meant the woman in San Diego he had a one-week fling with. But she couldn't know about that.

She tried reading his emotionally blank face. "Life's funny…and cruel, like that…sometimes…" she continued. "I take it…she's not someone who talks about…God or Jesus, like I do?"

Rico grimaced as he saw the effect he was already creating without even saying what he needed to. Sure enough no one he had met before referred to God with such passion and sincerity, let alone frequency.

"I promise…it's not another woman. There is no one else in my life that I…this is going to sound real corny…that I would want in my life…enjoying the kind of relationship you…we…have." He finally finished the flurry of stuttered words.

"You know, it'd be nice to define this *relationship* a little more precisely," Joey said after regaining her composure and gathering her thoughts.

"Huh?"

"Except for a time when you wouldn't talk to me, my feelings for you have been the same. You know very well that I'm madly in love with you. The very rhythm of my heartbeat sounds out your name."

Rico processed what she was saying. *Women speak like this for real? Do they practice these things?* He wondered.

"As for you, the most I can guess is that you are at least taken with me, perhaps infatuated. Or maybe more than interested, but you certainly don't give much by way of verbal expression. You're a…a closed diary…with…with…a double padlock, Jacob."

Joey looked at him inquisitively, yearning, waiting, for those words that make every woman's face glow and heart pound. She waited for what seemed an eternity, burying her face in the crook of his neck. Love could be so exhausting at times.

"It is to my shame Joey, that for the longest time I haven't spoken my heart. This Latino macho, man thing, just…You must have known." He paused to measure his words, mushy as they felt. It was not a good time to put his foot in his mouth. "I … thought…I didn't have to say it with words."

Her inklings were confirmed, yet she pressed for the words to flow from his lips so she could engrave them in her heart. With her broadest smile this morning, she playfully commanded him, "Come on Sergeant Rico, do your duty...please!"

"Oh, all right. You women are all the same. Joey, I love you. There...are you *happy*?"

Joey was too busy giggling and hanging on and kissing his neck to answer.

"Woman, get off of me! People are watching," he teased. "There *is* something that might affect our...interactions," he said, after a few moments. His expression plainly expressed that a serious matter was at hand, had she chosen to look.

"What new quirk would that be?" she asked, putting her head back on his shoulder. She hoped it was something that simple to deal with.

He elbowed her gently.

"There's no other way to put it...I have a medical condition that doesn't...uhhhm...let me perform...uhmmm...my manly...duties," he finished in a mumble and looked away from her peering eyes processing what he meant.

"How long have you had this?" She made a face of surprise at her question. "Wait! I'm sorry, that came out terribly. I don't care. I wasn't thinking when I asked that." She examined his eyes for the hurt she figured she had inflicted. She knew well that her macho Latino friend wasn't so invulnerable.

But Rico had rehearsed that exact scenario and didn't flinch—no open page there.

"Actually, there are numerous ways to deal with that issue. So if you don't plan to dump me for a more *complete*, though not possibly better, model...I think I can in the future...when appropriate...make use of my brain to..."

There was that little tinge of suspense in the back of his mind; she just might decide on doing just that; move on that is.

Joey blushed, looking radiant. "Yes, I get the picture," she answered with a half giggle.

He was really happy to be over with that chore, and needless to say, hear a positive response.

"I can tell you hang around those giggly girls a lot," was the most intelligent thing he could muster to say after breathing again.

"Yep, they keep me going. And they were right too. They said that you loved me when I...read them one of...Oops!"

"I can't believe you did that!" Rico said feigning anger. He mused for a moment about the awesome relationship Joey had with the two girls, and a tad of envy crept in. "They must be very intuitive."

"What a diplomatic way to say nosey. You're good at spin, aren't you? I'd better watch you closely."

If she only knew how accurate she was.

A gentle breeze continued twirling the birch tree leaves above them. The dancing of the leaves was so soothing; the alternating green and silvery colors matched the cadence of the leaves rubbing each other. Soon more people were out and about enjoying the same.

"Joey, I hate to say this but…there's another thing I wanted to bring up."

"It's okay…I always knew you were an alien."

"Funnnny. Seriously, there is something that I feel I have to do that may or may not involve you. It is a highly dangerous endeavor," Rico blurted. The impulse to just let it all hang out nearly caused him to burst.

Wow, his vocabulary has improved, Joey thought.

Thing, not endeavor, would have been his word choice in the past; the better to spin with maybe?

She figured nothing could top the other thing so she wasn't too concerned. And more than likely it had a punch line.

Still, she didn't venture looking at his face. "Look at the birds…and the bees. Isn't that a Monarch Butterfly? I bet they…" Joey said.

Rico frowned.

"You mean financially or physically dangerous? Are we talking a crime kind of thing?" she asked after giving his strange statement a second thought.

Now she took a peek at his face. *There's a story here.* Her head started to buzz. She couldn't believe how quickly her former investigative reporter's disconnected mindset had kicked into action. The impulse to pursue a story in the making startled her. She was perfectly happy at having moved on. Just then she recognized a suppressed, yet eager to surface cynicism that enduring good things were only meant for others. She would bring the matter up to God in her prayer closet, soon.

"It is dangerous in many ways actually…and a few broken laws would be involved. Your involvement would be minimal. Of course, I can't tell you a single thing for you to even consider, unless…" He stopped to think about the relationship and awesome person he was risking and involving in his crazy plan.

"Yea…go ahead, Jacob."

"Well, you and I would have to be married." He noticed a quivering half-smile. "That way, whatever I tell you can stay between us. Even if you decide not to know much about my plans, you could still be a witness against me. But, not if you're my wife, 'cause…"

"Yes, I know some law, Jacob. I feel slightly insulted. Is that the only reason for us to be married?"

"Actually, my plan is just a ploy to get you into bed. Plus, I couldn't find anyone with more freckles than you. Did I ever tell you…freckles get me…?"

"No, not in so many words, but I remember back then in Iraq…I could sense…"

"Oh, what do we have here, a psychic?" Rico whispered, softly touching her cheeks with his finger tips.

"Stop teasing me you ugly man!"

At that moment Joey threw caution out the window. She had decided that she was thinking straight—at least about whether real love was to be the primary ingredient of this "arrangement."

She waited until her thoughts were clear and no sign of having had any doubts would sully the glee in her voice. "So, when do you formally propose— cause I could still say no—and we get married?" she asked with a chirpy bounce in her normally brassy, sultry voice.

"Funnnny. Un dia señorita," he said trying to be charming.

Before he knew it, Joey's countenance dropped.

This was not the response Rico expected. Then he quickly realized that once again he had put foot in mouth. Before he could embrace her and say something else, she turned and pulled away.

Joey was more surprised than he was at her reaction. The vividness of one certain memory, one that had haunted her to no end for so many years, gave her another shock. Not an inkling or thought about it had surfaced for more than three years. She thought the torment was over. Shameful feelings of that day she suffered a sexual assault made her body tremble—as if it had occurred only yesterday.

Will that horrible voice that whispers in my ear ever leave? She asked herself for the millionth time. *No, those animals had no right! I fought them the best I could.* Her head spun and her knees buckled.

Rico embraced her and walked her gently toward the grass to help her sit, but she stopped him. She wiped her tears and looked him in the eye.

"I wish…for you…that I was still a señorita," she murmured. The odd thought that she had not suffered any flashbacks the one time Jacob and she had slept together came to mind. She had been with no other man since that day of horror.

Rico suddenly realized exactly what she was alluding to. A pang of anguish gnarled his stomach.

"Joey, remember this, you are not what people do to you, but what you decide to do with the events that transpire in your life. Define yourself and learn to live with the consequences. Good things and bad, Joey. I want you to know for you…that you *are* a señorita…in *every* way. To me, especially…you are a señorita of the highest caliber."

He couldn't read her face to tell whether he was reaching her. "And a lassie any leprechaun would yearn to hold, and he'd forget the gold!" he added with compassion and a gentle bit of wisdom.

They sat quietly for several minutes, her back still to him, but now their faces touching cheek-to-cheek. He gently caressed her hand and arm. She reciprocated in kind.

"I guess…" She paused to let Rico wipe a remaining tear and land a kiss on her cheek.

"You guess…?" he said quickly to interrupt her thoughts, trying to prevent another digression.

"I guess…you're not a poet, and the only one that doesn't know it." She smiled as she tried to escape his grasp.

"You Irish…Mexican…whatever…brat!" He wrestled her to the ground. They lay side-by-side on the grass, catching their breath, observing the people that had been curiously observing them.

"So, we get married *when*?" She pointed to a bald eagle soaring above—a rare sight. "That's how I feel right now, Jacob," she added when he didn't respond.

Thanks Joey, no pressure there! Rico was trying to figure out a safe answer on the spot—winging it some would say—as was his tendency.

"Come on, don't be evasive. It's elementary my dear boy. When do we get married?" she said in Spanglish.

"When…I'm able to do things the right way. That's when. Trust me, mujer."

The firmness and finality of his response seemed to satisfy her. He gave her one last firm squeeze and stood, offering a hand to help her up.

"Why, thank you handsome, gracious, caballero."

CHAPTER EIGHT

THE TWO lovers were still so absorbed in each other that they didn't notice a stranger approaching. A homeless man, who had been sleeping under some blankets some thirty yards from them, was now right up near them. The muscle-shirt-clad, ragged, scraggly looking man was quite tall—and absent any body fat. Rico deduced that he was or had been into serious weight training due to the bulging muscular forearms and biceps—not someone he would want to annoy.

Rico tried to remember how much spare change he had as the man approached with an obvious intent. Instead, the man demanded Rico's wallet. He must have noticed that Joey didn't have her purse because he didn't ask for that. Rico was about to let loose some stern words when he noticed a reflection of light from the polished blade of a sizable dagger the man was partially concealing.

Joey was closest to the stranger and off to Rico's side. She didn't move.

Rico tried to will her behind him. For some reason she didn't appear to be planning to subdue the stranger, or move behind her man and protector. She just stood there, no fear registering on her face. Obviously, she hadn't seen the knife, Rico was sure.

But then again, Rico wasn't planning any heroics either—though every fiber in his body wanted to grab the man by the neck and break it. Nobody threatened people he cared for. But he wouldn't risk that this might be one of those days—occurring more and more frequently—when his reflexes were as nimble as a ninety-year-old man's. He was not about to be the cause of the love of his life getting stabbed because of money.

"Listen mister," Rico said, trying for a voice soothing and yet firm, "I have three hundreds in my wallet. You can have two of them without any trouble."

The man seemed momentarily distracted by something behind Rico. Using some nasty expletives and a threat to cause Joey harm, the man again demanded the wallet. And he wanted it now, of course.

"Ok! Here, just give me my wallet back."

"Mister…" Joey said. She ignored Rico's look to hush up. He knew Joey less than he thought. "God doesn't like what you're doing. I can offer you work so you can earn it," Joey said firmly, but kindly. And she wasn't kidding. Her personal network was extensive enough to help, a fact she had not exactly been very upfront with Rico about, yet.

"Yea, right!" the man said while turning to run with Rico's wallet firmly in his grasp.

Rico felt stupid. For a second he wondered whether the man had responded to his remark or Joey's stranger one. *God doesn't like?*

For a split second he considered a pursuit. Then four other men sprinted from behind Rico and Joey, apparently joining their buddy. Rico figured that he had made a good move to appease the guy and let him go so that he and his cronies wouldn't slice them to pieces. He didn't feel so stupid anymore; or invalid as it were.

Nevertheless, each one wondered about the other's inaction. It seemed to Joey that Rico apparently had turned over a pacifist leaf somehow…but, more likely something was wrong. He wondered why the fourth degree blackbelt let the guy off…or if something was wrong; maybe the religion thing was for real. Would he come clean about the brain-cancer, and how, even dormant, it inter- mittently wreaked havoc with his reflexes and thinking processes? Would she come clean about having known what was going to happen to the hold-up man and the full meaning of her born-again life?

Rico and Joey watched with curiosity as the four other men corralled the assailant and attempted to coerce him to hand over the wallet. Their arms flailed in argumentative gestures. Their words were too muddled to be understood by the two interrupted lovebirds.

Rico could only conclude that it was an argument about the spoils. He was puzzled when Joey urged him to put away the cell phone; he had already keyed in 911.

The four strangers looked at each other and shrugged as they finished dia- loging with the suspected gang member. To Rico it looked as if the thief was refusing to share, so they pounced on him. Rico became saddened by what his former little town had been reduced to. Even to the battle hardened vet, the vio- lence inflicted on the one that had taken the wallet was appalling and dishearten- ing…and it was by the guy's own partners in crime.

Before Rico knew it, the men were headed back toward them. And he was now high and dry on cold cash. How would he appease them if they wanted more? If only he could get used to toting a gun again. He had every state's conceivable concealed weapon license imaginable; and an odd aversion to the things.

Joey wouldn't heed his budging, even when Rico—not feeling exactly like a knight just then—tried a harder push toward their car. He was stuck—no police, no running away, no fighting back, just standing. It was a strange state of affairs for him.

Joey, what the…? He was surprised to see the men strolling back with odd looking grins on their faces, fixing themselves up as they approached. *They want to be tidy for the next holdup. If we had three hundred, they figure we have more.*

"Hi, folks, top of the morning!" one of the men said.

Rico didn't know what to say. What was it with the Irish lingo? It was a long shot to have another Irish in Las Cruces.

Joey didn't let out a peep.

When is the full gang going to issue the threat, he wondered. *Just drop the hammer man.*

Joey didn't seem scared or even apprehensive; she just took it all in. She smiled a resistive smile and offered a nod in acknowledgment instead.

"Sir, I believe this is yours, courtesy of your local homeless safety patrol!"

"Safety patrol?" Rico finally muttered. Just then he noticed the group's racial mixture—a skin tone rainbow, white, black, brown, and light brown.

"We're not official or anything, but the cops respond fast when we call."

"Seems to me like you don't need them for much," Rico said, figuring he'd play along until the sucker punch.

"Sometimes strung out druggies or other unsavory types try to move in on our safety areas to peddle their stuff. We're poor and homeless, but not because of vices or lack of effort. This guy just rolled in from out of town—apparently hold ups is what he did in Seattle to get by."

"I see," Rico said, still only half believing. He decided to be courteous, nonetheless. It wouldn't be wise to antagonize the group for sure. "I believe what you said about not being homeless for lack of effort. Would I offend you guys if I offered you the *only* cash I have that's in my wallet—for helping out…I mean?"

At least one of men caught Rico's gist. The man's face registered a dislike for the insinuation. Rico realized by then that the real bad guy might have tried to make a point with a stab of the knife, if these men had not been closing in. The man had been antsy enough—juiced up on something.

The men looked at each other. A different one of the four spoke up. "We sure could use anything you offered, but we wouldn't want to make you think we do this for cash. This is our town too."

One of the men looked at Joey strangely. Rico found it suspicious—very. At first she was smiling in general, now there was this, this something.

"Hi, Robert," Joey said softly, looking sheepish all of a sudden.

Now what? He wondered.

"I knew that was you. You look a little different…uh, lost a few pounds, and…new do."

She did lose a few, Rico thought. *But that isn't any of your bee's wax, guy.*

Joey nodded ever so slightly in agreement to the man's comment.

"But, why didn't you kick that guy's…Sorry, I almost cussed."

Joey just shrugged.

Rico's mouth hung open a little. *Tell me she doesn't personally know this guy!*

"Jacob, here's your wallet," she whispered.

Rico didn't even blink. The wallet felt two Franklins lighter.

"Here's my card and here's a couple of bills. Say hi to the wives and kids, all right?" she said to Robert. She stepped forward slightly and reached out with the money and card.

Up to then everything was kind of kosher with Rico. But he started to get dizzy when she put her hand to the man's face and caressed his very bushy bearded cheek, then kissed it. He felt very awkward and glued his eyes to the ground.

In contrast, Robert's face lit up, a noticeable sparkle shown in his eyes.

Another man in the group yanked the card from the other and read it in haste. "You gone done yourself good, Joey!"

"Joey, we can't take this kind of money from you!" the main man murmured politely, eyeing one of the hundred dollar bills Robert was handing him. He didn't sound very convincing.

The guy's a con, Rico thought. *A good one, too.*

"Yes, you can. And if things get really bad, call me. Even if they don't get bad, just call…promise?"

The four men nodded as they walked away shaking their heads. One turned and yelled, "Mister, you got a gold mine there with that woman! You'd better treat her well. We'll be watching!"

She is…but, mind your own business. "Apparently, you have a fan club," Rico said to Joey, tugging at her arm to get going. "I…take it you served them at the soup kitchen or somewhere?"

Joey walked along, but her head was turned, apparently trying to spot where her *buddies* were camping out. She nearly tripped. She stalled taking baby steps while the four moved well past earshot distance.

"So?" Rico persisted.

"It's a long story and not very interesting at all. Besides…"

"Well, lassie, I have plenty of *tiempo* right now."

She cleared her throat to keep from laughing, and to stall some more. Maybe Rico would drop it. "Have I ever told you, what a nice behind you have? And your biceps are oh, so…" she said in Spanish.

His serious face told her there was no chance of distraction.

Joey gave up and continued in Spanish. "Hum…well its more like…we ate and slept at the same shelter for a little bit."

Rico frowned at her. *Slept, a little bit of…? Sure.* The punch line he waited for didn't come.

"Then, I met this pastor couple that helped me on my feet."

Rico was floored when he realized she was serious; then anger quickly reared its head. "You needed money and never bothered to call me! Gee whiz, Joey! What got into you? What am I…a second rate boyfriend?"

The acidy tone almost raised *her* ire; and they weren't even husband and wife.

"Look, it's water under the bridge. Let the dead bury the dead," she said matter-of-factly. She would not listen to another word. She wanted to make sure she lived up to the same saying by not bursting out in anger that he had the audacity to question her silence when for almost three years he had kept her at a distance. She didn't know that he had expected to be dead.

Let the dead bury the dead? He missed the irony. *I don't need idioms, Joey. Soup kitchen? Shelter?* His head spun. The love of his life had been homeless and he hadn't known? What did that say about their relationship? Why did she keep it from him? They had talked on the phone during that exact time frame.

Joey wouldn't bother to tell him that it was her mistake she ended up in the streets. She had plenty of cash initially when she made her move to New Mexico, but it had run out even as a major mix up occurred in the sale and cashing out of her stocks. On top of that, a denial of service attack—a computer-based virus used by hackers—had caused major confusion in bank transactions.

Even money wired to her account from friends disappeared. It seemed she was destined to learn first-hand what it meant to be in dire straights; especially after losing her purse with the plethora of ID's, including the credentials that tended to open doors for her quite quickly. Humility had not been one of her traits, until after that first appointment with a new destiny.

It was a quiet ride back to the dojo. The girls were there waiting; full of energy as usual. Rico made no qualms about wanting to avoid them—as much as he was growing attached to them. He didn't much feel like the knight they still believed him to be. He escaped to his place before they saw him and snuck into his bedroom sanctuary. They wouldn't go there; it was off-limits. He flipped the air conditioner on full blast, popped a pill or two, and collapsed on the bed.

CHAPTER NINE

RICO FRETTED about the heat as he walked across the street. The mercury was well above the century mark. He began to doubt that New Mexico, at least the south, was going to work anymore. The comfortable San Diego climate beckoned him back. But something more important quickly occupied his thoughts.

Rico got to Joey's place and went in. He couldn't find Joey, so he headed downstairs to chat with his new buddy, Michelle. Fortunately for him, the combination dojo-house had refrigerated air. At the time, higher than normal humidity levels had rendered the standard swamp coolers—like the one in his new place—useless. In fact, Joey's two small downstairs bedrooms didn't even need artificial cooling. Nonetheless, Rico was rather sweaty palmed...but not from the heat.

He edged into the room and tried not to rouse the sleeping Michelle.

"Is that the warrior I've heard of, walking to and fro all nervous for some reason?" Michelle asked sleepily. She was looking more like Joey every day as her body weight stabilized. She was nearing a hundred pounds. Her pallid and stark appearance was slowly giving way to a glow, so slight that a stranger wouldn't notice. Her conversations were lasting longer and becoming more lucid.

He zoomed in on her eyes like when he first met her—then only because that was the only agreeable part of her face—but now he was getting as comfortable being himself with her as with Joey. He sensed that Michelle knew this and at some level drew comfort from it.

"Yep, Michelle, I just want to do things right. I was really lousy at this romantic stuff with my first wife. I want to give your awesome sister nice memories," he said. He sat down next to her, some frustration showing on his face.

"May I share something?" Michelle politely asked, though she intended to share regardless. "If the romance you and my sis..." she clearly loved the sound of that word *sis* and stopped to savor it before continuing, "...have shared these couple of years were to end this day, I know she would still cherish it the rest of her life.

"And you know what? So would I. To know that my long lost sister knows love at the level she does, gives me more strength to live another day than you'll ever know, Jacob."

Rico tried to absorb the gentle, exhorting words of the person who only a month before was at death's doorstep and considered insane. He wondered if by destiny this person lay before him.

He would learn much later how much in fact Michelle's future was really tied to his.

"Well," he said after some moments passed. "That's laying it on heavy, Michelle. Thanks for making this easier, girl," he teased.

"Hello, down there!" they heard Joey yell. "*We're* here," she added, forewarning she had company with her.

"Jacob, are you decent down there?" she asked to give her an added excuse to keep the downstairs off limits. Rico wondered when curiosity would get the best of the girls, or at least one of the many youngsters who used to have the run of the place. Perhaps a bathroom emergency would send one of an otherwise obedient group of youngsters downstairs and discover Joey's secret, unwell visitor.

Rico wondered again why she had chosen not to reveal Michelle's presence, or even existence, to the caring people in her life. Later, he would figure out that it wasn't a secret Joey was keeping for secrecy itself, but initially to guard Michelle's dignity and then later to respect Michelle's odd wish to remain unknown.

"Yea, Joey, I'm decent!" he said loudly to make sure all parties could hear him.   "Come in!" he said to her exaggerated knocking on the door.

"Are you coming up, Jacob," she asked as she peeked into the room before walking in. The suspicious look Joey got from her sister, as she tried to shield the lower part of her face with the bed sheet, hinted that something was up.

"OK, what's going on here?" she whispered, looking at her and then Rico.

Rico's forehead suddenly sported sweat beads, which he wiped off with his palm as he gave Michelle a glance. She nodded, barely concealing a big grin under the sheet. Rico beckoned Joey closer to him then stopped her at arm's length.

"What?" Joey asked impatiently. It had better be something good, she hoped.

Rico got down on one knee and fumbled through his pocket. Joey's hands covered her blushing cheeks.

"Joey," he mumbled clumsily, as the little box decided to cling to its hideaway.

Joey bounced slightly as she looked at her sister, already teary-eyed.

"I would like to know if you …" he gulped, "…will give me your hand in marriage."

He didn't know what else to say as she looked at the open ring box. Reaching for it with a trembling hand, he removed it from the box. In turn, she, with lightning fast speed, nabbed the ring from his skinny fingers and ran upstairs screaming. Rico got on both knees not knowing what to do. Puzzled, he looked at Michelle and shrugged.

"I *think* that's a yes," he said to her, blushing under his beard.

She didn't answer because she was busy looking for a dry spot on the bed sheet to blow her nose. Rico dragged himself to a tissue box sitting on the floor and handed it to her.

Seconds later Joey came back into the room. She was rambling incomprehensibly.

Just like a woman, Rico thought.

Joey went over to Michelle. "You knew! You brat!" she whispered as she hugged her ever so gingerly and motioned to Rico that the girls wanted to see him put the ring on.

"You might want to tell him yes or no first," Michelle whispered and pointed to Rico, still semi-kneeling on the carpet.

"Ay, tonta yo! (Oh, dummy me!) Of course! Yes, yes I'll marry you!" she yelled as she ran and tackled him.

"Well, can I put the ring on then?" he asked in Spanish, almost begging and trying to take a breath under the weight of her draped body.

"Yes! But the girls want to see you do it," she added, nearly yanking his arm from its socket.

"No! Not in front of those giggly girls! I'll never hear the end of it."

Joey's fake pout melted him.

Unfair manipulation! Rico looked at Michelle and frowned as Joey nearly dragged him up the stairs. The scene upstairs made him try to go back down. But he was way too slow for the jubilant girls who grabbed him firmly by both arms. Had he foreseen this, he would have proposed on a boat, somewhere in the middle of an ocean—water aversion or not.

"Hurry and get it over with," he whispered to himself. He placed the one caret diamond ring on her trembling finger and gently kissed the back of her hand. The girls were momentarily speechless. Then Tina reverted to normal, bombarding them with questions about the wedding date and place.

"When will you move into Joey's bedroom?" Tina chirped, prompting waiting looks from the other two women.

"You're too young to be asking that question girl," Rico answered, wearing a sheepish grin. "Now about the wedding date." He retrieved an envelope from his back pocket and waved it in the air. "What I have here, ladies…and girl…is a travel package for four people to…" he stopped to look at the glee in Tina's and Rosangelica's eyes, savoring the rare moment he was actually in control.

"Ow!" he yelped when Rosangelica slapped his upper arm.

The girl was stronger than she knew.

"You brat! As I was saying…to Las Vegas!" Before they had a chance to start screaming, he added, "We leave in two weeks."

He noted Joey's pensive look. The girls were busy giving each other high fives and talking about where Las Vegas was. They ran off to get a map.

Rico leaned over and whispered, "Haven't I told you often to trust me?"

She gave him a puzzled look.

"My future sister-in-law will be in great hands. That embassy buddy of yours will be here that week…just for you," he said, his tone comforting.

She didn't have to say, but he could tell the weight was off her shoulders.

"If the guy wasn't such an old guy and didn't consider you like his daughter, I'd be jealous about how much he knows about your life. Including your homeless adv…"

"Only three years older than you, I'll have you know."

That was not what Rico had perceived from the man's voice.

"Tell me how you got a hold of him without me getting wind of it?" she whispered.

The newly engaged pair hugged and kissed…until the girls peering in from the kitchen started giggling…again.

"Tell me you bum…Ambassador Bailey is a very busy man."

"I have my sources too, Ms. Reporter," he offered.

CHAPTER TEN

RICO BARELY survived two weeks of dealing with a trio of giddy, tireless, demanding girls, Joey included. A break in the otherwise monotonous business routine came the Monday before the Friday wedding trip.

An unexpected job seeker knocked at his door. Rico's home and office building, still without furniture, wasn't exactly ready for visitors.

The man was an old acquaintance of his. At the time they knew each other, the then Sergeant Rafael Azerra was a rebel rouser, gung ho, super patriot that annoyed Rico to no end with his loud, verbose manner. Somehow, Azerra had gotten word through a mutual acquaintance that the former Sergeant Rico was assembling another bodyguard outfit. It wasn't as if Rico was recruiting old teammates, but everyone knew he'd give anyone starving a job.

With no real intention of even considering the Delta Force commando vet for a position, Rico had finally acceded nonetheless—over the phone—to granting an interview if the guy would fly in. Thinking he had rid himself of the guy by stipulating the at-your-own-expense visit, the knock—at an annoyingly early hour—proved him wrong.

At first, their past slightly acrimonious history made for an awkward start to the meeting. But as their conversation progressed, Rico became quite intrigued with the turnaround in the guy's demeanor and new outlook of life. He wasn't sure whether the man was spouting out tales, but they talked for nearly forty-five minutes.

A wallet full of pictures gave Rico some proof, though he half suspected the photos had come with the wallet. How could that guy have progeny like them, and the wife, well...a literally picture-perfect face? Rico finally had to concede that Azerra did have a family, with children, and a passionate desire to provide them the safest, most comfortable life possible.

Azerra proved quite amenable to the responsibilities of the job and the little pay and minimal benefits that came with it. To Rico's now pleasant surprise, he accepted the job. But that wasn't until after checking with Shelley, his wife of 16 years. She had also flown in, along with the children, to see New Mexico. They had two children; Eli, a bulky, sulky 15-year-old son and a rather reserved daughter, Kindra, 13.

Rico blasted Azerra for leaving the family out in the car. At times Rico tended to be melodramatic. He was concerned about the heat, which wouldn't have made a difference in the air conditioned rental vehicle. It was just one of Rico's many quirks.

Azerra considered that the old man hadn't changed much.

Rico found Shelley's wit and candor refreshing, and it had little to do with the fact that the picture didn't do the woman justice. He took an instant liking to the whole bunch.

On a whim, Rico asked the two parents if he could task the whole family with an assignment; he made an attractive offer. They were thrilled just to go to Las Vegas, never mind getting paid! Azerra's task would be to see to everyone's safety and enjoyment. Shelley's job was simply to keep him away from the craps table—an old vice Rico knew about.

The Azerra family's trip from home, Maryland, was extending even farther west. The kids hadn't been west of the Carolinas and the desert was quite a shock—and so far, not entirely agreeable.

Friday rolled around way too slowly. Finally, it was flying time.

The crew experienced no delays in boarding—except for Rico—and the flight from El Paso to Las Vegas was nice and quick.

Rico, on the other hand, ran into a small problem. As he was clearing through the airport terminal metal detectors, the attending guard noticed an odd looking object in his carry-on bag. Even before the object was removed for examination, it dawned on Rico what it was. Not good news.

Fortunately, minutes before, Rico had given Joey everyone else's tickets and ducked into the restroom while everyone else went on ahead. The girls were in a hurry to watch the planes land. Because of that it wasn't readily apparent that they were traveling with Rico. The group was slightly ahead when "Sarge"—as Rico had taken to calling Azerra—looked back at hearing a mild commotion on the guard's radios. The barely perceptible nod and eye contact between the two old warriors let Sarge know to keep the group moving. His assignment was the girls and his family, not Rico—at least not on this particular mission.

Sarge continued on and informed Joey of Rico's possible delay.

And Rico would be more than a little delayed. The mystery item was a high-tech device he had forgotten to remove from his bag after a testing session weeks before. There was quite a ruckus; the on-edge guards reacted rather aggressively. Upon identifying it they immediately pounced on him. His somewhat Arab looking features didn't serve him well this day.

The Homeland Security alert levels had been elevated due to an apparent attack at another airport two days prior; a planned chemical release was suspected. Even though only two confirmed foreigner-initiated attacks had occurred in nearly ten years, the hysteria often caused personal disasters of their own. Suspicious neighbors sometimes took action into their own hands. A flurry of police alerts and response activity would ensue, and then die down, only to be repeated in other places. All this, added to the chaos and crime sprees instigated by the catastrophic recession gripping the nation, made for overworked and tense security workers of all kinds—from small private security firms to the U.S. Secret Service. This would prove fortuitous for Rico soon enough, but not this day.

Strangely enough, the next two hours spent sporting shiny handcuffs and sitting in an isolated security interview room proved very informative for Rico. He would discover that apparently he had connections in high places. In fact, many former working associates of his had zipped right up the ladder of success in various government agency posts.

All Rico knew was that saying anything would only dig him a deeper hole. He only hoped that he would get his one phone call. An extended period in a tank somewhere—as had occurred to countless other suspected of terrorist connections—would really mess with his marital plans. The thought that perhaps Joey might even change her mind completely occurred to him. At the same time his mind registered how painful the cuffs and the guard's grip were.

"Would you like to try explaining away the fact that you were trying to board a flight with this device? Which, I might add, appears to be on closer examination something I've never seen before? This is some serious high tech," said Nathan Roundtree, the Airport Director of Security.

Fear gripped Rico. Up to then he had maintained a sliver of hope that the whole thing would be dealt with as a big mistake and he'd be released. Reality set in and he envisioned his wedding night plans heading down the tube.

Some thought Jacob odd, others crazy—and rightly so in some ways—but *stupid* he surely was not. Wisely, he kept his response short and free of any wise cracks.

"I forgot it was there," he said.

"Again, Mr. Rico, please tell me that you by *some* miracle have a good explanation for this thing. I would love to have the Marshals, who are on the way, leave empty handed. Though they'd treat you OK…"

This didn't help Rico's nerves much.

"You sound to me like a man desperate to let me go. So I'll play the fool and pretend you really give a craa…hoot." There went restraint. "Even though I'll eventually be cleared, the risk for not trusting you could delay a very, very important date with destiny. Actually, her name is Joey," Rico said, at the last finally making a readable expression.

The Director's face registered the slightest of smiles.

"So, get your notepad ready, Mister," Rico offered.

Without much delay he disclosed in rapid fire the story of his foul up. "…So, after completing the tests, I placed the non-lethal prototype in my bag for the drive home. I got home and forgot to put the device in the safe, and instead threw it in the closet inside this travel bag. I wrote my critique and forgot about it. End of story."

"Sounds plausible," the Director said with a thoughtful look on his face. "And whom could I contact about this fairy tale?"

"The person who is aware of my *fairy tale,* and could vouch for me, would be Joe Corral. He's…"

"The Homeland Security Weapon Research and Development Director," Roundtree interrupted.

He is? Rico thought. *I thought he was an aid to some guy there.*

"Dang, son…you'd better thank your lucky stars I'm so good at judging people. I knew you were legit, but I just didn't know if I cared.

Don't call me son!"

"Yea, yea, well let's see how well your story holds up. Remember, even if it's true, there will still be hell to pay with the FAA and a grand jury hearing. So don't blame me," he said pointing at himself with one hand, waving at the guard, peeking in from outside, with the other.

"Have Courtney get me in contact with this person pronto, please." Roundtree told the guard when he stepped in.

"Yes, sir, right away." The guard fumbled with the door handle and left. He looked confused.

Two minutes later he returned. "Sir, Mr. Corral is on the line."

"Thanks. You and Officer Rogers watch over this gentleman until my return. He is not to be removed from this room. Understood?"

The message to the officers seemed clear enough—the Marshals were not to take detainee Rico without his clearance.

But, not three minutes later two U.S. Marshals appeared at the door and entered, displaying an air of superiority and control as they had done on many prior occasions. The pair behaved like poster children for rankism at its plainest. Of course, the airport officers themselves aspired to achieve the station in life the Marshal badge signified. The guards' awe of them clouded their thinking for a second.

To their horror one said, "We'll take it from here, gentlemen. Please hand us all possessions confiscated from this suspect. We have already taken evidentiary custody of his luggage.

"Well, Mister," the Marshal continued, without a pause, but now in a different tone as he approached Rico, placing an arm under his armpit to lift him. "Let's go."

"I'm sorry, Marshals, but you won't be able to remove him from this room right now," muttered the one guard that had strained and mustered the guts to speak up. "This person is currently being cleared for release."

"Under whose direction?" the senior Marshal asked in disbelief, eyeing the confiscated device, aware of its sophistication.

"The Airport Director of Security," responded the same guard, though not very firmly.

"I have no earthly idea where he came up with that," the other marshal quipped, bitingly.

With choreographed precision both marshals stood Rico up and proceeded to walk down the hallway. One of the guards flew by them and hurried into the Director's office.

"Sir, the U.S. Marshals have our detainee!"

A scowl came over his face, the Director readied his radio while he spoke into the phone. "Hey, Joe, are we talking about the same man? And you say he has an active Top Security Clearance? Please, wait a moment."

He changed to a commanding voice, and speaking into the two-way radio, instructed all guards to stop the marshals and hold them until he arrived.

"Thank you old buddy," Roundtree spoke into the phone. "You've been very helpful. Now I need to grab him back from the marshals. Yep, they took him against my explicit instructions not to, arrogant jerks! Yes, I have a cell phone. My secretary will give you the number, because I gotta run."

Roundtree tried to leave, but Corral, on the phone, held him up. "He *seemed* like an OK guy. Yea, I saw the movie *Forrest Gump*. That's funny! But I have to run! Yes, Joe, my secretary just gave me the fax with your letterhead. Thanks, I believe this should do it. Why am I going to this extent for this guy? I guess…I don't know. The name rang a bell maybe. Honestly, I have no earthly idea. Yes, it turned out great that you happened to know the guy. God bless you. Ring me up sometime, Joe."

The Director left the office in a rush shaking his head thinking, *I'll be…I was right!* He laughed a little, a year-long rarity for him. Life had become a non-stop nightmare; a rollercoaster of alerts and crises to respond to, shadow chases mostly.

"Run Forrest! Run!" he chuckled.

As the Director approached the marshals, the higher ranking one released a tirade.

"Roundtree, do you have any idea what you're doing? You are impeding the progress of U.S. Marshals who are transporting a federal suspect! Now direct your men to step aside before they are arrested or shot! Do it now!"

The Marshals nervously pondered their options, since Director Roundtree didn't appear too shaken. And even though only half of the airport officers surrounding them appeared armed the Marshals were still outgunned 8-to-2. They were also aware that all of them, including the Director, were Homeland Security employees, or federal.

In a very conciliatory voice and calm demeanor the Director interjected, "Ruiz, please act rationally. My men were to hold that U.S. citizen there…" he said, pointing at Rico, "…while I tied up some loose ends about his story."

"That is irrelevant at this juncture, I have assumed responsibility for him and this device," Marshal Ruiz responded tartly. His was clearly annoyed at being interfered with by lower level walks of life, federal or otherwise. The standing rule was that any marshal's word was gospel.

"I understand that you were informed on your way in that he fit the profile. Let me assure you that he is an American citizen, a highly decorated military man, and currently holds a Top Secret Clearance. Above that I can vouch for him."

The Director thought he had gotten through when the senior marshal raised an eyebrow. "So please release him to me," he requested firmly, signaling with his hand to send him over.

"I will confirm everything you've said, eventually…" Ruiz said, a little less tartly, "…but all those details will come out in the wash once he's processed. Now, step aside"

He took a few steps forward to test the waters.

The Director shook his head, and none of his underlings moved. Fortunately, everyone showed great restraint at not unsnapping their holsters. Rico felt embarrassed at the crazy scene unfolding on his behalf. Rico wondered whether anyone besides the marshals, Roundtree, and himself knew that the Director was way off on a limb and probably off the regs on this one.

The airport underlings were face-to-face, mano-a-mano, against the very ones they looked up to and weren't even flinching—someone was in solid command.

"I'll make a deal with you. Make one short call, and when you're done you can take him if you still think it *wise*. Either way he'll still have to appear in court. But, that's later, how about it?"

"All right, I'll play your silly game," Marshal Ruiz growled. "We've done this going on two years now. This is one crazy stunt! I like you, Roundtree…but, your career is over. Nothing personal, mind you. You're top-notch, except for this major disaster," he added, regaining his composure and sounding somewhat sympathetic—as if Roundtree needed his endorsement.

"Now, who could you possibly want me to call?" Sarcasm flowed out with the words.

Roundtree handed him the fax. The Marshal acted unimpressed with Corral's letterhead or the content of the letter. He punched the number on his government cell phone.

"Yes, with whom am I speaking?" he asked quite cordially. "This is U.S. Marshal Ruiz with an urgent call from El Paso International."

Director Corral's secretary informed him that the Director had been waiting for him to call.

"Yes, Director Corral. It seems we have a situation. Somehow you have been contacted about a matter regarding…"

Director Corral sternly told the Marshal to cooperate with Roundtree, or else.

"Sir, with all due respect, according to your letterhead, you're just the Homeland Security Weapon Research and Development Director. And your veiled threats do nothing to alleviate this situation."

"Yes, sir I am saying that I will *not* hand over Mr. Rico to Director Roundtree.

I am aware that he is fully competent and authorized to handle these matters. But, he had not cleared Mr. Rico when we arrived. And even then I must inform you that pursuant to Section 15 paragraph 8b of the Security and Freedom Act of 2010, a U.S. Marshal may assume control of any detained person deemed a probable threat based even solely on a profile, let alone confirmed possession of an illegal device with the intent to board a federally protected means of conveyance, i.e. a commercial flight...Sir! Good day!" Ruiz hung up more determined than ever to end what at first had amused him.

"OK, Mr. Roundtree, I played your card. Now, please...call these nice folk off before I have to arrest them all...and you!"

Director Roundtree's jaw hung limp, not from the command, but the stupidity he had just witnessed. "You have no idea what you just did, Marshal Ruiz. Hope you like desk work," he said, still aghast as the Marshals loaded their prize *prisoner*—for lack of a better word—into their vehicle.

Ruiz's phone rang. He confidently answered it after viewing the caller ID.

"Yes, sir, I just talked to him a few seconds ago. Sir...

"No, sir, I feel I was very professional in speech."

It was evident that the caller was getting his attention.

"Yes sir, I did quote him a section of the Act...

"No sir, I was not aware that he drafted that exact piece of the legislation. Sir, with all due respect..." Ruiz moved the cell phone away from his ear to avoid the shouting voice on the other end. "Yes sir, I'll catch the next flight to your office...

"I agree, sir, it is very convenient to already be at the airport...

"Yes sir, I am at this very moment turning over custody." Ruiz signaled his partner to quickly get Rico out of the van and officially return custody to Director Roundtree.

"Mr. Roundtree, the Director of the U.S. Marshal's Service would like a word with you," the senior Marshal said, handing over the phone.

Roundtree wondered what the Director wanted with him.

"Good morning, sir," Roundtree said. He eyed the senior Marshal who was wiping his now sweaty forehead. "Well sir, it's actually a very *cool* morning," he offered. "Actually sir, both of these Marshals were very professional in their conduct. I have to admit though, that their lack of understanding of the spirit of the law is a little disturbing...

"That is true, it was their zeal for the law, and perhaps eagerness in exerting authority, that became an obstacle to good communication this otherwise fine morning...

"And to you also, sir…

"Yes, I have complete faith that you will ensure that miscommunications of this sort do not recur and that the spirit of cooperation we had established continues…

"Thank you much, good day sir." With that, Roundtree handed the phone over to Marshal Ruiz, then uncuffed Rico using his key.

Rico, mesmerized by the drama he had just witnessed had forgotten about the pain. Then he whined as the removal of the cuffs aggravated his swollen wrists. Rico retrieved his travel bag from one marshal. He quickly dug out and popped one of his pills, heading off the full force of another headache.

"We have some formalities to get done," Roundtree told Rico. "Numerous Hancocks. If you can't move your wrist, just scribble. I expect you have enough common sense not to leave the country anytime prior to your hearing date. You might want to sell your car…you'll need lots of cash," he offered bluntly.

"Thanks for the sugar. Now I won't whine about these things." Rico held up the pill bottle.

Roundtree gestured, asking what they were. Rico gestured back, never mind.

Rico had hoped that the legal part of the adventure would fade away like a bad dream. As usual, hopeful thinking didn't work. Even then, he would manage to iron everything out without any criminal mark on his record or even having to tell Joey about the final dollar tally for staying on the better side of a prison cell; a paltry thirty thousand dollars to avoid a whole year in jail.

Before parting ways Rico attempted to entice Roundtree to retire and work for him.

"Considering the grace God has shown you today mister…I guess I'll seriously consider it. Someone is watching over you Rico. You could have easily ended up in solitary or Guantanamo."

Oh, no! Another one of those holy roller, hallelujahs. I retract my offer, Rico thought.

"One year to retirement and maybe so."

Yippee, he thought as he observed the underlings behind the boss break out in smiles.

"All righty then," Rico said, fidgeting. The silence made him even more uncomfortable. "Cinnamon roll," he blurted.

"What?" Roundtree said.

"Cinnamon rolls. I smelled them in the hallway when I was being viciously dragged over here…and coffee…"

The three security people shook their heads. Roundtree tapped one of the underlings and had him escort Rico to where he needed to go. Rico tempered the unpleasant experience of signing countless e-forms by enjoying three warm, gooey, succulent rolls with a Columbian ground chaser.

CHAPTER ELEVEN

RICO DIDN'T do bad time getting to Vegas after all, arriving only five hours behind the others. He strolled off the plane feeling surprisingly relaxed. Ignorance was bliss, of course.

Joey was waiting in the hotel lobby. "Jacob, I have a cell phone, you have a cell phone. So…?" Joey asked, somewhat perturbed. She stood, tapping the floor, arms crossed over her chest, fingers twiddling her bicep.

It wasn't a posture she had used with him before.

Is she really mad? She must be joking with me. "Joey, I…I don't know. I'm a busy man."

Dumb answer. She rolled her eyes.

"It just seems like everyone wants a piece of me." Double dumb.

She gave up, wondering who she was marrying—and for the first time getting just a tinge of doubt. By eight, everyone, including Joey, was demanding to go to the chapel to make it final, *before* she changed her mind.

"Wait guys! I have to eat something first. And I want to see what you girls have planned for the night, while I…we…are busy…*seeing* the sights," he insisted, bursting their bubble.

He whispered to Joey to go back upstairs and arrange all her stuff near the door for the bellhop to move to *their* room later. It took a few seconds before it registered, evidenced by a big grin on her face seconds later.

The girls had their suspicions about why. Rosangelica's blushing cheeks and quick girlish glance gave a clue she knew too.

Once ready to roll, Joey hugged him from one side and Tina from the other. Rosangelica held Joey's free hand and gave her a nervous smile. Was this going to change their great relationship? Were they going to be relegated to occasional attention? Who could know those things?

They moved through the various casinos to the hotel restaurant. Sarge's family followed as the ex-commando clumsily tried to act like a super smooth bodyguard. Rico often spotted him trying to be nonchalant as he addressed potential *threats*.

Rico enjoyed the dorky behavior too much to tell him that the protection thing was just a pretense to entice the family. There was no threat to the girls or him that everyone else in Vegas wasn't also susceptible to. Big money still managed to keep the tourist traps reasonably safe. Other parts of Vegas were a different story. For this trip they just needed an adult babysitter so he and Joey could do the honeymoon thing.

Rico could see he would have to send Sarge through bodyguard school; probably twice. It was obvious why he had been relegated to only doing advance work with former personal security employers—not that it was unimportant work. It was just a different skill set.

As they left the lobby of the hotel, a super-long, white Cadillac Escalade limo drove up. Rico stopped as if to let it go by. The teenagers peered in trying to catch a glimpse of the star they guessed was inside. Rico stood closest to the door that the driver opened, apparently to let the star out. Rico enjoyed their wide eyes and shrugs when no one came out. Then he leapt inside while the driver was looking the other way. The driver shut the door, climbed in the driver's seat and started to drive off.

The kids and Joey screamed, "Jacob, you're crazy! The car's leaving, get out hurry!"

The youngsters got all excited as the limo rolled out and then stopped suddenly. The driver ran to the back door and pretended to chew Rico out. Through the tinted window Rico watched the others looking thoroughly embarrassed. They all stared at the ground and tried to disappear as people passed by.

Then Rico jumped out and yelled at the top of his lungs, "Attention everyone!"

People all around stopped for a second. Most were tourists expecting some celebrity sighting. The locals were easily differentiated from the crowd as they carried on without even a change in stride.

"There's this wonderful woman I'm trying to marry, but I can't get her in the limo! Those people over there…" He pointed to the red-faced group. "…are holding up my wedding! Will my bride-to-be and the rest of the slow pokes please get in?"

That's all they needed to hear. The teens sprinted over and jumped in. The adults tried to be, well, more adult-like. The limo driver had been laughing the whole time Rico was yelling. He hadn't met such a character in a while.

Everyone admired the luxurious interior and played with all the gadgets and controls in the limo.

Rosangelica was extra wide-eyed. She was clinging to Joey as she took everything in. But still, there was this look of angst Joey could detect. Could Rosangelica sense Joey's apprehension?

Rico, noting a confused look, asked her in Spanish, "Well, mija. I have a feeling that your buddy there might change her mind. What do think?"

Maybe he wasn't so dense after all. He was teasing Joey, probing really.

Rosangelica looked thoughtfully into Joey's eyes, turned to him and shook her head with a new found air of sophistication, which surprised Joey. She answered Rico in her broken, wonderfully accented English, "No, chee will no shange her mine. Een all da time I…know…Joey…her eyes no tweenkle…as mush as today." Her pauses took nothing away from her loving commentary.

Joey's eyes welled up with tears. Rico wondered about the baby talk; she spoke English well he knew.

"I no think your face will ever glow more dan now…'sept…" She paused as she slid down to Joey's belly and placed her hand and face on it "…wen dare ees a leedle bebe een here."

Rico looked at the two women hugging each other. Tears rolled down Joey's cheeks soaking Rosangelica's hair. The wet strands made it sparkle, burning into his mind an image of little shining tear stars of one who loved another beyond his comprehension. Their lives had become intertwined to a level of bonding only a mother and a daughter could experience.

I was just teasing, he thought, feeling guilty and confused.

His eyes met Joey's. Through the tears she still managed to give him a tender look that asked if he was all right.

He started to speak, but Joey subtly shook her head, indicating that Rosangelica didn't need to know about her damaged womb. There she went again, looking out for someone else. This behavior was clearly a contrast to tendencies he had observed years before. Not that she had been an ogre, but ulterior motives, selfishness, and gruffness often ruled. He managed to control the gulp in his throat. He regretted having asked the question.

But Joey was glad he had. In her arms she no longer held a child in an adult body. The child—though Rico would not have characterized her as one in the first place—had become a woman just then. Joey understood that Rosangelica had just given her approval for Joey to marry the man she also still loved—insofar as puppy-love went. Joey's romanticized version of Rico—*very* romanticized—and not that bad of looks, had won the budding woman's heart, even with his initial missteps.

To Joey, she had sacrificially given up the romantic love for him, and placed it at her beloved friend's feet. It was a treasure that only a mature mind could begin to place in its proper perspective. Then she laid her head on Joey's belly and anointed it with her tears. Joey felt that by doing so, she was ceremoniously sanctioning the expected sexual union her friend would be enjoying. That act also bestowed to Joey the wishes of the young woman to see her womb as Joey herself had always spoken about with wishful, though cryptic words—and more direct, private words and groans in her prayer closet.

That is until God told her His grace was sufficient for her—until her boy child arrived. Anxiety for that promise sometimes crept up…like now.

Rosangelica sensed that she would forever be Joey's first born, comforted to know she would never lack tender arms to be held in and rocked. Her place in Joey's expected quiver was secure. She would be right even if someday Joey's womb was healed.

Basking in the moment, *most* reservations Joey had held about marrying Rico evaporated.

They arrived at what the driver considered the nicest chapel in town. To conceal the reason for his teary eyes, Rico claimed he had specks of dirt in them—it *was* the desert after all.

"OK, someone get the groom fixed up. I'll be back here with my maid of honor," Joey said. At seeing Joey's hand extended toward her, Rosangelica realized that meant her. She was ecstatic. She hadn't thought of it at all, her mind had been on *other* things.

As the music from the boom box played the wedding song, the beautiful women walked down the aisle with big smiles, gently shoving at each other with their hips. Joey stopped next to Rico, and he placed his arm under hers. They faced the minister, or the person pretending to be the minister, who could know?

Rosangelica got an ill-timed giggle attack.

"There she goes again," Rico quipped. "Stop, Rosangelica. This is very serious. Marriage is nothing to giggle about."

At that she ran to the bathroom, face flushed and blowing snot as she tried to restrain her laughter. Was her sidekick Tina, next? Fortunately, she was busy making every effort to impress Sarge's son with more mature, lady-like, manners.

Oh, no! Joey thought as she saw Tina google-eyed over the boy.

Rico was oblivious.

Rosangelica returned, flushed, runny-nosed, but composed. Rico wasn't sure how long that would last so he urged the minister to hurry it up. The minister flew through the lines and got to the "do-you" part quickly.

"Yes, I do," Rico answered solemnly, eyeing his gorgeous bride.

"Yes, I do," Joey said just as quickly and firmly.

"You may kiss the bride," the minister said.

They embraced and everyone cheered.

The original plan was that Sarge would escort the wedding party to Circus Circus, while Rico and Joey would escape to begin the honeymoon part of the trip. But Rosangelica felt nervous about being alone in an unfamiliar place. After some pleading on both her and Tina's part, the newlyweds decided to join the party at the casino…momentarily.

"I think Joey and I can…cover the little one's ears…control our passion for a little longer," Rico said.

"Speak for yourself," Joey retorted, drawing oohs from the group. "Just kidding…women have lots of self-control when it comes to that…huh, Shelley?" she asked Sarge's wife, expecting support.

"Speak for yourself, woman. When I get in the mood, Rafael starts marching, or else!"

"Oh, Mom!" her teenagers squealed. "That's sooo gross!"

After both of the newlyweds felt all was well with Rosangelica, they snuck out during a trapeze act.

CHAPTER TWELVE

"I FEEL like a million dollars!" Joey exclaimed a few hours later.

"Well, let's see, at today's inflation rate you must feel like…a whole dollar." Rico had just finished the sentence when a pillow pummeled his face. "Hey, woman…what was that for?"

"That was for your sarcasm … and this is for bursting my bubble," she yelled as she slapped him with the other pillow.

They engaged in mock wrestling until both were out of breath.

Then Joey piped up, "I can't believe what just went through my head!"

"You mean about how you just married the most outrageously stunning, debonair man on earth?"

"No, something significant…and real," she said with a straight face.

He feigned injured feelings, adding melodramatic hand gestures to a sullen look. The sudden tenseness and tightness that always preceded a major headache suddenly announced itself. He felt vertigo and moved casually to hide it from Joey.

Unaware of his condition she chirped, "I feel like going to a casino. But, that's weird, 'cause I don't gamble. In fact, I abh…"

"Who knows, you got luckier tonight than any other woman on Earth. Maybe you could win a few million," he willed out of his mouth, his voice sounding strained.

She noticed.

"Well, go on to the lobby, Joey. Let me catch my breath. Anyway, it's been quite an interesting day already." *Is she buying it?*

"Maybe we should just stay here and relax then," she said, eying him closely. His eyes looked different; she tried remembering signs of a drinking or drug problem.

"Move along woman…" he mumbled, "…we can also check on the girls while we're there."

Joey disappeared into the restroom to change, the whole time musing about her husband's behavior and her own strange *urge*.

Meanwhile, he quickly popped a pill. The throbbing headache didn't stop Rico from doing a double-take at seeing Joey's snug, red, strapless, micro-fiber, mini-dress.

"Wow! If some rich guy makes me an offer for you, you know I gotta take it. Nothing personal, mind you, just business baby!"

It sounded like he had all his faculties. He even managed to gingerly roll to the other side of the bed to avoid her purse as it swung toward his behind.

"Next time I *will* whack you," Joey promised.

She primped and curled her hair, then decided to try on her new glitter lipstick. Rico insisted she never needed any kind of lipstick. But she *had* to use Rosangelica's gift or there would be hurt feelings, she insisted. It was one of those little lies people tell themselves to do what they wanted to do anyway. She bent down to kiss him. He glanced closely at her lips. Wow! He wouldn't discourage her anymore. She softly kissed him, then headed to the lobby.

Rico stayed behind, splashed his face with water and sipped some from his palm. Normalcy, for him, returned only minutes later. He proceeded downstairs to join Joey, arriving just in time to see a wanna-be Romeo making the moves on *his* fine looking woman.

Joey extricated herself with finesse, strolling over to Rico. She walked with reasonable grace in the high heels she despised.

Rico got more than a little frazzled as the gentleman she had left behind eyed her backside shapeliness, exhibiting no couth whatsoever. Rico's ire didn't register with Joey; at least she didn't let on.

"Let's play that game that has a spinning wheel...roulette...or whatever," she said after they entered the main floor of the ritzy hotel's casino.

Joey was playing the dumb blonde about the name of the game, but she really didn't have a clue about playing roulette, or any other game of chance. It had never appealed to her in the least, and she wasn't given much to impulsiveness, apart from hugging babies and puppies.

Needless to say, they were both a little curious about her *urge*.

"Over, there. Come on," she said, acting like an excited little girl in a doll store dragging Rico by the hand. "What do we do to get into the game?"

"Don't ask me. Let's see how others do it," he said, trying to be the voice of reason.

"No, just get me in," she begged impatiently.

"Wait a minute. Joey, if you have a gambling thing … addiction, you've kept secret, it's time to fess up. I think we should get out of here. I don't like gambling or the atmosphere," he said with a strained tone.

"No, I promise. I've played rummy for pennies and that's about it. Please trust me." She added sugar on top with a loving look and peck on the cheek.

Rummy? His frown didn't go away.

"Gee whiz! All right," he conceded. So much for the hero who stands his ground. "Ma'am," he whispered to a kind-looking lady already playing. "How do we get in?"

She told him about getting the chips at the counter.

He lumbered over and got a hundred, bemoaning tossing away hard-earned money.

Joey stared at the itty bitty pile of chips, her tongue expanding her lower lip. "I saved you at *least* fifteen thousand on our wedding."

Rico didn't bother frowning. He went back to the counter and got four hundred more, shaking his head as he plucked the last hundred out of his wallet.

Saved me under $15,000 now! Well…still a good trade off, but….

His frustration was quickly tempered as his waiting beauty, little dress and all, gave him a big inviting smile and a subtle move of a bare shoulder.

Hay yay yay! Better trade-off, he figured.

He didn't want to fold without whining some more. "I'm out of cash…you emptied my wallet."

"It's OK, lots of ATM's around. And I saw a recent deposit slip of yours… on the floor…in that trash bin that doubles as your bedroom," she added as he started making a face about her snooping.

Seemed like she held all the cards this day, his comebacks were lagging.

Joey proved to be a cool customer as she played; giddiness aside.

In contrast, Rico sweated bullets, whispering things into her ear regularly. "Joey, let's get our money. You've won a whole bunch, now let's go!" he said one time.

He embraced her from behind and caressed her tummy. She seemed oblivious to it…she was in the *zone*. The "Zonza Zone" Rico liked to say. It was a Spanish idiom, akin to stupid, dense, or moronic in English, depending on its context.

"Sir," Joey piped up all of a sudden, addressing the dealer.

For a second Rico was relieved, thinking she was quitting.

"Am I allowed to bet all this at one time?"

Rico's gut tightened.

"Joey, are you losing your mind? You have about…what…thirteen-some thousand dollars there!" he whispered sternly, releasing his stomach hold and turning her around by the shoulders.

"Jacob, just let me play," she whispered trying to calm him down.

"I can't do that, Joey. Come on let's go. Please Joey, we could use that money!"

"Jacob, please settle down. People are watching."

And they were. The obvious newlyweds with the stroke of good luck had become a focal point of attention. Just what Rico liked—about as much as a splinter in the quick of the nail, or cactus quills in the behind.

"Yes, I figured that, Joey. I'm leaving. I can't handle seeing a gambling addict in the making."

"Oh, Jacob…Mister Melodramatic," she said, squeezing his hand tenderly.

"Let the lady play mister," chided a tall, husky man standing next to them.

In a nanosecond Rico's countenance changed, though *almost* unnoticeably so, from consternation and loving concern, to a darker, more ominous one. Joey peered into his eyes; she instantly recognized the shadow of rage.

"OK! Here, Jacob, take these chips and get *our* money back," she said, making sure to emphasize *our*.

She handed Rico almost half the chips. At the same time she gave the man that had rudely intruded a look that made him nervous; mini-dress and lipstick or not, her mile-long stare was no less penetrating than Rico's. The man wisely retreated.

"I'll be putting all this into play. I'll put it on seven," Joey said to the dealer the second Rico was out of ear shot. She tried to act as if she knew what she was doing.

She had been going by the odds as the numbers displayed on a screen revealed a pattern. She had asked her neighbor at the table what the numbers were for. It seemed silly, but she pretended to know what she was doing after a mini-lesson from the fellow gambler.

The dealer closed the bets and rolled the wheel as he eyed the obvious non-player, or con, as he was thinking.

The wheel spun and spun for what seemed an eternity to Joey. *Please hurry before Jacob gets back,* she prayed. She was nervous about him returning and doing something stupid right in the middle of a spin.

"We have a winner! Lucky seven wins!" the dealer announced, subtly pressing the security button below the table at the same time.

Everybody around Joey was ecstatic and cheered for her like a returning war hero. Some even hugged her. One guy hugged a little too long for her liking. Fortunately, the crowd around her blocked Rico's view as he counted the money handed him, all the while trying to see the reason for the commotion at Joey's table.

"What's the big deal? I just doubled my winnings." Joey muttered to the lady who helped her.

"Well, it's a little more than that honey. Girl, you just won near a hundred K. From what I could see you placed ten K or so in the pot. That's a good ten-fold increase or so, I would say. People like seeing underdogs win, that's all," the lady finished saying as two security men approached and whispered something in Joey's ear.

Her freckled face quickly matched the hue of her red dress.

Rico approached from behind and tapped one of the well-dressed security men to move aside.

"Hey, honey, what was that ruckus about?" His mind processed the look the dealer was giving the security men. The security man in front of him took a step toward Joey.

"Gentlemen, I suspect…" Rico thought for a moment about his ironic choice of words, "…that you have a problem with my wife. Joey let's get any winnings you have left and go cash in…or whatever," he instructed Joey, tugging at her arm without waiting for commentary from the men.

He figured she had blown most of it and it would be a quick matter.

"Sir…ma'am…that won't be necessary, a runner is now doing that for you. The amount of one hundred and five thousand *may* be given to you after we clear up a security matter. Please, folks…this way." A polite hand gesture pointed in the expected direction of travel; that it wasn't an option was written on the two security men's faces.

Rico's neurons processed the words "security," "may," and "one hundred and five thousand" and almost short circuited.

At one point the senior man pointed in the direction of the elevators.

Rico's mouth still hung open as he followed in a daze. It couldn't be possible, in trouble with authorities twice in two days!

The group walked in silence; Joey and Rico from embarrassment, the security team because it looked good.

Joey finally spoke up when she saw the man that had been sent to cash in her gambling chips. He was intending to follow the group onto the elevator and leave the money bag in the security office. She felt a sudden sense of injustice at thinking of the looks from others as they were being cordially escorted off, and then seeing her money just out of reach.

"That's my money and I want it now!" she announced to no one in particular as she moved toward the now wide-eyed young man who was, unfortunately, in the wrong place at the wrong time.

Rico assessed the scenario that was unfolding. His mind went into sensory overload, sometimes called the tachy-psyche effect, when sounds become distorted and events appear to slow down. With extensive and continuing training, its distorting effects could be reduced and an auto response initiated; but this day his training didn't help much.

Rico's reaction to the events happening would make him doubt his mental capacity even more. The elevator had just reached their floor, the doors opened. That's when the lead security man was caught by surprise by Joey's move away from the elevator. She closed in on the moneyman, who had decided to wait for the elevator to the right.

"Ma'am, this way!" the security man said as he grabbed her arm. She broke away and grabbed hold of the money bag. The man carrying it held on with a death grip. At that moment the security officer who had grabbed her arm wrapped his arms around her in a rear bear hug, attempting to carry her into the elevator.

Rico could only mouth the words, "Don't do that! Let her go!" He really meant to ask if the man was suicidal…or just stupid. No sound actually left his mouth even as Joey yelled for him.

Rico moved toward her as the other guard grabbed his elbow and placed his hand into a hold that causes extreme pain. Had his instincts kicked into gear like on his good days, he would have escaped the hold with ease and the security man would have been the one in pain.

"Let go of me," Joey screamed. Her heels flew off her flailing feet just a second before she planted her feet on the carpeted floor. A judo technique executed with precision freed her from the hold.

Then, to Rico's horror, Joey took a stance he had seen weeks before at the dojo. With lighting speed she delivered a powerful blow to the man's chest. It sent him flying backward into the wall next to the elevator doors. The mirror wall cracked and the man's eyes rolled to the back of his head.

No one in the crowd moved. Then the senior man on duty, who had been monitoring on the closed circuit system, zipped through the crowd, panting. He had used the stairs.

"Everyone step aside, an ambulance is on the way!" he hollered as he glared at Joey, by then kneeling on the floor, already repentant of what she had just done...and from instinct had thought of finishing. The new man in charge was about to say something to her.

"Mister," Rico said through greeted teeth. "That is my wife. That's what she did...if you want to see what I can do, just say something stupid."

Rico's stare sent shivers down the man's back, shutting him up. But, it was obvious to Rico, from Joey's stare, that he had lost some of the chivalrous glimmer in her eyes. He in turn resented the fact that, even though she meant everything to him, *anyone* could draw out the rage in him that he had worked so hard to temper for so many years. And apparently, he considered, he was expected to summon it when convenient to her.

The second in command of security arrived seconds later. As she walked through the crowd and then touched the hand of the still unconscious agent, she took note of the profile of the woman the police officer was interviewing. The pointing crowd had made it easy for the officers to determine the culprit.

"*That* lady did this?" she asked, speaking to no one in particular.

A nod from the man still gripping the money bag gave her the answer. At first she thought it a lucky strike to her buddy, until she saw the large indentation made in the mirror wall, next to the elevator doors. She eyed Joey and thought briefly that the profile looked familiar, but no one came to mind.

Then she saw Rico. "Sergeant *Rico*? Jacob?" she said, not caring that she interrupted another interviewing officer.

Rico looked up. An appropriate facial expression for the situation escaped him. A blank stare threw the woman off for a second. Rico finally revealed a slight grin; that was all he could offer the comforting face in a jungle of fuzzy ones.

"Pardon me, lady," the Las Vegas Officer told her not quite tartly. Had the lady's face not be so striking he certainly would have been more caustic.

She ignored him. Without thinking, she firmly and unabashedly hugged Rico the moment he got up from the floor. It didn't matter that eons had passed since they last saw each other or that the relationship might have faded.

Rico acted stiff, caught by surprise, but was sincerely moved by her still loving spirit.

"Officer, is this man a witness?" the lady asked.

The pale face registered muted annoyance. A civilian was interfering with his work.

"Oh, I'm Jennifer Jordan, Assistant Director of Security here," she quipped as the officer appeared about to will himself to chastise her. She flashed her credentials.

"I'm trying to find that out now, Ma'am. Apparently your friends…this man and his wife…" Those words hung in the air and distracted her for a second; she avoided Rico's eyes. "…were caught running some con at the roulette table. We will…"

"Be releasing him…*and* his *wife* to me," Jennifer said.

"Excuse me?"

"I am presuming that you are in the middle of preliminaries and have not determined probable cause and arrested them. Therefore I am releasing you of the need to do so. If that version of events holds up, your department will be contacted when I see fit," she said with unequivocal authority.

"But, Ma'am. These two assaulted your security man. He might not even make…Well, at least he's conscious now," the officer corrected himself as the paramedics, using smelling salts on the agent, could be seen arousing him.

"I'll be back officer," Jennifer said as she walked away. "Rico, don't say another word." The first command she had ever issued him…as a civilian.

She walked away after seeing submission in Rico's eyes. Those eyes, he was as handsome as ever; her knees quivered some.

"Steve, can you hear me?" she said, kneeling next to the victim.

The man nodded.

"I need to know if these people attacked you."

The man's eyes rolled in various directions, his faced winced as his lips moved but said nothing.

"Why did the lady kick you, Steve?"

She drew closer to his face. She moved the oxygen mask and leaned in. One paramedic didn't look at all pleased.

"I think I screwed up, Jennifer. I grabbed her and she went crazy," he whispered.

"Steve, you're saying that it wasn't planned…to assault you I mean?"

"I guess it wasn't…sorry Jennifer…about the paperwork…and all," the man said, every syllable spoken with labored breaths.

"That's fine Steve, as long as you make it through this. You *do* plan to make it through this, don't you?" she asked nervously. "Just be glad her high heels fell off first…before…you know."

The agent nodded firmly and gave her a thumbs-up. The cracked ribs would heal just fine, he figured. With that chore done, a bigger one awaited her.

Using all the power of persuasion she could muster, Jennifer succeeded in keeping Joey and Rico from being taken into the custody of the Las Vegas PD. There would be no charges pressed by the injured officer or the casino, as far as she was concerned.

Then the Director of Security arrived and quickly made it plain that he thought different.

"Ms. Jordan…" he said, emphasizing the "mizz" and using a tone intended to induce fear, "…what do you think you're doing!" He had not *yet* seen anything in Jennifer's demeanor to give him pause and cause him to behave with more restraint. She was a dove.

"I've taken responsibility for these two individuals while I investigate this matter…and after we view the tapes together I will be releasing them," Jennifer said without looking up, still caressing Joey's blond, sweaty, hair. She had tried to calm Joey, who was still trembling. It occurred to Jennifer at that moment that it was a futile exercise.

"You have violated protocol!" he continued in an abrasive tone. "I am in charge here and I *will* be pressing charges against this…maniac woman!"

Those last words had barely trailed out his lips when Jennifer, who had already decided to stand and wait out Joey, moved toward him ever so calmly. The supervisor prepared to hear words to savor, like, "You're right sir. I apologize!"

Instead, Jennifer's hand moved up slowly as if to move several rebellious bangs from her eyes. Then with lightning fast speed her right hand grabbed his neck; she lifted him into the air about an inch, and backed him up about four feet, where his body slammed into a mirrored wall. Cracks spread like a thousand tentacles growing instantaneously. More repairs for the maintenance crew.

Bystanders, including a surprised Joey and Rico, watched as the five-foot-eight inch woman pinned the slightly taller and heavier man against the wall. As he struggled to disconnect her fingers from his neck, she was whispering things to his face. She was basically one with his throat, her sun-bronzed hand contrasting with the man's now blood red neck.

One young police officer was standing three or so feet away, apparently listening to the one-way conversation while chewing gum. He just stood there not twitching any of his ample muscles—to him it was just another street brawl, under chandeliers.

"Man, is anyone going to stop her!" Rico mumbled. He looked around hoping another cop would step in. For a second he thought that the young officer was frozen with panic. He quickly deduced that the officer was, in-fact, finding the scene a monotony breaker in this otherwise boring shift.

Then he saw the same officer step forward, apparently to take control. But he only grabbed the man's wrist. The supervisor's weapon was millimeters from clearing the holster and being put to use.

Jennifer saw the officer's hand clear their bodies with the muzzle of the confiscated 357 Magnum in hand—her boss's weapon of choice. Rico could see Jennifer subtly tense her fist. He heard her say, "You son of a...! You would shoot me?"

The officer could not have stopped the blow even if he tried. Either way, he wasn't alert enough to notice the change in her facial demeanor, even as the force of her grip ratcheted tighter. Nor could he know that her fists were lethal weapons. Rico knew of at least once this had been proven.

"Jenny!" Among the cacophony of voices, Rico's voice was the only one she discerned as her arm started backward for momentum. It registered crystal clear above the increasingly boisterous crowd of onlookers that were being pushed back by uniformed casino security people.

Jennifer turned for a second and looked into the surprisingly tender stare of her former sergeant and love interest. Even though every inch of her being wanted to release pent-up rage—including at seeing Jacob again, a *married* man—she instinctively digressed into military mode and obeyed the command, or plea, as it was.

Strangely enough, she missed the fact that Rico had used her romantic pet name; the one he used in the years they had dug foxholes together, battled side-by-side, and did other more personal things together. She learned quickly that when he got serious, romantic or sentimental, her name was Jenny. But he tended toward the informal with his male teammates as well.

The choking, gasping man in Jennifer's grip fell to the floor in a heap. His humiliation was tempered somewhat by the fact that the police had cordoned the area and the gawking was from a distance. That was more than fortunate for the man because the wet spot in his trousers did not look impressive.

Joey was on her feet by then; eyes, ears, mind, and heart engaged. She sensed the still immensely powerful connection between her husband and his former compatriot. Her heart skipped a beat...or two. Was it love...or military drill that had commanded such immediate, unquestioning obedience?

Joey was no stranger to deeply ingrained drills that would take over in-stinctively, almost robotically, during stress. She would ponder that question throughout the rest of the morning. She considered the combat bonds forged with others in her own past. But this seemed to her to supersede even that. After no small inner struggle Joey chose to take the high road, dismissing the potential romantic overtones, and moved to offer comfort to Jennifer, now the one trembling with subsiding rage.

"We are some nasty women aren't we?" Joey piped up.

"Oh, maybe a bit aggressive…" Jennifer said, accepting the hug and affection Joey offered.

Joey seemed as surprised as Jennifer at the warm and sincere affection she was showing.

"But …" she paused again to think whether what she was going to say was appropriate, "…at least I just have Anglo blood running through *my* veins," Jennifer added.

Joey was puzzled for a second and then made the connection—the heritage thing. It was in her blood to be subdued, not in Joey's, at least as stereotypes went. But how would Jennifer know about Joey's heritage? They met briefly once. It hadn't been exactly a bonding moment either.

"Anglo blood? Well that is kind of bland, and I don't have a problem with that, mind you…just…please don't say…English blood."

It was Jennifer's turn to be puzzled. She would have to wait to solve that one.

"OK officers, who's in charge here?" Jennifer asked in her in-charge tone. She needed to take control if she was still going to keep her friends out of jail. Tissue had cleared evidence of tears from her face. Now it was all business.

"That would be me," piped up what turned out to be a transplanted Englishman, of all people. That he still had a British accent was an understatement.

Jennifer and Joey grinned at each other. The cool casino air wasn't enough to keep the very fair-skinned Brit from turning red with embarrassment. He had heard a little of the women's conversation.

"Ladies, please," Rico said to support the poor fellow. His own blood pressure and senses were back to normal tolerances. Any more adventures on this trip and he would have a heart attack for sure.

"Well, Ma'am…" the officer turned to Jennifer, "…at this time the Las Vegas Police Department has no jurisdiction since you have chosen, if the decision stills stands, not to pursue charges."

"That's correct. And they, I'm sure, being tourists here in our fair city…," saying it with little sincerity, but for effect, "…want to continue their visits to other casinos and such. Is that right folks?" Jennifer asked, looking at the Rico and Joey, edging them to follow her lead.

"Yes…yes, this has been a most traumatic event for us." It really had been. "We would hate for this to be the major event to tell our many, well-traveled friends…sir," they both chimed in.

"Hmmm, I see. Well apart from the smoke in this room, it is beyond me to direct where you go," the officer said to the couple and then turned to Jennifer.

"Miss…Jordan, is it? I expect an incident report that indicates you declined to press charges. OK?"

"That's the procedure, Officer…?" She squinted trying to read his nametag.

"Roberts … Officer James Roberts," he offered kindly. He was letting his guard down.

"You're pretty handsome. Are you single?" Joey piped in out of nowhere, glancing playfully at Jennifer.

Jennifer noticed and pretended to be offended. She couldn't be too put off, a sly smile showed. She had noticed his charming demeanor…and looks.

Joey peeked at his left hand—no ring.

Rico noticed and quickly deduced her conniving thoughts. *Joey…we gotta talk…soon.*

"You Brit men are cold blankets," Rico blurted out just to shake things off. "Maybe I could give you some romance lessons some day … old chap."

"What?" the two intrigued women piped in.

Jennifer continued admiring the Brit's features from the corner of her eye. It suddenly dawned on her she might actually be over Rico. Her heart had pounded for sure at getting closer and then hugging him, but not that often agonizing yearning she had suffered through in the past. It was now, she pondered, only a feeling of great joy at seeing a long lost loved one—a brother maybe, or even a father figure of sorts. She knew her romantic love had been real enough. The sexual yearnings and thoughts she had entertained were from a fully mature woman's mind. Now, she was happy to be discovering that those feelings had transformed into a *still* yearning love for the man and his image, but now…*mostly* a platonic love. Maybe she didn't have to run from him any more. And maybe her private oath of celibacy, or at least extended relationship break, could be forgotten—conveniently.

Strangely enough, it was what Joey had prayed for minutes before—

almost willing it into being. It seemed that someone was answering prayers rather quickly…perhaps. Joey's motives were less than pure, albeit understandable, if one had sensed the electricity in the past between her new husband and this woman. As much as it bothered her to have such insecurities, former romantic interests were always a threat in her mind.

Cemented in Jennifer's mind at that moment was thinking of Rico as family. From the outside though, especially from Joey's vantage point, her clinging to Rico was not discernable as romantic or just *very* friendly in nature. Jennifer was oblivious to what it might look like to others. She finally felt at peace. She was satisfied that life did not have to mean, Rico, or no Rico. Her old buddy had dropped in from out of the blue. And it had to be destiny. Trying to make the break months before, she had purposely not told him that she was moving to Vegas. First of all, he would have chastised her. Mostly, she just wanted to sever the hold of her security blanket.

It was not lost on Rico that the two closest people in his life had hidden things from him. It was rather perturbing and disturbing.

In Jennifer's mind, she had no doubt from that moment on that they were intended to be family. She was happy. Rico and Joey would agree soon enough; that she was sure.

Rico noticed Joey give Jennifer a subtle nod and the two headed to the ladies room without saying a word. Rico barely had time to wonder what they could possibly be doing when the two returned after five minutes of *freshening up*. It was obvious they had hoped the crowd had dispersed.

At the same time they arrived, the man Jennifer had terrorized returned from his own absence.

"May I speak with you, Ms. Jordan," he said, this time cordially, or perhaps cautiously.

Jennifer excused herself from the group. Rico gave Officer Roberts a subtle nod to get close to the pair, to help avoid another fiasco. What a chore, having to keep an eye on the pretty lady.

The Brit stayed close. He heard the man say tentatively, "I want to tell you in person that I am letting you go. I will not press assault charges if you don't make a scene. You'll get paid to the end of the month. The head boss said to throw in six months severance *if*, and only *if*, you cooperate."

"Let me get this straight…you're saying that Robert knows about this already and he agrees with *you*?"

Her use of the boss's first name caught him by surprise. Nobody on staff called him that, ever."

"Yes, he wants this over with quickly and quietly. He'll be arriving in an hour or so. Please, Jennifer…"

"Jennifer is my name with friends; *don't* call me that again," she said through gritted teeth. "Guess what, Mister Ted Jones, wanna-be-Ceasar." She added to his guardedness as she drew closer and whispered, "I'll be leaving quietly out the front door…with my integrity and dignity intact. Yours is nowhere to be seen."

After savoring the injury she inflicted, she continued. "You can take your pathetic job. I resign! Oh, and tell Robert to use that money of his and…you know. That's what his money means to me. I thought…" she swallowed hard, "…he had some integrity and guts to come and fire me himself, in person! You know very well …" her voice began to rise, then she lowered it again, "… that those people didn't deserve the treatment they got.

"I'm hoping for your sake that man over there," she turned and pointed at the attentive Rico and company, "who taught me everything I know about killing people quietly…decides to only seek legal recompense. If he does, please for your sake, be very persuasive with Robert to pay his demands the first time. Even though an *accident* happening to a cruel and arrogant jerk like you would please me, since my…best friend…just got *married*, and wants to start a new life, I'll *try* to stop him.

"To use a phrase from this God forsaken place, 'Do you feel lucky…well do you?' Oh, wait a minute, that's by someone else who reminds me of my old sergeant," she said and nodded her head at Rico again. "We understand each other, don't we?" She turned away and then stopped, "By the way…nice new pants."

Perspiration streamed down the supervisor's face.

"That's Sergeant Rico?" he confirmed with a big gulp, not entirely missing the reference to his pants. When Jennifer nodded yes, he made a wise decision. "Consider it done. I can't promise Robert will buy it and not drag it into court."

"That would be stupid." Jennifer stepped away as she finished her sentence and gave him a sinister stare..

She noticed Officer Roberts watching closely and deduced Rico had something to do with it. *As protective as ever*, she thought.

Well, if Officer Roberts here…" Jennifer commented to the newlyweds,

"…is done, maybe we can head out, to where ever? I'll need your card, of course, for my report."

He nodded before she even finished, fishing for his wallet with haste.

"Let's hurry guys," Jennifer urged, turning toward the main entrance, casually making the card disappear into her slacks pocket. Rico and Joey followed, quickening their pace as they turned a corner.

Outside, the temperature was a refreshing sixty-five degrees and an unseasonable mist hung in the early morning air. Everyone looked at each other awkwardly and wondered what to do next.

The honeymooners, Jennifer was sure, were anxious to make the remainder of this day a more pleasant memory. "Uhm, I'd better get going," Jennifer muttered in the general direction of Joey. "It was a most unusual way to have gotten to meet you in person, again."

She took a deep breath and continued. "Jacob mentioned you in his letters every time," she said speaking to Joey in a whisper. "Congratulations! I can tell that Jacob made a wonderful choice. Perhaps…" she looked down, "…we can stay in touch. Maybe, let Jacob continue writing…you know…about family…" the word caught in her throat, "…*things,* and such." Her voice was dry and raspy. "Maybe keep me in mind for a God mother…or whatever Irish or Mexican people do."

Joey knew more or less that Rico corresponded with her, but she wasn't aware that he had shared any details about her with Jennifer. To Joey he made mention of Jennifer often in his letters; often enough to foster uneasiness at times. Those subtle jealousies aside, Joey felt good at that moment. She surprised Jennifer and Rico as she grabbed Jennifer, hugging her firmly.

There went those goose bumps again. Rico had always felt odd enjoying such seemingly mushy things, like seeing people in the park showing affection for each other. He wasn't sure if it was a normal, *manly* emotional response. He also *thought* he hid it well from others.

Even some women had reservations about him when his defenses were down, at times even allowing a tear or two. Sometimes it was a spontaneous sob that sneaked out at seeing a kindness somewhere. Other times it was a muted groan when witnessing an injury, especially emotional, but he had always managed to avert a full-fledged outburst. It was difficult for him to reconcile these two sides of himself; bouncing back and forth between tenderheartedness and the more prominent state of inner anger and self-loathing had made him an able mental gymnast.

The increasing level of pent up anger had become a growing concern during the last year. But, there seemed to be still waters up ahead; he sensed that the woman he had chosen had a great destiny and could help set him free. Free from what he really wasn't sure. Yet, he already felt a sense of belonging. Finally, he was beginning to enjoy pleasant moments like this one with great, though somewhat awkward, happiness. Maybe it *was* Joey, or age…or just mortality knocking.

"Jennifer, he got married, he didn't die! Listen, even though I happen to be closer to his age, you were…no, you *are* and always will be someone that would also be the perfect woman for him. He would have done great to have married you instead. Please don't ever doubt that.

"Remember this though, twenty years from now he and I will be using walkers and speaking with trembling voices, like this."

Joey used a little voice she normally performed for children. Jennifer started half-laughing, half-crying.

"And I don't think that you would like changing your husband's diapers or asking him to insert his dentures to give him a kiss."

The two women looked at each other and laughed the same instant.

"Oh, no! I've got corny-itis! Jacob, you've infected me! Help!" Joey mocked.

"Me too," Jennifer added, "…'cause I actually thought she was funny!"

The women were having a ball at Rico's expense. It wasn't funny to him, because he knew well that, statistically speaking, Joey was accurate about who had to care for whom in the sunset years. An uninviting image of an *older* him came to mind for an instant, it made him queasy. Time was really gaining on him after all.

A taxi drove up and Rico opened the door for Jennifer.

"You know, people…I'm really, really offended. Me, the best jokester in the world, just might change his mind about inviting you to a fine restaurant for breakfast with us. That woman I have to live with, but not you," he said to Jennifer."

Jennifer managed quite successfully to sweet talk herself—as always—and Joey back into Rico's good graces.

"OK, since I see that you have truly humbled yourself, and are sufficiently contrite," he said.

Joey and Jennifer rolled their eyes.

Contrite? Joey mused.

"Therefore, with one last pucker right here…" He pointed to his lips. "… from this outrageously gorgeous, but *humbled* girl, we can move beyond this shameful, tragic moment … and meet in one hour at…at…" he looked expectantly at Jennifer.

"The Excelsior will work," Jennifer offered quickly. She gave him one final kiss and bounced into the taxi.

Whoa! That sure didn't look like a friend kind of kiss. Jennifer, he's married now remember! Joey thought.

Rico waved and turned to face a glowering Joey.

Oops! "What?" he asked, waiting for a rebuke. Was it the kiss, or the smirk on his face from the kiss?

"Jacob, I didn't think it was possible, but your behavior is getting more eccentric by the day!" she said, laughing quietly as they walked side-by-side until they reached their room.

They hugged and loved on each other like typical newlyweds, as if nothing out of the ordinary had occurred on their wedding day.

He was really happy she had been kidding, that face he had seen was scary. And the promotion to eccentric from crazy was really nice too; moving up in the world.

"Now listen, woman, we have one hour, so…" Rico said as he gently hugged her more passionately and edged her into their room.

The anxiety about his *little problem*, which had caused the delay in proposing, vanished the moment her arms were wrapped around him in complete acceptance. He could finally let go of his reservations; Joey's disarming, warm laughter helped a little.

CHAPTER THIRTEEN

THEY ARRIVED at the restaurant freshly showered, Rico in casual attire and Joey in a less revealing, but classy, bright blue dress. Much to her surprise, she was beginning to feel at ease—sexiness wasn't so difficult to recapture after all. She had no intention of abandoning her modesty, but did intend on being extra pleasing to her husband's eyes.

Rico wasn't the slightest bit surprised that she could wear sensuality so effortlessly. He enjoyed the scenery from every angle. The lady he had just married was looking extra fine—not skinny, but not chunky either, just healthy—a very well proportioned five-foot six indeed.

Rico almost gulped at the sight of the nicely outfitted Jennifer gliding toward them, in high heels even. Unlike Joey, Jennifer had always been aware of her hypnotizing sensuality and made use of it. Some would say that at times she had misused it. She obviously had something to learn about when to tone it down.

Rico, used to seeing Jennifer in more revealing evening attire, wasn't *too* stunned by the raving beauty in the satin white slacks and blue halter top; but then again, it had been a while since he had set eyes on her. Something about those brown eyes and the warm color of her cheeks. He knew it was a natural glow—though less glowing than earlier—because Jennifer never wore make-up apart from lipstick. He had long concluded that she didn't need that either. Her naturally red, shapely and full lips were always in fashion—even under black and green shades of camouflage.

Rico stared absentmindedly at those very lips; some habits were hard to kill.

Joey elbowed him firmly, annoyance showing on her face.

"What?" he blurted out. "I was just trying to figure out the color of her… shiny lipstick!"

Jennifer had been too engrossed in thoughts about having gotten fired to notice Rico's stare.

Joey wasn't about to let him continue what she perceived to be lustful staring. She stood to offer Jennifer a seat, purposely obstructing his view.

"Jacob, maybe you should go check on the girls?"

What girls? Jennifer wondered. *Do they have kids already? Rico never....*

"Buth...I'm noth done," Rico muffled through a mouthful of eggs and ham.

"Oh, all right. But, hurry up! I want to talk with Jennifer."

"Yeth, Honey," Rico said with a mouthful of pancakes. He rose to his feet obediently, but wondered what in the world his wife wanted to talk with his old buddy about.

"Oh my goodness, Joey, in all my years working with this man, I have never ever heard such an obedient tone of voice coming out of him. Not even with generals...well, he was even more belligerent with them," Jennifer said. She exaggerated of course. "But, wow! You have him well trained already!"

Jennifer tried to restrain her laughter to no avail. She was already having one of the most interesting and fun-filled days in years. But her hee-hawing stopped abruptly when she spotted her former boss approaching. Her face became instantly closed as she greeted the man in an uninterested, almost disrespectful tone.

"Mister Robert Jones. What brings you here?" She knew he had made use of his power and influence to direct resources, security people and cameras, to search for them. Even casinos he didn't own would have obliged him. It perturbed her to have been hunted down like a common criminal.

"Jennifer, may we speak in private for a moment?" Jones asked softly.

"These are my friends and anything to be said between you and me can be said here."

"I should've expected that," he commented without hesitation, a tinge of hurt registered n his eyes. The stately Anglo man was the owner of several casinos in the city. He was not used to being the odd man out as he was just then. It was obvious he was out of his element; speaking to *real* people who actually didn't give a darn about his status.

"Look Jennifer. I want you back. I've fired Ted and his second fiddle. Is there anyone else that I can let go to convince you to come back?"

Jennifer shook her head.

"How about the Director position?"

"No thanks," she said flatly. .

"Ummm…just for curiosity's sake, how much does a director make?" Joey blurted.

Rico frowned at her, though he waited for the response too.

"Right now it's slightly more than one hundred and ninety thousand plus benefits and perks," he said without blinking.

Joey shot Jennifer a look. *Are you stupid or something?*

Jennifer eyed her right back.

They had barely become friends and were already trading looks that could kill.

"Sorry, Mister Jones, but I've not been comfortable in this town since I got here last year."

Last year? She must have forgotten to forward her mail. But, why didn't you answer my E-mails? Rico privately fumed. *Girl, we gotta talk.*

"I stayed because I thought the place would grow on me. It hasn't, and I'm glad." Her tone and sense of finality made Mister Jones concede defeat.

"Very well, Jennifer, God speed to you. I expect you will succeed no matter where you go. I just hope that next lucky boss realizes what he has in you before it's too late."

Mr. Jones turned to leave.

"Mr. Jones. One last thing you need to settle," Jennifer whispered. She pointed at Joey and Rico. "These folks will be visiting their attorney upon returning home. Perhaps we…ummm, you…can cut your losses and settle matters here."

"I'm sorry, I didn't know these were the folks that had a problem in my casino," he said sincerely. "I was going to my office to review the recording with my attorneys. Some of my gutsier men broke rank with Ted and told me what really happened. He lied to me when I was in L.A."

The man had left the investor meeting only because Jennifer was involved; and he was running the meeting.

"Would you like to save those attorney fees and pass them on to these people who didn't do a da…arn thing wrong last night?" Jennifer said.

"Sir, Ma'am, I would like you to consider settling this out of court for let's say…two hundred thousand even…and my sincere apologies for the conduct of my security people."

He waited patiently, thinking he had a cheap winner as he eyed Joey's wide open mouth and Rico's wide grin.

Just before he blurted yes, Rico noticed Jennifer's two fingers oddly moving her bangs side-to-side. "Considering you would have had to pay mine *and* your attorney's fees, plus damages and other stuff, I think the most fair and equitable amount for forgiveness and silence about this matter would be double that…or four hundred," he said matter-of-factly, expecting to be talked down to under three hundred and change.

"You drive a hard bargain, Mr. Rico. If you are a man of your word and agree to sign forms attesting to the fact that you have been satisfactorily recompensed, and will not pursue further legal action of *any* kind…consider it done.

"My lawyers can have a cashier's check in six hours, *after* all papers are signed."

All Joey and Rico could do was nod in agreement. Jennifer sat wide-eyed. After some awkward moments, Mr. Jones dismissed himself and went to a nearby bar, apparently to quench his thirst.

"Jennifer, promise not to hit me if I say something," Rico whispered.

"Maybe…OK." She was still taking in the amount Rico was going to be collecting.

"It really bothers me that you are letting that man…who, from what I could tell, you had something going with…whether you knew it or not…go without a proper send off."

Oh, she knew it, but she had maintained a completely platonic relationship because she wanted to succeed on her own. No special treatment. Then again, maybe the man's advanced age had something to do with it, though fifty-two was hardly over the hill.

"I wasn't mean or anything!"

"You just ripped a man's heart out and you weren't mean! It wasn't a fair fight. I know, I know, he'll recover the financial loss in a day or two of business. But, he probably agreed to this pay-off because the fight he would normally have in him is gone…at least for the moment. Normally, that would be a good thing, but I have this gut feeling that he's a more or less an honest man—and a very, very, lonely one inside." *And in that I'm a field expert, girl.*

And how would you know that? Jennifer mused, her eyes closing for a second. Her mind considered the extravagant, busy lifestyle the man led.

Jennifer and Rico didn't know each other as well as they thought.

"Jacob, you're butting in …" Joey started to chastise Rico, but wisely stopped short as she noticed a facial hint that Jennifer wasn't happy with her interference.

"And what do you suppose I do?" Jennifer said, looking at Rico and then Joey.

Seems like Jacob has given someone some lectures before, Joey thought, even as she offered a shrug.

"Pardon my forwardness," Rico said.

Why stop now? Joey and Jennifer thought at almost the same instant.

"But, I think going over there while you can…and, and giving him at least a goodbye hug would be a great relief to him. At least that's what *I* think," he said, shrugging.

Hesitantly, Jennifer left her comfort zone and joined the broken man at the bar. After all, the man had jumped on a jet just for her. Never mind that it was always at his beck and call. They talked for some time and then she bid him farewell with a hug. Perhaps they would stay in touch they each said, both fully aware of the symbolic nature of such parting agreements.

"Well, I hope I said the right words," Jennifer pondered aloud as she rejoined her friends.

"Jennifer…" Mister Jones said when he revisited their table. He held out an envelope for her. "Sorry, I forgot to give you this. If it isn't enough, please let me know."

He was about to leave when he stopped and, speaking to no one in particular, said, "Jennifer is the most wonderful woman I've ever met. It must have something to do with the company she keeps."

With that he walked away, wondering if he would ever find friends of that caliber.

Perhaps in Rico he already had.

"Not a bad guy," Rico mumbled under his breath. "But…what was he talking about?"

"Oh, nothing…I just mentioned that you guys *forced* me to…you know…"

Each one of the foursome twiddled their fingers for some time. Jennifer picked up the envelope and played with a corner.

Rico, for one, had already mentally spent the money that had *fallen* into his lap.

"Well, Jennifer, aren't you going to open it?" Joey insisted. Rico gave her a little elbow love. "What? I can't help it. Being nosy is in my genes," she proudly announced.

"Yea, I've heard about your investigative reporting," Jennifer chided. "You

won't find any dirt here." She playfully waved the envelope in front of the old
reporter.

"Truthfully though, I'm kind of worried. What if he insults me by short-
changing me—or what if he insults me by giving me too much. I'd feel like he
was trying to buy me like an everyday prostitute," she muttered.

"Listen, sweetie," Joey piped in impatiently. "If he was paying you like a
prostitute, that envelope would be much fatter. So…"

"And what exactly do you mean by that?" Jennifer asked, hoping for a direct
compliment, or at least, an explicit jab if that was what Joey intended.

"What I mean is…you, like myself, would be in extremely high demand
if…we…you were…you know."

"Oh…uhm, that's so much plainer. Thank you."

"You go fishing, sometimes you catch something," Joey said matter-of-
factly. "Now, open the doggone envelope!" Joey urged.

Feigning fear, Jennifer opened the envelope. A huge grin painted her face as
she leaned over to show Joey.

Joey turned red with excitement. "Holy cow!"

It was Rico's turn to show interest. Jennifer wouldn't let go of the envelope
when Rico tugged at it. She put it up to her nose instead.

"It says…" Jennifer read out loud from the statement portion of the business
check. "…thirty thousand severance, seventy thousand for contract services."

Jennifer made a thoughtful pose; she couldn't remember what the contract
services might have been. She glared at Joey. "Not a peep out of you!" she whispered threateningly.

"Not a peep…as in…?"

Jennifer turned beet red and then the two laughed hysterically.

Rico slipped away from the attention they were drawing. He returned after
paying the tab and stalling at some slot machines, losing a quick five dollars.

Then Jennifer remembered what the contract services were for. She explained to Joey how she had traveled all over the states on a security detail for
the rich guy and his teenaged step-kids; the real mother had long been out of
the family picture.

Jennifer was slightly insulted when Joey noted that it seemed like an awfully good way of having her nearby—like courting. No, it was because of her
security acumen, Jennifer insisted. Just then she realized that Joey was right, and
she was full of malarkey. The guy had tried to sweep her off her feet and she had
been oblivious.

JACOB RICO: CHINK IN THE ARMOR

As happy as he was to see Jennifer again, Rico felt exhausted. "Well, Joey, we ready to go?"

"Sit down for a minute more. It seems that Jennifer here wants to set down roots somewhere once and for all," Joey said with a hint of secrecy in her voice. She expected Rico to be way ahead of her. But, he hadn't a clue.

"That's good, and ..." he didn't want to say anything stupid, "... that involves me how?"

At least he tried. Joey's stinging glare and Jennifer's frown let him know how unsatisfactory his response was.

"Well, anyway, she tells me she likes the desert, but not this Nevada desert..." Joey gave him a look with a raised eye-brow. "And...?

"And...*maybe*, you would be interested in visiting the great state of New Mexico?" he piped up proudly, thinking he finally understood.

Joey lowered her shaking head.

"Or ... or better yet, Las Cruces, where we've ..." he paused to savor the, *we*, that he was really part of now. "...made our homestead. Nuestra habitación," he said with a sense of satisfaction.

"Yea, but I do have to make a living, you know. I don't think there's much of a market for high priced security or bodyguards in that part of the country," she said.

It dawned on Rico what Joey had been hinting at. "Jennifer...do you want a job?"

"You know someone in the security business in that little town?"

"As a matter of fact...there is...this little itty-bitty, upstart company of a soon to be half-dozen or so folks that might need your services; protective services, of course," he quickly added.

"How much?"

"Pennies, for all practical purposes. A little over fifty-K. I know, I know, that's less than peanuts for someone like you. But, think of the fringe benefits... you get to work with the best looking dude you ever met. And to work with that wonderful woman there," he said in a full blown sales pitch. Rico figured there wasn't a chance in million she would take the slim pay and leave what appeared to be an easily recoverable relationship with the rich, and relatively young guy.

His thoughts wandered off to some of the incredible, even superhuman, things he had seen Jennifer do. Her talents were innumerable and invaluable to say the least—and came in a package of the highest caliber of character and ethics. Except of course, those misguided searches for love mentioned before. Now that, seemingly by fate, the opportunity to have her skills at his disposal had presented itself, he just had to convince her. He was about to toss in some extra enticement when Jennifer spoke up.

"Well, the pay *is* way short of a hundred-K. But, I would get to work alongside my new buddy." She acted like she was in deep thought. "I'll take it!" she declared all of a sudden.

Rico was elated, but he decided to savor it inwardly; for safety's sake.

"Well, I guess I don't have to throw in Joey's old place for you to stay in, or the health plan, or …"

"Or maybe you do," she said quickly.

"Well…I don't suppose I'll have a need for my old adobe place," Joey said, kicking Rico under the table. "Though, I would miss my nice, cool, one-of-a-kind basement bedroom."

That brought Michelle to mind. "But the extra room is…temporarily occupied. I need to make a call. Excuse me." She started to leave. "Oh. Welcome to the company, girl!" she said, leaning over to give Jennifer a hug.

Joey was gone and back in minutes. From the look on her face, all was well. The group chatted about various things for nearly half an hour, until the girls calling on the cell phone interrupted. They were up and ready to work somebody's legs into the ground. But, Rico had to finish some business first.

"You have kids…already?" Jennifer asked.

"Oh, yea, but adopted, kind of, sort of. You'll meet them today," Joey offered.

"Jennifer, I'd like you to get to work right away," Rico directed, as the others gave him a look. "There's stuff you can manage from here. In fact, it would be great if you could get down to Las Cruces in the next two days. I could have a list by tomorrow morning. You can fly over while we get a rental to take a road trip back to catch the sights. If you don't have a PC tablet, get one. And make it a good one."

Jennifer quickly got into the business mode herself; it started feeling like old times. She ignored Joey shaking her head.

After the requisite farewells and exchange of cell numbers, Rico took off quickly, signaling Joey to follow.

Jennifer hurried to her apartment to pack.

Meanwhile, Rico's entourage did the sightseeing thing until he decided to end the *fun*; but not the fun of paying Mister Jones a visit at his office regarding the matter of a four hundred thousand dollar check.

The next day the gang packed into a rented suburban and bid Jennifer farewell. Rosangelica and Tina were dying to know who the raving beauty was who Rico introduced them to in a purposeful rush. No need to risk Jennifer letting slip certain aspects of their past.

The girls also noted that Sarge seemed to know her. They watched Jennifer and Sarge interact for a few minutes standing a few feet away, both wearing big grins, saying good-bye a minute later with an awkward half-hug that Jennifer initiated. *That* really intrigued the girls.

Joey promised Jacob would offer all the details while they drove to the first adventure ride they could find. For some reason Rico was more talkative than usual. His recounting of some of Jennifer's combat exploits mesmerized them.

Joey listened too, intrigued at how passionately her husband recounted the stories; noting how much he raved about Jennifer in general. Joey didn't have the heart to interrupt when Rico inadvertently revealed some probably classified events. He was going a mile a minute—like a broken dam. Rosangelica seemed not to blink; it seemed she had a new hero.

The stories ended when Sarge drove up to the first of the several thrilling rides they would enjoy the next two days; a sightseeing helicopter ride from which Rico abstained. Some memories were hard to forget.

After those two exhausting fun-filled days—stopping only to rest in a hotel bed for about five hours—they headed back to New Mexico.

CHAPTER FOURTEEN

THE FIRST morning after arriving back in Las Cruces, Rico and the Sarge separated ways. The Azerra's went house hunting; Rico went looking for and then spending money. Aside from depositing the four hundred thousand from Vegas, spending money proved more successful than acquiring it. One bank took a serious look at his proposal, but only momentarily. Rico watched the amenable lower manager walk into the senior bank manager's office. Through the window Rico could see the woman's head shaking adamantly, an obvious no. What did he expect? His was a risky business; much more so in this relatively small burb. Fortunately, he had faithfully stuffed twenty percent of all company profits into a reserve fund. After three years he had accumulated $295,000. His client list netted another $200,000, and then some, after taxes.

Along with those assets, his stock portfolio profits offered a sufficient sum for a reasonably comfortable retirement—if only that was his plan. The sale of his stocks had netted him almost $575,000. In his eyes, the bonanza had to officially qualify him as an eccentric.

Joey had some idea that her new husband was out and about eyeing and buying things. It wasn't that he bought quantities of useless "things," as she called them; it was more his tendency to buy the most expensive model and brand, or make in the case of vehicles. Actually, all the vehicles he had purchased for his company in San Diego were from auctions or other firms upgrading. Yes, they were top of the line, equipped with armor and electronic gadgets, and still cost a pretty penny; but it wasn't like she thought.

Unknown to Rico, though, a few agents on his staff had confided to Joey, whom they got to know over the phone, that it was rather serious over-kill for the threats their type of clients faced.

Joey wanted to address this propensity, though she felt like a mother just thinking about it. When he got home that day she told him she had something to discuss. She didn't dare say "budget," a bad word for Rico since she had known him. Her ambush would catch him unprepared and fresh out of ideas for excuses. He would just have to bite the bullet.

It was 4:00 p.m. and Joey promised an hour maximum on the topic. She was anxious to make a good impression on the newest team member, Jennifer, with the first formal dinner she had cooked since returning from Vegas. A veritable cornucopia of Mexican delights—enchiladas, chile relleno, rice, beans, and, oddly enough, a home-made coconut cream pie (Jennifer's favorite)—overflowed on the table on warming plates. And with the girls out of town for two days at another tournament, Joey would be taking more than her usual *accidental* extras to her buddies in the park.

Rico would make sure—being the good husband he was—that he didn't allow a simple budget discussion ruin the homey atmosphere. Missing out on the pie by upsetting her wouldn't do either.

"Wow!" Jennifer said. "About all I can manage is heating water."

Rico shot her a quick glance with the obvious intent of saying something. Jennifer shot him back an unspoken threat.

Sure Jennifer, you don't cook, Joey mused. *Unless a certain someone is coming over?*

"So, Joey, are we going to talk budget stuff while we eat, or after? Jennifer offered, taking her eyes off Rico.

Rico wondered why Joey decided to include Jennifer in the budget talk. He was about to find out that the real boss had decided to post Jennifer as comptroller. As such she needed an overview of the numbers, once some semblance of a beginning balance could be determined. Of course, Joey had already taken an extended peek at some of Rico's bank statements.

The balances seemed healthy, but looking at her husband's seemingly erratic and impulsive spending habits, she wondered how long it would last. She made it clear that she would have little to do with the fiscal matters of the company. Except for expenditures over $10,000, she wanted minimal involvement. Running her martial arts business was already a handful, not to mention her many other commitments.

What other commitments? Rico wondered. "But how am I going to manage this stuff without you?" he whined.

"Do you have wax in…oh, never mind. I told you I'd be mentoring Jennifer.

She'll manage the books, and I'll do a monthly audit. I *expect*, don't ask me why I know, you'll be throwing Jennifer a lot of curves. This type of business has quite a complexity to it as it is. So try and take it easy on her."

"That's what I mean! I was counting on you to…"

"Well Joey, I guess Jacob forgot about my stint as our unit's supply sergeant. So if he wants to find someone else…that's fine with me," Jennifer interjected.

She *had* handled millions in inventory after all. And, aside from one case of four mortar rounds gone missing, she excelled at it.

"I didn't mean…"

"He didn't mean anything that made sense is what he was going to say…" Joey cut in, "…right Jacob?"

"Yes, ma'am," he said, humbly.

Jennifer viewed Joey with extra respect after that. She tried hiding her grin. Someone had really tamed the rebel of rebels.

Rico playfully scowled at her when Joey stuck her nose in the fridge.

"Let's get to the nitty-gritty, shall we?" Joey urged, pouring some juice.

The other two nodded in agreement. Rico went to grab another soda and more fig bars.

"Don't over-do those or you won't have room for a healthy supper," Joey insisted.

"Yes, Mother," he retorted, only half joking. *Joey, we gotta talk.* "Yuppee, they're whole grain," he murmured. She had pulled a switch.

"I'm serious…if you leave food on your plate tonight," she said shaking a finger at him. "You can eat out the rest of the year."

Oh, that would be unbearable Joey, he thought. *Did she think he cooked a meal in San Diego? Then again, I'd miss out on this awesome company.*

He dropped two of the four large bars back into the bag. *Joey, we really, really need to talk.*

Jennifer hadn't seen the two interacting as a husband and wife and was doing all she could to keep from laughing. Joey noticed and blushed.

"Anyway, here are your current balances, Jacob."

Joey displayed the figures on a spreadsheet on her laptop. On the split screen she displayed the savings and checking balances. "If every check has cleared you have $470,000 in checking. You had $250,000 in savings a week ago and today you have $450,000. Where did that other money come from? Or *any* of it for that matter."

The Vegas money deposit had not posted yet.

"A loan from the Prince…which I'll be paying back in a month…or so."

"You borrowed two hundred thou, Jacob?" Jennifer asked.

He just nodded sheepishly. He decided on not mentioning the fifty plus thousand he kept in his briefcase upstairs in cash and travelers checks. Joey would nag about that too. He had heard enough nagging on the phone the previous three months.

"Do you want part of the winnings from our Vegas adventure thrown in there?" Joey asked. She thought she concealed her glee when he said no. Grand plans for the cash churned in her mind—polar opposites to Rico's.

"But I'll keep the payoff from Jenny's old boss…if you let me, of course." Jennifer grinned.

"Maybe half, but don't spend it. We'll discuss that later; now back to the matter at hand please. Do you have a receipt for all these purchases shown here on your bank statement? You'll need them in the event of an audit. Otherwise, we should just start from this balance. I don't want to back track."

"That sounds good to me. Isn't it time? The food might get cold," Rico offered in Spanish.

She ignored him completely. "To keep things straight, Jennifer will need to have a memo for everything you ask her to buy or pay for. She'll photocopy each receipt, annotate what it was for, and post it in the correct ledger. Right off the bat she needs a thousand bucks for a decent accounting program. Later, you can hire my accountant or whomever."

Rico's head was reeling. Jennifer didn't even blink.

"She in turn must give you a photocopy of everything for your review and filing. You have to make sure you look at it in case she received a bill for something that you didn't purchase or order. Electronic theft is booming nowadays. Do you understand that, Jacob?"

Jennifer sensed that he was being chastised again about past practices. This wasn't her best buddy's day. She couldn't help chuckle inside.

"Yes, of course I look at important papers…a lot more, now," he mumbled, a crumb of fig flew from his lips, landing on the table. "I think we're almost at the big five," he hinted dutifully again, subtly swiping the crumb to the floor.

"Jacob, can you focus a little, please? About managing employee work hours, do you plan to use some form of time card?"

Rico took his time to answer.

"Well?" Joey urged.

"I don't think so. All I want to know is when they are on post…for legal reasons. The control center operators, currently Jennifer and Sarge, will maintain a running blotter of operational matters. That's about it. I prefer to run this company on trust."

"Then you'll pay them on salary," Joey said. "One last thing…you must agree to have an executive meeting on budget matters every single month, apart from planning and training sessions. Agreed? I don't want to have to clean up a fiscal disaster. The IRS *is* kinder and gentler…but not *that* much."

Tell me about it! "Agreed…and I promise to pay attention. Really!" he added quickly when Jennifer almost choked, spitting droplets of water she had been drinking. Rico closed his eyes and calmly wiped his face.

Joey, intrigued and slightly envious about the almost spiritual interaction between the two closed down her laptop, let out a sigh and headed upstairs. *Lord, I understand it's a blessing for my husband to have such a connection with her…but…Yes, Lord…I'll try to remember you're in control.*

"Jennifer," Rico said.

"Yea."

"Women are…" He wisely chose to leave instead of finishing the sentence.

Minutes later they ate dinner, sharing all kinds of memories. Rico mostly listened.

CHAPTER FIFTEEN

SOMETIME THE next morning Rico was cruising around town, glad to escape the confines of his office for awhile. On Roadrunner Parkway he noticed a newer building. A small sign read, "Doña Ana County Battered Women's Shelter, Inc." On a whim—still a positive habit from his perspective and still a negative one from others, including Joey—he decided to offer his services. What better place to reconnect with the community's pulse.

An attractive high arching overhang led to the front door and reception area. "Hi," he said timidly to the receptionist. It was too late to put better thought into what he was doing. "Is there someone I can speak with about volunteering?"

"Sure, let me get the director."

A few seconds later, the director walked up to Rico.

"Hello," she said courteously enough, extending her hand as the security door closed behind her. Both of them were now outside the secure door and in the lobby. "My name is Antonia Guerra. And you are?"

"Jacob…Rico, Ma'am," he replied. His mouth was as dry as the desert air. *What am I doing here?*

"I understand that you would like to volunteer?"

"Yes, actually I would. I would be willing to provide personal protection for anyone who needed it while they do things around town or go to court. I can also provide tutors for kids, or adults. And my good friend could provide instructors to teach karate or other activities," he blabbed on.

Getting started had been easy in San Diego because it had fallen into his lap; the future chief of police had been his credibility and biggest cheerleader.

"Sounds like an expensive endeavor, Mr. Rico."

"Yes, it can be. My company would pick up the tab for the instructors and body guards."

"Like I said, it seems like an expensive…" *What's in it for you?* She paused and looked him over with her eyebrow raised. "You realize that most of the women and children in this facility have an aversion to men due to trauma. Sometimes they won't be very courteous, and truthfully…sometimes they'll be downright nasty."

Rico concealed his worry. He was extremely sensitive to rejection and second thoughts flooded his mind. Was she trying to say no thanks? Her look seemed to point that way. What was he doing creating more stress for himself?

The lady continued without missing a beat. "There is an extensive background check we would have to run on you before we can even talk seriously about any actual services you could provide."

"I hadn't thought of that, actually. Surprise! But, I promise that won't be a problem," he said, trying to seem undaunted. Again, his buddy had whizzed everything through back channels in San Diego.

She eyed him intently for much longer than Rico thought was reasonable. What was she thinking? Rico began to sweat.

"I have to be honest, Jacob. It is not every day a man comes in here for good reasons. Even though many do come for court-ordered counseling alongside their estranged partners, most come here trying to bring down the place when they somehow find out that their spouse is here. You do know that everything that goes on in here is confidential, right? You can't even say hi to people out in the streets that you meet here…unless they approach you first."

"That makes sense."

Rico didn't want to sound smart-alecky about already knowing the psychology of battered women, so he kept quiet. When she told him to fill out the paperwork and give it to the receptionist he was sure he had just been brushed off. As it was, the director took his offer seriously and when it turned out he was associated with her good friend Joey, she expedited the clearance procedures and soon put Rico's company to work. Again, his connections proved very helpful without him knowing it. And once again he began a new life, though sometimes it was a little more exciting than he expected.

After making it back to his office, a guilt-ridden Rico felt obliged to visit Michelle. Days had passed since his last visit. He wasn't exactly ready for her reaction when he suggested having Joey introduce her to everyone else in the family. Up to then only Jennifer, who obviously had to be filled in about Michelle's existence and presence since her bedroom was next to Michelle's, plus those Joey had contracted to tend to her sister, knew about her even now. Rico's logic for suggesting the "coming out" was that the girls' for sure would cheer Michelle up and help with her recovery.

Michelle recoiled at the idea, even began trembling. "No, because anyone that knows me can be in danger!" she said to Rico in a hoarse whisper.

Danger? Danger from who, Michelle? Hasn't Joey told you that we're in the protection business and can take care of ourselves? he thought. "OK, Michelle, you're right."

Her face softened and she became calm. Rico had that effect on people, seeming to express a genuine concern after thoughtful listening. He was often told that he had a nurturing sense about him; a gentleness and softness that starkly contrasted with some of the things they had seen in him in combat—and to this day when he got riled.

Rico considered Joey's sister was delusional, or someone was over medicating her. "Could you…I mean…if you want to, tell me about this danger you're talking about?" he said.

She cowered a little less this time.

Rico waited a while after he got closer, sat down and gently caressed the still very thin, bony hand. It was everything he could do not to cringe at the feel of the skeletal-like hand. Research he was aware of pointed to the healing effects of touch and prayer; and this woman needed lots of both. At least he could manage the touching part.

Michelle sighed and stopped trembling at his touch.

"A drink precedes a story," she said.

Joey had mentioned earlier that Michelle seemed to favor street Irish, proverbs or vulgarity when stress levels went up. She insisted Rico avoid any serious subject matter. Of course, she forgot she was talking to Rico.

"It is sweet to drink, but bitter to pay for," Rico whispered back, in case Joey was eaves dropping on his disobedience.

"I take it my sister has put a bug in your ear. You said that like you know the heart wrenching second part…when the liquor is gone the fun is gone."

She stared at the ceiling.

"Some."

He was being honest, having dealt with only occasional digressions to alcoholic binges.

"But thirst is the end of drinking."

"And sorrow is the end of drunkenness," Rico said, finishing the proverb. "Please tell me your story."

Her extended silence made *him* uncomfortable. Had he messed up and sent her to her shell again by disobeying Joey? Michelle closed her eyes. His heart palpitated.

"Wine divulges truth," she pleaded one last time. Her first sober weeks in more than twenty-five years were proving overwhelming. Without the medication she would have gone searching for some spirits.

Rico's compassion for the obviously troubled soul made him drop pretenses. "Please, Michelle, I...I want to help. I know you barely know me, and I you, but you're Joey's sister. I love her so much, and you're...well, part of her. So..."

His sincerity overwhelmed Michelle. "I'm afraid to scare you away, Jacob. I don't want to tell my sister either because she might send me away to keep the girls safe. Not that...not that I would blame her, but to tell you the truth...I don't know what's real...and what..." She stopped to catch her breath. "...what are simply my imaginations."

"It's OK Michelle. I guess Joey hasn't told you that we are in the security business. Not only that, all four of us in my company are former Special Forces and can take care of any danger. OK?" he said, tenderly, but with authority.

Michelle's countenance changed a little and she gave him a strange look. Rico could swear it was one of pity, and then fear.

"Jacob," she labored to say, "...if half of what is in my head has any substance to it, we would all be in harm's way." She was exhausting herself but wanted to warn the ones she loved. "When I am well, I will leave here...and none of those animals...will know I was here. You will all be safe...then. But right now..." She ran out of breath.

Rico wanted to let her sleep, but he might not have another chance to talk with her in private, without Joey there. "Please, Michelle, just give me a hint about what you mean."

She grimaced and moaned. "These people...animals...control people. They use addictive and other sorts of drugs and torture to keep the women in line. One girl...or woman...I can't remember clearly, who got out of line was given a box with a finger from her mother's hand. You..." Michelle was almost blacking out. "Another time, as an object lesson to the rest of us, they demonstrated...some, some, nasty kind of poison. They made a show of using the tip of a pin...in a drink...the girl...horrible!"

Rico considered the matter a delusion and was about to leave. The idea that

Ricin—a poison, of which just 500 micrograms would prove fatal—would be used in such a way, and by a non-terrorist group, seemed a major stretch to him. They had to be drugged induced thoughts. They had to.

"You might wonder why they would do that?" she continued. "Instead of beating bunches of them into submission? Well, its simple…you can't market broken *products*," she almost regurgitated, "so one…the impact…"

Rico's heart dropped. Could it be a coincidence that he had once read a classified report about what she was alluding to?

"Where is this happening, Michelle?" Rico asked.

Michelle opened her eyes wide, surprised that Rico had not dismissed her off hand. "If my mind is not delusional, and sometimes I wonder, those…are ruthless. Jacob, do not start turning rocks over."

Rico's firm look made her give in.

"From London to Dublin to Sweden to China…America. Lords and highly…"

Rico nodded as she faded to sleep. He softly patted her hand. Minutes later he headed upstairs, knees quivering, and avoided Joey. Walking into his house he felt a familiar dull ache creep up the back of his neck. Soon the throbbing would engulf his head, and the smallest glimmer of light would feel like red hot spikes piercing his eyes; nausea would follow.

CHAPTER SIXTEEN

Later in the day Rico sat in his office thinking how to rationalize away what Michelle had told him. Pretty well convinced that he had overreacted, he told himself that a call to Prince Michael was long over due anyway. Just in case, he would subtly broach the topic. What if they were in danger for real? He made a mental note to do an internet search for European organized crime syndicates. He quickly chastised himself when his earlier thought came to mind; that Michelle's existence could be of use for what he was planning to carry out very soon. He felt dirty; evil.

Online shopping proved a way to get his mind off the matter. Rico was reading the specs on a product when Jennifer hollered at him from her lobby desk.

"Jacob, you have a Mr. Joshua Cohen. Says he has an interview at ten today," Jennifer, now at the doorway, informed Rico.

It was Rico's office and nit-picky protocol that the front desk person communicated with him face-to-face. He disliked the impersonal feeling of the intercom; or so he said.

Jennifer was sure that it was really so he could see her pretty, and usually chirpy, face. She leaned against the outside wall and peered in with a smile.

He was thankful the smile was back. His lack of enthusiasm, or confidence, about her taking over the finances had stung her more then he knew.

"But, but it's only nine," he answered, disbelief on his face.

He motioned to her to look at his PC monitor screen. She leaned over him and wrapped her arms around his shoulders and chest, chin resting on the crown of his head.

"What? Looks like a juiced up Chevy Suburban to me," she whispered, exaggerating her Dakotan country accent, if there was such a thing. As much as she played the accent up, she played dumb about the vehicle; she knew exactly what the vehicle was. She thought he was just window shopping.

"Jenny, if I didn't know better I'd say you were trying to get fresh with me, wearing that *very* nice perfume! Won't it make Joey a tad bit unhappy?" he said.

She smelled herself and agreed with a nod. "I'll save this one for a future honey," she said coyly, kissing him on the forehead. "…and that's not you!

"Now, what about this vehicle?" she said. It was only because a professional didn't engage in chit chat, even with the boss, while on duty—the body contact notwithstanding. Only during a short period in her life had she deviated from consummate professionalism—and that was in a distant past the two in the room relegated to the Sea of Forgetfulness.

The sergeant and the airman, with the apparent fondness for each other, had caused misunderstandings and heated arguments among the detachment commandos at times. Not one of the other team members believed the truth that the pair hadn't slept together. Though the He-Men on the team would have considered her conquest a badge of honor, Rico vehemently denied it…sometimes shutting them up with choice words.

One unfortunate time, Jennifer overheard the whispering back and forth and internalized what she thought was disgust on Rico's part about them being a couple. And where she stood with him only got blurrier. When another commando had said that since Jennifer was free, he was going to….

What the man *almost* finished saying caused a free-for-all between him and Rico, which landed them in the brig's medical unit. Needless to say, confusion prevailed in her heart.

Thankfully, things weren't so fuzzy any more. The lack of sexual tension between the two since a *talk* they had had was proving to be very liberating for both of them. The ever present reservations of being the *real* them were gone. Now they were like family and totally open with each other. It created a great working environment for everyone, especially between Joey and Jennifer.

"Here, take this printout, go to this web site and order me one with the color changing option. I need it in no more than four weeks," he insisted.

Jennifer gave him a look of disapproval. Rico figured Joey had been sharing about his fiscal practices, again. "Irresponsible," was the word she, he was sure, tossed around plenty.

"All righty…about your visitor?" She smartly resisted any comment about the money topic.

"Let him stew about fifteen and watch what he does with his time," he said in a hush. She nodded to Rico with a look of understanding.

"Mr. Cohen, it'll be about fifteen minutes. Please, make yourself comfortable," she said.

Jennifer stepped back in Rico's office minutes later and informed him that the man had been reading *Scientific American* and that another magazine she noticed in his open brief case was *Voice of the Martyrs*.

"Don't ask me!" Jennifer answered his non verbal question about the strange sounding magazine. Every once in a while Rico also read *Scientific American*, so he knew what *that* was about. The other magazine, a Jewish, Evangelical religious publication, stumped him.

Jennifer informed him before leaving that the Smart Truck he was looking at was over two hundred and seventy-five thousand big ones.

"I must've gone to the wrong site, boss; especially, since it says that it is available only to government entities, authorized foreign governments and domestic security agencies authorized by the Department of Homeland Security."

He told her he knew about the price. She was to get to ordering it from the equipment testing budget. He handed her a paper with his user name and password to the Homeland Security Directorate technology clearance office. He pulled an odd looking contraption out of his safe. "Here, plug this retina and bio scanner into your computer after you've entered the site. Once you've filled out the on-line forms I listed on that paper, I'll go over and scan my eye and thumb when it prompts you. Got it girl?"

Jennifer's head was spinning, but she nodded anyway.

Four minutes later she called him over and he scanned his eye and thumb. Cohen watched Rico raise the handheld cup-looking device up to his left eye. The screen said the scan and match was complete and flashed that the application would be processed. Rico just nodded politely to Cohen as he passed on the way back to his office.

Cohen observed closely, though he appeared disinterested.

Some minutes later Rico asked for Mr. Cohen. Jennifer directed him in, then mulled over the instructions she had just been given about the truck. Now she had to fill out the on-line order form at the manufacturer's web site. They would only fulfill the order if final approval was received from the appropriate Homeland Security section.

Mr. Cohen and Rico exchanged pleasantries about being from here and there.

"So, why would a Jew straight out of Israel want to move to New Mexico to work for a small company," Rico asked bluntly. He wasn't sure he liked the answer.

"Actually, New York is currently my home. I'm really only looking to moonlight and do contract work out of there," Cohen replied. "I've lived there for ten years and already have guaranteed executive security work, but I'm looking to branch out on my own. Since I usually have weeks off at a time, I figured I could fill in that time offering my quality work to a small company that normally wouldn't be able to afford my fee scale."

Weeks off at a time, huh? "Can you give me the names of some of your current clientele that I can call for a reference?"

"Sorry, that's privileged information."

Rico didn't like that answer either, appropriate as it was.

"I have done some checking about your former company, though," Cohen continued. "And I've heard nothing but good things about some of your now successful former employees."

"Coming from a man with your dossier, that really means something to me Mr. Cohen," Rico said, paying a rare and sincere compliment to the man. "I would like you to return for a full interview if my staff agrees that we could use your services. If not, where can I contact you to inform you of that?"

What about the Mossad? Rico thought. He couldn't ask the man why a former Mossad operative would be interested in his little company because he didn't want to reveal to the stranger how deep his own intel was. Rico considered off-hand sending Cohen down the road, but then thought about the possibilities.

"Two things before you leave, Mr. Cohen. One is, whether you do come back for a full panel interview or not, I want to extend an invitation for dinner here at five-thirty or so. Seems like everyone in this company can cook…except for me and that woman out there…and they love to compete and show off. RIGHT, Jennifer?" Rico said toward the open door without changing volume. He knew she was eavesdropping and hanging on every word.

"Yes, it's true, you can't even boil water!" She did an admirable job of concealing the surprise at being called on.

"She exaggerates. I do instant oatmeal, and she can't do *that*." Rico couldn't help grinning.

"Anyway, the second thing is that the questions you would be asked would not be standard questions. It is important that you take them seriously, and not think they're intended to insult you. If you don't like them, obviously, you would be free to walk away."

I wish I could do that already, Cohen thought. *But, I have my instructions.*

"No hard feelings either way. You have your interests, we have ours." With that, Rico extended his hand and stood.

"Jennifer, call a staff meeting, we have something to discuss," he instructed casually, escorting Cohen to the door.

Jennifer was aching to rib Rico back about him suddenly being so formal, but she said nothing.

"Remember, Sarge is in the field," she said instead.

"Have him come in...or we'll do a teleconference."

Mr. Cohen waited for a taxi under the shade of the splendid cottonwood trees in the building's manicured front lawn. The cab Jennifer called arrived in about five minutes.

Two hours later the staff was assembled in the conference room. Fruit and finger food platters crowded the serving table, a fringe benefit for the staff and family. Rico had a nontraditional practice of having open meetings, though planning and operational sessions took place behind closed doors.

It was rare that a child whined about hunger pains, and that's how Rico liked it. He planned for the young children (of staff and various friends of Joey's) to play in the upper level, supervised by a parent or Rosangelica and Tina, while the back yard was being dug out. Older children shot hoops or roller bladed in the neighboring apartment complex parking lot. The corner of the lot was rarely used and so far from the apartments that Rico negotiated with the owners, paying a small fee for its use.

The goal of this particular meeting was to match the company's tasks—the ones he would divulge, at least—to the skills the Israeli brought to the table. Rico asked everyone to brainstorm some reasons to hire the man. If they could find no substantial match with the man's skills and character traits, then no contract offer would be considered.

After an hour of munching and talking, the group identified some tasks that someone working out of New York could do for the company. They spent another half hour matching tasks from the applicant's dossier and the standard personal file Rico managed to assemble from who knew where. The man's claims corresponded with Rico's file records—minus facts that the man excluded, since they were likely restricted by his former organization.

Finally, they considered man's overall character and suitability to work with others, especially children, pre-adolescents and teenagers, as well as battered women. Some questions obviously would have to wait to be answered in person. Rico gathered everyone's input and would make a decision, after privately consulting with Joey.

Rico realized he would have to rely more and more on Joey to make crucial decisions about people's characters. Even though his instincts were as sharp as ever, the headaches frequently impeded clear thinking. Detecting deviancy was even more essential now that his business directly involved vulnerable women and children, and not combat. He wisely deferred to Joey's take on the man.

Rico wondered when her motherly attributes had first surfaced. Only now was he noticing that she had somehow reconciled her past, seeming to possess a peaceful spirit and purposeful direction. He at times thought *he* was finally getting a grip, only to digress in a whirlwind of self-loathing and overwhelming guilt, often without an external trigger. He dwelt at the edge of hell quite often; permanent relief always seemed *just* around the corner.

After conferring with Rico, Joey decided that she would need a follow-up meeting in person. He got on the phone and informed the Israeli that further informal discussions over dinner would be necessary, *if* he was still interested.

And Cohen was definitely interested, especially in home-cooked Mexican cuisine. It was a go.

Later, just past 4 p.m., the ladies, and even Sarge, contributed to a monster buffet dinner. The contrasts between Mexican and Irish music made for delightful dancing and conversation. Cohen seemed to fit right into the festivities, joining unabashedly with the dancing children. The conference room served well as a combination dining room and dance floor.

After almost two hours of socializing, everyone had a chance to get a sense of what Mr. Cohen was all about. Then Rico casually solicited a final yea or nay from everyone on the staff and the adult family members. As had already been established, he would get the one that really counted last—Joey's.

Thankfully, they unanimously chose to offer him a contract. Rico couldn't have been more relieved. He had taken a quite a liking to the man, and would've had to argue vehemently with the *boss*.

Even though the question of the Mossad lingered, the two men quickly sensed the other's penchant for joking around. Rico tested the waters by ribbing him about Jewish culture. Cohen's quick wit pleasantly surprised him. Rico wasn't about to hire somebody with anal-retentive tendencies and no sense of humor.

Cohen indicated he was very interested. Rico directed him to the office and, with a look, directed Jennifer to follow.

A smidgen of jealousy bit into Joey as she observed the three leaving the room without her. She quickly snapped out of it. *There's no need for me to be there. They're just setting up an agreement. I've done my part. But still, he could've…* She took that thought captive and chastised herself. *Forgive me, Lord.* She picked up one of the children and hugged herself back to the important world.

"After seeing all these wild people, who I must tell you didn't drink a drop of alcohol, you're still interested?" Rico asked.

"I don't know if it's company policy not to drink, but it sure is refreshing not dealing with drunken fools," he said bluntly.

His reaction caught Rico and Jennifer off guard. He was definitely spirited.

Cohen alluded to the culture of overindulgence that agents in the business frequently witnessed. They then had to keep their mouths shut about their clients' indiscretions because they were sworn to protect their privacy, along with their lives. Never mind the notorious tendency for excessive drinking and machismo by the disillusioned, mostly male agents.

"It is not company policy, but because I don't hire people that drink more than a beer a day, I don't have to make it one," Rico clarified.

The man nodded. He eyed Jennifer and seemed puzzled at her presence instead of Joey's, introduced earlier as Rico's wife and company vice president. Rico noted his expression. He liked the man's apparent transparency—a refreshing change. Overly closed-faced, secretive people populated the protection business, as far as he was concerned. His company would move away from that mold as much as possible.

But…was the man naturally that way; or was it a calculated move intended to ingratiate Rico and then burn him? Either way, the once wary Rico chose to trust him—to a point.

"Before we negotiate a contract, there is one last thing we must agree on. And that is regarding who you would answer to. This young lady here is my right hand regarding security operations. She executes the plan we all agree on. If she's not happy, I'm not happy. Do you have qualms about taking orders from a seemingly less experienced troop than yourself?"

"With all due respect," Cohen said after some thought. "This woman's reputation precedes her. I would be honored to serve under her direction."

Rico's and Jennifer's eyebrows rose. Jennifer's posture, already contest perfect, improved a bit more.

I can't believe she needed a positive stroke, Rico thought. "No, Jennifer, you can't have a raise because you're famous. He must be talking about that sexy, bikini pose of you that I posted on the web," Rico said, dodging Jennifer's backhand. Even as he pretended playfulness, Rico was sure Cohen's surprised look had been more a look of recognition. But where could they have met? Jennifer gave no indication of recognizing him in return.

"I guess I'll take that as a yes," Rico said to Cohen, shaking off his thoughts. "If I ask you to elaborate on your source, Jennifer's head won't fit through that door!"

Rico considered for a fleeting second mentioning what other part of her wouldn't fit. He left well enough alone. They had a quick laugh and moved on to discuss the at-will contract Rico had in mind. The man's skills were so much in demand that he could have commanded many times what Rico was predisposed to pay for each contract job.

Rico caved in to the impulse to ask Cohen about the sources that knew about his company and Jennifer in particular. Of the names Cohen cited, Oscar Villas kept ringing in his head. He recalled all the others, but the fact that Villas was now, according to Cohen, in the top ranks of the US Secret Service, gave him pause. He had been very close to the top-notch airman and not surprised at his success. But he was a little concerned about running into him again. Rico thought that Cohen seemed awfully well connected with the very tight-knit world of U.S. Secret Service agents.

In fact, Cohen was an outsider and less than embraced by most. But much to their ire, he possessed unusual access to the oval office, the nature of the visits a mystery to all of them.

Once again, doubts about hiring the man crept in, but only for a second. It really troubled Rico that the man seemed to know many of his own government contacts—too many. Any slip on his part, and though his friends, they would pounce if they found him out as quickly as any other threat to national security. Nevertheless, Rico decided to follow through hiring him. Maybe later he would broach that topic. How and when he had no idea. The bothersome thought lingered in his mind for several days until other pressing matters moved it to the background.

Cohen left the get-together with an at-will contract; he left a discounted fee list for various contract services he offered.

Rico already had plans bouncing around in his head.

CHAPTER SEVENTEEN

LATER THAT evening Rico sat in his quiet office, his mind racing, planning—or conniving, depending on one's perspective—his next moves, and then recanting, doubting, chastising and other things. To add to the mix, thoughts of Cohen intruded. Why had the man not mentioned his Mossad background? Was it possible he was still an active agent? Could someone have overheard his drunken tirade in a San Diego bar? But what had he said about the President? *That's* why he didn't drink often any more.

Then the dilemma about Michelle's apparent memories came to mind. Rico postponed the unsavory call to London this time until midnight. But, a long nap and three hours spent watching a rare late movie with Jennifer and the girls didn't help him forget this time.

I can't believe I'm wasting Z time on this. Even if there is anything to Michelle's story, she did say not to be nosing around. I've got enough problems of my own making without...Boy, the girl has an imagination. The girls would be in danger? What's that about? Too much TV, maybe? Probably American reruns running in England, Ireland...wherever.

"Hi, it's Jacob. Is the Prince available, please?"

"Hello Mr. Rico...Jacob, just a second please. Yes, he is available. God bless you sir, have a great day."

Rico thought she did fine for being new, till the last part. He made a mental note to let Michael know that his new help was likely to offend someone's sensibilities.

The Prince would know quite well who in particular would be offended, thanks to Joey. He couldn't exactly tell his friend Jacob that he highly encouraged his help's salutation; nor could he offer, on Joey's admonition, that he had had an encounter with God more than a year before. Fortunately, by the end of their conversation Rico's mind would be too confused to bring the topic up.

"Hello, Jacob. Top of the morning to you…I mean…midnight."

"Hey."

"Don't tell me you need more cash?"

"Naw, just had some questions. They might make you think I'm…strange… or something."

"A *tad* late for that," the Prince said, being quite honest. "Would I no longer be your friend if you couldn't pay me? Would I be furious for a while? Would I eventually get over it? Yes cubed."

"I lost all your money," Jacob said, stalling figuring he could still bail out of the questions he intended to ask, and keep lots of cash. But two traits Rico valued were integrity and honesty…mostly.

Michael surprised himself with his reaction to the news he thought was for real. Without a pause he answered, "Oh well, I'm sure you have your reasons."

"I'm kidding…but, do you think England has a problem with organized crime…the slave-trade kind?" *There*, he got it off his chest.

The pronounced silence at the other end said volumes, or was the Prince just caught off guard by the seeming nonsense?

"I…I…where in the world did that come from?"

"I have this nagging feeling that your M4 or M5, whichever applies, is keeping things under wraps. Of course, I could just as well be mental or something." The silence this time was deafening. "What would Lords, or high…something, or whatever, have to do with something like this?" Rico continued, sensing something was up.

It couldn't possibly be Rico's questions that caused his silence. Maybe he was in a meeting again and was multitasking.

"Did I interrupt something?" Rico asked wishfully.

"No." That answered that. "But listen, I do have to run. You were right. Those were strange things to ask. I'll…I'll look into it though. Give me a couple of months on that."

"Listen, it might just be gibberish sh…stuff, I conjured up. So don't put much into it, you being busy and all."

"OK, Jacob, good day."

Rico mused that that was one strange exchange. He was sure he had touched a raw nerve, or something. It made him shudder for a second to think Michelle had even half her mind straight. And there he was; turning rocks she told him not to.

But across the Atlantic, Prince Michael was experiencing more than a shudder—it was more like an outright panic attack. He wondered why God had used an unsaved person, according to Joey of course, to confirm what God had told him during a meeting with important members of parliament—lords. "Evil is in your midst," the Spirit had spoken softly, though not audibly through his natural ears. "Many suffer in shackles in the Lion's land. One of my sheep is with the Young Lion now. What will *you* do? Count the cost and act to save the Lion from utter destruction. When will the Lion arise from its slumber? The Young Lion shames you praising the Most High God more than you."

Michael had been totally confused about the biblical term for his country at the time. And the rest of the Words of Exhortation had gone over his head, until Rico called. Then a classified report he had read, *mistakenly*—he believed—placed in his possession three years before, came to mind. Unknown to him at the time was that this was exactly what had happened to Rico ten years before. It hit home now what the phrase "numerous cases of involuntary servitude" was supposed to mean. The report had mysteriously disappeared, and follow-ups never came. But the thought of acting, even on the matter of the missing report, made him tremble.

CHAPTER EIGHTEEN

SLOWLY RISING to consciousness at about 2:00 p.m. the next day, Rico felt quite lonesome, and alone, in the large building he called home. Joey's normal rising at five-thirty for morning-prayer hadn't even stirred him. Normally, he would turn and mumble and grumble why anyone would rise at such an ungodly hour. A pat on the head like a puppy always worked to settle him down so Joey could scoot to her private place.

Waking up to this quiet house—every day everyone was long gone before he rose—had particularly roused his ire this particular morning. He could barely tolerate himself.

The conversation with Michael fourteen hours earlier ran through his mind while he showered and brushed his teeth. Finally, he managed to will it out of his mind. Skilled mental gymnastics made the memory a permanently distant thing after just a few more days.

But this day, overcome with boredom by three o' clock, he headed to Joey's dojo; for the first time actually intending to walk in during classes. He walked over and held the door knob. Things always sounded lively from outside.

Today, Jennifer was there too. She forwarded the office phone since she was on duty. Students sat on the floor, leaning against the mirrored walls. The weekly advanced student session was about to begin. Around twenty people in their gees chatted away as mats were laid out.

Joey finished the opening prayer, a practice she did over anyone's objection. In Jesus' name she would conclude each time. That day would be the first time in a long time that there was anyone who would complain. A former Los Angeles police officer, six-months-new to the LCPD, sneered, but didn't say anything. He figured he'd show the small town hicks a thing or two instead…about something better than prayer.

Rico edged through the front door. Sneaking in unnoticed wasn't going to be as easy as he expected.

At seeing Rico, Joey shot a look at Jennifer and shook her head. Joey mouthed, "You brat!" *I have a feeling this is not a good day for him to come*, she thought. She had seen the LA cop's sneer.

Rico wondered what the facial exchange between the two women was about.

Jennifer, sitting on the floor near Rosangelica, covered a grin with her knees. She had chastised Rico about not having shown any interest in how Joey made her living, or about her life in general for that matter.

He took it hard, so there he was.

She was glad to still have some influence on him.

Rosangelica elbowed Jennifer, also wondering what the exchange with Joey was about. Before Jennifer could respond, Rosangelica quickly turned to Rico and excitedly waved him over to her.

Rico turned bright red under his beard and tried with all his might to become invisible. If that wasn't enough, Joey announced that her husband was in the house and pointed him out. He stiffened, but managed waving sheepishly as a few of the students applauded.

Great, get all these people to stare at me, Joey, he thought, then sat quickly.

After a few opening remarks, Joey demonstrated some defensive moves on a volunteer. Everyone seemed impressed. She made it look easy.

Rico took out a super-size candy bar. Rosangelica ribbed him and pointed to the No Food or Drink sign taped above them.

He took a bite and mumbled through caramel, "Its okay, I know the owner," and grinned.

"Do you really?" Rosangelica said, wearing an undecipherable expression.

Then the "I've-seen-everything" former East L.A. beat cop spoke up. "Nothing personal, but I don't think those moves would work where I come from."

Joey liked a lighted-hearted atmosphere, but the room suddenly became dead silent. The officer's supervisor shook his head, slowly slumping further down the wall.

"Where are you from?" Joey asked, arms crossed, lips pursed, a toe tracing meaningless circles on the mat.

"East LA, six years LAPD," the officer said with a smirk, adding a puffed-out chest to the statement.

Rico didn't notice the subtle shift in Joey's expression. Maybe he was too busy seething at the man's rudeness.

Instead of addressing the man again, Joey turned to his boss. "Captain...do you mind?"

The man shook his head and gestured with his hands to go ahead.

Captain? Do you mind, what? Rico thought. He didn't know that half of the students were police officers, most from in town, some from El Paso and some from Albuquerque.

"This is your lucky day," Joey said, speaking to the officer. "You'll get to show us here in little 'ole Las Cruces how the big bad wolves do their thing in East LA. We just happen to be a little ahead of schedule today."

All who knew Joey, except Rico, thought, *Oh no, the other Joey is in the house...again!*

"Rosangelica, full contact gear please."

Even though she had spoken only to Rosangelica, and without even facing her, others rose and moved about like busy bees, grabbing large pads to put between them and the sparring partners. They formed a complete circle with the rectangular shaped pads touching edge to edge. The officer stood there, head cocked, and arms crossed.

Joey stood in a relaxed, carefree manner; she closed her eyes and seemed to be praying. Then she let out a strange question. "Captain, did he sign the waiver and does he have any days off?"

"Yes and yes, sensei," the captain whined, his fingers interlocked over his head. "But...only two *short* days."

The whispering in the room stopped again. The arrogant subordinate still didn't get it. He was busy stretching and putting on the gear Rosangelica offered.

Joey slipped on her last piece of gear and held her mouthpiece in her hand.

Rosangelica unwrapped a new mouthpiece for the officer. She was very helpful, and a different kind of quiet, Rico observed; his curiosity was fully piqued.

This is odd. These people sure act serious, he observed.

"The officer here will choose a scenario and play the part of either the officer or perpetrator. Here are the contact rules—full contact, no holds barred. 'Alibi' means surrender."

The officer nodded in agreement. The man's supervisor sunk even lower against the wall.

"We'll do three scenarios where there are no stun guns, weapons or sprays. If you win two of the three, I'll buy you and your wife, or girlfriend…are you attached?"

The man shook his head.

"Can't imagine why," she said through pursed lips.

Joey had just taught the officer his first lesson and he hadn't even seen it coming. But he felt it, which was the point. The others in the room watched the officer's countenance change from bored to agitated.

Joey asked for the scenario. The officer suggested a real life example in which he had subdued a large aggressive suspect in an alley after the man had knocked his weapon away. He had received a commendation for it and much acclaim for collaring the violent offender, a dangerous, skilled jail bird.

Joey played the suspect. The officer got her in the same hold his suspect had not been able to escape from, according to him, and asked her to say, "alibi." Instead, Joey spun and kicked, propelling the officer toward the waiting pads. She followed through delivering another blow as the man turned to get back in the fight.

Rico gawked at the man now laying flat on his back. Rico determined never to anger his wife again.

Joey, one; officer, zero.

To add injury to insult, she decided to find out how the officer had lost his weapon and rescinded the no gun rule. This time, she played the role of officer and used a dummy hand gun another officer handed her from his bag. The *suspect*, the officer in this case, was to disarm her the way the felon had disarmed him. They reenacted the surprise attack from around a blind corner. The split second the *suspect's* hand touched the weapon she jammed her head into his nose, then delivered a knee high into his abdomen. Rico could only identify the Crav Maga move as some kind of martial arts move.

Though wearing pads, the officer winced in pain.

Joey, two; officer, nil.

"OK, for the last scenario, choose a partner and the two of you are to apprehend an unarmed suspect in a domestic abuse situation," Joey said. "You can use a simulated stun gun; the kind that gets placed against the body."

Sweating and breathing more heavily than before, the officer looked around.

The others in the room tried to shrink and avoided direct eye contact. Instinctively, the officer picked the huskiest of his fellow officers, who then glared at him.

Rosangelica rose and quickly got him suited up. She fought the urge to giggle as she looked at the man's disgusted face. This was the third time it had happened to him. Being tall and husky just wasn't paying dividends.

Joey thought otherwise; he made for memorable object lessons.

They began the scenario with Joey boxed in and the two *assailants* ready to team wrestle her down and stun her. The former LAPD officer grabbed her from behind and the other officer moved in. But Joey twisted around, used the man behind her as leverage for a winding kick, and knocked the weapon into the air. Before it hit the ground, Joey forced the officer, who had her in a bear hug, face down on the ground in an elbow lock, and then caught the stun gun and put it to his neck. When the other officer threw a roundhouse at her face, she flew up, did a back flip and landed on her feet. She grabbed the man's follow-through punch and pretended to break his arm, then followed with a blow to the back of his neck.

Rico grimaced. It reminded him of a time something similar happened to him, for real. Fortunately for him and his partner at the time, the rear cover man took the hostile out with a shot to the chest.

Joey, three; opponents, still zero.

"In the end, the best offense is being right...with God," Joey said, murmuring the last part too low to be heard. She casually walked away from the two moaning heaps on the floor.

Rico was speechless and Jennifer's eyes were as big as half dollars. Jennifer expected her friend to be good, obviously, running a dojo and all, but what she saw seemed like something out of Hollywood. Even choreographed, the blows would have hurt plenty. The two gawked at each other.

Rico resolved...again...never ever to make Joey mad...face-to-face at least. He gave Rosangelica a dorky grin as he slowly rewrapped the last half of his candy bar and secretively stuffed it back into his small tote bag.

She nodded and whispered, partially shielding her lips, "¿*Ahora* si verdad?" (*Now* you do it, huh?), she said, referring to the *illegal* candy bar.

CHAPTER NINETEEN

"Training meeting tomorrow morning, eight a.m. sharp," Rico later said to Jennifer, some time after leaving the dojo. "That includes Joey. Got it?"

"Yes," she replied. *Oh Jacob, what a sacrifice for two women who get up before six a.m. seven days a week!* "She might be busy tomorrow. Why don't you tell her? Chicken."

Rico conveniently ignored her. "You'll be taking notes about what we conjure up."

"Why so formal, boss?"

"Well, for future certification of agents, we need to document training hours. And, to write some useful manuals if we come up with some nifty stuff." *And for continuity when I'm…gone,* he thought.

"Eight a.m. it is," Jennifer said. Standing to leave, she kissed him gently on the cheek. "You okay with you know what?"

He nodded and waved his hand dismissively. He knew she meant about the flashbacks. Occasionally, he mumbled to her about them. They were getting more intense. He wondered what brought that subject up. He realized that probably the slightest change in his demeanor made her think that he had had an episode.

"I'm fine, woman."

She only half believed him.

"Remember, *Honey,* not too many fig bars before…." She rushed around the corner before the fig bar aimed at her hit the wall.

Eight a.m. came as rudely as usual for Rico. He started to ask himself which genius made such early plans before remembering who the guilty party was. At least he had retrieved the equipment from storage the night before.

"Sorry for being a little late folks," he said. "Please, take your seats."

He displayed a floor plan of the building they were in. Everyone paid close attention to the procedures he outlined for surviving a hostile entry. He demonstrated how the portable, spring-actuated, bullet-proof shields were to be used. Once cornered, he instructed, with no plausible escape route, they were authorized to offensively engage until they could disengage. That was the only recourse to the fundamental concept of never allowing oneself to be cornered. But survival was survival. Things tended to happen after all, and one didn't just lie down and die; an admirable fight against Murphy was a requisite.

The staff agreed that if all the non-lethal measures at their disposal had failed, then they owed it to the client to use lethal force. There was not a high probability; but they agreed, though they all knew that a lawsuit could break the company if Rico didn't have enough coverage.

Rico went on to demonstrate the use of a stun-gun, sleeping gas, electric net, and other non-lethal incapacitating instruments. He mentioned the type of round they were to carry. The zap round had all the penetration characteristics of a lead round, but normally inflicted only a non-lethal, temporarily incapacitating charge. Legally, it still fell in the category of deadly force. The upshot was that a fired round that didn't otherwise hit a vital organ would only cause sufficient muscle disturbance to allow time for disengagement—even if the assailant was on PCP or other similar substance—eliminating the need for continuing fire and a possible long, dragged-out wrongful death suit.

Still, each agent was to carry at least one magazine loaded with standard hollow point rounds; clearly marked as such.

The last portion of the training involved familiarization with the numerous types of surveillance and intrusion detection devices Rico had installed in and around their building—laser and motion detectors, infrared and standard cameras, a wireless Internet accessible camera network, as well as audio monitoring. He *had* been busy after all.

The crew studied the device layout schematics on the screen—minus some super high tech devices he would keep to himself, just in case. But they weren't looking at any equipment they hadn't used before, until Rico pulled out one of two highly restricted pieces of surveillance devices. He was keeping the second unit stored for a particularly sensitive mission, which would also remain undisclosed for the time being.

He placed what seemed like a small portable DVD player/viewer on the conference table. Two things that differentiated it were a small joystick and a switch protected by a plastic flip cover.

"This device will only be used when a penetration is probable by high danger individuals or suspects, if you will. The legal consequences would otherwise land us in the poor house, or jail. Once you suspect or can confirm an action against the location you are using it at—normally a safe house—you flip this cover open. The light on the tip will flash green if it is ready. If it is, you flip the switch. If it isn't, wait for the self-diagnostic program to correct the malfunction, and then flip it."

"And it does…what?" Joey asked impatiently.

"Someone switch on the big screen please."

The controller's six-inch screen wouldn't be as impressive.

Sarge obliged.

"Watch this," Rico said, grinning. He flipped the cover open; it flashed green. Then he flipped the switch and the plasma screen flickered slightly. The roof of their building appeared first, then several others, then the city block, then almost the whole city. It would have kept going if not for Rico pushing the hover button on the control.

"Will you look at that, we have our own eye in the sky," Sarge blurted.

The two women looked at each, rolled their eyes and shook their heads.

"Yep, this little black box can digitally record four hours of high fidelity video. But the flight time on the hover cam is only fifteen to twenty minutes. If it can be parked on a tree or something before flight power dies, you can still monitor—and record—for the remainder of hard drive space. It can also transmit a live video feed for monitoring and recording indefinitely on these dedicated battery backed-up hard drives." He pointed at three small suitcase-sized plastic carrying cases. "The default operation is a vertical take-off and hover, directly above at 300 feet."

He paused to take a deep breath before continuing. "Now this is why this machine is highly restricted." Rico maneuvered the hover cam and zoomed into some windows. "Unfortunately, I didn't get clearance for a model with laser audio monitoring."

"Oh, too bad," Jennifer teased.

Then he aimed a laser onto a particular car and locked on. At the push of a button the camera zoomed in on the license plate and the machine dropped to a height of 500 feet. It followed the vehicle without any input from Rico. GPS equipped vehicles could be located and tracked from even greater distances.

"I'll bring it in before the SETI people get flooded with UFO sighting calls. Remember, this device is to help track or identify a hostile…so we can run the *opposite* way. And, of course, to provide the law what they need to prosecute whomever manages to…well…rub one of us out, to use an old cliché."

"Yea, real old," Joey murmured as she eyed the view on the screen. The craft had turned toward their building again and was guiding itself to the tiny landing pad Rico had placed on the roof. The GPS and artificial intelligence programming enabled it to find its own way home. It would sit there on the pad recharging its batteries via solar panels until needed.

"Isn't this slight overkill, Jacob?" Jennifer asked, Joey and Sarge nodding in agreement. "This is NSA and HID stuff," she concluded. She meant the National Security Agency and Homeland Intelligence Directorate, charged with providing the president with substantial intelligence information on which to base national security policy and response.

"Yes, it would be *if* I wasn't doing it for an article," Rico said matter-of-factly. "And you never know, the shelter says they have four tricky cases for us to take on starting tomorrow." That seemed to allay their concern that he had lost a screw. He was telling the truth…mostly.

"Have you received permission from the local police, Jacob?" a very concerned Joey inquired.

She wouldn't tolerate anything even remotely illegal—at least by choice. Magnanimous as she thought he was, it really wasn't a concern.

"As a matter of fact, I forged an agreement with the LCPD chief of police. If I provide them a receiver," he pointed at the cases, "that receives all images we see. The catch is that we must agree to deploy it in the event of an Amber Alert or other serious emergency. I figured it was a win-win scenario. I love those deals!"

Joey would trust *and* verify—the late Ronald Reagan's Cold War philosophy at work—and call a certain Chief.

"For now, I will carry this extra controller with me. If I'm out of the office I can deploy it remotely…in the unlikely event we ever need it."

Secretly, he worried that a legal opportunity to test it fully wouldn't present itself, risking drawing attention when he did test it like he had to. He forgot about the current state of affairs and the increasing problem of abductions nationwide.

At the end of the meeting, Rico told Sarge to attempt to make an undetected after-hours entry into the building sometime during the next four days. Then they would iron out any bugs or fix any blind spots in the entry detection sensor layout.

CHAPTER TWENTY

RICO WAS driving back to the office after returning two clients to the shelter from a court appearance. He had the sudden urge to get out of town and sight see. He rang Joey and asked if she wanted to go to Caballo Lake for some jet-skiing.

As much as she wanted to spend time with him, she asked for a rain check. He wondered what she could possibly have on her agenda that was more important than him. Jennifer's chirpy request in the background to join him soothed his bruised ego.

Jennifer privately asked Joey if it was okay. She hesitantly said yes, but no itty-bitty bikini permitted. Jennifer agreed, much to Joey's surprise. Weeks before, she would have lectured Joey on insecurities and envy. Now she was beginning to understand the benefits of modesty—less ogling for one. Besides, an unsightly gash across her belly near the belly button didn't show well, except when recounting war stories to the girls.

Rico drove to the storage facility and hitched up the jet-ski trailer.

Jennifer had forwarded the office phone to her cell and was patiently waiting with a nicely packed picnic basket. She made no effort to conceal how thrilled she felt to have him all to herself for spell. It was just like old times.

Joey bid Rico an extra affectionate farewell, while Jennifer hopped in the passenger side.

"You behave yourself," Joey directed Jacob.

"Always," Rico answered as he hopped in the truck.

If that is not the lie to end all lies, Joey thought, shaking her head and looking skyward. *Please don't strike him down, Lord!*

Jennifer talked incessantly about vision, strategy and other things. Rico just nodded in agreement here and there. As they approached the lake, however, she stopped mid-sentence as she stared wide-eyed at all the water. She had expected a little watering hole. Colorado's snowmelt this year offered generous amounts of water. The Rio Grande likewise saw higher levels of released water, for which Texas was very thankful. Unfortunately, that still didn't address the long term water issues in the region.

Joey would be pleased to know that her husband had insisted that Jennifer put on a wet-suit. Jennifer didn't have to know that he did it only to minimize the gawking by the other water sport enthusiasts, and *maybe* him. Of course, the wet-suit did nothing to alter her curvature. But he didn't have a gunny sack to offer her, so that would have to do.

He annoyed Jennifer when he asked to see her belly scar again.

She refused. "You know better."

"Sorry, just wondering why you don't try those new surgeries."

Sure Jacob, don't you have a flashback and ruin our time together. "Five others is enough surgery for me thanks. Can we get off this subject and go have some fun now?"

Two hours of tricks, and plenty of wrecks, on the jet-skis helped both of them forget that day Rico and Jennifer had to wait for a medivac flight, her insides laying on top of her while he shielded her from ricocheting rounds. All he had been able to do was brush her disheveled hair off her face. Wide open, scared eyes told them both she was a goner. He had cried and cried, even when the others told him to shape up.

Now here they were, exhausted and happy to forget. He had said he loved her then, not expecting to have to explain in what way. The other commandos hearing that only threw fuel to the fire when she bounced back in short order. With bulldog ferocity she volunteered for Afghanistan again to quench the rumors she wished were true.

Rico had called it suicidal tenacity and had flown in a rage. He was on the way out with or without her.

While walking back to the dock Jennifer exhausted herself with laughter, while Rico tried everything possible to flip her off the mini surfboard he was towing her on. It was his turn to laugh when she finally went sailing into the water.

The unrestrained laughter felt good. He was going to have to let himself cut loose more often. He determined this day that his head pain, and other matters, weren't going to control his life every second.

The two grabbed a bite at a little shore-side diner. It was Rico's turn to talk incessantly. Jennifer didn't know what to make of it. Sometimes what he said was way out there, while other things made perfect sense. It gave her goose bumps to see glimpses of the Rico she had once known. This was the Rico who would let his hair down—mostly when the two were on a stroll, whether in the middle of a desert, on a beach, or on a military installation—talking about family and sentimental stuff. It had always gnawed at her how he would change as soon other people came into the picture, almost as if he was ashamed of her interest in him.

They locked eyes for a few moments and studied each other. In an eerie sort of way each knew what the other was thinking at that moment. *Are we the same people we were before? And if we are, is that good? And if not, do we know who we are?*

She thought to tell him that he was still the light of her life. He wanted badly to tell her that even though Joey was now his wife, she still meant the world to him. As it was, they comforted each other with the unspoken affirmation of a loving look. And they had been commandos? Well, at least she had.

They finished eating and walked to the truck, hugging each other like buddies. Jennifer wondered whether Joey would think it proper; and wasn't sure she cared.

Thirty minutes north of Las Cruces, on the way back from the lake, Jennifer found a reason to forget about what Joey might think. Joey called and said the police had initiated an Amber Alert—a police initiated alert when a child was abducted. The time lapse was ten minutes from a confirmed abduction from Young's Park.

Rico worried that he wasn't ready to deliver on what he had told the police chief. He pulled the truck over. Jennifer booted up the laptop to use as a monitor. The screen on the surveillance remote monitor was designed for portability and stealth, not detail, which is what he knew he would need. He hoped it would be enough detail; someone's life was on the line. Rico readied the hover cam remote control device.

"We're airborne, Joey," Rico said into the VOX microphone. "Do we have a vehicle description?"

"A red, late model, maybe 2012, Dodge Caravan. A playmate witness saw a moon roof on it. Our *friends* from the park called it in."

Good job. Rico and Jennifer studied the landscape video being transmitted by the hover device that had taken flight seconds before. Rico's heart felt tight. He knew that the ten minute plus head start could put the vehicle well on the way to El Paso and then no-man's land, Mexico…or anywhere else.

He also knew the Border Patrol checkpoints would have been alerted and on the look out, but there wasn't one to the south. And what if there was a car switch. Could it be an organized thing? Things like that were circulating in legislative circles, but confirmation was hard to come by.

"There!" Jennifer almost screamed.

She pointed at a vehicle, really a speck, on the dirt road paralleling I-10, the Interstate they were on. The two quickly switched seating positions and Jennifer gunned the engine. Rico confirmed the partial plates witnesses gave.

They were more than fifteen minutes away at legal speeds. They neared the exit to Doña Ana six minutes later. Rico had called 911 and patrols were on the way, but he sensed something wrong with the picture.

He had studied the screen and zoomed in and out many times. A vehicle that looked like a Cadillac, Escalade drew his attention. But it was back near the edge of the screen, farther back from what they had confirmed as being the suspect vehicle. But the Escalade seemed out of place out in the desert hills he knew so well.

"Turn left, Jenny."

"But, Jacob the van is just blocks from here…that way!"

"Left. And hurry!"

He was strangely collected now, his minding working at hyper-speed. He called the police again for a helicopter. It was out of commission and units were at least ten minutes from where he had specified. The dispatcher corrected herself and said a Border Patrol chopper had volunteered and was on the way, ETA ten minutes.

Rico felt they didn't have ten. He watched the Escalade pull over and the driver walk into the desert. Rico zoomed in. The guy was looking into…a cave of some kind.

I know where that is!

Rico guided Jennifer through arroyos and various short cuts, cringing each time the Mesquite bush thorns scraped along the sides of his beautiful truck. He had no choice; he wouldn't be able to direct police ground units to the location with any precision. He was going totally by instinct and a visual memory borne of hours and hours exploring, or escaping, while a teenager.

The man, he had zoomed in enough to tell, was now going back to the Escalade. Rico's blood pressure rose. The man was going to get something to transfer the kid to the car, Rico was sure. A powerful pang of fear and anxiety hit him. What if he was misunderstanding what he was feeling, or what if his brain was being *creative* again? He may have sent valuable patrols after an uninvolved person, the Cadillac driver.

He felt slightly comforted when he saw the patrols on his screen evenly split, two nearing the red van three miles away and three others headed toward the Escalade, which Jennifer and Rico were closing in on. At least they had the confirmed suspect vehicle covered...just in case.

The man Rico had observed on his screen was bending into the Escalade when Jennifer brought Rico's truck to a stop some fifty feet away. Rico had already retrieved a 9mm he always carried in the locked glove box. He jumped out of the truck. The man that had been leaning into the Escalade looked at them quickly and dropped the phone he seemed to have been about to use. Then the man reached into his vehicle.

"Hey mister, get out of here!" Rico yelled, about to walk toward the man. Before Rico knew it the man had raised a weapon and fired a round. The man had yanked the trigger and pulled right, hitting the windshield. Rico cursed about that. Then as he pulled back to get behind the door, the man shot another round into Rico's open passenger door. Rico cursed again.

"Jacob, for heaven's sake, take him out! Why is he shooting?" Jennifer screamed.

She was confused as to why Rico was reacting the way he was. She had fought next to him before when they faced multiple aggressors using automatic rifles. Rico didn't flinch back then.

"Just get down!" he instructed as he hid behind the door.

Just then a round went through the door panel and into his thigh. He had just caught a bullet, something she wasn't aware of right away.

Jennifer saw him wince.

Blood gushed out onto the door panel and then the seat. For the first time Rico didn't give a hoot about stains in his truck.

"Police...detectives, hold your fire!" Rico yelled at the man.

The man's hand seemed to be trembling. Pretty shaky bad guy, Rico thought, mashing the pressure point of his leg with his left palm.

"Police?" the guy yelled back. "If...if...you are police officers...let me...see your badges."

"OK!" Just as Rico waved his wallet above the door frame, and Jennifer waved hers out the window, they heard the Border Patrol chopper.

"Oh, man, just in time," Rico said to no one in particular. "Jenny girl...take over will you? Disarm the guy and quickly go see what's in the hole he was looking in."

He was the boss. Rico grabbed the jumper cables from under the seat and busied himself with a tourniquet. His thinking was getting fuzzy very quickly.

Meanwhile, Jennifer walked calmly toward the man and easily coaxed the guy into handing over his weapon. She rushed to the hill the man pointed to as he said, "She's in there, in there!" The man was hysterical.

By this time she calculated that Rico was going into shock. She waved aggressively with one hand as she talked to the dispatcher on her cell and requested medical help for a gunshot victim. "I need a medivac for one, no two," she said, correcting herself as she yanked a board covering a hole in the hillside. A sand-covered, very pale-looking twelve-year-old girl cowered in the hole.

Jennifer peered at the man who had shot her friend. He was frantic. Jennifer busied herself rendering first aide to the girl. The duct tape that covered her mouth was not the problem. Dirt had collapsed and was suffocating her.

The Border Patrol agents arrived quickly and took over rendering aid.

Jennifer was ready to collapse herself. Returning to the truck, she found Rico trying to apply the defibrillator pads to the already unconscious Escalade driver. The excitement had been too much and he had gone into cardiac arrest. An arriving Doña Ana County Deputy quickly took over for Jennifer, who had managed to resuscitate the man.

Three people weren't going to fit in a medivac so she loaded Rico up and flew in the truck to Memorial Medical off I-25 in Cruces. She almost collapsed on top of him as he lay on the gurney outside the Emergency Room.

An hour later the news media reported that, through a combined effort of community members and highly efficient inter-agency cooperation, an abducted victim had been rescued and two suspects arrested.

The governor was to visit the victim's family and hold a press conference to inform them and the public what he was going to do about the issue of abductions.

The reporters also made mention of a misunderstanding between two co-incidental passersby that had led to gunfire. One thought the other was there to transfer the victim as part of a trafficking ring or something of the sort. The district attorney was quoted as saying no charges would be filed against the man who injured another man and damaged the same man's vehicle.

Fortunately for Rico, his wound was more superficial than it had looked.

The shooter had only been a scared bank executive who had happened to notice something strange while looking through binoculars at potential future real estate, and had gone to investigate. Rico was glad that the news agencies had respected his need for privacy, but the mention of the damaged truck really hurt, now that he was going to be fine.

Joey insisted he get over the truck, and being shot by a *banker*. She sent the truck to the body shop to stop his whining. What to do about his ego she didn't know. Maybe he needed the humbling.

The hover cam had returned on its own as the manufacturer designed it. Joey was glad she didn't have to deal with damage to that. But, she also wondered for the first time whether this team could handle this much excitement very often. Soon enough, many more clients than the six they had—and the police—would end up thanking God that the little crew that could, would.

CHAPTER TWENTY-ONE

TWO WEEKS later, back at the office from a checkup at the hospital clinic, and after a nap, Rico finally did what he was supposed to have done weeks before. He would only be dealing with terrible bruising if he had. He contacted a sales representative for a military and police sales company that had developed a prototype for bulletproof, full-body armor.

He identified himself and gave his authorization number. The representative made a connection between the name and magazine articles by Rico. Rico told him that he was interested in writing a review article and wanted to purchase five prototypes or final versions if they were available. The rep told him he was a fan and to call the next day.

By noon the next day the rep had already received permission to ship five units at $2,000 each, half of retail. The apt sales rep didn't miss a beat and sold him on testing the just developed prototype helmet that was proving to be quite effective; those could be loners only. On a whim Rico ordered five of them with a damage deposit of one grand each.

After conferring with a senior exec to clarify Rico's clearance status with Homeland Security, the order was approved. The rep emphasized to Rico the need not to exceed the intended caliber of round when he conducted his tests. Rico considered the warning reasonable; though he would more than likely test it for himself.

As much as he needed the stuff, had Rico realized even such a minor purchase would trigger the flag he feared, he would have waited to order the armor. In the CIA's operations center at Langley, the computer initiated a low-level flag. Special software received input from companies that manufactured various kinds of chemicals and arms or explosives. The software also monitored security devices and equipment sales, though only in general terms. All follow-up actions fell to the FBI, NSA, HID, local authorities, or a combination thereof.

When a flag event appeared, a threat analysis ran automatically, which then initiated different levels of response actions. The officer in charge examined the flags for Rico: a high tech surveillance device, an armored Smart Truck, cutting-edge body armor, and a plethora of sophisticated communication equipment. It merited a simple query and wire dispatch to the other agencies in case they were already running some black, or covert, operation on him—or with him.

Fortunately for Rico, his company showed up as registered and clean of any violations, plus this possible alert was only one in thousands that landed on the follow-up pile of one of many exhausted agents' desks. The query report sounded no alarms anywhere and appeared dead with only a simple memo for-warded to the Regional Homeland Intelligence Directorate—the one on Rico's front steps in El Paso, but still not fully operational. This action marked the item of interest as having been dealt with, awaiting final disposition.

For two weeks Rico kept himself busy looking for a suitable permanent safe house. He found a solid possibility that he would be making an offer for—already forgetting his promise to consult the wife, and partner, about major purchases. How could he explain he was even looking anyway? The apparent paranoid need for one would surely raise questions about his mental state. He'd figure out how to tell Joey later.

As the sales rep promised, the body armor equipment arrived two weeks later, delivered to the office before Rico returned from breakfast. Curious, Jennifer broke open the large box. The appearance of the odd-looking body armor intrigued her. If she had not been told to expect them, and then not seen the shipping list, she would have thought they were just some interesting weighty, spongy, sweater-like shirts.

The helmets were full-faced, motorcycle types and wouldn't have garnered a second look either. But they were nice though. The wearer could lift up the front flap to expose his face. They also had a built-in WI-FI radio and communication system, an added feature Rico would be very happy about.

Jennifer had stuffed everything back in the boxes, placed them in Rico's office, and filed the warranties and receipts by the time he showed up. She had also stacked some unopened boxes, electronic gizmos Rico had ordered weeks before, with the rest. Had she opened them as well, she would have been quite surprised by the sophisticated, cutting edge—and *very* pricey—radio equipment Rico bought.

She might have started asking questions about why they needed this NSA grade communication equipment—two-way radios sewn into light-weight mock turtleneck shirts. They used nanotechnology; a throat microphone that picked up even barely audible speech; sound output via built-in vibrating devices in the neck area of the shirt; an optional wireless ear-canal device was also included. That shipment of encryption-enabled transceivers, a set of five, exceeded ten grand. Rico used his personal credit card to conceal the expense from Joey.

Jennifer didn't pay much attention to Rico when he walked in the front door. She was engrossed in the somewhat complex technical literature that came with the armor.

"Earth to Jennifer," he ribbed softly.

"I'm busy, can't you see?"

"Well excuse me!" Rico intoned . He went around the desk to give her a squeeze and a peck on the cheek, but more to stick his nose into what she was reading. "Hey! That looks like the specs for the armor I'm waiting for."

Jennifer nodded as she pointed toward his office. He dashed off like a kid at Christmas.

Joey had finished her stretching and workout routine at the dojo and walked in. She found it odd that her husband wasn't sitting in the front office yapping away with Jennifer. She too found Jennifer trying to decipher some pamphlet that read, "The Science Behind Carbon Tube Armor."

"Jacob!" Joey called out.

"Over here, mujer," he answered chirpily in Spanglish.

He had been rather melancholy for a couple of weeks since the shooting, which she figured was at the root of it. She eyed Jennifer for a clue as to why he was so upbeat all of a sudden.

"It's his Christmas," she murmured without looking up to see Joey's questioning face.

Joey went into the office and found Rico modeling a new sweater in front of the full-length mirror, posing like Mr. Universe.

"Wow! It makes you look a little fuller. Even gives the impression you have a chest and muscles."

"Actually, this *sweater* accentuates my muskles very well, thank you."

Very funny, she thought.

He tossed her one to try on. She rubbed the strange material. It felt rubbery, not the woolly feel she had expected. It was heavier than it looked too.

"I can't put this on in here," she whined, not wanting to undress in an office.

"Oh, don't whine, just close the door in case Sarge comes in."

Reluctantly, she obeyed.

"Wow! This is weird stuff, Jacob. It feels like you're not wearing anything. I can feel the weight, but the airflow is amazing! I figured it would be hot as heck."

"That's not the only part that's true about it. It's also touted as 'form fitting.' Look in the mirror," Rico instructed with a smirk.

The thickness and the clinginess of the material gave her a fuller, perkier appearance. The cutting edge carbon fiber was making a big splash in the security business, though not for *that* particular reason. The chest and back areas obviously contained added material; it just happened to have the nice shaping benefit.

According to preliminary field tests he had studied, they exceeded expectations. Rico was about to provide input from his own, unbiased testing methods—rather dramatic ones at that.

"Not bad. Of course Jennifer is gonna look like an Amazon woman," she added.

"Yea, like that girl in…in…Tomb Raider…What was her name?" he mused aloud.

Joey grabbed another of the *sweaters* from the box and tossed it at him. "Angelina Jolie…but, that's *not* what you're supposed to say! You're supposed to say, 'Oh! But honey, no one can compare to you.' Or something *like* that!"

She purposely took her time slipping on the pants portion of the set.

"Hey! Rico thought. *That's not playing fair!*

"Hey Jennifer, check this out!" she announced as she stepped out of the office to model for Jennifer.

"Oh, girl! That almost looks like you could wear it to a party. It's like that vinyl stuff women wear. It's weird how the material helps you look so much… well…perkier!"

"Girls! This is body armor! Not lingerie *or* party clothes!" Rico announced loudly from the other room.

"Oh, be quiet and come out here so Jennifer can see the new, more muscular you!"

"¡Estas loca, mujer!"

Just then Sarge walked in and his jaw dropped. A red-faced Joey scrambled back into Jacob's office. Since Joey tended to dress conservatively, he had not realized how curvy she was.

Jennifer laughed hysterically. She finally stopped long enough to remind Sarge that the protein shake he liked was waiting in the kitchen.

Joey avoided eye contact with Sarge for the next few days. Even though she didn't stop being affectionate, it would take her a little time to get over her embarrassment. Jennifer found it so very amusing.

"Sarge!" Rico called through the closed door.

"Yea," he said, his tone revealing that *he* was still somewhat embarrassed.

"Working lunch at noon and firing range after that at about...three thirty."

Rico stepped out of the office and closed the door, leaving the still red-faced Joey acting like she was busy. Rico looked at Jennifer who was grinning. To avoid another laughing fit, he motioned to Sarge to follow and the two hurried into the conference room.

Rico briefed Sarge about a high-risk client they were about to pick up and the new armor and equipment that they would be testing just for these kinds of clients. At least that was Rico's story.

Minutes later, back in his office, Rico loaded up some weapons and told Joey to get her side arm. It was nine-thirty a.m.

His tone let her know that she needed to acquiesce quietly. She watched as he withdrew a box of real bullets from the safe. Why was he not going to use the non-lethal shock rounds they normally carried? She noticed his pensive mood as he put on his shoulder rig and readied his 9mm Glock to holster.

Rico reluctantly packed a piece every day, but normally in a hip pack or small tote bag. The holster tended to be bothersome, but Joey rather liked seeing him wear it. He had a good idea about it, her friskiness tending to correlate with the days he wore it. He wondered if things would change after today.

"Jennifer, Joey and I will be at the range. We are going to be indisposed. Except for emergencies or urgent calls from government types, don't ring us."

His tone to her wasn't any more placid.

"Want to trade?" Joey whispered to Jennifer as she walked by.

"No thanks! I think he has male PMS," Jennifer answered with a wink of good luck.

"You're fired!" Joey said, echoing Rico's oft repeated dorky phrase.

"Thank you!" Jennifer said. "I'll be in Hawaii."

The newlyweds drove north toward the Doña Ana Mountains.

Joey grew impatient at the extended drive. It was rough going after leaving anything that resembled even a dirt road miles behind. She had *very* important things to do. But this didn't seem a like good day at all to pick a fight about priorities with her...husband. Silent, fervent prayer for patience proved more constructive. Of course, she had forgotten that patience was granted by God when asked…and tested through trials…and refined by fire.

Once at the site, Rico unloaded a scarecrow looking thing he had pieced together with milk jugs and chicken wire he had grabbed from a construction junk heap. He had fitted his scarecrow with one of the armor shirts.

"Save that thing after this for Halloween," Joey said. She didn't celebrate this particular holiday, but she wanted to break the silence.

"OK. If it survives," Rico said, slightly annoyed, thinking she was serious.

He hung the odd looking contraption on a mesquite bush about fifty feet away. He looked around the surrounding desert to ensure he wouldn't attract attention—or worse, accidentally hit someone with a stray round. At a real firing range, he'd have had prying questions to answer. The arroyo, a floodwater cut waterway, would serve just fine.

The half-filled water jugs caused the branch the scarecrow was on to bend over and sit flat. He let out an expletive as he saw it and walked to fix it. Joey had asked him to be respectful regarding the minimal and very rare, but still there, expletives he would use. He didn't care to be courteous at the moment. She wisely chose to ignore him.

"I'll shoot first. Your gun will probably shred it," he said after setting the scarecrow upright again.

She just nodded, looking up at the cloudless ten a.m. sky and wiping a sweat bead.

Rico practiced a holster draw. He missed both shots. Shaking his head, he re-holstered and drew again, then fired. Both hit center of mass. The hits were good, but he knew that his draw was getting slower than molasses.

"Let's see the damage," he murmured as he walked toward the scarecrow. He wasn't expecting anything close to the manufacturer's hype.

"Not bad. None of the jugs broke," Joey commented, analyzing the impact points.

Rico nodded with concealed relief.

"OK, Joey, it's your turn," he said, situating his behind on the tailgate.

Joey was ready. With lighting fast speed she drew her thigh-holstered Desert Eagle and tossed the scarecrow end over end with three rounds that sounded like one long ear-piercing shot.

"Hey, you all right?" she said, moving toward Rico while re-holstering the sizeable handgun.

He had slumped over on the tailgate, appearing to have fainted. He was just asleep. Joey quickly opened a bottle of water and forced him to sit up.

"What?" he asked as she slapped him gently on the cheeks.

"Fell asleep…or fainted?" she whispered.

"Oh! Don't be silly. Una siesta solamente. Hey where's the thing?" he asked as he looked around.

Joey signaled him to stay and left to retrieve the scarecrow. "Looks like that stuff's magic!" she announced.

Rico examined the results. "What was the load?"

"Standard, low penetration hollow point, minimal powder load."

"It might have been a quirk. That fifty cal round should've torn this thing to shreds. All it did was pop the top and evacuate the water from the impact."

Joey nodded in agreement.

"Put the armor on this plywood, and I'll give it a couple of rounds with mine," Rico said. "The real thest will be against some rethistance on impact." He didn't notice a few labored syllables from his mouth. Joey did.

"How about if I do that and you sit?"

She was being motherly and risked annoying him, but she didn't care. To her surprise, he acceded without a word, and with a shaky hand offered her his sidearm.

"Honey, there's a soda and a doughnut in the cooler," he mumbled.

She grabbed them for him. He gobbled them quickly as she took the armor-attired piece of wood and leaned it against the arroyo wall. Without fanfare, she fired off three rounds. Each one landed on chest center, give or a take a nano-meter. She took the board to Rico. There were only minor pressure indentations where, if the armor had not worked, there would have been pinky-sized holes; only three little black rings were faintly visible.

"Try yours just for kicks," he said. He repeated the statement more loudly when she leaned over and raised the cup of her ear protection off one ear.

Without a word she went to hang the board, walked back, and stood at the ready. She drew, again with lightning speed, this time firing four rounds in rapid succession.

She retrieved the board. Walking back toward Rico, she studied it. Three rounds hit dead center without penetrating the carbon fibers; the fourth round was a rare miss. Of course, it was clear from the results, the dented and distorted piece of plywood, that any wearer's internal organs would not have survived the vicious impact of the larger and more powerful rounds.

"Well…" Rico commented as they gathered the shells and some extra trash they hadn't brought. "…at least the guy wouldn't need stitches."

"That really wouldn't matter in the morgue, would it?" Joey's unexpected subdued tone threw Rico off.

What's up with you?

She didn't give him a chance to say anything as she hurried to make sure she beat him to the driver's seat. Not that she was in a driving mood; she figured he was in no condition to drive. It didn't elude Joey that her partner seemed less tense now. The fact that the armor actually worked seemed to have something to do with it. She didn't think it was such a big deal. It was a curiosity that the equipment worked as advertised, but she also knew that no one in their company expected any actual need for the stuff. They *had*, after all, agreed that only in extreme cases would they take on any high-attack probability clients—ones that were at high risk of a planned attack even for short time frames. It began to nag at her why this had been so important to him. She planned on asking, perhaps later.

Rico had just dozed off in his office recliner when Sarge knocked on the open door and woke him.

"It's twelve, boss."

"Figured that," Rico said, as he headed to the bathroom. He noticed that Jennifer was not at the front.

"Can you page Joey? Tell her we'll be headed back to the firing range in about two hours."

Sarge nodded and took care of it right then. He was as proficient as Jennifer at the administrative stuff, but unlike her, hated every minute of every day in the weekly rotation. He liked the outdoors, with lots of room for constant motion.

"ADHD," Rico had murmured to Joey at least once. Must have been difficult for him during the constant hurry up and wait operations they used to go on, Rico was sure.

"I bet she whined to get out of it, right?" Rico commented, heading out the door toward the deli.

"Boss, you know your wife well. But, I didn't say a word."

"I'm gonna tell her you told me all the whiney stuff she blurted on the phone. Speak of the devil! Here comes Joey and the other she devil!" Rico said raising his volume as the two women approached.

Joey ignored the comment she knew was intended to illicit questions.

Instead, she squeezed her husband firmly and kissed him tenderly on the lips. How it annoyed him when she wouldn't play into his little game. She squeezed him mainly to get close enough to check his eyes under his sunglasses, but also because in spite of everything she still gushed like a school girl when she saw him.

She grabbed a hold of his hand to check for shakiness. Rico was fully aware of her motives and actually appreciated it—*this time*.

"Excuse me!" Jennifer chirped, sliding in to give Rico a hug and a feather peck on the lips of her own.

That annoyed Joey. Friends or not, she and Jennifer were going to need a heart-to-heart talk soon. She could easily kiss him on the cheek like the Honduran women do.

Jennifer quickly gave Sarge a solid squeeze too, but no kiss. Even with him her close hugging bothered Joey a little. She would do that even though Sarge tended to be on the tentative side when she did, especially in front of his wife. He hadn't figured out that being eye-popping gorgeous like Jennifer didn't make a woman loose. Besides, if he really knew his wife, he would have realized that she didn't have the least bit of concern about his affectionate coworker's intentions.

"All right girls," Rico said. "We men have appetites to attend to. And Joey, don't forget. We go out to the range again at about three."

"*If* I have to and if Tina's soccer game is over. You said you would be there. I'm sure you remember it starts at two," she said. She shot him a look that hinted at what she wanted to hear, or else.

"Yea, well of course I remembered," he said, sounding convincing.

CHAPTER TWENTY-TWO

THE TWO men slipped into a booth at Gino's Deli.

"OK, Sarge, what's in that head of yours?"

"Did you really remember?"

"Remember…?"

"You know…Tina's soccer game."

What does that have to do with the price of tea in China? For heaven's sake! Rico was annoyed but figured it was a *somewhat* reasonable question. Sarge wanted to know whether he was working with a liar. That was fair.

"Are you kidding?" he said , running a hand through his hair. "These days I'm lucky to remember my name. If it wasn't for those two, I'd be in a world of hurt." That was more than an accurate assessment. "Between Joey and I, there's this eerie connection. She already knew I had forgotten, but she…let me off the hook. Are all wives like that? Was that just to soften me up for something?" he trailed off, speaking more to himself than Sarge.

Sarge found himself resisting the desire to delve into the couple's connection thing some more, but he didn't want to push the sharing thing *too* far; Rico could draw the wrong conclusion. The secret need for intimacy among men hadn't exactly become part of the common American consciousness as yet. Sarge wasn't any more equipped to tackle the vast divide between the psychological needs of men and their bravado—especially men of valor such as himself—than anyone else. But he sure could use some advice on creating better chemistry with his wife.

"So, what's the plan?" Sarge asked, sipping on a third refill.

"I'm testing the armor that just came in. Joey and I have determined that the stuff really works. But now we have to test how capable or conscious the wearer would be after impact."

"Normally too incapacitated to stay in the fight," added Sarge, thinking ahead. "How exactly will you be testing that?"

"I have this life-like, remote control, full-sized robot. It can measure the severity of impacts and somehow gives a response capability factor."

"Yea, right."

Rico was not about to leak clues. He knew Sarge would not participate if he knew what was really going to happen. Since he had a somewhat limited capability of sustaining stories fabricated on the run—oddly enough—Rico just nodded and evaded more questions by getting up to get a fourth refill. Spin had grown to be a socially acceptable practice for the common man, joining the politicos in mastering it; discernment was never more difficult than now. Even then Rico's faint recollection of a mother's admonition to honesty and truthfulness tightened his stomach each time spin, or an outright lie, left his lips. Perhaps one day he wouldn't have to deal with regrets.

When he got back to the booth Rico subtly redirected the discussion. "So, how's your idea of taking two or three clients shopping at the same time working out?"

Sarge didn't want to change the subject, but he wasn't going to test the boss's temper. Reluctantly, he said, "It has actually worked out great. I decided to use them as look outs for each other."

Rico raised a brow.

"I had each one study each other's spouse's photo. So now, when one is relaxed and browsing the others give me an extra set of eyes."

"Whoa, porque no pense yo de eso. Smart move hombre. (Why didn't I think of that.)

Rico tended to be conservative with praise when it came to adults. For some reason it was different when it came to children; he praised every little thing. He always wondered why. This tendency served him well winning over the girls at home and other youngsters at the alternative high school, where even the tougher characters softened a bit. But with adults he tended to expect excellence in the work product, and wasn't about to praise good work. This often *didn't* serve him well. So this day Sarge was pleased his boss was pleased.

"I also had a break-through with this kid … Mario," Sarge offered.

Sarge had been pressed into service a few times when Rico couldn't make it to teach the fifty-minute life skills class. It was an innovative idea that offered community volunteers several opportunities to bring their life experiences into the classroom to expand the students' horizons.

Sarge said , "Yea, he came up to me and said hi, then shook my hand!" Sarge paused a moment reflecting. "I think … unless it was my imagination … that he was going to give me a hug."

"You gotta be kidding me? I've worked on that kid for two months now, and you get to be there. You bum!" Rico got goose bumps thinking about the sight. "He shook your hand?" he said, trying to seem interested.

Sarge gave an affirming nod, adding a smile.

"With no blade in it?"

Sarge shook his head that time.

Mario, barely in seventh grade, had grown so angry at the world that he had almost killed his abusive father with a knife and a bat. Insufficient mental health services and two years in a juvenile reform institution staving off attempted rapes didn't help the least bit. Every man after that was a prime target for his wrath. Especially, Hispanic looking ones like his dad.

Apparently, the boy's surprise defense of his mother had only temporarily startled his father. The fear that gripped him at seeing the rebellion in his son's eyes that fateful day had apparently been short-lived. Now that Mario was out from behind his protective steel bars, ironically, the man was on the prowl in search of revenge. The police were legally powerless and out of resources. They couldn't follow the boy for even a few hours, much less days and nights.

Rico, against his better judgment, acceded to Joey's pleas. He took on the job pro bono and gave him a shadow on and off from then on. It had been four weeks and Rico was getting weary of the logistics it took to manage the coverage; even with the boy enrolled in the alternative school where Rico spent that hour or two every day—usually tutoring in reading and Social Studies.

Joey had found that very odd; did he have a hidden desire to be a teacher?

Rico was concocting a plan in his mind even as Sarge and he spoke. They finished their lunch in silence while Rico's mental gears churned and engineered a skeleton plan.

Minutes later, back in the office, Rico convinced Joey to physically drag him out of his office at the appropriate time for the soccer game.

Being glad to have him back in a chirpy mood, she wasn't about to turn down the offer. She was glad Jennifer had left because she would have for sure said something smart-alecky and annoyed him. Minutes before, Jennifer had responded to a call from the contract security company they used for external building security and back up at the rental apartment that served as a temporary safe house. It turned out to be a simple case of mistaken identity.

At the soccer game they had trouble getting to their bleacher seats because practically every person made sure to stop Joey to say hi. Rico thought that waves would have sufficed. Perhaps it was from feeling awkward about the attention they drew. Then again, perhaps the slight tinge of jealousy, and loneliness, had something to do with his unease.

He really didn't know anyone anymore. Everyone he had known and associated with was dead or had moved on, literally *and* metaphorically speaking. The few former *acquaintances* he had already run into didn't count as friends. They had seen each other around was all that could be said. He wondered how in the world they could remember his face and name.

They finally sat at an empty spot on the bleachers and chatted while they waited for the game to start. Joey yelled and waved at Tina as the team passed by. Totally disallowing the coach's stern verbal admonition, Tina left the lineup, bolted to the bleachers, and gave the two a hug and a kiss. She took off just as quickly and got back in line under the coach's semi scowl and shaking head. Tina's drooping shoulders gave Rico a pang in his stomach. Apparently, she only had self confidence when Joey was nearby.

Watch it coach. You'd better drop it, the wanna-be father-hawk thought.

Just in time, the referees called the teams onto the field to shake hands for the game to begin. To Rico's surprise, and angst, Tina left the line again and flew through the bleachers to hug a person neither of them had met. Joey whispered to him that she looked like Tina's mother. She knew this only because she had nosed around Tina's stuff and found a tattered picture. To Joey, the lady barely resembled the pretty Asian face in the photo.

Tina, pointing to them as the lady looked where she pointed, gave them a clue that Joey was right. The hollow-eyed, frail-looking lady shook her head as she pried her hand loose from Tina's, who was begging her to move next to Joey. Rico readied himself to deal with the coach when Tina got back on the field. Fortunately, she seemed to have surrendered any attempt to reform the little rascal who had no respect for the *important* things. The coach just hurried her best player—who happened to be Tina—from the sideline onto the field.

Joey was worried about a possible emotional meltdown from Tina. Both their fears diminished when Tina dashed back to the field wearing a big smile. The milder than expected scolding she got from the coach didn't even faze her as she nodded understanding. Joey's face glowed as she watched *her* little girl.

Rico actually enjoyed the game. It helped him to forget some of his troubles. He figured the soccer dad thing wasn't too bad.

The lady, who was indeed Tina's mom, left after a short conversation with Tina. She was on probation, again, earlier than expected. She felt too ashamed to meet the woman who had apparently assumed her role. "Later," she promised Tina. A promise no one expected her to keep.

Joey and Rico would have to broach the subject of a sure meeting, and maybe the mine-laden topic of adoption, eventually. Good things could be costly.

CHAPTER TWENTY-THREE

SARGE WAS at the office waiting for them. It was time for the *real* world again.

"Stay here until I call you on the radio. I've got things to get ready at the range after Tina's game," Rico instructed him.

Both of them were glad clouds were rolling in. Unexpected, spectacular thunderheads appeared on the horizon.

"What do you want me to do while I wait, boss?"

"Rosangelica will…Speak of the devil," he murmured as she walked in from her afternoon class. "You can help Rosangelica unpack and test-run the five new laptops I bought. Setting up the wireless connection on them should be simple. If you have trouble, call the tech center."

"I have no earthly idea what we need *more* computers for…but okay," Rosangelica quipped.

"For the kids at school to borrow, for homework," Rico said, an eyebrow raised as he looked at Joey. *Are you training her or what?* He thought.

All he could do was say bye to Rosangelica and leave; he had important matters to deal with.

Joey followed dutifully. She knew he was up to something. Her suspicions were confirmed when he drove directly to the desert after watching Tina's team demolish the other, courtesy Tina's three goals. And Rico didn't make a stop for a remote robot like Sarge had mentioned to her. She didn't want to perturb him by asking anything. The ride was pleasant, though absent verbal communication. Her thoughts were on having seen in person for the first time Tina's mother—just out of jail—who surprised Tina and her. Was she about to rip Tina away from her?

"This place will do for the firing range," Rico announced, reminding her of another stressful issue.

He called Sarge on the cell phone walkie-talkie and gave him the coordinates for the GPS locator. Sarge arrived fifteen minutes later. Rico and Joey still hadn't spoken a word during the wait.

"Well, it's out here," Sarge commented when he arrived.

"You and Joey will be staying here," Rico said. "When I tell her on the radio to get ready, that means I'm ready to send out the armored dummy.

You got that right, Joey thought, trying to conceal her concern from Sarge.

"You're both gonna stay behind the vehicle when you're firing … in case something goes wrong. To test reflexes after impact, it'll be firing at those boards over there."

"How many rounds do I fire?" Sarge asked.

"One to start with…then what I tell Joey on the radio." He nodded to Joey who was already retrieving the radio box.

She quickly retrieved an earpiece from the radio box and placed it in her ear under her ear protection.

Good, she's in all business mode, he thought.

Lord, you gave me a…something…husband, she thought.

Rico disappeared around a sharp corner in the arroyo wall and parked the truck. Within ten minutes he gave Joey the heads up that he was ready. Sarge gawked as a very life-like, expensive-looking robot lumbered into view. Rico had stuck a car cell phone antenna on the helmet's top.

It seemed to Joey that he had practiced because he looked very convincing. Once he even acted as if a leg froze up and then broke free.

Why am I not stopping this? She wondered.

Sure, she had seen the stuff work, but to actually get hit to test it? Silent, fervent prayer flowed from her lips.

Rico signaled for one shot to the right shoulder.

She paused to calm her nerves, then turned to Sarge and unemotionally as possible relayed the instructions. Milliseconds after the shot's report, Rico let out a few choice expletives into Joey's earpiece. Joey's heart skipped a beat or two before she could inquire about the robot's status.

He told her *it* was fine.

Nothing muscle cream couldn't handle she effectively rationalized…so far.

That was the test round for pain. He called for one to the left shoulder and a follow up to center of mass. He informed Joey that this time he would be returning fire and to have Sarge duck after firing. He waited patiently and directed her again after she didn't move. She finally relayed the firing instructions.

Rico's mind instantly processed that Sarge's aim was as good as ever. The hit to the left shoulder and chest registered almost instantaneously with a slight puff of dust to the shooter, pain to the target. Disregarding the pain for another fraction of a second, he managed to fire three rounds of his own.

The two shots he fired, before the full impact of the blunt force registered in his mind, hit center of mass in the people-shaped plywood boards. The third went wayward, into the ground as his wrist had moved down when he doubled over. Even though it was quite painful, he was surprised at how much less it was than what he had expected.

The robot ceased to look like a robot as it stumbled forward. Sarge let out some choice words of his own as he rushed to help Rico.

Joey had seen the impact, and though she knew it had not likely penetrated, her knees felt like rubber. She stayed leaning on Sarge's truck listening, but not listening, to the more than heated argument that ensued between the two newest men in her life.

As soon as Sarge knew Rico was in no real danger, he let out some more choice expletives. Rico responded in kind and topped them.

Halfway back to his truck Sarge turned around. "You know, I'm the one that is supposed to be crazy. This freaking takes the cake. I can't believe that *Mr. Reserved* would do something this stupid!"

Tell me about it, Rico thought, as he fought to maintain his equilibrium and keep from fainting.

Sarge turned away angrily and shot Joey a glare. "What are you *doing* with this crazy idiot?" he said tersely as he climbed into his truck and sped off in reverse. "I quit!" he yelled as he aggressively slapped the shift lever into drive and sped away.

"I'm asking myself that very question," she murmured, starting toward the stranger that was her husband. "But…don't call him an…."

They didn't see or hear from Sarge for three days after that.

Rico insisted on driving; Joey had no energy or inclination to argue the matter. The trip not only proved quieter than the drive there, if that was possible, but much slower and more tense.

Joey did everything in her power to keep from saying what she wanted to say, knowing it could rile him up. It wasn't her fault she couldn't manage long.

"Why didn't you let me fire my gun just now?" she murmured.

"*What?*"

"You heard, good and well," she said, staring out her side window.

He unconsciously gave her a glare that if she had been looking his way, she would have whacked him good.

"Remember what it did to the plywood?" It was stupid to ask it. Joey never forgot *anything*—except on purpose. He couldn't stay quiet either when he should have.

"So?" she retorted in a biting, Irish tinged tone.

He had asked for it after all.

"I'm crazy…not stupid." He looked out his window to wait for a sure-to-come stinging rebuttal.

"That former employee of yours who just quit, thinks I'm one…and you're the other."

Joey's last words faded away. The matter was closed.

Which one am I, Rico mused. *He didn't quit! What's he whining about any way, I'm the one in pain. It's better this way. I didn't want to hire him anyways. Better than having to fire him. And anyway…*

The self-deluding, self-talk continued the whole trip like a broken record. He was well on the way to believing his own malarkey.

For Joey, the fierceness of the deluge that had begun to pour on them was a useful distraction. The awe inspiring lightning streaks and ground strikes, some landing slightly too close for comfort, made her focus shift to the girls for some reason she couldn't understand. Then traversing the rushing waters flowing through the numerous arroyos proved a little more distracting, taking her thoughts away from the girls again. Thankfully, Rico's truck was heavy enough and the four-wheel-drive did its job, though barely.

The standard flash-in-the-pan southwestern thunderstorm came and went by the time the two drove up to the office driveway; nothing was worse for wear. But Rico did walk around the truck and grimace at a couple of dings caused by some fast moving logs in the water.

When they entered the office, Jennifer sensed that the two honeymooners were in no mood to deal with energetic youngsters. She literally grabbed the girls and dragged them out for pizza. It would be a very pensive dinner, at least for her.

Jennifer passed the time puzzled and concerned. They had just gone to the firing range. What kind of squabble could a couple possibly get into at a firing range? Maybe Joey out did Rico again, she was thinking. Or money came up. Who knew, she finally conceded.

Upstairs Rico gingerly undressed. Joey generously, but unceremoniously, started the bathwater for him.

"I'll be in the guest room. Don't go in there without knocking." Joey said, more tempered than before.

"Joey," Rico said softly, "You know it was safe. One day you'll know that it wasn't some macho thing. I needed to know for a good reason. But, I'm sorry. I should've found another way."

Not exactly what she wanted to hear, it didn't appease her. She was exhausted. Emotion, including anger, evaded her.

"On second thought, don't even bother knocking. Just stay out of my prr... guest room altogether." She looked at the ceiling as she spoke in a labored whisper and gently closed the door.

He shook his head and considered chasing after her; instead he gasped for air. He waddled to the tub and gingerly climbed into the steamy Epson salt bath.

Rosangelica didn't see Joey slip into the prayer room. It surely would have garnered a question. Early evening prayer was only common for her during crises; usually someone else's.

When Rico got out of the tub, three hot water refills later, it was already slightly past seven. In the mirror, he noticed a horrendous sight. It looked like his entire upper body was one large greenish-purplish mess. Fortunately, the pain was much less he expected—thanks to his morphine savior. Slow movements helped keep it a mere nuisance.

Morphine didn't temper his troubled thinking though. He took three sleeping pills to force his extremely agitated mind to take a break. After some twenty-five minutes, he was fast asleep. He didn't know what to expect from Joey the next day. For now, sleep would delay his knowing.

But not even sleeping pills could halt the varied, ever intensifying, incessant dreams that had begun to haunt him. These weren't the usual fair of combat dreams. Though those were definitely bothersome, they no longer strangled his heart with lasting panic. The new nightmares were much more bizarre and scared the living daylights out of him. Joey's prominence in them caused him to awaken many restless nights, drenched in sweat. Was there no end to the torture?

Meanwhile, at almost eight, Joey was still in the spirit, interceding for her two good friends' souls—Jennifer and Jacob—and getting recharged for the next day's challenges. Including what her husband could possibly conjure up next.

CHAPTER TWENTY-FOUR

"JOEY, I'VE changed my mind," Jennifer said, peeking into the imposing foyer. It wasn't a fancy place, but it *was* a church—and she had avoided entering one since turning sixteen.

Joey, Rosangelica, and Tina stood at the front entrance to their church building, looking back at their indecisive friend.

"Well, OK. It's your choice, but yesterday you said you would come in for a few minutes. Here are the keys," Joey said. With a kind but disappointed smile, she turned and, hand-in-hand with the girls, walked into the building.

Jennifer got in the car and started backing up. *What am I doing at a church on a Tuesday night? These people are probably all zombies.*

She glanced at the people going in. She didn't remember people looking so genuinely happy at the last church she had attended. But, it was more than a lighthearted kind of happy that she sensed. Even individuals walking in alone and of all ages had this glad, peacefulness about them—a genuineness. They didn't *look* like zombies.

I thought it was just Joey and the girls who were like that. She slammed her open palms against the steering wheel. *But, why did I open my mouth and say I would come? I can just see Jacob's reaction when he finds out I went to church, and on a Tuesday!* "*Oh, no Jennifer, are you one of those Holy Roller freaks now?*" *he'll probably say.*

She got out of the car and slithered in.

It was much more imposing inside the six hundred-seat sanctuary than she expected. It didn't look that big from the outside. The K-12 academy she thought was part of the main building was actually a structure all by itself on the opposite side. She slipped into a seat in a row near the middle. It seemed, as she watched, that everyone was voluntarily bunching up into the front seats. That definitely wasn't what she remembered from way back when. She did remember that Joey had said that a two-week crusade was coming; this was the start of the second week. She couldn't recall what significance crusades held, but was very curious about what Joey and the girls were up to without her those many nights out of the past week. No doubt Joey's lack of attention to his needs had contributed to Rico's most recent acerbic mood.

The furnishings and architecture were as plain as could be. Jennifer thought it odd that the place wasn't lavishly decorated. Yet, as she thought about it, she wondered why other church buildings were. The natural wood trim and minimal furnishings were rustic Mexico. The flowers and other added touches gave the sanctuary a warm ambiance all its own; some were silk and others real, all tastefully chosen. She would learn later that the pastors spent the members' hard earned and freely offered money on more important things, like feeding the hungry and tending to widows and orphans.

Before she could sarcastically muse that the place was empty, by six-forty-five p.m. waves of people began rolling in. A man sitting across the aisle from her quickly managed to creep her out; as if the chills down her spine from just being there weren't enough. She had told Joey she wouldn't be at fault if the place burst into flames when she walked in. Joey had said that the place did that regularly anyway. Joey was strange sometimes, Jennifer had thought.

Jennifer scrutinized everything with a fine tooth comb. It struck her again how people seemed so genuine with each other. They hugged and laughed and carried on. Still, a voice told her it was just a facade—an aspect of her childhood church days she did remember all too well. She shook it off; these people deserved a chance to prove otherwise. Perhaps things had changed.

Jennifer noticed the first two rows on each side of the church had signs that read, "Pastors Only Please." She couldn't believe Joey's church had thirty plus associate pastors. When Joey came by she planned to ask about it. She was starting to feel reasonably at ease about being there. After all, everyone so far had been congenial, at least. They really did seem sincere…and normal. Well, for the most part.

"Hey, lady…you new here?" the man across the aisle to the right asked.

Jennifer politely smiled and nodded. *Don't edge him on, Jennifer!* she thought. *Scowl, growl, or something.*

"I'm Bill. Billy Bob Jackson, some people call me."

Get up and leave this place, a little voice screamed in her ears. She wouldn't do that and insult Joey, but considered a seat change. Too late, a family sat down a few chairs away to her left; she was trapped! If she moved that way, the lady there would think she was interested in talking to *her*.

Dang, too slow! she chastised herself mentally. Then she remembered the man that had greeted her, the strange one. Her conscience wouldn't let her be rude, as much as she wanted to, or even ignore the man, who, she thought, was more than likely, homeless.

"I'm…" *Don't do it!* "…Jennifer…. Hi."

Just as she suspected, he took it as a license and started yapping. "Look at this!"

He's taking off his shoe and sock!

"Look at my foot!" He showed off the nice clean foot, changing the angle for her to see its fine form from all sides.

Yippee! she thought. *But, it is a nice one,* Jennifer caught herself thinking. *You really ought to leave before you get infected.*

"It's new. I only had part of a foot last week," he said.

Jennifer's eye brow shot up. She looked again. The man gleefully wiggled his toes at passers by. It looked as new as a baby's foot. *Where does the prosthesis start?* she asked herself. *I don't think organ bioengineering has advanced that much.* Biology and anatomy was a fascination of hers.

The man answered her thoughts. "See, I didn't have anything from here on." The man touched his ankle bone. "A sheet of steel fell on it at a construction job, chopped it right off cleanly, boot and all. Haven't worked in three years, 'cause of the foot…and my, my…nerves…you know."

That she could relate to.

Technology has really advanced, Jennifer marveled, still looking for the connecting point.

Then he dropped a bomb shell on her. "It started growing back last Sunday when this lady prayed over it. Truth be told, I was a little…well, more than a little…juiced when I got in the prayer line. Even told the lady I didn't and wouldn't believe in Jesus. Know what she said?" Jennifer shook her head and considered moving again. "She said, 'I'll pray that you'll reconsider believing and calling on Jesus. For now, be healed and enjoy it.' Can you believe that nonsense?"

Then the man stopped talking, just like that.

The man was about to put his sock back on when Joey and the clan reappeared from behind a door marked "Intercession." Something about that word rang a bell.

"Hey, Bill! Let me see that foot," Joey instructed in a whisper. "Look girls, remember this guy." The girls didn't bother to answer; they just covered their mouths in surprise. Jennifer knew they wouldn't joke around like that in what *they*, at least, revered as God's house.

The girls patted and hugged the guy then turned to Jennifer and loved on her too.

"Bill," Tina offered, "You need a bath, *today*."

"You're absolutely right young one, I'll do that today," Bill quickly said to keep Joey, who made an upset face, from chastising her.

"Thank you, thank you," Tina whispered to Bill, with a polite bow.

They murmured to each other as they squeezed into the seats next to Jennifer. Joey sat farthest from her. Then Tina stood and insisted that Jennifer move over so she could be next to Jennifer too.

Now the foot guy was a little farther away. That made Jennifer more comfortable, though not necessarily feeling peachy-keen, as Joey would say often. But just then, with all the commotion from Tina wanting to be close to her too, she felt more loved and wanted than she had felt in a long time. It dawned on her that maybe she had found home; perhaps in more ways than one?

Jennifer leaned over and asked about all the pastor's chairs.

"Oh, we only have six associate pastors," Joey said.

"So, who are all those well dressed men? I count almost forty. And those two…Catholic priests?"

"Twelve or so are local pastors, ministers, reverends, and what not. The others are from out of town. They're doing a shut-in with our pastor during this campaign, and then some conference thingy next week."

"I guess they're all from your denomination, except the two?"

"Naw, this church doesn't belong to a denomination. Some of those pastors are Baptist, some are Methodist, Lutheran, Catholic, etc."

"But, when my father pastored…"

Joey's expression changed only subtly. Jennifer had never given a hint about her family, much less about having pastor parents.

"He was shunned by those very people. They called us…bad things."

"I hear that's the way Las Cruces was even five years ago. But God has been setting pastors straight. The high price they pay for going unorthodox, or astray, cannot begin to compare to the manifest presence of God and anointing they enjoy; once their hearts let go of dead religious tradition, at least."

Jennifer was sure there was a veiled message in what Joey was saying. *Where does she get those terms from? Unorthodox? Manifest presence?*

"Those that have obeyed and crossed the ungodly denominational walls have been seeing incredible things happen in their congregations. Some of the stoic looking pastors you see will be hucking and bucking before they know it. Just watch girl. But then again some won't and will still be caught up in the Spirit; we're all different."

Hucking and bucking. Now there was an antiquated phrase. Jennifer didn't have to ask what to look for; she knew it well. But she didn't want a soul to know she knew.

"Any more questions, Jennifer?"

Jennifer shook her head.

"Maybe we can talk about those parents of yours…sometime?"

Joey hoped she hadn't moved too early in wanting to know a little about her friend's parents. She excused herself and left to roam about, shaking hands and hugging practically all in the sanctuary.

Jennifer just watched. She couldn't tell if it was Irish passion Joey was sharing or something else.

When the singing started, Joey went back to her seat and sang along with everyone else. It quickly became apparent to Jennifer that singing was *not* one of the gifts God had bestowed on Joey.

At least Jennifer actually remembered one or two hymns they sang. Some Negro spirituals quickened her soul and memories. Even with some fond recollections coming to mind, she still felt uncomfortable, but tried to fit in by clapping along on some songs. She could hear Rosangelica and Tina singing next to her. Rosangelica's voice reverberated in her ears; an operatic voice polar opposite of Joey's. Moreover, the conviction with which her three friends sang was digging into her heart. She wanted to leave right then, but her feet wouldn't budge.

Then smack in the middle of a chorus, the place became instantly quiet; the drum cymbals resonated ever so slightly, then profound silence.

A lady up front spoke loudly, "Behold, says the Lord God of Abraham, Isaac and Jacob. I Am that I Am. He that worships me must worship me in spirit and in truth. My children, this day I am well pleased with your worship. Three years ago I told you that you would see signs and wonders as never before. And last year I released upon you my latter rain. Today, I am well pleased that my children in this body have not turned to glory at gifts, signs, wonders and miracles, but to Him that gives them and does them. And you have done as my Son told you to, 'Do not rejoice that demons are subject to you, rather that your names are written in the Lamb's Book of Life.'

"I have come this day to be before my people who have turned from their wicked ways, and gone to the byways and highways to preach the Gospel of Jesus Christ, making disciples; teaching them of my beloved Son, who died and is resurrected that all may have life, and have it abundantly. Do not believe for the signs and wonders you shall witness this day; rather believe I Am the I Am. And now my judgment is here for those in the household of faith whose hearts have waxed cold and continue in wicked ways and turn not toward me who created them. I shall start with pastors and leaders. Let he who has an ear to hear, hear. Thus saith the Lord of Hosts."

There was another moment of profound silence before a wave of applause literally shook the fan lights. Jennifer wondered what the haziness behind the choir was, less pronounced now than during the singing. It was like a transparent cloud that just hovered there. As the applause died down, Joey walked up to the front in response to her pastor's subtle hand gesture from behind the podium.

Jennifer wondered what that was about. Joey had never mentioned holding any post in the ministry or pastoral staff. The pastor leaned down from the platform and handed Joey a microphone.

Joey spoke softly at first. "Tonight we will be doing things somewhat differently. To maintain order we will have those who want to testify of, or are still seeking, healing or deliverance line up along the outside aisles. The two lines will converge up there on the platform. Those of you who want a touch of the spirit, or are otherwise already overflowing, minister to others next to you and offer your own praises to the I Am from where you stand…or where you fall as the case may be."

The crowd's laughter caught Jennifer by surprise. *An inside joke?* She didn't have to wait long for an answer.

"I'll wait until the lines are fully formed and our pastor prays to get things rolling. Then I'll tend to those remaining in place. After that I'll come back here. Those who get in line, please allow those unable to stand for extended periods to move up in line, just so that any doubts don't convince them to leave without the blessing God has for them. Pastor, seems like they're ready," she concluded.

The pastor offered a short, quite simple prayer. From what Jennifer could gather, it wasn't supposed to be Joey's night to minister, but it seemed God had a plan and Joey acknowledged the pastor's urging to take over completely. This kept Joey from sitting next to Jennifer again. Otherwise, Jennifer would have been peppering her with a million questions about what was going on. She wasn't about to expose her ignorance to the two girls next to her. They still seemed to think that the adults in their lives had all the answers; and had all issues nice and tidy.

Out of the six hundred plus standing-room-only crowd, almost a hundred, more or less, lined each side of the building. Jennifer concluded that the reason the lines formed on the sides was so visitors who stayed in their seats could see the platform…and the supposed miracles and testimonies to take place. She tried managing her cynicism, suppressing at the same time a faint recollection of things one could classify as miracle healings, that *maybe* she had witnessed as a child.

Joey didn't say anything else after the pastor finished the prayer. She just walked down the center aisle and waved her arms. She started to move toward the back of the church intending to stop to touch some people on their foreheads and ministering to people, as was the practice. Then she stopped, turned, and went back to the altar.

The pastor edged over and inquired. God told her He would be doing all the work from now on, she informed him. After a moment of puzzlement the pastor sat back and grinned. That sounded real good to him. He had stopped trying to figure God out three years before; now he just moved out of the way quickly. It didn't matter to him who got the word from God first. And God would regularly tell him that though he'd prepared a wonderful sermon, He'd be taking over from there.

Minutes later, Jennifer watched utterly amazed and perplexed. Before she knew it, some people fell over on their sides, others jumped up and down, and others did both; many more others simply held their arms up in complete reverence. A translucent cloud of something rolled toward the back of the building.

Joey must have influenced these people somehow, Jennifer was thinking just then. She didn't think so in a bad way, just that maybe the people didn't want to seem *unspiritual* or something, and were maybe weak minded and needy. But Joey was now seated on the altar step facing away from the pews. She wasn't even close to Jennifer or Bill, the other skeptic, when something akin to a paradoxically gentle, yet forceful, wind knocked them both off their feet.

What was that? Jennifer, clearly shaken, forced herself back onto her seat. *So far they haven't taken out any snakes, but I wonder if these are those people my parents used to warn me about.*

She turned to watch Joey. It reminded her of her father who would go into trances at the altar, eyes open and not breathing. But right then she couldn't see Joey's eyes to know if that was what had her motionless. It was just so odd; so *very* odd…and strangely familiar at the same time.

Then it became clear as day to her that other congregations in the town of her youth had considered her parent's ministry like those very people. Attributions assigned in ignorance, like what she had just done. Guilt overwhelmed her.

Jennifer stood there dumbfounded as Joey finally rose to her feet and started toward the pews. Jennifer's heart stopped when Joey stopped right by her and then looked right through her with piercing eyes.

"Girls, did you fast all yesterday and today?"

They both nodded, Tina not so emphatically. She had only given her life to Christ a few weeks earlier, and all of this was still very new to her.

Fasting? Jennifer thought, cynicism making a quick comeback. *How archaic.*

"Are you sure?" Joey asked. "I don't want anything to go wrong up there."

They nodded yes again. Joey signaled her young disciples to follow.

Jennifer sat when they left. *Wrong? What is she talking about?*

There was the matter of angelic and demonic forces Joey had purposely avoided discussing during some already lively interactions on spiritual matters. That was meat for another season—at least this was Joey's thinking—meat Jennifer remembered more than she allowed her mind to bring to the fore.

Then there was the drastic change Jennifer had seen in Tina, the seething bitterness about life in general that often crept out without warning seemed to have faded away over just a few week's time. Now, what had been a seriously broken little girl was before her, offering substance to what Joey claimed to be possible in anybody's life; to *anybody* who went to the foot of the cross. But then again, people *could* heal and change that quickly when they wanted to. Couldn't they? The pain of years of neglect and abuse of all kinds could disappear in a whiff, through self-will, right?

Most people went up to testify of a healing or miracle God had done for them the night before or as they entered the building this night. Others shared a revelation God had given them. Others went up merely seeking. Joey laid hands on some and just spoke a word to others while the girls prayed nearby. When it was a little child or a female their age, they stepped in to minister.

Some of the people shook strangely or broke into weeping when Joey touched them or simply spoke prophetic words to them; others gave no outward indication of anything happening. Some, God wouldn't allow Joey to touch. Some got out of wheel chairs completely healed; others didn't but received instructions from God on what to do to receive the healing he had already completed.

Jennifer couldn't hear the interaction with Joey and those that didn't get healed immediately and wondered if those were too heavy sinners; or maybe this *thing* was a hit and miss proposition?

She rose out of her chair to take a chance when she saw a young girl's arm uncurl from a horrendously twisted state, something difficult to attribute to slight of hand. Hollywood couldn't begin to manage special effects to match what she had just seen. The fact that Bill had edged over into the line on the right helped give her a little extra nudge. She got into the line on the left though.

Jennifer tried the fly on the wall thing. *This is utterly ridiculous. Maybe even Joey doesn't know she is being psychologically manipulated. Besides, I don't understand how God could possibly love me, who...*

Before her thought was finished and a muscle had twitched to turn her body toward the exit, she felt a tender touch on her arm. The person in front nudged her one spot forward, then another, and so on until she was facing Joey's back. Joey was at this time gently touching a woman's severely hunched back and began to prophesy.

"My child, your children and your children's children unto the fourth generation have turned to Me through your love. Go and minister in joy until I come for my bride, soon, very soon."

The lady didn't appear to be repaired after getting up from lying on the ground. Jennifer had serious doubts. What was the use?

Joey seemed to almost faint when she tried to turn to the next person, who was Jennifer, standing behind her. Jennifer thought that maybe she was drunk, but she had witnessed this same anointing in her father. He would often fall into a chair when it grew too heavy and continue ministering from there. She had secretly attributed it to stress.

Upon exiting the building, out of Jennifer's view, the woman raised her hands to the sky and praised God with a shout. She did this seven times. Suddenly, she walked upright as gracefully as royalty. She hummed a brand new tune to a brand new testimony; another added to the many, many others in her humble walk with the Lord.

But Jennifer's attention was glued on Joey.

"You are right my child, it is beyond your capabilities to comprehend how much I love you...even now in your rebellion. Know that I set you apart before the beginning of time. That which you came for Jennifer..."

Hearing her name startled Jennifer, and she tried to leave. Her question was about to be answered and she was fearful of the answer.

"…I give freely to you that you may protect he who I sent you to protect; a hard-hearted, conniving man, but beloved nonetheless. You shall dream dreams my child, simply trust me…and know that I AM."

If that wasn't enough, the girls were about to pour olive oil on her. She stopped them.

"Wait! Look, I don't believe in this…anymore…OK. I'm sorry," she said, looking at the ground.

Joey finally opened her eyes and looked at her friend. "It's OK. God has freely given you healing and rest to your tormented mind. But, returning to him is totally up to you. Don't wait too long."

Jennifer couldn't believe this meek and gentle person talking was the same woman who tossed men around like toys in her dojo. The girls were about to put their hands on their friend's head, but Jennifer hit the ground first. She missed the flame-like redness and smoke all over the ceiling…at least with her natural eyes.

The fire department wouldn't be responding to passersby calling in the smoke. Not unless someone from the church called in a natural fire. Three false alarms were enough. Besides, one of their department firefighters was there in church.

Back at the office, Rico worked from his bed all day and into the evening—the same evening and moment Jennifer was at church. Rosangelica had generously made him some sandwiches before leaving. He typed away on his laptop, nibbling sandwiches and gulping soda like any other day.

He wondered what the women were up to. Knowing that Jennifer had found relief from her torment would have warmed him, though he would have vehemently doubted the means. He would be sure to make a point of derision if he found out about it…*if.*

CHAPTER TWENTY-FIVE

THE NEXT day brought a bright, shining, should-be-chirpy kind of morning. But time was pressing in on Rico and he wasn't thrilled. A tender, achy body didn't help the crankiness; neither did two more pills. To add to the sour mood, it was past 8:30 a.m. and Jennifer wasn't at her desk.

It was her rotation week he was sure. "Dang it, Jennifer, you making your own hours now, or what?" he mumbled, temper flaring.

Joey and Jennifer meandered into the conference room, just off the kitchen, yapping away and fired up about something. They didn't notice Rico in the kitchen pouring honey into his tea. Rico heard Jennifer say something to the effect that it was an incredible experience just seconds before he came out to join them and have a talk with Jennifer. It roused his curiosity when she stopped her sentence short, looking at him wide-eyed, like a kid caught with a hand in the cookie jar. Otherwise, he would have ignored the yapping; he had mastered that already.

"What was?" he inquired, managing a reasonable tone.

"What was what?" Jennifer responded, shooting Joey a look Rico couldn't read.

"An incredible experience?" he asked, eyeing Joey as he gingerly lowered himself to a seat.

"Oh! Just something really enlightening I might tell you about sometime," Jennifer offered reluctantly and followed Joey to the kitchen.

"Whatever, woman! We have an operation to carry out three days from now, on Friday. You'll be on point."

Jennifer gave him a look.

I need to brief you both, and Sarge, if I have too, he thought.

He wouldn't get to it until the next evening though. He decided that facing Jennifer just then, considering his mood and Joey being around, was not a good idea.

Perhaps he was growing wiser with age. Maybe.

The phone on the receptionist desk rang once…twice…three times.

"Jennifer…the phone's ringing!"

Rico's annoyance rang clearly in her ears.

"You might want to get it! It might be important!" she said.

Her voice resounded in his head—just as calm and absent of concern as could be—and almost caused him to blow his top. This was very unlike the Jennifer he knew. Her job was her life. At least that's the way things had been. Rico was missing little bits and pieces of what was happening around his world.

The phone stopped ringing and the answering machine picked up; the leave-a-message message was very professional, not that he cared.

"Jennifer, I'd like to speak with you…right now!" The bite in his voice made her brace herself for a chewing out.

"Yes?" she asked softly, stirring a cup of Joey's lentil soup while walking cautiously around her lobby desk. She sat down gingerly.

Her voice might have been soft, but the be-careful-what-and-how-you-say-it look on her face quickly diffused Rico.

"Listen, we need to get something straight. I'm the boss here and if you want to change your office hours, that needs to go through me. At least inform me when you're gonna start late…or whatever."

"Of course, Jacob," she acknowledged, a face and tone overflowing with sugar and spice.

Is she being condescending? 'Cause…

"If…you would have read the sticky note on your desk, you would have known that I was going to be doing something this morning until about nine. And you can, just as well as anyone here, answer a phone every once in a while."

Now there was a hint of a tart tone. It hurt his ears more than the condescension. He wanted her to go back to that. She didn't oblige.

"Perhaps you don't realize how heavy the phone traffic is getting," she continued. "I might have to do this full time because when Sarge and I switch…this switching back and forth causes confusion. I think it's time *you* stepped up to the plate and took control of the rudder for this company."

The *you* really stung…and she wasn't done.

"I think Joey has other more important commitments she would like to get back to."

That was like a love tap given by a giant wasp. Rico looked on, wide-eyed and speechless. An employee had just dressed him down. Where could he find some salve? What could Joey possibly have going other than to serve her husband's company? He searched for a reasonably diplomatic way to say…something. He kept thinking.

Joey strolled in and sat next to him—two against one, great. Now that he appeared wounded, surely his loving, protective wife would set the employee straight.

"Did you hear what she just said?" Rico asked her quietly.

"Yes. Everything," she whispered back as she looked at Jennifer, who was still a little flustered.

"She has good lungs…and good diction." *And from what I heard last night, perfect pitch.*

Huh? Well, set her straight, Joey. "Did you know Jennifer felt that way?" Rico finally asked when Joey just sat there calmly, legs crossed, sipping something annoyingly, obviously choosing to say nothing—or at least taking her sweet southwest time.

When should I ask her to join the choir? I just know she's coming back to the Lord; hopefully soon. "No…but, she made sense," Joey said, snapping out of her important planning.

Two against one was right, but against the wrong one as far as he was concerned.

"About what? This *thing*…about you having *more* important things to do doesn't make sense!"

"Jacob, I…*we*…love you…," Joey said, signaling with a wave whom the "we" included. She took a deep breath—the kind that usually preceded bad news. "…but, I have a newsflash for you," she started saying in English, then finished in Spanish. "The whole world doesn't revolve around *you*."

The wasp nest dropped.

Narcissism. I'm not narcissistic! "You mean … you *do* have more important things than to help me?"

He had aimed for manly indignation, but sounded more like a wounded puppy. Things weren't going well. The bedroom refuge was calling.

"Just like Jenny mentioned. I'm going to leave it at that. Now what are you going to do to start deferring some of the tasks you've had me doing, as well as getting Jennifer some help?"

The women waited patiently and tried to seem unaware of the strain on his face and the gulps he was hiding. He summoned the military man in him and assumed control.

"Well, I have a solution for that. But I think that setting some goals and a developing vision for this company is what is really needed. If you help me with that complex part, I can construct a logistical plan to deal with the direction you guys think we should go."

"We can do that," the two women said, agreeably.

What? No victory celebration? No rubbing it in? Aren't you going to gloat? Rico waited.

"I think that in reality we have ninety percent of it done," Jennifer added in a chirpier mood.

How convenient that they had discussed the matter, or rather complained about it, already.

"It should be a simple matter of putting it in black and white and polishing it up. We've talked about the possibilities for this business so much, it'll be a breeze," Jennifer added, knowing her boss wasn't going to chew her butt for speaking up.

And he found himself *actually* listening to her needs. It was a pretty good start.

"Could you give me a general outline by around eleven o'clock this morning then?"

The two nodded.

"OK. I'll be out meeting with a realtor for something," Rico said after a long silence. "Maybe play some golf."

The two women seemed to have tuned him out, eyeing each other with knowing looks.

"I'm a little concerned about Tina," Joey lamented, showing no indication she was getting up.

Rico had almost made his escape. It sounded bad already. He rationalized Joey must have been addressing Jennifer. It sounded like girl talk to him. He took one step. Jennifer gently hooked his arm and nudged him back down.

"Well, I'll be out and about…grass needs mowing, toilet…" Rico said.

"She's starting to develop and get flirty," Joey said.

Rico stared at them, grimacing. The two women waited to make sure he correctly processed what they meant.

"Oh! I get it. Umm, and…?"

He had noticed that very thing the last time they had been at the pool. Rosangelica had nonchalantly commented, among other things, that Tina was going to need a new swimsuit. Rico forked over fifty bills for a new one after letting Rosangelica know that he had *quite* enough information already.

Tina had been aware of her changing body and would cover herself with crossed arms when an "un-cute" boy veered and steered too close. She had wanted to ask Rico for some cash but hadn't because she was sure he would ask what it was for.

After Rosangelica's comment he wouldn't ever be asking anything of the sort, no matter the amount she asked for. If necessary, he would tolerate Joey's muttering about spoiling the girl with ridiculous amounts of cash.

"And...Sarge's son is beginning to notice, too. I don't plan to interfere with what her foster mother, or her mother, allows her to buy, unless it gets any more on the sensual side than it already is. I gotta draw the line in this home somewhere," Joey added.

"And you want me to talk to Sarge...or Junior?" Rico wanted to redirect the subject to real important matters. "Well ... anyway ... I, I don't understand what this girl stuff has to do with running a company?"

Both women rolled their eyes and banged their foreheads with open palms.

"Like I was saying earlier, the world does not revolve around you *or* this *company*, Jacob! This is real life," Joey said.

Her suddenly flushed cheeks didn't bode well for him. The Irish tint of her verbiage made her point extra clear. And he really didn't like it when she spoke his name like that.

"Ok! I'll try and process this. Just give me time." Rico aggressively rubbed his beard. "Since it's not a crisis then, I think I can manage. This stage will pass...by...next week? Soon? Please tell me yes!"

The two women shook their heads and made unequivocal facial gestures. *What planet is he on?*

"And did I mention Rosangelica's budding romantic love interest?" Joey had to add.

"I'm leaving for a five year TDY...tonight." Rico put his hands to his ears and walked off to the kitchen.

There wasn't anything like temporary duty assignments for him anymore, though he would have loved one then.

"Information overload! Information overload!" he mumbled.

The ladies could only laugh. It was true, but the details about Rosangelica could wait until later. Details they thought they knew. In fact, Rosangelica had no real romantic interest in anyone. She just loved to see Joey squirm. She was using one of her close male friends as a ruse to do just that; then again, the young man had great potential. She and her male friend had agreed to forestall romantic involvement until a serious commitment to marriage was forthcoming.

The concept was making a dent in the Christian dating scene, preventing many broken hearts and shattered lives. Rico would have told Rosangelica that it was an utterly ridiculous supposition.

Likewise, as one would expect, the majority in the hunt for mate found it difficult to seriously consider being so different than even the majority in the faith. And Tina, struggling with leaving the world behind just when she was discovering certain *feelings* for the opposite sex, was no different. She made a cross with her fingers and shoved them forward whenever Rosangelica broached the subject. Rosangelica knew what kind of miserable pit her little *sister* was digging and was interceding fervently for her in her prayer closet. Tina had recently laid out an elaborate eloping plan to her wide-eyed big *sister*. Rosangelica didn't know if the groom was even aware of the plan.

Oblivious to all these deeper matters, Rico was kind of gelling with the family thing nonetheless. At least like the grease in a bowl of chicken soup. It doesn't really mix together with the water, but together they sure taste great and work wonders on the soul. The interaction with the girls and other energetic youngsters brought much satisfaction, though the idea of getting in the middle of the girl things the women were discussing was less than inviting. He did like the fact that Rosangelica had seen fit to bring him in on the romance ruse. At least he was on the inside of something, he thought. And she *thought* she knew what she was doing.

Interesting as he found this man of the house thing, the well-intended efforts to be there for them taxed his stamina. This family thing was one thing he didn't want to mess up on. But the company and other goal needed attention too. And now his energy levels day to day were becoming more and more erratic. The two disparate focuses began taking their toll.

"Will you guys be prepared to present at our first official company meeting, tonight at six?" Rico asked before leaving, already exhausted.

They nodded again, sure their part hadn't gotten the necessary attention in his mind. But what were they to do?

CHAPTER TWENTY-SIX

LATER THAT evening the conference room was buzzing. The mood, as usual, was light hearted. Still, the main topic of discussion was about the company's vision and goals.

The top three executives agreed to make permanent the family welcome mat policy for meetings. Joey proposed the idea during a previous talk to help keep priorities in line. Rico was sure there was a hidden meaning he was supposed to glean.

Rosangelica and Tina gained more responsibility to manage the youngsters during those same meetings. At the same time, they also got more and more leeway in deciding how much of their personal time they wanted to put into other aspects of the company's business.

On a whim Rico instructed Joey to begin a pay sheet for the two. Perhaps they would consider a career in the business. "God forbid!" Joey had said, jokingly. Over time she would grow to be mortified for real about the prospect. It would have been better for her to be more direct about that fear. Had she done so, *another* set of misunderstandings may have been averted. She couldn't—or chose not to—see that Rico wasn't running on all cylinders.

CHAPTER TWENTY-SEVEN

EARLY THE next morning, Joey was headed out just when Jennifer finished scribbling a note to Rico.

"Well, Jenny, are you ready to make a decision?" Joey asked.

Jennifer knew exactly what she meant and shook her head.

"Don't wait too long," Joey warned, adding a serious look. "So…where you going lassie?"

Jennifer gave her a pretend annoyed look, then quickly smiled and said, "I have no idea. I got this hare-brained idea to take a casual drive. I woke up with Valley Drive and north stuck in my head. This is weird."

Jennifer waited for Joey to respond, but she was too busy concealing a grin with her hand.

Joey hugged her and started out the door, "Well, have fun Jenny girl. I love you."

Jennifer was still trying to get used to being shown affection so directly and verbally like that. She liked it, though there was a smidgen of embarrassment she felt when strangers were nearby. While it felt less odd with Roseangelica, it still felt strange. Tina was a more subtle hugger, and *never* spoke the "love" word above a mumble.

Heading north on Valley Drive, Jennifer felt a stirring in her spirit. It was getting a little uncomfortable. An overwhelming sense of loneliness hit her. It grew stronger and stronger as she passed onion field after onion field. The engine on her recently purchased new car suddenly died. Very annoyed, she pulled over and planned to offer the dealer a piece of her mind.

She dug through her purse searching for her phone, while at the same time watching field workers labor away harvesting the onion crop. In between some mild cursing, she wondered why anyone would work in blazing heat for the pennies they made.

At the far corner of the field a fifteen year-old Hispanic girl stood from her kneeling position on the hot ground. She stood and looked around. A much older sister next to her asked her where she thought she was going. In Spanish she answered that she was about God's business and continued trudging along, raising tired feet over row after row. She would have conserved more energy had she stayed where she had been and made money filling up some more gunny sacks; but she walked on. It was just like in a dream she had had months before.

Jennifer saw her through a combination of unexplainable teary eyes and heat waves rising off the hot Mesilla Valley ground. The petite young woman of Tina's age seemed only a blurry illusion. Jennifer looked around for help from a real person. She continued stirring things around in her purse looking for the cell phone—forgetting she always clipped it on her belt—all the while promising to clean out the junk filled purse. She angrily twiddled her thumbs on the steering wheel after she checked her belt. Realizing she had forgotten it on her desk, she hoped just then that Rico didn't try calling or that no emergency happened. Today was not a good day to deal with chastisement—not at all. Anger one second and lonesome heartache the next were already beyond coping with.

By this time the young migrant woman had made it across the field and was tapping on her window. Jennifer turned the key and tried the window. It lowered. The young woman gestured with her hand to ask if she could climb in.

A puzzled Jennifer nodded. What else could she do?

The raggedy clothes and strong onion smell made Jennifer uncomfortable. She couldn't believe that her own boss, Rico, had earned his spending money the same hard way when he was little.

The girl spoke in broken English, not even trying Spanish first. "Your car works now," the girl said and pointed at the air conditioning button.

Jennifer thought the comment odd but tried the ignition anyway. It started right up and the A/C turned on. It was 9:30 a.m. and already blazing hot. The girl showed appreciation with a smile. Of course, Jennifer hadn't noticed the heat while she had wandered all over town before surrendering to that still small voice and compelling feeling to head down Valley Drive.

Jennifer grew even more uneasy. She didn't know that one of God's messengers was sitting next to her.

The messenger wondered what in the world she thought she was doing. The girl thought she had just become delirious in the heat. It must not have been God. The dream was just that, another of many. She reached for the door handle.

Jennifer noticed the ever so subtle twitch of her hand and secretly edged her on. She reached in her purse to grab some of the plentiful cash she always carried; some of Rico's tendencies had rubbed off on her. It made sense to her that that was what the young lady had hoped for.

Instead of opening the door the young woman turned and with a powerful sense of conviction looked the very well dressed and refined-looking Jennifer straight in the eye.

Jennifer froze with her hand in her purse.

"Jesus wants to know if you are tired of the emptiness inside you. You keep running away, Jennifer. All He wants is to fill you to overflowing with love and power. Today is the day of decision, to return to Him or not," the girl said, now in perfect English.

Jennifer's jaw dropped; her heart torn. She could only give a slight nod to the young woman, who had become a mirage again through Jennifer's tears.

"But, I've done so many horrible things…why would he want anything to do with me now?" Jennifer said, sobbing.

Killing in combat was not the worse thing she was thinking about, but that was part of it.

"Jesus died on the cross for every sin you did and will ever do. Do you want to be unbound, delivered?"

Jennifer nodded again with more firmness.

Right there, beside a hot, New Mexico onion field, a young Mexican migrant girl guided Jennifer back to the straight and narrow path. Jennifer repeated a rededication prayer as the girl said it. She agreed to reread Romans, Chapter 10, as the girl suggested.

In the same unassuming manner as she had come, the young woman exited the car, humbly accepting the two hundred dollar gift and business card Jennifer held out. At first, she refused, but Jennifer insisted. She watched the young lady walk away with more energy than before, raising the money gift up to heaven; it equaled one month's sweat-earned wages and a fourth of the money she needed for her mother's cancer surgery back in Mexico.

Jennifer felt freer and more unburdened than she had ever had. She drove back to the office, joy bubbling inside her spirit. Somehow, the desert green looked a brighter green. She thought about what she would tell Joey. She had expected lightning and stuff, but she didn't see or feel anything supernatural happen…well, except for the unburdened soul. Now she knew that she knew that God was God, and a major change had occurred inside. She was ready for her new life. First she had to deal with Rico.

Jennifer stepped into the office and quickly got an earful from Rico, bellowing from his desk. Ignoring him, she hurried looking through her desk drawers for the Bible Joey had given her; the one she had *warmly* and *graciously* accepted before hiding it in a *safe* place.

The short dedication Joey had inscribed took on new meaning; deeply touched, Jennifer smiled as she read it again and again. Quickly, she found the table of contents and pointed at Romans. The girl had told her to read Romans 10:9, in particular, for assurance of her salvation. The girl must have known Jennifer would want to complicate things and think there was something else she had to do to *re-earn* eternal life. According to what she read there wasn't. In fact, she had only left her walk with Christ—a direction of travel which could lead to eternal separation. But now she was back on the right path, headed in the right direction and reconnected with the Holy Spirit. Jennifer felt ecstatic.

Rico, on the other hand, was rather perturbed. He hollered that she wasn't where she was supposed to be.

On the contrary, Jacob…I was exactly where I was supposed to be; for once in a…an eternity.

CHAPTER TWENTY-EIGHT

MERCIFULLY, AT least for Rico, Friday came quickly. He was getting antsy. The team, including Sarge, had been prepping and drilling for the operation for days. It was, for all practical purposes, a military op.

Mario's aggressive, dangerous father had tired Rico. It was time for the man to come face to face with the boy's source of protection—his guardian angels. Rico had finally caved to Joey's pleas to get involved. Joey thought the boy needed someone to care for him to turn out different from his father, and find God. Rico was one hundred percent sure the boy was incorrigible, but everyone deserved a second chance to prove others wrong.

This strange little company of people was going to offer Mario a chance to open his eyes to a kinder world—and a different standard of existence. Rico's and Joey's policy was that they would spend the full force of their resources on a few people they were able to take in as clients. It made more sense than scattering resources all over the place with no focus. They knew they couldn't save the world; but they would, at least, attempt to stop some cycles of destruction and set into motion more positive, constructive, and possibly functional, ones. Mario was one of those fortunate few people to experience such concern.

The multifaceted roots of the problems that plagued the people they protected and helped were daunting. Without employing every government and private agency's help, as well as consoling one another when things got bad, they would have to close up their not-for-profit shop and declare the world lost. The condition they found some children in horrified even this group of hardened vets. Some of the youngsters were extremely aggressive and violent. Because of that, even though Rico greatly appreciated the unreserved—and unearned—affection Tina and Rosangelica had offered him from the moment they met, the contentment he felt after each breakthrough with some of the aggressive youngsters was immense.

But achieving each little breakthrough tortured him emotionally. Waiting for legal authority to act on behalf of clients drove him into fits of anxiety and anger. Agitated as he was, Rico never bothered to consider how quickly Joey managed to navigate the normally sluggish bureaucracy so efficiently and speedily. The police, even with somewhat expanded police powers, were often hogtied. He would find out much later—by then it would matter little—how God responded almost instantly to her prayer-room petitions. All *he* experienced was frazzled nerves and testy days; then unbeknownst to him God's hand invisibly moved things…*just in time*.

Mario's case would prove the first of many great and complex security challenges in which the company would excel. In this case, Joey completely placed in Rico's hands the seemingly insurmountable task of keeping the boy safe—the first order of business always. God told Joey to submit to Rico's plan. She wondered if she could manage that; his plan was rather aggressive. She respected his skills without question, but this seemed like a spiritual matter to her. God told her ever so clearly, "Be still."

Weeks earlier the first official collaboration between the police and Rico's company had begun with this boy's case. In an intensely debated meeting, where an *unofficial* hands-off understanding with the police was reached, Rico plotted a confrontation meant to deliver a forceful ultimatum—or make a bad decision by the aggressor very painful. The police had balked at several options Rico had previously offered. Finally, this one seemed agreeable. Of course, it was the one where plausible deniability by the police was possible if anything went wrong.

After some advance work at likely hangouts, the team made their move. A copy of the man's rap sheet *accidentally* left open on the Lieutenant's desk saved Rico lots of leg work finding the man's favorite spots—often for arrests. Rico picked a time when the man and his rag tag entourage would be expected to be totally sober. Rico missed the mark on that—a *near* state of soberness would have to do.

Jennifer backed the cycle into a parking spot. Rico insisted she wear the new armor underneath the form-fitting leather suspender pants and equally snug tee-shirt. Even before returning to the Lord she had started heeding Joey's counsel and had begun to gravitate toward more conservative attire. But she had worn such stuff for less honorable reasons, so she didn't complain adamantly. Not as vociferously as Joey did when she saw the outfit, and found out who insisted on it.

The parking lot just off Valley Drive was dimly lit and slightly isolated. Her cycle was aimed at the escape route—the alley. Jennifer, leaning back on her cycle, quickly drew the attention of the arriving bogey, as expected. The bullet-proof helmet obscured much of her face, though her piercing eyes still made the men gulp as their headlights shown on her.

They seemed undecided about approaching her once they got out of their SUV.

Jennifer feigned disinterest. To Rico she had seemed disinterested about the whole affair during the briefings, but the acting parts piqued her interest finally.

Testosterone quickly edged the not completely sober pack into an unwise decision—the game was now in Jennifer's park.

Rico felt a sudden wave of panic. Had he prepped her properly? Was she ready?

"Hey boys, would any of you happen to be Javier Santos?" Jennifer said.

She expertly created more distraction as she gingerly dismounted the cycle. Joey, watching from nearby, almost gagged; obviously someone had practice. Jennifer placed her Bible, which she had really been reading by flashlight, into the right side leather saddlebag.

The other men stopped in their tracks—as intended—and cajoled the man, who had quickly identified himself as the man she apparently *wanted*. *It's my lucky day* was written all over his face.

"How 'bout a minute with you…in private?" Jennifer said.

The other men hooted and hollered. The now puff-chested Santos turned to the others and grinned.

"Honey, all you want—unless you're a cop."

Jennifer shook her head and said it was a personal matter. The catcalls grew louder.

"These boys…you'll want some private time, too…after *we're* done," Santos said, turning back to grin at his buddies.

Jennifer forced herself with everything in her being not to puke right then and there. Cleaning the helmet would be too much trouble.

"Yea, whatever!"

"Maintain, Jennifer!" Rico ordered over the radio. "Draw him in, don't re-pulse him!"

She realized she deserved the terseness in his voice, but it still stung.

Rico whispered into his mike, "Now is the time to ask the others to please hush up, while keeping the bogey from looking back."

"Wilco," she said without moving her lips. She grabbed the man's arm teasingly and calmly told him she was going to get the "boys" to quiet down. At that moment, he didn't care the least bit about his companions.

"Boys," she whispered in the direction of the men as she firmly held Santos at the elbow. "Will you please keep it quiet and stay right where you're at."

At that exact moment tiny red dots appeared, one on each man's chest and forehead intermittently; each laser emanated from a separate rooftop. The suddenness of the silence piqued Santos's interest and he tried, against Jennifer's resistance, to turn.

"Let him turn in two seconds…one…now!" Rico said.

The man gave the other men, frozen-in-place, a puzzled look. Jennifer quickly distracted him again and forced him to turn so that the dots could reappear.

Jennifer stepped away and did the Jekyll and Hyde thing. Her posture hinted a new game had started. She was ready. In a very different tone than before, she turned to tell the *frozen* group that they were not to move, regardless of what happened. "Do we understand that gentlemen?"

They all nodded in agreement, even as the now slightly annoyed behemoth of a man turned to show them his distaste for taking commands from this woman. The dots disappeared again.

"Mr. Santos, it seems we have some business to attend to," Jennifer said, deflecting Rico's terseness on to him.

Jennifer's open hand on his chest stopped the now tense Santos from joining his friends. This clearly agitated him. He released the standard macho gibberish; a tirade of expletives.

The moment he was done, Jennifer spoke. "I'm here to deliver a message to you. A one time, free of charge warning if you will." She got on a roll. "You are to leave your son *alone*, from here until you see the other side of eternity."

"Almost poetic, Jennifer," Rico said with a slight light-heartedness in his voice.

"Thanks…shut up," Jennifer said under her breath, of course relieved to hear a calmer boss. Again, her lips didn't move, and she was sure Rico hadn't heard the last part because she had barely even heard herself.

"I heard that!"

"This dang radio system is too sensitive. By the way…why am *I* here and not you?" Why didn't she leave well enough alone and keep him in a good mood?

Good question, the others thought.

JACOB RICO: CHINK IN THE ARMOR

"Focus," he ordered. That worked.

In that split second the man turned to leave in outright anger. "Why that little piece of garbage. I was taking a break from finding him today, but now that he sent some stupid girl friend to fight his battles, I'll find him tonight!"

It struck him odd how his buddies didn't seem to want to move, weren't saying a word, nor were showing any emotion. Their eyes looked strange. They must have juiced up and not shared with him.

"Maybe you would like to see what this *girl* intends to teach you?" Jennifer asked. "Or perhaps you're chicken?"

That worked, again. The tired cliché seemed always to work.

"As a matter-of-fact!" The man stopped and turned in his tracks. His face took on a sinister look; eyes got bigger, an open palm rubbed his chin and mustache.

Jennifer wondered how many times little Mario had to endure that fearsome look. For a split second it even shocked her.

"After I'm done with that loser…I'll be in the pen for a lonnnng time, so I'm gonna have me some fun right now!"

The man gruffly grabbed his crotch, mocking her.

"I gonna kill him!"

"No!" a chorus of barely maintained whispers boomed through her earpiece, almost bursting ear drums. She jerked her head and said, "Ow."

The man became suspicious.

She spoke again through gritted teeth, "OK, Mister, today is your kinda, sorta lucky day."

Good, she's back to her senses, thought the three on the roof tops.

"Today, I might break only one or two legs…and then again, maybe an arm…or two…*if* you don't cooperate. But, by *accident* you might find your pitiful self in traction for a long, long time!"

The three on the roof tops groaned, "Oh, no!"

The man reached for her with a wrath burning in his brains and loins. "Let me get a feel of that firm body I'm about to enjoy!"

Within seconds the man was lying prostrate on the ground. He used his arms to drag his body and face from out of the puddle it ended up in; two fractured legs kept him from standing or even kneeling. The man writhed, barely able to groan. Even if Jennifer hadn't struck his throat with a solid blow, the man's screaming would not have been heard much above the blaring music emanating from the bar. It was a gruesome sight, even for the veterans on the roof.

Jennifer walked over to the man's side just as a police patrol sped passed. Blue and red lights reflected off buildings as the patrol looked for a place to make a quick u-turn. It jumped the center divider instead.

"Mr. Santos," Jennifer said loudly through gritted teeth. "Are we communicating more clearly now? Are you going to want traction today…or tomorrow…or the next day?" The man could barely answer. "If you do not answer me in two seconds before the police get here, I'll take it as a no and make traction a fact of life for you, free of charge."

"Jennifer! Get out of there now! What are you doing?" Rico ordered.

The three *snipers*—armed only with sleeper-dart loaded rifles—were loading up their gear by then.

"Finishing the job. You didn't see this man's face!"

The three shook their heads. They hoped she was bluffing the man, hopefully out of town.

"No! No! I don't need any more pain," Santos huffed out just in time. By then he was sobbing. "Who the hell are you?"

How many times have I heard that? She had heard it often in Arabic and Farsi, albeit without the hell part. "Just someone that wants you out of town; but, if you stay…" she paused to consider if she wanted to give him that leeway. "…I highly recommend that when you see Mario out and about, that you cross the street quickly. I live here and I'll be watching. You leave him alone and you… well, get to live a normal life, if you can call this pathetic life of yours normal."

Jennifer mounted her iron steed just as the police patrol drove up with its lights flashing.

"Hold it right there!" The PA boomed.

Jennifer didn't…she just yelled that the man seemed to be in need of an ambulance. She casually pointed at the still writhing man, then made the cycle scream and screeched the tires all the way into the alley.

The man's friends edged toward the whimpering lump as the cycle smoke cleared.

"Hold it right there!" the patrol officer yelled again over the PA. The siren blared as he finished calling in for an ambulance. The pursuit ended before it started as the dispatcher directed him to abort the pursuit.

"But…I have a fleeing assault suspect!"

The man reluctantly obeyed. The officer's frustration grew as he waited for the ambulance. Someone at the department had forgotten to brief the on-coming shift about the look-the-other-way *arrangement*.

The ensuing interview of the witnesses conveniently proved useless. They refused to offer any information. The cover team was now driving three separate cars back to base.

Joey and Jennifer had a long into-the-night talk. Jennifer's aggressive tendencies had Joey worried; Jennifer's aggressive tendencies? Jennifer had her own observations to mention. The point well taken, the two agreed to be accountable to each other. They ended with prayer, forging an eternal kind of bond—one that would be tested soon.

Nevertheless, it was a very productive night indeed.

CHAPTER TWENTY-NINE

ONE WEEK later a Lieutenant Barrientos called.

"It's about what?" he asked Joey who was filling in for Jennifer and was forwarding the call. His voice didn't reveal the tenseness he felt; Santos had discovered Jennifer's identity and had filed charges he was sure.

"Something about an urgent case."

Joey kept from Rico that she knew the man personally. She asked the lieutenant to keep her out of it and deal with matters pertaining to her husband directly with him—but a little information leak was acceptable. The lieutenant didn't know what the big deal was, but he agreed. She didn't offer that someone like Rico would want to build his own reputation and not ride anyone's coattails, especially his wife's.

"Oh! That. All righty…I'll take it then," Rico said.

The lieutenant wanted to meet with him for lunch to discuss and meet a potential client who was currently in police protection. The two agreed to meet in Rico's conference room. Rico thought the man sounded strangely excited about that. Perhaps they didn't let police lieutenants out of their cages much.

In reality, the lieutenant was enthusiastic about seeing the 120-inch diagonal plasma screen Joey had mentioned, or whined about Rico buying, at a meeting with him earlier in the week. He tried to get an invite to watch a game. Joey told him that was Rico's domain, knowing already that she was in deep doo-doo.

The lieutenant and the potential client arrived at noon. A plain-clothes officer remained outside and roamed about. Barrientos entered the conference room, stuck his nose up in the air and took a deep whiff.

"I'll take a cup of that Columbian, Jo…Mrs. Black, I mean Rico. Oh, would you like a cup too ma'am?" the lieutenant asked his charge.

He seems a little nervous, Rico considered. *Rather cozy with Joey, too.* "A coffee connoisseur, I see," Rico said to break the ice. *Of course, you're a cop.*

"And besides that nice smelling herbal tea I can discern something cinnamony in the kitchen."

Yep, a veteran, Rico thought as he grudgingly rose to bring the leftover morning rolls from the kitchen. His expression when he placed the now steaming rolls on the table told the lieutenant that Rico's warmth had expired.

"Mr. Rico, this is Jessica Putman. Mrs. Putman, Mr. Rico," the lieutenant cordially introduced.

Rico and Putman shook hands lightly. Rico tried not to let his eyes wander to the large bruise above her left eye or the bandaged right cheek. Never mind the purple bruising around her neck. A slightly off canter nose gave evidence of the woman's previous sufferings. She didn't look at him, at least not directly.

"Hello, Mrs. Putman," Rico's voice crackled just enough for Jennifer and Joey to notice.

They shot him a stern look he could feel more than see. He could just hear them thinking, *Jacob, get it together!*

"I told the lieutenant," Rico continued, "I would have my associates at this meeting. I hope it's okay."

The woman nodded.

"This is my wife and vice president, Joey. These are my people, Jennifer, and Rafael, known as Sarge. These agents, along with an armed private security company I use, would provide for your safety."

Rico waited for each to shake hands with the overwhelmed lady. It didn't help his nerves as her shirt sleeve slid up to expose more purplish bruising. He felt embarrassed … no, pain … for her. Did anyone in the business ever get used to these kinds of things? Joey hid her discomfort much better than he did. Jennifer just had a blank stare. Sarge seemed unmoved.

Doubts overwhelmed Rico about whether he could protect her without killing the person who did it. His agents' roles would be to whisk her away from any danger. He had all the confidence in them; would *he* be able to control his rage if a confrontation occurred in his presence, was the question.

Get a grip Jacob! They're just bruises for heaven's sake! Rico thought, excusing himself to the restroom.

Jennifer figured he was dealing with a nasty memory. She followed him to the restroom doorway, avoiding Joey's glare.

Rico whispered in Jennifer's ear that he needed her to cover for him in the meeting while he managed. He didn't tell her, but he was trying to suppress a resurfacing memory of when he had to pull a commando, a good friend, off the wife who by then had died from a single blow to the face. A fit of anger and PTSD induced delusions had overcome the Iraq War veteran. Rico had warned the woman, his friend as well, to seek shelter until the man sought help. She thought she could turn him around alone.

Rico remembered that his dead friend had not had too many more visible bruises than the lady now seeking his protection. This was his new company's first case of this sort; one where the other side had boundless financial resources to cause harm. He considered the potential for hired guns to get in the mix. Though not a real probability so far, it gnawed on Rico. He wondered if he had the stomach…to fail again.

Jennifer returned with a drink in hand to defer attention.

Rico followed a minute later. "Sorry, Ma'am, the jalapeños were more than I bargained for."

That seemed to ease the visitor's nerves—and Joey's.

Everyone else did their best to help Mrs. Putman feel at home and insisted she grab a sandwich. As they ate, Joey and Jennifer outlined to the woman their extensive qualifications. That alone did wonders for her nerves.

The lieutenant courteously served her some coffee while he inspected the plasma screen TV. Rico noticed, but wasn't the least bit in the mood to make nice with the stranger. His mind still raced.

All chatted quietly until they had enough to eat. Rico waited to be sure the lady was reasonably at ease before unloading some tough questions on her.

"All right folks, if everyone will take a seat, we'll get started," Rico announced. Everyone who hadn't been sitting did as he asked. Joey sat, wondering why he sounded so solemn.

"Mrs. Putman, I have some questions for you. Some of these questions will not be very pleasant. They are, however, crucial for me to be able to keep you, as well as my crew, *safe*." They all knew what he meant. "Are you willing to answer truthfully as best you can?"

Before answering, the lady looked at the lieutenant for reassurance. He nodded an affirmation.

"Yes, Mr. Rico," she whispered.

"First, are you willing to agree to and sign an agreement with my company to never reveal to anyone the procedures, safe-houses or identities of myself or my agents? That would include giving out the name of this company, except in a court of law, or to a possible client."

"Yes, I'll sign the agreement," she said tepidly, avoiding eye contact again.

"Good. Now…to the first of the tough questions. Are you prepared to abandon every aspect of your relationship with your former spouse until such time as you are under our protection, and to obey our directives when we sense danger?"

The ambiance got a little tense.

"Yes, I'm done being abused and fearing for my children's safety. I will follow your instructions."

Children? No one mentioned children. Rico felt she was being too agreeable, too soon. From his research and stories gleaned from the field he knew many women in this stage of separation tended to digress after some persuasive speech from the estranged spouse. For many, the decision to give their partner one last chance, an average of fourteen times, had proven fatal. This particular man, according to the lieutenant, besides money, had enormous clout, influence and certain kinds of connections—the level of these connections beyond the newly promoted lieutenant's imagination.

"I want to clarify something …" Rico paused to consider what he was about to say. "… if you decide to return to your spouse sometime in the future, and you tell him what we did to protect you, these people and our future clients will all be in grave danger if that person shares that information out of spite…or whatever. Do you understand me ma'am?"

Joey didn't understand why Rico was being so blunt, and seemingly harsh.

"I think she already answered that Jacob," Joey whispered into Rico's ear.

His face didn't display the ire she had aroused, though the eyes couldn't completely conceal it.

"It's, OK!" The lady announced softly. "I wouldn't trust this man with my life if he wasn't so concerned for those that work alongside him, or his loved ones. Why would he give his everything to protect me…which is what I need, if he didn't first care about his own," Mrs. Putman finished, tapering off into the softest of whispers; it looked like exasperation to the others.

They watched her with compassion burning in them, even Sarge. Everyone waited in silent thought.

"Thank you…for understanding, ma'am. I take it that you will not disseminate any information to anyone then?"

She shook her head.

"I am told that you are also to be protected as a state witness against your estranged husband. Since he has the means to hire some help, we would like to keep you in a safe house. Are you in agreement with that?"

"Where?"

"Excuse me?" Rico wasn't prepared for the lack of resistance in leaving her long-time home. Where was the argument about creature comforts, and the loss of identity; or at least her bed?

"Where is your safe house?"

"Well…uhm…Joey."

"That would be here for now. The apartment is maxed out at the moment. We have a bedroom upstairs. You would have freedom of movement and one of us can escort you on errands. In a day or two Jennifer will sign a lease at a gated apartment complex," Joey offered.

"Good deal. Is that acceptable to you Ms. Putman, lieutenant?" Rico said, very relieved logistics he had forgotten about were going so well.

"Yes," Mrs. Putman said. The lieutenant only nodded in agreement.

"The only thing left is for you to get some of your belongings. Then the team will orient you on some safety procedures. The first is to carry this cell phone at all times. If you get separated from your escort you can call us; or if under duress, conceal it on your person and we'll track you through the built-in GPS."

Mrs. Putman quietly signed the three electronic forms Rico provided her.

"Well, that should be about it for now. We will be back in about an hour with Ms. Putman's bags and a small mountain of my department's paperwork," the lieutenant announced.

"Can I talk to you in private for a second, Lieutenant? Joey, could you show Ms. Putman the upstairs room?" Rico asked quietly.

Joey graciously guided the lady up the stairs.

The lieutenant waited. *Here it comes! He's going to invite me to a game,* he thought gleefully.

"I need you to stall entering the transfer of Ms. Putman to my control into the database," Rico said.

"Say what?"

"Bury the documents that show the transfer to me and enter them into the electronic database later. If your superiors direct you to do it right away, that's fine, but I'd like to be informed when it happens."

"Joey never mentioned you had a paranoid side," blurted the man in a murmur.

"What? What does Joey have to do with this?"

Oops! "Oh…I know Joey somewhat, and I called her when I saw her name as a reference on your background request from the shelter," he muttered, hoping he sounded believable.

Rico sensed he was blowing smoke, but figured it had to do with Joey keeping some secret; probably that homeless thing.

"Another thing, for our purposes my client's new name is…uhm…Marcy. Yea, that'll work."

"Marcy? He couldn't come up with anything else?" the lieutenant muttered as he started out the conference room door. "Oh! I was admiring your big screen. It's a beauty. I…"

"It's for training and meetings," Rico interrupted.

The deflated man had his answer; no sports at the casa de los Ricos…yet. The lieutenant and Mrs. Putman, now Marcy, departed.

One hour later they trudged in with several large suitcases. She seemed resigned to a new, and possibly extended secluded, life on the run.

Rico's alarms went off again when he noticed what looked like children's suitcases. His antennae had gone up when the lady had mentioned children. Up until the time she got back he had shrugged it off. But something felt wrong. The lieutenant was leaving something out. The understanding was that the company could handle up to a medium and short-term risk. The short-term part would prove accurate; but the risk assessment sitting on the police chief's desk was off the mark and conducted by an overworked officer.

For now, as far as Rico and his agents were concerned, prudent caution and minimal exposure would suffice. His staff would deal with Mrs. Putman and he would step in when the children appeared. Somehow, the nagging foreboding wouldn't budge when his thoughts turned to the kids. He decided right then on being the only agent assigned to them if they came into the picture. He had excellent agents, but for surprises? After some self-talk, Rico settled in his mind that his crew was totally skill ready, but wondered a lot whether *he* was ready. He'd just have to wing it.

A dismissal or an indictment was only four weeks away. Rico and company had gone through this same process before numerous times with other clients. The police department quickly saw how aptly the company handled each client that they tasked him with; each one with unique needs and levels of protection requirements. Private clients likewise received excellent protection.

The techniques and procedures Jennifer and Rico developed on the fly worked extremely well. And the confident, yet gentle, demeanor Rico demanded of the protection team made the clients obey some of the more arduous security procedures they had to follow. Then there was the Hyundai contract price for the Cadillac product. The only charges were incidental expenses and overtime for particular cases.

Rico noticed that Joey had a magic touch when it came to calming new female and male clients' nerves—a one eighty compared to the tempers she roused as a beat reporter. They seemed strangely serene to him after Joey had her one-on-one talk with them; and, to his dismay, always done in private. He wondered constantly what the talk could possibly entail.

So went the next two weeks in Rico's small company—many quiet days—with the exception of response exercises and two minor run-ins with much less financially endowed, though no less hostile, estranged spouses. They proved easily managed inconveniences.

CHAPTER THIRTY

FIVE WEEKS had passed since Jennifer had ordered the Smart Truck. The process had taken a couple of resubmissions and Rico speaking to representatives of the Justice and Homeland Security departments to finalize the order. It was either a huge bureaucratic blunder that the purchase and delivery were approved, or someone very high up in the food chain had kindly cleared it through. Since ignorance was bliss, Rico was going to be in bliss. Actually, the vehicle was ready at the nearby Fort Bliss Army Post.

Rico was unaware that in the months while he was in transition from the coast to the desert, even orders of a few Taser-guns by any nongovernmental agency triggered alarms in the halls of the security apparatuses. For all practical purposes he should have been put through the interrogation ringer regarding the intent to purchase the heavily armored *tank*, albeit only defensively equipped. No matter how it happened, the juiced up vehicle had come just in time.

Joey drove him to the Army post and dropped him off at the gate. Rico returned to Las Cruces later that day and stored the vehicle at a storage unit. He grabbed a taxi home.

The next day Rico gave in to Joey's and Jennifer's daily badgering to conduct another company meeting. Conveniently, since it was their idea, Rico tasked them with organizing it. He had critical things to do, after all.

Working efficiently, the two organized a sophisticated electronic presentation elaborating on the earlier vision statement, adding a mission statement and the year's goals.

Meanwhile, Rico faded away into his new preferred reality, learning about the intricacies of his most expensive toy to-date. He didn't tell Jennifer where he would be; but she would get snoopy.

Rico drove the Smart Truck to the Rio Grande and parked at La Llorona Park. He began browsing through the various sections of the voluminous user's guide. He noticed a tab, *Using the voice controlled computer*. "That sounds interesting," he mumbled.

Suddenly, Joey's words rushed in from some deep—really deep—recess of his mind and hammered him hard. "The world doesn't revolve around *you*." Joey's voice had been low and with a measure of tenderness when she had said them, but just then they boomed and cut to the quick. Rico shook his head to make the words go away—as if the truth just up and leaves that easily after announcing itself. He had to get to his important work. A little rationalizing here, a little there, and the booming words were but a fading echo. The world, his world, was again placid.

In minutes he was ready for the basics. He recorded his voice as the primary or master voice as per the written instructions. According to the guide, his voice would override any other authorized user's commands if they contradicted. The standard accessory commands were entertaining enough, but he was quickly drawn to the Battle Station Control Console. The manual used the acronym BSCC. It offered a redundant system consisting of parallel control panels.

The driver's control console was an overhead duplicate of the battle station console that was positioned just behind the passenger seat. Each one had a rolling titanium cover that was opened independently via voice command, key, or the thumb print reader.

"Computer…" he said. The computer acknowledged with a beep. "…open control panel one."

Without further response from the computer, the panel rolled open in a silky smooth, silent second.

"Nice!" he blurted as he stared at the fully equipped panel. Only two switch and light slots had dummy covers instead of operational devices. The fire buttons for the not included rocket tubes and their respective rockets belonged there. Even then, way more stuff was operational than he had dreamed of. He had thought he was going to get a totally barebones, stripped down model.

Apparently, the government is taking a more lenient approach, he thought. He was impressed at having only to whisper and tested the sensitivity at various volumes. He acted like a kid in a one-child family who had received a large Christmas bonus check.

Rico was ready to close up when, as he admired and brushed his fingers along the lit up rocker and flip switches, he accidentally flipped one. He closed his eyes expecting a bang. Instead, he heard the clanging of metal for a second.

The tiny lettering on the switch read, "Tire PD."

"Whew!" he sighed. He would have to read about how to replace the road spikes, or piercing devices. Gingerly, he gathered them up and tossed them under the driver's seat. Before closing the cover, he studied some of the other buttons he might have to use in the near future: front, rear, left, and right strobe light; oil; smoke; electronics disrupter; tube-launched vehicle electronics disruptor; and finally, an internal and external radio emissions disrupter. He studied the table in the manual and did mental drills on the acronyms and corresponding flip switches.

"Computer…"

"Beep."

"…close control panel one," he whispered, wearing a big grin…until Joey's words resounded again. "OK! OK! I'm selfish and I need to change. I'm trying Joey!" he blurted.

Rico tried shaking it off during the drive back to the office. He took some sleeping pills along with some more pain pills before he went back in the house. It was almost 1:00 p.m. Rico passed by Jennifer and said a wimpy hello on his way upstairs. He asked her to wake him at around five.

Jennifer considered stopping him and forcing him to talk it out; instead, she talked herself back into her seat. She hoped and prayed that it was such a simple matter as *just* another headache. But, then again…Now her concentration was shot and her studying went out the window. It was time for some recreational reading anyway, she figured.

CHAPTER THIRTY-ONE

IT WAS 6:15 p.m. Everyone of consequence was there: Joey, Jennifer, Sarge and his crew. Rico trailed in last after checking in on Marcy who was upstairs. She seemed quite calm and peaceful enjoying Rosangelica's gracious company.

Cohen was already on the screen via video link from New York—Joey's idea. Rico hadn't intended for the man to be part of this particular meeting and right then decided to keep him on line only until they finished with the vision, mission and goal statements.

Rico still had a nagging in his gut about the man's deeper motives. Because of that he wasn't ready to make him privy to operational matters.

Joey motioned to Rico to take the podium—a nice, microphone equipped, modern looking one Jennifer had picked out. He just nodded and remained seated, a look of deep thought on his face. *What is it about this guy; I trust him...but.*

Joey grew impatient, and then remembered how nervous he got when he had to speak in front of groups of people. Thinking that was it, she casually and gleefully stepped up and slightly adjusted the microphone. "Hi, folks. In a couple of minutes Jacob...*Mr. Rico*..." she teased, "...will initiate our first official company meeting." There had been other, unofficial, planning type meetings, but no official business meeting.

It was about darned time, she wanted to add.

Her smile got bigger as everyone whooped and hollered.

You're not helping, Joey! Rico thought.

"I would just like to say, Shelley, that we're glad you are supporting your husband, Rafael. By doing so you're helping this little company to grow and do a fine job for people," Joey continued. Though she was sincere, she wondered how long she would have to extend the chatter.

It was then or never. Rico stood, taking in a deep concealed breath. Joey took the cue. "Folks, please welcome the founder and president of this corporation."

The group applauded and offered large smiles. Rico noticed on the teleconference screen that Cohen was also smiling and applauding. *Is the man really enthused or a good actor? The guy seems sincere enough.*

"You people are too much!" Rico blurted as he shook he head. The group got even louder. He waited to steady his knees. "I want to also thank you, my team, for doing such an outstanding job from the very beginning."

The room grew respectfully silent.

"Now, I would like to formally share with you what this company is about and where we're headed. We all heard last time what the two brains of this organization conjured up for a vision, and I'm sure you were all as impressed as I was. I want to preface what new things they will be presenting in a minute by sharing a little something with you folks. And that is this; we are here to help keep people safe. Yes, we need to be proficient at making money to do that, but that will *not* be the overarching reason for our existence.

"We will be serving an extremely varied group of clients. We do that through three companies. The primary is the nonprofit one called Domestic Abuse Protective Services. The two profit making ones are the Southwest Executive Protection Services and Protective Technologies Testing Company. They are incorporated under the umbrella of National Security Agents, Inc.

"I have no doubt that I've assembled the most professional, and respectful, group of agents in the business. The family members assembled here are just an added bonus whose value cannot be measured by any standard I know of. I hope it continues to be that kind of company, even if the head honcho is out of the picture."

Joey and Jennifer looked at each other, each with a slight shrug. Rico eyed Cohen's face on the screen—nothing but an attentive look.

"I just want to say welcome to National Security Agents first corporate board meeting."

Rico waited for the hoopla to die down. He thought he caught a hint of feigning in the smile on Cohen's face. The digital image on the screen was so clear that Rico couldn't also help notice the wrinkle of concern in the corner of wise-looking man's eyes when for a microsecond he dropped his guard. Was Rico imagining things or had he also noticed a foreboding sadness almost that same instance?

Rico had stolen a quick peek into the man's soul, and it seemed, after Rico thought about it, that this was not coincidental. What did it mean? Maybe more of the delusional stuff his mind had started conjuring up. He had to brush it off before he lost his bearings.

"The two real bosses will now quickly review the company's vision and structure. Then after we bid Cohen farewell, they will provide some general information in the area of our current client status and some operational field and office procedures. As if you don't already know them, here are the Vice President, Joey, and her partner in crime, our DSO, Director of Security Operations, Jennifer."

The place went wild. Rico was glad to fade to background. Everyone got a good laugh when the two wives in the room started chanting, "Girl power...girl power!"

Cohen applauded along with everyone else. *This is a corporate meeting?* he mused, chuckling privately. He wore a subdued grin; one Rico, eyeing the screen from the corner of his eye, couldn't exactly make out.

Rico was pleasantly surprised at the two women's preparedness. He had heard many high-powered presentations given before Pentagon officials and congressional committee members. In his mind the two were easily of that caliber.

Regularly, he felt like a boy scout among pros when he was around them, though they would never have guessed. It was interesting how less able persons could conceal the fact; or did they compensate?

They gave a concise thirty-minute briefing, then opened the floor for questions. They asked about the company structure, mainly about positions that would be forthcoming. The vision and goals had been clearly outlined and no one asked for clarification.

Cohen was about to be dismissed from the meeting, when things got interesting. Jennifer spoke into the camera and informed him that she was going to cut the feed. The man nodded in response and let out an extended blurb in Hebrew. Apparently, he had inadvertently slipped into his mother language. He realized it when he saw the puzzled looks on the crowd's faces and was about to translate when Joey, to everyone's surprise, responded.

Joey spoke in what sounded like the language Cohen had spoken in. It seemed to be the correct response to whatever Cohen had said or asked as evidenced by his more than surprised smiling and nodding. The two held a thirty second tête-à-tête and then Joey signaled Jennifer with a nod to cut the feed.

Joey seemed perplexed, or troubled, about what Cohen had said at the end. She stared at the table top.

Everyone else was just perplexed period, and gave Joey puzzled looks. She thought it was about what she was puzzled about.

"What?" she asked no one in particular.

"How did you know what he was saying, and how come you could answer him back?" Jennifer whispered in her ear.

Rico leaned in, very interested in her response. He was sure she had been holding out on a little secret or something.

"Duh!" Joey said, thinking it was some joke. "Everyone here speaks English."

"Uh hum." Jennifer mumbled. "Yes, Joey we all do. Mr. Cohen, however, was speaking what had to be Hebrew."

Joey blushed and took a seat to avert everyone's stare. Jennifer proceeded with the meeting while Rico shot Joey a strange look.

Was he angry about something? Or was he playing along with what must be a practical joke, Joey wondered. Rico would later avoid the subject, but Jennifer would drill her about the matter. Joey was no less curious about her apparent linguistic secret. Little did they know that speaking anything other than English or Spanish, with broken Arabic sprinkled in, wasn't her doing, or that it hadn't occurred before then.

Meanwhile, Jennifer moved on to the particulars of the current clientele and the security procedures established for each. The women had wisely structured the tail end of the meeting as a strategy building open forum. Anyone, including the spouses, could comment on weaknesses or incorrect assumptions in planning.

Then Joey stood to continue directing the meeting. "As you all know, Jennifer coordinates all tasking for client protection. She'll fill us in on the current picture regarding clients. Jennifer."

The two didn't miss a beat. When they had business to attend to they took care of it.

"I decided it would be wise to divide our clientele for tracking purposes," Jennifer said.

Rico smiled. She was getting to be a sage of sorts lately.

Jennifer laid out the client load. She mentioned three particularly challenging ones.

"What type of threat is posed to those three?" Sarge's wife asked.

The others were surprised that she was showing interest. In fact, she was quite intrigued by the protection stuff. Sarge hadn't seen that side of her. It passed through Rico's thoughts that she was an agent in the making. Sarge would have something to say about that.

"Estranged lovers for two of them," Jennifer said. "And a whole family of ticked off druggies for the other. Her former in-laws were vicious. Even though they aren't sophisticated enough to track this client, a chance encounter would most likely result in some serious bodily harm. The rap sheet for each member is extensive. They seem to think she turned snitch…I mean…informant, with the cops."

"Why do we only have ten of these Group GSC's (Government Sponsored Clients)?" Joey inquired. "I know the police department is inundated with protection requests."

Rico wondered how she knew that tidbit of information. She sounded as if it was first hand knowledge.

"I ask this because we should have enough funding for more," Joey said. She gave him a passing glance. *Yes, Honey, you bet I'm keeping an eye on the books.*

"The size of our force," Jennifer explained. "But, the real show stopper is housing. The apartment we use right now could hold six clients and one of us. The owners wouldn't stand for that though. And, cabin fever is setting in on the three we have there. We take them all over town as needed, but the risks and vulnerabilities are high…Cruces isn't all that big. Wintertime is going to exacerbate the cabin fever problem further. The second apartment is too small, but more secure."

What winter? Rico wondered.

Everyone was mulling over a possible solution. Each solution offered only provided temporary and limited improvements to the picture. A few minutes passed and everyone was stumped. Joey noticed Rico had a smirk on his face.

"What's on your mind?" she said in Spanish without realizing it.

Jennifer found it interesting that they could switch languages and not know it. She asked Joey what she had just said. Joey thought it funny that Jennifer was asking, because she had just said it.

"Habla en ingles, mujer," Rico answered teasingly.

"Oh!"

"I have good news about solving that very problem," Rico offered, remaining in his seat. "It's amazing how things fall into place. We have a positive coincidence at this juncture. *But*, I'm only going to share it *if* Joey promises not to hit me."

"Promise, Joey, promise!" Rico had assembled an interesting group of people. He thought perhaps they were crazier than he had intended. But he realized that he had a darned good thing going. Then a wave of melancholy suddenly overwhelmed him.

Can't say I didn't enjoy a fulfilled life when I pass on to the great beyond! he thought, realizing via an almost physical pain in his chest what he was really putting on the table of sacrifice.

Reluctantly, Joey assented. That wasn't enough for the crowd. Again they let out a chorus.

Rico was glad the Mossad veteran, Cohen, wasn't still watching.

"Oh! Ok!" she finally said. "I promise not to hit Jacob…today."

Rico half smiled while the others grinned.

"I have papers ready to sign," Rico offered, "to close on a nice safe house a few miles south of here. Once Joey checks it out and approves, that is."

He stopped and gave most everyone a glance.

That's great, but no big deal, everyone thought. Respectful silence filled the room, their faces for once expressionless, looking at Joey.

"I'll try going tomorrow," Joey belatedly said; that made everyone jubilant, except her.

Something told her he probably went overboard on a house; a near million dollar one certainly fit the bill. She would argue adamantly for days, but the group ganging up on her would break her down.

For everyone except Joey, the night ended on a chirpy note.

Later in bed, Joey's slightly agitated look about what Cohen had said during the meeting was still bothering Rico; and then scolding him for not consulting with her about the house first wasn't very nice. Couldn't she have waited until they were alone to chastise him? *After all*, he *was* doing a good thing!

CHAPTER THIRTY-TWO

RICO WAS growing accustomed to the relatively slow pace of family life since the lively meeting days before. Now, partially by his design, things would speed up exponentially starting this morning. He needed to gain some ground on the bigger plan.

Armed with information from some contacts back in San Diego about some helpful technology minded blogs, he went fishing. He had a hunch that the computer whiz—a.k.a. hacker—he was going to need could be found in one of them. He couldn't very well advertise for a hacker in the newspaper.

All I gotta do is find a blog that geeks who like challenges would gravitate to, he thought.

He monitored the politically and technologically oriented dialogue for a few minutes. *Intriguing combination,* he thought. Just as he was about to enter into the fray Joey stepped in.

"Hey Sweetie Pie. Let's go eat," she said as she hugged him from behind.

"I'm working right now, can you wait please?"

The tartness in his voice and stiffening body threw her off balance.

"I don't like that tone of voice, Jacob," she snapped, standing to leave.

"Wait!" he blurted out. "I'm sorry. I just get into what I'm doing and sometimes it's sensitive stuff. How about if we come to an agreement that if I'm on the computer, or phone, you'll test the waters to see if the timing is good. Agreed?" he asked, waving her over to sit on his lap.

She hesitated an agonizing thirty seconds, but an urge for a hug and a smooch overcame her agitation. Love, and the need for it, conquered her Irish ire *this* morning.

"I have my two cents worth to add," she whispered after catching her breath from a lip-lock. "If you *ever* talk to me in that tone of voice again, you can kiss your chance of touching this fine body again…for reals." The piercing look in her deep blue eyes gave a solid clue that she really meant it; *more* than last time.

He responded with learned wisdom. "Yes, honey."

"Te vas para Gino's Deli while I finish up here…about ten minutes."

"Bueno, mi amor. Of course, the more you delay, the more those young college guys will try hitting on me."

"I ain't got no competition in this one-cow town. College boys or not, uno mas guapo que yo, no existe," he teased, slapping her hind parts as she left.

All attention back on the monitor, he did what he had been taught for getting onto blackboards. He wrote about how technology seemed to be helping the lower classes very little. On that blackboard the typing by the other people online stopped, until someone asked who the new person was.

Rico typed the moniker "Lion1." He thought about what to say when they asked why he was hiding behind such a dorky screen name. The others were using cyber names too, but more techy-type ones.

Rico cursed himself for being so obvious. He responded that he was in a sensitive position that required staying in the shadows. The effect those words had on the activity that followed intrigued him.

"Government?" they asked, among other things.

The unknowns communicated via code words, typing at lightning speeds back and forth. He was only getting bits and pieces. The back and forth stopped when one named Q Factor advised the others to get off line. Another named Chimira Moon didn't seem to like the apparent directive very much. After only Rico remained, Q asked Rico for his real name and e-mail address. If Rico wanted to talk business, this was the only way this hacker would talk to him.

Rico reluctantly gave both and waited.

Not ten minutes later Rico opened the e-mail from Q. He scrolled down the e-mail and read what sounded like techno babble nonsense. He was about to delete the supposed practical joke when the computer begin to shut down.

At first he was mad thinking the power had gone off and he hadn't plugged the PC to the power back-up unit. Then his heart stopped when the PC completed its restart.

"What do you want Jacob Rico, former USAF GI?" scrolled across the screen. The Trojan horse Q had sent was working just fine.

The startle Rico got was paradoxically invigorating and scary at the same time. He realized instantly that the person who had typed it was using his *own* screen saver! He would have been more in shock had he known that the person on the other end had every bit of his life history in front of him on another screen. This included every gunshot wound, every bandage, every run-in with the law, and ticket in the government's supposedly secure national database. The most spine chilling of all, Q had the name and address of every associate and friend he had in his e-mail address book.

I can't believe I'm following through with this. "Need top notch geek to help with a sensitive private matter," he typed.

"Roswell. You set me up I'll bankrupt your company…and turn your life upside down!" came a chilling reply. The ghost quickly signed off.

Rico couldn't decide whether to celebrate or cry. What a stroke of luck. Like a bolt of lighting, the fact that now he had a family struck him with a jolt. He couldn't continue living like before, passionately and frequently seeking to intercept deadly pieces of shrapnel or hoping for a parachute to fail; he realized he had a responsibility outside himself now. He watched his mouse hand tremble as he shut down the computer. A bead of sweat formed on his forehead. He ran to the bathroom for a swig of stomach medicine.

The buzz of the belt-clipped walkie-talkie gave him a startle; his trembling hand raised it to his ear. Joey suggested he hurry because all the hunks were hitting on her. He knew she was kidding, but it gave him a reason to get riled up and regain his composure. Before leaving the building, he shouted up the stairs to Jennifer. She yelled back for him to wait. She wanted a hug. The girls stomped down the stairs for one too. Rosangelica and Tina shot back up the stairs just as fast as they had come and didn't even pause their yapping.

Jennifer lingered. "You OK?" she whispered as she embraced his tense body a second time, more firmly this time.

She's getting awfully mushy, he thought, instinctively squeezing back. At the very last second he caught a sob trying to escape. It had snuck up out of nowhere. He covered it up well and tried to separate. She didn't budge.

"I'm okay…now," he said, making no effort at concealing that he felt comforted. *She's getting mushy?*

She pulled away whispering, "There's something you're not letting on. Before…that would make me angry. Now, it saddens me, Jacob. I'll always be here. Please don't build a wall just because you're married. OK?"

Before? Before what? He nodded anyway and turned quickly to leave. The stomach medicine wasn't working on his troubled soul. At least a dose of Jennifer tempered the ache a little; not as much as it used to though.

Jennifer didn't move until he was well on the way. *That's not the Rico I knew,* she thought. *Or is it just me that's different?*

Rico hastily walked down Solano Drive, Jennifer's words occupying his thoughts. Their echo brought him back to earth. He had a deep suspicion that God, metaphorically speaking, had sent Jennifer to save him from himself. An almost supernatural sereneness he couldn't explain always prevailed when she was around him.

Oddly, this was the same unspoken thing she unconsciously thought about *him*; God, as of recent, representing more than a metaphor in her case.

How he had come to be surrounded by such affection was beyond his natural understanding. Perhaps he was looking for an answer in the wrong realm. It was a thought he occasionally entertained—a momentary lapse into nonsense.

He quickly covered the few blocks to the deli, stepping in once he felt prepared for some good cover up acting. "Did you see that hunk of a man that just walked in?" he asked Joey, referring to himself.

"Yea," she said, smiling. "That one over there, right?" She pointed to a muscle-bound, tank-topped, tight-jeaned hunk of a young man of some twenty-two; a boy to her.

"Pleeease!" He gave the young man—boy—a "She's with me, que miras, hombre?" friendly look since the *boy* was giving Joey an "I want you" look of his own.

The young man looked without the least bit of respect or trepidation right past the much older Rico. That would not cut it; Rico gave the young man a healthy stare. That worked.

Joey chuckled. "See! I still got it. I'm not as old as I thought," she said with a twinkle in her eye.

Rico knew very well what she was doing. But he was puzzled about the attention she garnered. It had to be something about her quick smile and gentleness that made people notice her; because, except for the piercing blue eyes and cute freckles, she was a plain looking girl. Nonetheless, he was completely hooked.

Joey was doing a little acting of her own. Underneath she was feeling pensive, having on more than one occasion in the previous week allowed her mind to consider how much calmer her life would have been had she married the deacon who had shown considerable desire to court her. Her soul ached for those long discussions they had shared about God's greatness and goodness, about mercy and grace evident in their lives. It nagged at her spirit that eventually Rico would find out. More disconcerting was that she knew God wasn't pleased with the less than pure and very recent thoughts she had entertained about the man, or with the withholding of information from her husband. Soon, she knew, she would have to confess her faults to God; but Rico didn't have to know about the thoughts she reasoned. And eventually he was bound to discover the Dodge Viper ST10 the man had given her; and which she had recently grounded and stored in her back alley detached garage.

But why did God choose Rico? To what end? Had she misunderstood God? Had she let sentimental feelings cloud better judgment? She knew better than to be unequally yolked.

Seemingly out of nowhere, to Rico at least, she had to ask the question that no man wants to hear, "Where are we, Jacob?"

That question could mean many things. Communication? Love? Sex? Money?

Rico sat, hopeful that she didn't mean health or money. He mulled over the question, twiddling his fingers. She twiddled her shorter, pudgier, freckled ones.

He finally had to answer as her big eyes and hand signals said, "Well!"

Even when she was annoying him, her eyes were captivating. "I can only tell you that I'm supposed to go to Roswell."

If she had forgotten about getting involved in his business matters before his tart response just that morning, his temper slip had been a good hint that he was getting into something deep.

She raised two palms toward the air. "I won't even ask." *See God, he hasn't a clue about what my concerns are. That's why I wonder about…*

Now, that's a good wife, Rico thought, while Joey secretly continued her mental digression and one way argument with God.

"When?" she finally asked.

So much for that. "Don't exactly know to tell you the truth," he said shrugging.

"Is that when you'll tell me the whole plan you're concocting?"

"By then I'll tell you about ninety-five percent," he mumbled.

He stood and reached for her hand.

It was an obvious diversionary tactic that she chose to play along with; the better to bury the bothersome thoughts. "Where are we going, lover boy?"

She started to give the tank top guy one last *pretend* look when Rico playfully wagged a finger at her. The Holy Spirit did more and said, "Why are you playing with temptation, child?"

Her lips barely moved when she muttered repentance, and her eyes looked up and closed for a split second.

Rico thought she might be getting a headache.

After leaving the deli, they meandered, hand-in-hand, toward the house. Their affection came naturally and words were only intrusive guests. Rico especially liked the quiet.

CHAPTER THIRTY-THREE

JENNIFER HANDLED the only incident the company encountered during the week. The estranged wife of a male principal had attempted to stab her husband at the mall. Jennifer disarmed her, and mall Security quickly took control.

A lawsuit wasn't expected since Jennifer had done everything possible to avoid the woman and evacuate the man, but the lady was just too quick on her feet. Her athleticism, coupled with a serious inner rage and some illicit substance, gave Jennifer a tougher fight than she had expected. The violence of the encounter left a good part of a store's woman's department in disarray. The store video camera captured clear evidence for the company's defense if it ever went to court. And one of the Security guards, a moonlighting police officer, would be great on the stand for Jennifer, if it ever went that far.

With no other emergencies to respond to, Rico's increasingly lengthy midday naps went more or less unnoticed. He had reduced his teaching time at the alternative high school to two hours every other day. Outings with the girls filled parts of some days. A day trip with Joey, the girls and Marcy, the client, to the City of Rocks State Park, the Gila Forest and Elephant Butte Reservoir proved relaxing, and very tiring. But it was the earned kind of tired; it felt good for the exhaustion level of his body to match his mind.

At other times, he watched the laborers and supervisor complete the finishing touches on the garage, testing the electrical system and the steel rollup door's operation. Joey had yet to ask him directly about why the previously exposed lower areas looked so much like a basement apartment taking shape. He was sure she hadn't missed it. There was a good chance that because further construction had covered any evidence of the outline, she would soon forget to bring it up. She was rather busy after all.

Like every other night, Joey did her nightly routine, tiptoeing across the hallway, trying to avoid waking Rosangelica. The sitting room she prayed in—

something Rico was not yet aware of—was across from the master bedroom.

"I hear you Joey. I hear you every night. You don't have to tiptoe," Rosangelica announced in Spanish.

"Buenas noches, mija," Joey whispered through the closed door.

Like every other night, she had already tucked her in. She was way beyond the years when it was considered normal, but the two weren't much for upholding rigid conventions of behavior. They shared each night about what God had done for them that day. Just mother and daughter stuff.

Each night, at least forty-five minutes after starting her devotions and prayer, Joey would tiptoe back to her and Jacob's bedroom; all prayed up and armed for whatever Satan—or these days, maybe Jacob—could conjure up to throw at her.

"Oye, mi amor," Joey, gingerly climbing into bed, whispered in Rico's ear.

He was barely awake while reviewing defense equipment and weaponry periodicals, specifically *Jane's Defense Monthly* and *R & D Quarterly Guide*.

"You and I are going to Roswell next week."

"We?" he said, slightly more alert. "Why next week?"

"Yes, we. According to my sources there's a Trekki and technology convention…"

"And, that means…?" He shot a quick look at her glowing face and quickly turned back to his reading.

"That means, the person you're looking for…" she said, stopping at his nodding.

"I smell a catch to this helpfulness," he said, ceremoniously putting down the periodicals.

"I would really love to see you as a Star Fleet officer…like Number One," she whispered, eyeing him with a look dripping with desire. "I just *love* a man in a certain uniform."

"Ah, I don't think so. I'm not wearing a…N and O spells…." he announced firmly, attempting to resist the power of her come-hither look. "If I have to low crawl to avoid that, I will. I'll get there on my own, woman!"

"Darn," she whined. "That means I won't have a chance to wear my Counselor Troy outfit."

He was had. He'd seen a few reruns.

"You…um…have one of those?" he asked, almost concealing the wistfulness in his voice.

"Yup! Well … I'll send it back tomorrow. It's a shame! I actually looked

rather shapely in it, too. Not exactly as shapely as Troy, mind you, but mighty
fine anyway," she whispered. She rolled on her side facing away from Rico, smiling wide.

"Don't you have to try it out…you know, to make sure it fits?"

"Fine, fits *mighty* fine. Now let me sleep, some of us work you know," she
mumbled into her pillow.

"Well, I guess if we're out of town…and no one else would see me…espe-
cially Jennifer…or Sarge," he murmured to himself. "Where would I get one of
those…tights or uniforms…if I were to decide to…?"

He had all but surrendered; just the reeling in remained.

"Are you sure you can't wear your outfit without me?" he pleaded.

"Can…won't! Troy and Riker were a couple. Doesn't it sound romantic to
you, mi amor?"

She punctuated her whisper ever so devilishly, now facing him to make sure
he could see her practicing her lipstick model pose.

Rico rolled his eyes, shook his head, and snuggled up to her. Snoring something awful minutes later, she nudged him regularly, like every night, to shut him
up. And like every other night she would wait patiently as he passed through cold
sweats and groaning. Hers had ended abruptly three years before, like Jennifer's
had only recently. She prayed fervently for his to do the same—and soon.

The next morning Joey was already long gone when Rico woke up. He
washed up and headed downstairs for breakfast. As usual, he took his breakfast
to the waiting room where he and Jennifer would chat for almost an hour before
Jacob got properly dressed to do any real work. Usually, Jennifer talked incessantly about nothing in particular.

Somehow the topic veered toward their relationship. Rico wasn't uncomfortable about it. In fact, several times since she had arrived he had tried to steer
it in that direction. He had something to get out in the open—or rather, off his
chest. It wasn't so much a longing desire for her anymore, but nagging questions
that hung in the air—nice questions as far as *he* was concerned. He wanted to
view things from her perspective; he was somewhat sure at least.

"So Jacob, did you ever consider me a possible…uhm…wife?" she halfway
mumbled.

"It's interesting you brought that up," he answered, as he considered how
not to stick his foot in his mouth for the millionth time.

"No kidding! And I missed all those times you tried to hint that you wanted
to discuss it," she said.

"I'm a man, Jennifer. Men don't discuss relationships except under threat of...."

"Of course, we know that you don't fit the normal mold. And to tell you the truth, I constantly flip-flop between thinking it a good thing and a bad thing," she said straight faced.

He analyzed what she had just said and meant. "That's borderline mean *and* rude."

She bit her cinnamon roll and gestured, "Why?"

He ignored her. "Anyway...if you had been anywhere closer to my age...I would have," he said.

"So you *did* fall in love with me at some point?" she asked, walking around from her desk. She peered into his eyes, snuggled up to him, and draped an arm around his shoulders.

"Cinnamon breath!"

There was no escaping a final firm answer, since she waited patiently. A smile revealed a bit of roll between her two front teeth, humanizing her perfection a bit.

"Yes. I thought I loved you at one time. You brought all sorts of excitement into my life. And..."

"And now?" she interrupted, slightly surprised, confused, and a little agitated about the newly resurfaced tinge of romantic interest in her gut. Her face was frozen with anticipation and none of these emotions were obvious to Rico; not that he was looking at anything but a tiny speck of rock on the otherwise spotless hardwood floor.

"Now? Hmm."

He faced a veritable mine field; it was time to weigh words carefully. But the matter needed to be brought up to the surface and dealt with head on.

"I unequivocally love you more than ever. It's just that...now it's like...the love for a real close friend, or cousin; while before it was more like a...well...sexual...*infatuation*. So...you know...now it's not *quite* like that any more. And yet I am still aware of your physical...uhm...attributes...yea attributes. The more I get to know you, over again, the more I like you for you...like a sister; which makes it very unnatural when...you know."

Jennifer enjoyed seeing him stumbling over his words; he looked so helpless. She sighed. "I'm glad about that. I always thought you might think me a dork if I ever let the real me come out. I used my looks as a distraction. When we made out, I enjoyed it...of course," she stopped to gently slap his grinning face and head moving up and down, "…a lot. But, I was actually just looking to get to know you better…some intimacy. I never considered a different approach. And now that things have changed I'll dress more conservatively like Joey asks to avoid…you know."

"Thanks, it'll help…I think. It's probably just me though. Well, anyway we sure were confused. I'm glad we talked about this. But, you never said whether you still love *me*. The still dorky *me*, I mean," Rico said.

"Even as you get dorkier every day, I love you very, very much," She leaned over and gave him a longer and more tender than necessary peck on the lips.

Rico felt a little spark, only a slight heart rate increase, but quite enough. With one finger he pointed at his cheek.

Jennifer's heart ached ever so subtly. At least now it was *really* finally, settled. She got up, pecked him on the cheek and walked back to her desk; things were clear and all aired out.

"In that case you have my permission to marry some nice guy," Rico said, wearing a big grin.

"Permission, oh, thanks Dad. I'll keep that in mind … *if* one happens to propose," she ended in a murmur.

"We both know that any guy would have to be a complete dolt not too. Un estupido," he added, walking over and giving her a squeeze.

"Thanks!" she whispered as she hugged back. "I feel so at home here, Jacob. Joey has made me feel so welcome. I never thought it possible to love and like another woman like I do her, even when we've argued. And especially after stealing my honey, but she makes it so easy. You picked an awesome lady."

"It takes one to know one," Rico whispered into her ear.

He considered entering into a discussion about what love meant, exactly. He was having some trouble figuring it out, tangibly. Instead, he turned and hurried up the stairs.

"That makes me love you even more, honey!" she announced loudly one more time to squeeze the most out of the moment; which happened to be the moment Joey stepped through the front door.

Jennifer felt silly. Joey felt something else.

"What was that about?" Joey asked, looking ready and hopeful for a reasonable explanation.

"He's expecting some hunk to sweep me off my feet any time now. He's feeling separation anxiety," Jennifer offered nonchalantly, tidying up her already too neat desk.

"Oh, how sweet," Joey commented. *Has she been seeing someone?* She heard a soft still voice in her belly tell her that things were ok. All she could do was take a deep breath and quickly head toward the kitchen. She shelved the groceries while she tried humming through a not very loving thought. *I hope she finds someone soon.*

CHAPTER THIRTY-FOUR

ONE WEEK later Joey and Rico landed at Roswell in the rented Cessna Piper II twin prop. The two avid fliers traded landings and take-offs; Rico drew the landing straw on the eastward leg. Because of the air space restriction over the White Sands Missile Range they had a longer flight than the forty-five minute straight-line flight.

A drowsy Rico almost crashed the craft when he reduced speed too much instead of increasing the pitch of the plane. He aborted the landing quickly when Joey snapped him to.

It was a cooler than normal, but sunny mid-summer day. They sat quietly and enjoyed the scenery as a taxi drove them through town, quickly forgetting the little landing adventure.

"Interesting town," Rico commented to the driver.

The driver just nodded.

He's not one for conversation, Rico mused. *Been here, done that, just trying to be cordial.*

Actually, the man thought Rico was Arab—less than fond words twirled in the man's head. Arab-Israeli affairs were causing the entire planet to get antsy; it almost seemed like lines were being drawn in American's minds. Most, though, were quite indifferent.

"Boy, they really get into it," Joey chirped as she eyed a very believable space alien strolling along a walk. "And we'll fit right in tomorrow," she added with a big smile.

"Oh, yippee!" Rico quipped sarcastically.

The taxi came to a stop at the hotel entrance. After checking in, the couple quickly unloaded their very light luggage in the room and took advantage of their alone time.

Before Rico knew it, his mind wandered off to thoughts about how vulnerable a position he was in, not knowing a single thing about someone who probably already knew how many hang nails he had had. Or worse, about that one combat incident he was still trying to forget.

"It's no fun kissing a cold fish," Joey mumbled.

"Oh, I'm sorry, Joey. It's just a feeling of uneasiness being in the dark with this guy," he said before catching himself.

He wished he could recall those words. Rubbing his beard he walked to the window.

"Some guy out there knew who I was in seconds. That's spooky. It's one thing having the government do that, another to have someone else…in an instant…zoom in on you like that. Even when I worked with spooks in Afghanistan and here in the States, I don't recall them doing that so fast," he pondered, his voice trailing away.

"Jacob, you've been out a long time, this is 2013. That spook equipment is probably available to any weirdo out there who wants to snoop." She regretted that comment the moment it left her lips.

"That's exactly it! I…we are at the mercy of…possibly a 12 year-old, maybe a crazy one at that…and I just opened up myself to be a target."

His pacing began to show a repetitive pattern. She had not seen that behavior from him before. Obviously, it wasn't a physical threat that seemed to concern her able husband; so what could it be?

"Ease off with the paranoia, Jacob, we'll be fine."

"I'm worried about the business, but mostly about the girls and your sister. I couldn't live knowing that I lead some wacko right to them and made them victims…of whatever."

He was actually thinking like a father.

"Stop!" she urged as she stopped his odd pacing with a hug from behind. "If it wasn't really important for you to do…whatever you're doing…you wouldn't be doing this right?"

In the mirror she noted a blank stare come over him.

He figured she really meant whether he had counted the cost. His new family deserved that much, he was sure she wanted to add. In fact, he had given it less than sufficient thought. He nodded anyway.

They moved back toward the window and peered out. A warm sunset tempered both their moods.

He looked at her face and wondered how many unanswered questions she was hiding behind her serene, loving, contemplative look; questions he would have liked answered too.

She looked at him and wondered how in the world God expected her to keep the man she loved out of trouble and possibly even danger. Was that knot in her stomach related to that…or regrets?

They both slept very soundly that night. Perhaps it was because Michelle, and then the girls, had sounded very chirpy on the phone when they called. Or…perhaps, Joey's and Jennifer's prayers were being answered. Regardless of the reason, Rico slept more soundly than he had in years.

The convention proved more elaborate and sophisticated than the two expected. It kicked off the next morning at 10:00 a.m. Rico's apprehension about his costume faded away as he admired countless shapely female Star Fleet characters.

He wasn't so gleeful about some of the very fit looking male characters roaming about in *their* tights. Something was very, very wrong in the world when geeks were looking more like jocks—*healthy* jocks.

Even though they both found the convention entertaining, with Rico grabbing all sorts of technology fliers, they grew impatient. The two began to think they were the object of a malicious prank, and that they had made a wrong move. It was after 4 p.m. and *way* too many galaxy-class-starship chili cheese dogs…and still nothing. They figured the whole trip was a wash, but at least they had had a good time.

Just before they called it quits, a stranger approached and made small talk. They tried to judge whether the nervous mannerisms of the baby-faced, female alien were from being unpolished or from a person about to scam them. Facial features didn't reveal any clues since they were mostly concealed behind green paint and glitter. From her voice, they concluded that she was reasonably young.

Rico's and Joey's danger bells went off. They stood ready to protect themselves from a possible pick-pocket…or worse. The *professionals* had inadvertently walked to the fringes of all the activity as they chatted with the girl. They ended up away from the brighter lighting in the hangar-turned-convention center. They were slightly cornered, and both knew they had made a small error. Obviously, they were fully capable of disarming any threat with ease…at least Joey was. They were a little uptight nonetheless, for having made the need for defensive thinking necessary.

Joey casually snuck her hand into her waist pouch and grasped the stun device Rico insisted she carry. Evasion and escape were priority one. Her dangerous roundhouses and potentially lethal blows were to be avoided at all cost.

Joey made small talk. The girl seemed to dislike the short moments of silence.

She asked, a tremble detectable in her voice, "Are you cops? Is that your gun in there?"

She pointed to the pouch Joey's hand was in. Joey and Rico figured it could be a good sign or a bad one just as well. Rico felt down in his gut that he had found who he was looking for.

"Why would you ask that? Are you a criminal or something?" Joey asked softly.

Good approach, Rico thought. They were in Joey's domain.

"Who do you think we are, FBI, NSA...CIA, maybe?" Joey added.

Rico rolled his eyes. *Say, what? U-turn, Joey.*

"Well...I know the FBI...the others I...But...I asked first..." the alien muttered. Her demeanor changed and her voice showed real stress.

That's helping, good going Joey, he thought, sarcastically.

Joey looked at Rico for a hint about whether to open up or not. He nodded. What was there to lose?

"No, we are far from that. I'm Joey and this is..."

"Jacob Rico," the girl blurted out. She still thought they were some sort of law people.

"Yes, of course you would know that,"

"You're much better looking in person...you...have a, uh, very muscular body...and um...nice thighs...and...buns..."

Rico might have asked what visual or picture her friend had of him available. Maybe, if he had asked, she would have spilled the beans about her boyfriend high-jacking Rico's Internet cam; the one mounted on his monitor; the one with audio; always accessible through the Internet link when the computer was on. Right then Rico was busy wondering about the young girl's seemingly lustful eyes for him—and Joey's coming reaction.

Joey's cheeks became flushed, jaw opened wide. "Excuse me!"

Rico gently placed a hand on Joey's shoulder.

He whispered in her ear, "Joey, settle down. I have this feeling it's out of her control...Tourette's syndrome or something. Trust me. Please! OK?"

What in the world gave him that idea he didn't know, but it proved to be accurate.

She gave him a biting look of, "Now you're a doctor too?"

His look tempered her.

Of course, he knew it could be a con and mulled it over. He'd rather end up a sucker than injure her. It wasn't *really* a request he had made, and he knew Joey had gotten the message.

The girl, near tears and covering her face, leaned her body forward to make a break but, her feet wouldn't budge.

Rico subtly nudged Joey over to the trembling, green-skinned, green-eyed girl, age somewhere between 15 and 19, tall and lanky, almost frail. The girl winced as Joey inched toward her.

Joey gently offered her hand. "Listen, somehow I can't believe that you would say what you just said to my husband on purpose. Am I right, that it wasn't on purpose?"

The girl nodded nervously, eyes wide; she accepted Joey's hand. Joey drew her closer.

"It...it...takes over...when, when, when...I, I, I, get nervous. I hate it!"

Rico's mind had already conjured up the theory that his mystery guy was using the helpless girl to flush out any law hounds. It riled him, nonetheless acknowledging the solid move. Sympathy would move any jury to acquit the poor girl as a pawn.

The girl paused to stare into Joey's eyes to catch a hint of deception. She couldn't detect any guile.

Joey forced her heart into the right spirit.

Meanwhile, Rico had gone the opposite direction mentally, hoping to get away quickly. It wasn't as if they had anything else to do.

The girl continued, barely above a whisper, "People...people...either...either...mock me, or, or, or, or hit me. I wish I could...could...make this stop! I, I, I, just want to be, be, be...norrrmal!" she said, sobbing throughout, taking a huge breath at the end.

"Listen," Joey whispered back, fighting back tears of her own. "We, Jacob and I, are hardly normal, so we can relate. How about if we sit?"

Oh, no Joey! Let's go. Jacob thought.

The girl made an effort to sit, but couldn't.

"If, if, if y, y, you...*are* cops...d,d,d don't,ttake mmy boyfriend...bback...bbback...ttto...jail...ppppleeeease!"

Her chest heaved and her breathing grew extremely labored. Rico feared a heart attack, or something. They couldn't get her to stop talking. He wondered about the "back" to jail part.

"Thhththey took hhhhim, away...one ttttime bbbbecause...he, he, he wrote something bbbad, about the government...I, I, I, try to make him stop! But, but, he says they lllllie a lot. And it, its freedom of speech. I, I, I, caaan't live without hiiim. Heeee...heeee's the only one thhhat has never laughed at me...annnnnd lllloves me." A long breath saved her from fainting.

"Young lady," Rico interjected. "It seems like we made a mistake. We were looking for someone to help us with something. But, it would be..." he considered his words for Joey's sake. "...very tricky. I don't know if it is totally legal and all ... so I would not want to cause your...boyfriend, any trouble."

He tried a different angle. "Are you sure you're with this person voluntarily? Because, if you're not, we can help. Our business is helping people in trouble, so please call if you ever need anything. We can help you start a new life. Here's our card. OK?"

Only after he finished talking did it dawn on him that the girl could be wired. A flush came over his face. Then again, it would sound good to either a law agency or the guy he was searching for, depending on *their* spin on it.

The girl wiped a tear, controlling one last sob as she took the business card. Rico inched closer and offered a hug. To his surprise she accepted and hugged him tightly. He got the impression she didn't get many. He couldn't see or feel a wire while hugging her.

"I get this sense that you are a very special person," Rico whispered as he tried to pry himself loose.

His intuition had served him well over the years, having to judge people's character in seconds. He was also especially gifted at sensing lying and, oddly enough, when someone needed a hug or kind word; conversely when someone required a hostile look, or action.

"You're an important person, don't listen to ugly people," he said.

Ever so gently he peeled her off him.

Joey watched closely, feeling reassured that the compassion she always thought was in Rico, was really there...*even* with nothing to gain. It was a strange moment to get that confirmation, but she had needed it after hearing part of what Rico was up to, and the previous week's thoughts about the Godly other guy she walked away from. "Not perfectly legal," she had heard him mumble to the girl. Never mind the general secretiveness about the whole deal.

"We have to go now. Call us, even if just to talk," Rico said.

Joey also gave the comforted, tear-free, but still stiff, teenager a motherly hug. She added some words too. Some things she whispered so low that Rico had to strain to hear. But all he could overhear Joey say at the end just when she let go was, "…pray that prayer soon."

Why is she forever whispering in people's ears when I'm around?

"Bye, young lady," Joey said more loudly.

She pried her hand from the girl's grip. Rico looked at Joey's beet red hand and shook his head.

Once out of the girl's hearing range Joey commented, "Well, hombre…back to square one."

"Ah, yes, Counselor. But nothing was lost and much was gained today," he said in Spanish, pretending to be undeterred. His sullen stride said otherwise.

As they were about to reach the exit, an individual approached, donning an alien mask from some episode neither of them had seen. Without any exchange of words, he handed them a small folder that at first appeared to be another advertising packet.

They concluded it had to be something else as the stranger headed toward the corner where the young girl was still standing, arms crossed in a self-embrace. They saw the interesting couple embrace and walk hand-in-hand into the darkness. Bingo!

Rico kept the lightweight package close to his body. They opted to open the package once safely in the hotel room instead of right then. Strange events were not uncommon in either of their lives; the bizarreness of what had just transpired was ranked right up there with the oddest. They were both a little out of sorts. If they had been conned, the kid was really good.

Emptying the contents on the bed, Rico found a note, "Insert this cipher into the USB port of your computer **ONLY** when you enter the discussion area you did last time and after you have entered your name and started chatting. Otherwise, keep it in your safe. Destroy when no further contact is expected or when instructed. Do not allow it into the hands of *anyone* else…including your wife. "

Rico took one last look in the package and pulled out another sheet of folded paper. It was a picture of Rico, taken by his *own* internet camera mounted on top of his computer in his office. It showed Rico's face wearing a slight grimace apparently captured, he concluded, when he was reading the threat the guy had typed on the screen the one time they had interacted. So much for the top-of-the-line firewall he thought he had.

So he wasn't joking about my firewall being a joke. "I don't like this," Rico muttered. "It brings back too many memories."

"Then stop…stop whatever you're planning, Jacob! Let's just live normal, tranquil lives," she said.

She remembered who she was talking to the moment the plea left her mouth; she looked at the ceiling in surrender. But she would still persist, to Rico's dismay, repeating the refrain with some frequency.

Rico reclined on the bed, not bothering to acknowledge that her request was heard. Frown folds lined his forehead. Of his own accord he tried to conjure up the resolve to abandon the still hazy plan like she said. As yet particulars weren't clear in his mind. What *was* crystal clear was how utterly a ridiculous, disaster bound course it was. But, he considered, since it was bound to unravel in the earliest stages there would be no harm done…more or less. Sound reasoning eluded him still.

"Honey, call the airport to move our flight plan to today and confirm refueling was done," he murmured as if he wasn't all there. He closed his eyes.

Joey grimaced and offered a silent prayer when Rico popped one more *migraine* pill, as he called them. "Hope they don't start in full force," she said softly. She sat by him, put the back of one hand to his forehead and picked up the phone with the other.

Rico wondered where she had picked up the nurturing and motherly tendencies. He remembered her clawing and clamoring for news stories. Later, *she* became a prize story while as a British chopper pilot she terrorized enemy forces in Iraq.

Right now, life was throwing him so many twists and turns, Rico struggled to keep things straight.

"All set for an hour. Looks like a sunset view this trip…you want take-off or landing?" Joey asked unenthusiastically.

Rico didn't answer. This only served to heighten her suspicions of the increasingly frequent headaches. At first she had thought they were what he received military disability for. It turned out to be a most fortunate cover. He had made sure to show her once during a visit to San Diego the whopping three hundred and ninety-five dollars a month VA check. She had shrugged it off thinking maybe in Iraq he had been exposed to something she hadn't.

On the way to the airport Joey adamantly insisted on some action to get another check up or brain scan.

Rico, by now wearied of being badgered, told her he had a P.E.T. scan scheduled at the VA hospital in November—his very first outright lie. Of course, he would make a real appointment the very next day, so it was only a fib. And he did plan to give her all the news then, good or bad. At least, that was his honest intention.

Rico ignored Joey's first disapproving and then solemn look.

Still, it was enough for temporary appeasement. It helped too that she had a nice distraction to sooth her worried and flustered soul; a romantic flight into another brilliant, orange, red, and purple New Mexico sunset.

CHAPTER THIRTY-FIVE

A WEEK later Rico sat in his office. The phone rang. Jennifer answered and asked twice who it was and then was silent. Rico's stomach knotted instantly. Jennifer's slower than normal appearance at his door and absent smile didn't help.

"Jacob..." she said. "FBI."

The acronym processed in his brain letter by letter. *Oh man, are they on to me already?*

"Regarding?" he asked, keeping a blank face.

"Don't know. Says he's Agent Brooks."

"Then why the ashen face?" he managed to whisper, waiting for his pulse to startup again.

"Just a feeling...I guess."

Must be going around, he pondered.

Hearing that wasn't any comfort. Last time she had a *feeling* they had to fight their way out of a very well concealed Al-Qaeda ambush in the Kush region of Afghanistan. Had the commander listened to her, two men would not have perished.

"Hey, girl, I'm sure it's nothing. Make me one of those Iced Mocha thingies you and Joey drink, will you."

She obeyed and left, no less ashen faced, eyes looking up, arms hugging her belly.

"Rico here," he said to the caller on the phone an instant after Jennifer turned to leave. The grimace he allowed was more about losing influence over Jennifer; before she would have chirped right back up. Even when one time, way back when, she thought she was pregnant—by someone other than him—he quickly had her shedding tears of laughter. He knew darn well who had her ear now; for chastisement *and* comforting.

"Yes, Mr. Rico, the Las Cruces PD referred me to you. I have orders from

Washington that involve you in protecting two young principals. Where can we meet?"

Rico's mind locked on the word Washington and barely heard the rest. At least now he had a faint pulse.

Whew, it's about her. "Inside the new federal court house…in thirty. Give the security folks my name," Rico said and hung up. *Orders from Washington?*

It was high time to have a direct and stern talk with the lieutenant about clarity and integrity; just as soon as he could get his grimy hands on the man. And Rico wasn't even aware that the case had grown into a federal Grand Jury matter with serious political undertones.

At the court house, Rico was quickly ushered into a private conference room that had a U.S. Marshal standing guard. Inside, two FBI agents sat waiting at a long, natural oak conference table that had only a triangular teleconference device and a coffee pot sitting on it. Boredom and indifference shown on the slim, black female agent's posture and face; she wore a rather unstylish suit that Rico could only snicker at silently. A shorter white male agent wore wire rim glasses and a more business like expression, though not necessarily a thrilled-to-be-here one, and a rather pricey looking Italian cut suit. Rico wondered if the odd pair was really FBI.

The children were secure in another television-equipped room. A large one-way mirror divided the two rooms; Rico could see the two were engrossed watching *Monsters, Inc.* How ironic he thought, monsters *were* everywhere…real ones. *Believe children…and run!*

"OK, gentlemen, when is the transfer to take place and for how long," Rico asked, attempting a cool, detached demeanor while pouring himself some coffee.

The two agents looked at each other, rolling their eyes. They didn't seem impressed with his casual manner.

"Sometime this evening," the same one said instead.

"Whoa, wait a minute…today?" Rico wished he could recall the squeak.

At least it lowered the testosterone level in the room; or hormones as it were for the one agent. The male Doña Ana County Deputy Sheriff had entered the room and stood against the door arms crossed, but slightly fidgety, almost edgy.

"That's correct," the white agent answered, annoyed that Rico wouldn't look him straight in the eye.

From the corner of his eye Rico couldn't make out if the wince on the man's face when he spoke was an arrogant jab or an expression of worry. Another gut feeling told him the guy was really worried. But this was just a low level matter, he remembered. By now he was too frazzled to analyze anything accurately. Maybe it was standard procedure, but why a sheriff and a U.S. marshal on guard? An unidentified man, wearing raggedy attire with sunglasses and sitting quietly in a corner, rattled his nerves even more. He knew better than to ask the man's identity or agency.

"That's not enough lead time…I, I agreed to post trial security…because I needed the lead time."

"Intelligence points to…"

The black agent signaled to the one talking to tread carefully.

"This guy needs some help. He can't operate in the blind," the white agent said, slightly annoyed at the other.

"Yea," Rico said. *What's going on? This is giving me the heebee geebees.*

"This is strictly confidential…understand?"

Rico nodded. *Can I bail out instead?*

"Mrs. Putman would not testify unless independent evidence was found first. Well, guess what? U.S. Marshals are right now taking over Mrs. Putman's protection from your detail."

Sure enough, Rico's radio-phone buzzed.

The agent signaled he should answer it. Rico answered and authorized Joey to hand Mrs. Putman over.

"Tomorrow morning," the same agent continued when Rico put the radio away. "The Grand Jury will probably indict and then seal the case airtight. Since the kids have no information to provide, they are in little danger. Hence, the higher ups refuse to…"

Rico's underarm perspiration was flowing like a river. "Uhm…not to sound ignorant and all…but, all this for a domestic abuse case? Maybe you can find another company to handle this."

He made a wish. At least he could tell Joey he tried.

The two agents looked at each other. The senior FBI agent's mind raced. The man had been there when Rico saved the San Diego mayoral candidate's life, and had a good inkling that it had been a fluke. It was officially noted by him, but not included in the final official report, courtesy editing by his superiors. The career FBI agent felt sure Rico was back then just a very, very lucky novice. Unfortunately, this knowledge was of little solace on this second improbable occasion to deal with the man Rico. The agent knew his superiors would nix his recommendation to find someone else; never mind that Rico happened to be his best, and only, option in this one horse town.

The white agent considered the matter, secretly ringing his hands under the table while his partner stared at him, waiting. *Another failure by this man would do more to ruin my career than vindicate me. I have to make sure this jerk succeeds!*

Rico would no doubt have gone for the jugular had the man verbalized his thoughts. But right then, he evidently was getting all he would get; little information and no way out. There were positives in this situation somewhere; but they escaped him.

Rico's mind went into overdrive to find at least one. "OK, then…I just put the kids under wraps and that's it?"

The two FBI agents nodded.

"Except…"

Just sock it to me. Why stop now, Rico thought.

"…that the mother wants the kids to say goodbye to their father, before they…disappear. Bring them here tomorrow at 10 a.m. We'll take them from the lobby and let you know when to pick them up. Within the week they'll go on to new lives," the black agent said, finally speaking.

"Agreed," Rico said. *Retirement? There's a thought!*

The agents introduced Rico to the children, a seven and nine year-old.

The two girls' somber demeanor told Rico the movie hadn't helped them forget. Did they know that their father, who by all accounts had been a good, loving one, was probably prison bound? Rico assured them that they would see him tomorrow. That didn't promise to be complicated at all; at least with Joey's help.

On the drive back to the office, talking on his cell phone, he was informed about how the transfer of Mrs. Putman to the marshals had almost turned ugly. They didn't want to wait for them to call Rico who was then in conference with the FBI. Joey, the fighting Irish, wouldn't budge, so they caved in and let her call.

He called an emergency meeting for 10 a.m., thirty minutes away. Once everyone arrived, Rico ordered Sarge to rest before a later graveyard shift. The contract security company was enlisted to man all NSA's posts. Joey had duty from the time they picked up the kids until midnight. Jennifer had motorcycle rover duty the next morning. Rico was to be the sole escort for the kids to the courthouse when the time came—an executive decision.

CHAPTER THIRTY-SIX

MORNING PROVED a treat for the visiting children. Joey's home cooking and the company of lively girls had them in stitches. Tina dropped the pretense of being miss grown up sexy girl long enough to engage in silly antics. Rosangelica was glad to have her old little sis back, at least until Sarge's son made his appearance minutes later.

Meanwhile, Rico and Jennifer met privately in the conference room after donning the cutting edge armor. In case of a situation, Jennifer would run interference or provide cover fire, if necessary, while Rico escaped with his charges.

Jennifer wore a long face, her legs feeling strangely rubbery. Rico's extra emphasis on leaving the scene quickly, no matter what, reverberated in her head like in a dream. Though maximum caution was a cardinal rule with him, the look on his face this day portended something ominous. She hoped beyond hope that her sixth sense was fooling with her and that her newfound emotional, physical and spiritual paradise would remain undisturbed. But a one hundred percent hit rate on premonitions couldn't be ignored.

Both loaded their side arms with shock rounds. Rico quizzed Jennifer on using the spring-loaded bullet shields he had installed on all the motorcycles. The dialogue between the two had a graveness to it that neither wanted to acknowledge, verbally. When they were done, Jennifer offered a clingy hug. He didn't exactly resist.

Rico didn't say anything to anyone, but the day before he had upped his term insurance after his visit with the G-men and had secured various powers of attorney relegating authority to Joey, Jennifer and Sarge for all his business matters. He gave life-support matters exclusively to Joey of course. Sensibly, he concluded that two million in insurance would hold her over better than one.

Rico brought the Smart Truck and a cycle up from the underground lair. Jennifer, at his direction over the radio, escorted the two girls out to the garage.

The principals—the children—found the monster truck a real trip. Jennifer noted they tended to the tomboyish side; like someone else she knew.

Rico didn't have the control panels with all the lights and switches open yet. He did open the overhead panel one in the front compartment once they were strapped in and the dividing window was closed. No need to give someone a reason to threaten the little ones for tactical information.

Rico took off first. Jennifer followed. She peeled off from trailing escort duty at Solano and Amador streets. A minute later she was roaming around and about the fairly new federal courthouse. Having notified the dispatcher to advise all units about her presence and purpose, she wasn't pulled over about the cannon-size handgun she wore on her thigh. Neither did her looking around with binoculars concern the already notified feds patrolling the courthouse.

Jennifer, distracted by two mysterious vans, missed a movement on the rooftop of a two-story building one block north of the courthouse's main entrance. The minivans, parked in the second row nearest the court entrance didn't portend anything good. Then two armed guards, who for some reason suddenly headed toward the courthouse building, passed near to those same vans and seemed to have missed the suspicious occupants—several out of place, stoic looking, binocular-equipped men and a woman. Jennifer figured they had to be legit. Bad guys don't usually hide in plain site.

Jennifer felt her skin crawl. She forced herself to not call Rico to abort. What would she base it on anyway? Maybe other guards were around the corner and these were getting a quick briefing to receive Rico's two-person package.

Rico arrived three minutes later and received a radio all-clear from Jennifer. He, in turn, didn't miss the less than authoritative way she had spoken, but also shrugged off the odd feeling. Things looked fine as he turned the corner.

Meanwhile, Joey was at home obeying the unusual, but unequivocal, instructions her husband gave to sequester Rosangelica and Tina in her basement bedroom in the dojo. This was of course next to Michelle's room, whom the girls still didn't know existed.

But Joey wasn't exactly guarding them. Instead, she had them praying hard—for something she couldn't quite put her finger on. Nothing came to mind, though the fact that her husband had been concerned enough to send her into cover was a clue. She was about to start praying when suddenly a strong spirit of fear tried to overtake her. Her entire body refused to respond; her heart almost went into shock and felt as though it would stop beating. She mustered all her energy and all she could manage to force out was the name "Jesus," and that barely in a guttural whisper. But it was enough, the spirit fled; just as that same Jesus promised her in the Scriptures.

Joey's body still shuddered seconds afterward. *What in the world was that?* Several Bible verses came to mind and she had her answer. This was the first time she had been attacked so directly or by such a powerful being. If it never happened again she would be quite happy. But a strong servant in the spirit was always a prime target; and a strong servant of God she was. She hunkered down for more warfare.

Rico sat in his truck. He looked around. The inner alarms rang despite the serene, sleepy view; it was paranoia he continued reasoning. Even then he seriously considered disappointing the principals by denying them an opportunity to see their father one last time. The chaos he might create by alarming the mother and causing her not to testify against her abusive tyrant of a husband helped set his mind straight.

An alert Rico disembarked, looked about one last time, opened the sliding side door and offered his hand to each child to help them down. The two almost instinctively clung to him. He had parked illegally because the closest parking was rather far, and the front of the court house was blocked off to vehicle traffic. A six-story bank was located directly across the street. He gave each window a quick glance. Nothing out of the ordinary; roof looked clear too. He didn't look back to the building one block behind him.

Not more than fifty feet from the minivans, Rico realized he had forgotten his bullet proof helmet. He was turning the girls around when he heard the comforting sound of a revving cycle engine, echoing off the buildings. The comfort he felt evaporated instantly when two men wearing sunglasses flung open the van doors and emerged from each vehicle, about twenty feet behind him. They discreetly held silencer-fitted side arms against their thighs. One of them subtly revealed an Uzi submachine gun, also sporting a silencer, from under a windbreaker. A red dot bounced around Rico's belly. It aroused nothing in him.

Then the still mostly concealed Uzi's laser brushed over the two kids. Rico's throat tightened and prevented him from speaking into the sensitive VOX throat mic he wore. He drew the children behind him as they backed up toward the Smart Truck, also a long twenty feet away. Closing within six feet from him and the children, the men discreetly cocked their weapons and told Rico he could walk away if he handed the kids over.

Rico locked eyes with the apparent lead man. *Great! A wanna-be tough guy.*

"Delta Force? Don't look tough enough to break through a paper sack," the man annoyingly said, sounding more in control than he was. "Either way, don't do anything stupid…or then again, I wouldn't mind…"

Rico noticed fidgeting from the other hired guns. *Let me guess, the boss' son? This can't be happening…it only happens in the movies!* Rico was thinking as the woman in the group interrupted the man and spoke up, promising they wouldn't be hurt.

The father wanted them safe while the DA grew a brain and *dropped* the charges; or so the woman said.

"He doesn't want to have to find them if the mother leaves the country with them," she said, adding to the obvious ire of the leader.

Rico determined the men were clearly professional muscle, probably ex-military, and more than likely just wanted a quick, quiet and uneventful payday; except for the lead guy who, even with Rico's mile-long stare, still appeared intent on some action.

Killing was messy, in many ways, Rico knew. And maybe the others would knock out the brash youngster and keep things quiet the way the boss ordered; and avoid casualties. The others were obviously more seasoned in their work; they had to be cognizant that surprises were likely lurking under the ex-Delta man's plain exterior; a single man and easy to deal with to be sure, but dangerous nonetheless. And the Jordan they had studied in their prep was no push over.

Rico nodded. He needed to stall somehow. "Kids, do you want to go with your dad?"

They both nodded and said yes.

The radio better be transmitting, Rico thought.

Sweat now raining down his forehead contrasted with his otherwise effective poker face. "They're yours…but if you hurt these two kids…I'll find you. So drive the green and the white minivans safely."

The men scowled and signaled for him to cut the bull and hand them over.

Jennifer heard the last part of the conversation clearly. Flabbergasted, she revved the cycle and looked for a fed to alert. None were around. *Something's wrong*, she thought again, now having something concrete to substantiate her suspicions. The cycle jumped a curb toward the minivans.

I refuse or stall, I die…and they still get the kids. Rico released the girls and backed further toward his truck. He felt the urgency to get to his bulletproof helmet, but could barely see where the truck was for the burning sweat in his eyes.

The sniper Jennifer had missed during her recon, and still couldn't see, set the crosshairs.

Rico reached in the truck, felt for and grabbed his helmet and proceeded toward the minivans. The gunmen were about to shut the doors. The children, insisting on seatbelts, and a couple of the bulky assailants trying to fit in slowed their progress a bit.

The bad guy that was assigned rear security noticed the repentant Rico approaching while trying to place the helmet on and draw his side arm. The man fired a puff emanating round, hitting Rico in the abdomen.

As the helmet flew out of Rico's hand, he instantly came to the grim realization that the round had penetrated the armor. *Armor piercing…great…just great!* he grimaced, falling to the ground.

Staying down meant he lived, probably. If he didn't make it, it would eliminate the heart aches he was seemingly destined to create later; except the kids under his charge needed him first…before…

Jennifer slapped the buttons that actuated the protective bulletproof shields Rico had installed. They swung up like wings and covered the majority of her frame from the sides and the back. She felt like a dorky Bat Woman, but drew comfort that Rico had thought ahead. She fired from atop her cycle, with the machine skidding to a stop.

The would-be kidnappers were slightly annoyed, thinking the two former hero pests just needed to scoot along for their own good. The annoyance quickly turned to ire in the others when the hostile that had shot Rico caught Jennifer's single round through an eye socket; really an errant shot when she dropped the cycle to its side. The normally non-lethal Shock Round proved otherwise this time. The background on the lady was obviously right on the money, the crew concluded.

Rico lay on his side, in a fetal position, holding his belly, and barely able to consider any options; the thought of doing nothing dismissed as easily as it had come. The prescription morphine pill he had popped thirty minutes earlier served double duty and partially numbed the sting of the round.

"Disengage, Jenny, that's an order. Just get help!"

I would love to do that, Jacob, she thought.

With still no sign of the authorities, she wasn't about to leave her charge. Who had priority just then, the kids *or* Rico, she wasn't sure. She prayed for guidance and protection.

Rico willed himself upright and hobbled toward the minivan that was backing away from the attacking Jennifer, feverishly unloading his magazine into the tires and windshield.

Jennifer did the same, ignoring orders. She quickly ducked behind a car as Rico mentioned the armor piercing rounds…a little late. A round had just taken a good chunk of flesh off her right shoulder.

That's why the wings weren't stopping the bullets. I thought Rico got burnt, Jennifer thought, finding it interesting that such a silly thought could pass through her mind in the middle of all this.

From her pinned down position she managed to assess that the getaway for the hostiles had been complicated. She took another cautious peek and realized Rico's truck door was open. She panicked when she saw Rico catch another round and collapse to the ground.

A mere ninety seconds had transpired since the first shot had been fired. Passing cars and pedestrians thought it some sort of exercise since the silencers and closed, air conditioned car windows prevented even the puff sounds from registering. It might as well have been a paint-ball fight.

The hostiles fired in her direction while dragging the children toward Rico's truck—a perfect gift-wrapped escape vehicle; a fair trade for Rico disabling their vehicles.

Where are the feds, or cops? Rico thought in a state of fuzziness, increasing pain, and looming sense of finality. No sense of doom; just finality.

He didn't know better.

The apparent ring leader walked past Rico, who was trying to play possum; a little difficult when in agonizing pain; morphine could only do so much. The man stopped in his tracks, turned and placed a green laser dot on Rico's forehead.

Jennifer watched in horror and said what amounted to her very first panicked cry for help from above. "Jesus!" she mouthed.

She couldn't lift her weapon with her good arm above the car roof in time to fire a shot. Jennifer could only watch as the man, aiming at Rico from only a foot away, suddenly winced and reached for his neck at the same time he yanked the trigger and overshot Rico's head by inches, then fell over and hit the ground.

If anyone could choose a sniper in whose crosshairs to find themselves, they couldn't have picked a better one. The sniper, apparently intending to let his or her targets live another day, used sleeping darts. Normally, this same sniper would have used a lethal round and fired at the target's fatal funnel, a circular area at jaw level from the mouth around the to the back of the neck. If he had, the signal to the target's trigger finger would never have made it past the severed spinal cord.

Could this be a law enforcement sniper? Or was Rico the actual target? But why shoot the other guy? Maybe to toy with Rico before shooting him, but with a bullet? Jennifer's thoughts ran away like a freight train. She grew dizzy.

When Jennifer had been watching the ring leader steady the dot on Rico's forehead, toying with him, another of the would-be *kidnappers*—as Rico and Jennifer had mentally classified them by then—had unceremoniously snuck up on Jennifer to terminate her. Before he could execute her, he also went down in the same manner as the first sniper's mark.

The sniper, yet to be identified as friend or foe, had just fired two split second shots at two separate targets. It was an incredible feat in the best of conditions, and this sniper had done it firing darts from almost a hundred yards. Jennifer had been peeking through a windshield, almost blacking out from pain, and had witnessed the results of the sniper's first shot a second before she heard the thump of the felled sniper's second target. The man's skull hitting the pavement made a rather pronounced cracking sound; louder than any of the shots that had been fired.

By this time she had given up helping Rico, and had instead quickly targeted and shot the man sporting the Uzi. That hostile had gotten in her line of sight and had been shoving the children into the Smart Truck. She hit center of mass in the back. This time the round worked as designed and the man lay on the ground, alive but incapacitated by the electrical charge.

The two remaining hostiles dropped their weapons and raised their arms high. A male and female pair in an equal opportunity business, apparently.

Jennifer wasn't egotistical enough to think that the arms raised were in deference to her instead of the X factor on the roof. Holstering her weapon she reached for her cell phone and pretended to be talking to someone.

"I've ordered my cover to switch to full metal jacket," she informed the two reaching up to the sky. "Federal courthouse, shots fired," she said for real to the dispatcher that answered and then hung up.

The two visibly stiffened, and after looking at each other dropped to their knees. The newest team members had gotten into something deeper than they had intended. They never really expected to use their side arms. "They are for intimidation," they had been told.

They tried explaining more but Jennifer wasn't listening. Still, she somehow felt sorrow for the two and decided to pray for them; maybe she would visit them in jail. She couldn't believe she had actually had that thought.

Jennifer zigzagged toward Rico's motionless body. She called 911 again when she remembered she hadn't asked for an ambulance. Her mind wanted to shut down, the ground seemed to be moving.

"Jennifer? Is this you?" the dispatcher asked. "This is Rosemary! But, I can't make out what you want."

"Hi…Rose…I, I need an air-evac…for, for Ja…right now, I'll…pay for it. The federal courthouse…parking l…. Hurry, pleeease."

"Why, Jennifer?"

"Something went…wrong, terribly…wrong."

She was at least ten feet from Rico before falling to the ground. The dispatcher knew Jennifer's occupation and made the connection without any more questions.

Sirens blared, and feds and local police flooded the parking lot.

It had to be a dream; the noises came and went in waves; fading in and out, like someone playing with the volume knob on a radio.

Finally, Jennifer thought, getting to her feet and shoving her way past them to get to Rico. She angrily shoved one marshal aside who asked her where the sniper fire came from. So the shooter wasn't one of their own? She had spotted the shooter's outline on the roof just after the last round, but she wasn't about to help the ones she suspected had a hand in what smelled like a setup.

Instead, she hit the ground again next to Rico. Her head on the pavement, she watched blood trickle from his abdomen, a shallow wheezing coming from under his hand covering the entry wound. The bullet hole in his right chest, the second round that hit him, had gone right through without hitting bone, imbedding itself in the Smart Truck.

If she had seen the size of either of the exit wounds, she would have lost even the pretend ounce of hope that remained in her. Another big brother and soul friend taken away. *Is God still mad?* The notion tore into her soul.

Rico came to and started mumbling.

Jennifer crept forward to hear Rico's last words before crossing over.

"Tell her I've loved her from the first…and I love you…and the girls. And tell my ex sorry for me. But…to be honest…Jenny…I don't exactly…know what…love means. I, I'm sorry…You know…you really are…more beautiful inside than…." He took a deep breath.

It seemed strange to Jennifer that he didn't seem in pain, just out of breath. His eyes closed, throat contracted and convulsed.

"It's just a word some people say with their lips. But you've lived it, Jacob... and...and it has surrounded you a long, long time," she cried.

His eyes didn't open again to give a clue of understanding, only a slight wince showed on his face. "Anyway...tell the doc, Joey only needs to know... about today's little...problems...okay?"

"You're gonna make it, Jacob," Jennifer said, not very convincingly. "If you don't, I..." Her anguish quickly intermingled with rage, she seethed at the sight of SWAT officers flooding onto a rooftop, the sniper's abandoned perch.

"Jacob, I'm sorry...I messed up...I didn't..."

"Shut up," he said and reached for her hand. He squeezed as hard as a ninety year-old grandmother. "You...uh...great. The kids...safe...right, Jenny?"

Jennifer turned her head to see the children, encircled by marshals and being rushed into the federal courthouse building. She nodded and whispered, "Yes, boss," as the paramedics readied Rico for the air-ambulance.

Rosemary came through again, she thought. *I gotta get her a gift or some....*

Everything looked okay now, security wise, as she rolled onto her back and closed her eyes. The objective had been accomplished after all, the two principals safely tucked away. Somehow, she analyzed even as her brain registered another round of searing pain, it wasn't supposed to have been achieved. Nevertheless, another mission accomplished.

Another paramedic prepared a morphine shot for her. The dangling piece of flesh on her shoulder, speckled with bone fragments, would have made Rico faint if he had been able to even look sideways at his panicking friend. Seconds later she watched the paramedics carrying Rico stop just feet from the chopper and ready the paddles. She tried reaching for him, then blacked out.

CHAPTER 37

THE NEWS reached Joey ten minutes later. Rosemary had finally caught a break to make the somber call to Joey, her good friend, sister and mentor in the Lord. She told her Rico had regained consciousness momentarily in the chopper and had demanded to be sent to the UNM Medical Center, farther away from the undetermined danger. Jennifer was taken to Memorial Medical.

Joey quickly called for a plane at the Las Cruces airport. After Jennifer snuck out of the hospital, Joey picked Sarge and her up and drove to the airport.

On the way, Jennifer recounted what had happened, often slurring words. She counted two dead assailants by her hand and two unconscious ones by an anonymous sniper.

In fact, only one hostile was dead by her hand, the one she shot in the back only had some residual pain, thanks to her listening to Rico weeks before to drop the powder load by half. Now she would only have to stave off one unlawful death suit. Fortunately, Rico believed in lots of liability insurance. And prayer would keep her calm during the trying Grand Jury hearings that would follow and drag on and on.

A sniper that hit the wrong marks? Or highly proficient? And protecting who? Joey pondered. By then it was clear the individual had no affiliation with any branch of law, as a massive search had been initiated and announced on the local TV networks.

Based on what Jennifer had told her, Joey ordered the team into tactical mode. Each was already armed and armored. They would be circling the wagons around the downed knight. Joey called the governor and begged his help.

Immediately, he dispatched two of his State Police security detachment officers to her husband's side, declaring the situation a state security matter. A safety and public relations nightmare had landed at his doorstep. He was furious with the FBI and Marshal Service. And of all things, his high profile friend was smack in the middle of it.

Once on the ground in Albuquerque, Sarge finally made contact with Cohen. The man said he had engagements he could not break and apologized. He would contribute from afar and pray.

So much for loyalty, Sarge thought. He wondered how in the world this religious man got past his boss' anti-religious screening process. *And so much for support from the faithful. Prayer? Yeah, right!*

Jennifer broadcast her agony at every pot hole the rental car drove through. By now she was lucid enough to observe Joey closely, without Joey's face contorting and looking fuzzy. As Sarge drove, Joey just looked about like an every day tourist seeming to enjoy the passing scenery. At a red light an almost smile crossed Joey's face even when she spotted some kids playing in a corner lot, laughing their hearts out about something. Her interwoven fingers and just slightly moving lips were the only evidence Jennifer could see that prayer might be going up to heaven. Maybe it was a well developed coping mechanism; what Jennifer wouldn't give to read her mind.

Even as the small entourage entered through the emergency entrance, Joey continued her biblical example of serenity. A look of deep thought kept everyone else from speaking.

Jennifer, on the other hand, fell apart the moment she saw Rico on the operating table. The blood soaked clothes he had worn were in a plastic pan near the window from where they watched. The doctors worked feverishly. Jennifer found herself kneeling over the trash canister she had reached barely in time.

Joey emptied her purse of tissues and wipes, handing them to her. Joey snapped to all of a sudden and swung into action, dispatching Sarge for coffee and scribbling some notes for the bodyguards to deliver to the governor. The guards balked at first, but finally deferred to Joey's orders.

She could be very persuasive; some would say intimidating.

The nurses had reacted immediately at seeing the holstered side arms on the apparent civilians, especially the two women's large ones strapped to their thighs. The armed guard had been alerted to escort them out. Joey directed Jennifer, who had by then composed herself, and Sarge to go concealed. She then had to convince the arriving duty officer that *he* did not want to create a scene.

Fortunately, the governor had just arrived and prevented an escalation. He had met with Joey's messengers in the lobby and been briefed. Joey asked him to

J. F. ARIAS

provide intelligence about the men who attacked her husband and to assure the safety of the children he had tried to protect. He promised help and soon left to an important luncheon.

Minutes later Rico was moved to ICU. According to the surgical team, that Rico had made it alive to the operating table had been nothing short of a miracle in and of itself; that was the good news. The prognosis was not. The internal trauma and bleeding, along with bleeding from the two exit wounds should have killed him minutes after the shooting. Some organs they simply left untouched because they were beyond repair. Machines took over. Hours were optimistic; minutes likely—absent a second true blue miracle.

When one surgeon mentioned how long Rico had been in shock, and thereby probably suffered serious mental impairments, Joey mentally calculated backwards to the time of the shooting. It would have been the exact time she and the girls were in the basement praying ... for what, at the time, they didn't know.

Jennifer and the surgeons watched Joey as she went to a corner of the temporarily crowded ICU room. She seemed to be talking to herself...almost arguing.

"Oh, God! Oh, God!" Joey was saying under her breath. "I'm sorry for covetousness. I didn't mean it when I said Jacob was being too much of a burden. It's just that...he made me mad that he didn't turn down this job...like I asked him to. That's why he's dying! Did *you* do it God? Are you teaching me a lesson? But he's not saved. I thought you told me...he would be. I wanted to share my faith with him and you said no. And instead I wished I hadn't married him ... fantasizing, wishing I had married...Oh, I'm so sorry Lord! God, what am I...no, what are *you* Mighty God going to do?"

Joey started pacing in a circle. Her hands couldn't cover the flushed face and wet cheeks. Jennifer watched the less together Joey, and it wasn't pretty.

"Be still, I AM near."

For only the second time in her Christian walk she heard God with her natural ears. He gave her some instructions, speaking only into her mind after that, not audibly.

Jennifer felt compelled to comfort her. As she approached, she heard Joey say, "Lord...I don't know if I can do that. They are going to think I'm in shock... or just a wacko."

Jennifer was about to put her hand on Joey's shoulder when Joey turned, still talking.

"Yes, I'll do it L…Oh, Jennifer. Please excuse me." Joey unceremoniously and without any attempt at being subtle wiped her face and blew her nose firmly into a pre-used tissue she managed to salvage from her purse.

"Sorry, Jennifer, I gotta go do something before I change my mind." Joey hurried to the surgeons who were about to leave. Looking very reserved and staring at the floor, Joey raised a hand to signal them, her mouth didn't seem to want to move.

Jennifer followed closely behind. *Please, Lord, I can't possibly handle losing Jacob and Joey losing her mind on the same day! Oh, no, I'm gonna throw up again!*

"Doctors, nurse…" Joey started. "…I want to confirm that you have MRI's and video of his insides…you know, when you were operating?"

For liability reasons hospitals had taken to recording procedures of all kinds.

The surgeons were disturbed and dealing—each in their own way—with seeing a patient slipping away, but all in the group nodded.

"Can you please send for the tech that did the MRI."

The doctor's spirits weren't very high so acceded to her request to at least accomplish something. The puzzled tech arrived minutes later.

"Will you agree to personally sign this man's MRI printouts and send me a copy, at my expense, sometime today?" She waved a power of attorney, the one Rico forced on her the day before.

The tech agreed, sneaking a look at each of the doctors, one at a time. They didn't respond to his perplexed expression.

The doctors weren't wearing their masks any more, only long faces. Was there something they were missing? Were they counting the mangled man in front of them down and out prematurely?

"This will only take a few more minutes, doctors. Trust me please, it'll be worth your time. Remember that what you are about to see still falls under doctor-patient confidentiality laws and you can only tell others with *his* explicit permission."

The man on this bed? The one who will be dead in an hour at the most?

"We are all in agreement he has hours?" Joey asked.

The group reluctantly affirmed that that was their medical opinion. Jennifer almost let out a sob at seeing the nods of concurrence. But her friend lying on the bed would not have wanted to make it anyway, if someone had to tend to him.

Just then the monitors beeped and the EKG line went flat. The doctors were about to start CPR when Joey waved them off. One of the doctors actually seemed to agree and didn't even budge.

Jennifer was ready to explode with anger that Joey wasn't giving Rico a chance. She was just giving up, doing nothing but holding up Jacob Rico's Living Will to the doctors.

"You didn't touch his exit wounds." Joey asked, looking up at the ceiling.

The doctors shook their heads. *How could she know that?* They wondered.

"How big?"

One doctor made a large circle with his hands, about nine inches. The others concurred with nodding heads.

"We…placed coagulating pads on them to stop the bleeding and planned skin grafts if he made it."

"I take it that was going to be a challenge all by itself?"

They chose not to mention, even though Joey knew it, the hospital could generate any quantity of skin they needed for skin grafts in minutes. The inkjet-like tissue printing machine could also generate other types of tissue and several body parts. Lots of skin would have had to be generated for this patient. But that option was for probable survivors only, and insured ones. Rico was only one of those; the blood loss shock alone gave him less than a ten percent chance. The doctors just wanted to leave and put salve on their own wounds, hoping for a brighter outcome with the next patient, already prepped in the ER—perhaps also because their hearts went out to the strange-acting spouse of the unfortunate man.

Joey said nothing else for a very uncomfortable, tense-filled minute; eyes closed and lips moving in silent talk. Then she started talking aloud.

Jennifer didn't know whether to hide or indicate agreement.

"Lord you say that by your stripes we are healed. That greater things than you did, *we* would do. You gave me the gift of healing and you say that with a mustard seed of faith I can tell a mountain to be removed…and it will," Joey said.

Jennifer didn't know what to do. The doctors watched and waited for a courteous way to make tracks.

Joey continued, "…for your glory, and your glory alone, Lord God, in the name of Jesus, let this mountain be moved. Let this unbeliever experience Your mercy and grace." Joey didn't say another comprehensible thing. The rest of what came out her mouth for some ten seconds sounded like gibberish, with Hebrew in the mix.

Joey dug into her purse. She seemed almost in shock, or a trance. "Put my husband, as is, into a private room. In three hours he'll need a bandage change. Until then, do not resuscitate…here's the other notarized order that states that."

This only confirmed the doctor's, and Jennifer's, suspicion that she wasn't all there. Nevertheless, there was silence and then a sigh of relief from the doctors. They had done their best.

Before anyone knew it Joey began acting like her normal self; the level-headed friend Jennifer remembered. But her words were still out there.

"OK, doctors…soon after my husband resuscitates, he will begin to grow sinew tissue in the most damaged internal organs…those you could not have possibly repaired. By tonight, only the parts that you sewed up will remain to heal in a natural time frame. The exit wounds will also heal completely, and on their own, in three days, leaving only one inch memorial scars. All of this is so that you can know that the Lord is God. Apparently, God wants one of you folk's attention. Never mind my husband's attention," Joey added as an afterthought.

"Do not tell him anything about dying when he wakes up. Understand doctors?"

The group shrugged their shoulders as if embarrassed, not wanting to be the one to burst the loony lady's bubble.

Joey, faith in uncurling a crippled arm is one thing…but…Oh, Joey, just say bye, Jennifer thought.

"OK, Jenny, you're in charge of security and documenting the progress your boss makes, recording the *doctor's* words please. A recorder would do too. I'm headed home…there are things there I can plow."

Jennifer didn't have the wherewithal to ponder Joey's odd vocabulary.

Back in Las Cruces, Michelle was beginning to leave the bed and to be out and about in the room; she needed Joey's physical and emotional attention. Her physical therapy was grueling, and Joey wanted to be there for her. Joey thought it time to let the secret out and make use of the girl's energies, but Michelle kept nixing the suggestion.

Joey's words were hard for Jennifer to swallow. Joey was exiting the room when she stopped in her tracks near the door. Reluctant to turn her face, looking straight ahead, she said to Jennifer, "By the way Jennifer…God wants you to know that you will do greater works than what you are about to see happen to that man, who is like a second brother to you—a gift He had for you, since *before* you were born."

What are you talking about Joey? Do you know about my real brother? Of course, my parents told you.

In fact, they hadn't mentioned him yet.

Jennifer stood speechless, wide-eyed, and unable to decide whether her friend was being perceptive, cold, full of faith, trusting of her, indifferent, rude, drunk…or what. Sudden throbbing from the shoulder injury distracted her from her confused mind for a moment. Joey took advantage and vanished.

Jennifer once again felt the force of the loss of her brother decades before; as if it had happened only yesterday. She wanted to let out all the pain with one great wail, and yet she also wanted to praise God for loaning her Rico. Then again, there he lay…lifeless too. Her soul weighed a ton, the pit of despair called her name. She hugged her belly and sought a seat. Finding none, she slid down as she leaned against the cold wall; almost as cold as her heart felt. Her heart could not conjure up of a single word to say to God; on her behalf the Holy Spirit groaned prayers that could not be uttered.

For a second she almost allowed herself to pray in tongues, but she wasn't ready to believe in that strange thing again and restrained her tongue. After being baptized in the Holy Spirit at thirteen and speaking a beautiful sounding heavenly language, she had since refused to speak in a language she couldn't understand; never mind her parent's ardent explanations.

The doctors, by this time finished rationalizing away the whole event, quickly arranged for a room for the *corpse* and a cot for Jennifer, then hastily they left for the ER. All this and they still had ten hours left on their shift. Still, they were really worried about the bundle of tears that was Jennifer balled up on the floor, big gun and all. One of them informed a nurse on that floor to monitor her. She seemed not used to traumatic events he told the nurse. Maybe she'll hand you the gun.

The nurse was very patient and helped Jennifer come back to life and recover some of her senses; the effort to take the gun didn't go well. She recommended a hotel for Jennifer and offered to call a taxi. But of course Jennifer would have none of that. She stayed with her friend and alternated between groaning, moaning, and sobbing while watching her friend's lifeless body. She rocked back and forth like a child. Her frequent chills worsened when thoughts that Rico had died not knowing Jesus pummeled her.

Sarge walked in. He avoided eye contact with Jennifer. He paced for a short time at Rico's side, saying nothing; he knew a dead man when he saw one. When he snuck another peek at Jennifer, she had sat upright and was wiping and blowing her nose.

"I'm, I'm really sorry. I know how close you two were since way back when…."

He couldn't understand her look. It seemed to him the comment almost got her mad.

But, she was just curious as to what he could have heard about Rico and her, since they had never told him anything. Waves of memories came roaring in. She couldn't muster the strength to ask.

Jennifer changed the subject and mentioned Joey's earlier behavior. Sarge thought Joey's conduct in the ICU and subsequent sudden departure odd also. They considered that Joey might fly the plane into the ground in her disoriented mental state. Jennifer felt a tinge of fear and guilt at letting her go.

Jacob Rico had been to hell before, figuratively speaking; but even as his wife prayed for his life and the surgical team hovered over him wearing solemn faces, Rico began a descent toward hell…literally. The moment his heart stopped, a shadow on horseback approached; extending the shadowy form of a hand, the being reached into Rico's body and pulled fiercely on his soul. Horror filled Rico's eyes as he peered back at his motionless body on the ICU bed. As the horse rose up to the ceiling, Rico had time to see Joey below. He tried to yell at her but quickly realized that the paper she was waving at the surgeons was the Do Not Resuscitate directive he had given her only weeks before—too late for a change of heart, or mind.

Rico doggedly, wildly resisted. It was to no avail as the horseman jerked him through the hospital floor. They plunged into nothingness for a few seconds and then they floated skyward. It wasn't dark like he expected, at least not yet.

The horse suddenly broke into a fierce gallop as if racing time itself. Ahead, Rico spotted dark clouds surrounding black hot doors. Horrifying wails thundered from behind and beyond them. The full force of what the place was, and its significance, finally struck Rico. He screamed for Joey and Jennifer. The horseman ignored him. Darkness enveloped them.

The horseman stopped at the doors and shrieked. Barely had the doors creaked open when the screams from within shook Rico with the force of their anguish. He peeked ahead to see flames rising from a gigantic pit. Millions of condemned souls turned to see the newest one to join them. "Mercy!" they cried.

Fortunately, just before Rico was yanked past the threshold, he noticed four shooting stars streaming toward him from above. He determined that they were angels when one struck and broke the chains on his wrist with a double edged sword.

The horseman shrieked with anger. The shriek brought an instant response from ten hideous, vile smelling creatures that surrounded the angels.

Rico shuddered. His eyes bulged at the indescribable sight before him; a forceful smell emanating from the creatures shocked his nostrils, their hissing and gurgling was maddening. Obviously, his senses were going to be with him for eternity he considered.

Three of the angels engaged the beings with their swords and with words from the Lord of Hosts.

"The man of flesh belongs to Satan," the grotesque doormen of Hell screeched.

"It is not his appointed time, thus saith the Lord of Hosts," commanded the angel spiriting Rico away.

The creatures hissed as they caught up. One flew by and grabbed Rico's arm, ripping off flesh and leaving an acidy fluid that had dripped from the very unsanitary talons.

Horror filled Rico's heart as he stared at his dangling bicep muscle and visible bone underneath. The pain was excruciating and real; and apparently, morphine had no effect here.

Before the creature could follow through with a second swipe of his talons, an angel appeared from behind and smote the creature with a skillful swing of the sword. The creature screamed, evaporated into black smoke, and then reconstituted itself next to the lake of fire. The other creatures broke off the battle and flew toward the doorway and through the threshold, slamming the door shut behind them.

The eerie, dark spirit-being named Death, walked alongside the heavenly angels for a time, mocking Rico. "You'll be back there, sooner or later," he hissed.

Then Death veered off; off to another dimension, and Earth.

The angels turned toward a gleaming cloud surrounded by iridescent walls. Rico saw gigantic doors made of what looked like one solid piece of pearl. Rico figured he was about to enter paradise since his arm miraculously healed before his eyes as they drew closer to the place. Then the angels stopped near the entrance, encircled him, and assumed defensive stances.

Rico conjured up the courage to speak. "Angels of the Lord Most High…"

Being an unbeliever, he hadn't a clue how those words could come from his mouth. "Why don't we go in there if those things are coming back?"

"Thou Son of Perdition," one angel said. "Knowest not that thy name is not now written in the Lamb's Book of Life? Yet three hours has the I Am said that thou will remain in this the Third Heaven, then thou shall be returned to flesh until your breath ceases again."

Rico processed what the angel said. "Angels of the Lord Most High," he said, again puzzled by the ludicrous words. "What was beyond that door back there?"

"Son of the World, that is the door to the many pits of the Lake of Fire. Death and Hell will be cast therein. This was to be a place solely for Heaven's fallen angels. Many human souls have chosen to join them. As such, a soul that dies without a relationship with the Lamb of God goes there and is placed in the pit according to the primary sin it served while yet flesh."

Rico shuddered again. "And…and I was going where?"

"Is it not enough to know that thou had prepared a bed there, having refused a place freely offered at the table of the King of kings?"

Rico had a thousand more questions, but God restrained his mouth. He fought to force his mouth to speak. He had so many questions.

Three hours later—Earth time—the angels lifted him as they rose. He could see inside the walled heavenly place. He saw streets of iridescent gold, flowers and trees. He saw adults and children of all shades walking and playing. It was so bright, and completely absent of shadows. One very large, centrally situated circle of light, surrounded by what looked like a crystal glass mote, radiated light of unimaginable brilliance. By God's grace he was seeing into the future; a post rapture view of heaven.

No shadows! How can there be no shadows? Have I read that in a fairy tale some where? Could that be where I'm getting this dream? My imagination is getting just too creative. What are those light beams coming up from Earth into that bright, bright circle of light?

"Thou son of Israel, thus saith the Lord, those lights rising up from earth into my presence are the prayers of the righteous; even now three hundred and four of them fervently intercede on your behalf."

He considered that as far as he knew he only knew *one* person on the face of the Earth who would pray for him. Rico's last thought—before the four zoomed straight down from space like meteors through the stratosphere, into the atmosphere, toward the western hemisphere, North America, New Mexico,

Albuquerque, the hospital building, and finally through the ceiling and floors—was that *someone* could read his thoughts.

Finally, the angels gently placed Rico's soul back into the corpse that was his body.

What was that son of Israel thing? He still wanted to ask.

No angelic being would answer that for him. There was only One who knew the meaning of that.

Even though he was now back in the physical realm, his body wouldn't respond and let him wake up. He lay there, immobile, but with the full sense of hearing intact. In that state he felt touched at hearing Jennifer's fits of sobbing and words of endearment.

He listened intently for his wife's voice, hopefully crying. When he realized she wasn't there, his heart grew heavy.

Rico finally woke up three days later in his private room. The vividness of the gripping *nightmare* still remained and he considered telling Jennifer about it. The continuing chills down his back puzzled him. Talking with Jennifer would surely help. Fortunately, for Jennifer, he didn't. Instead, he focused on finding out about Joey's whereabouts.

Had he told her, she would have panicked and told him he had really died; even though Joey had explicitly said not to. Jennifer still couldn't figure that out, but she had just seen a miracle that confirmed God's power. But she obeyed what Joey's pastor had taught her, to listen to a man or woman of God's instructions, even when they seemed odd. And odd things Joey definitely said, often. God responded to obedience and faith with wonders and honors, the pastor had humbly offered.

No matter what, she was glad to have her *brother* back. That didn't erase the fact that she was perplexed not knowing the reason for God not letting Jacob in on his death.

Who can know the mind of the I Am, popped into her mind. Her earthly father had repeated those same words to her so many times when she was young. Nearly erased memories of so long ago; they had been such frustrating, ire invoking, empty words then.

But joy overwhelmed her now. She doted on her friend. Now she felt more secure surrendering the matter to the God she was quickly getting reacquainted with. Jennifer made for an overly helpful patient-protector roommate. Had Rico been able, he would insist she stop embarrassing him by her around-the-clock doting; her seemingly endless energy annoyed him so.

In contrast, Sarge grew bored quickly and was getting relieved from his hallway post by one of the governor's guards every eight hours. He stayed at a motel. Seeing a limp body didn't appeal to him.

Jennifer determined to have Joey pray over her too. She couldn't believe what she had seen, right at the three hour mark. Rico's chest had heaved once as if a giant breath had entered him. His chest then started rising and falling with normal healthy, steady breaths; the monitors had also suddenly sprung to life. The surgeons arrived in a rush and personally started changing the dressings on the *resurrected* man, three hours after Joey had left. They kept shoving each other out of the way to peek at Lazarus's, as they took to calling him, amazing sinew growth.

Rico continued in his unconscious state during this time of tedious bandage change, after bandage change...*another* merciful act of grace.

To Jennifer, the doctors' behavior was bizarre in so many ways. Then Joey's voice rang in her head, "...greater things than these..."

CHAPTER THIRTY-EIGHT

As promised, the governor initiated a special investigation into the lapses in security at the court house. His investigators briefed Joey one day after the incident about their preliminary findings. Joey wasn't happy that they had more questions than answers, but she held her peace, with a little help from the Holy Ghost.

The authorities hadn't a clue whether the men attempting to take the children were kidnappers, intent on keeping Mr. Ontiveros, the accused, silent about some incriminating knowledge involving an unknown person, person or group. Or maybe, they also considered, they were hired guns acting on Ontiveros' behalf to likewise give his wife a case of amnesia. Or, maybe still, he so loved his children—a plausible consideration—and was concerned about their safety; which begged the question in danger from whom?

The sniper matter was even more puzzling. The matter of the feds being called off their posts pointed to a supervisor who had gone missing and was still unaccounted for; lying either in an alley dumpster, dead...or on a beach, tanning? Had that supervisor hired the sniper, and if so, why did he shoot the hired guns? The case promised to morph into one of the many great conspiracy theories.

CHAPTER THIRTY-NINE

RICO ARRIVED in Las Cruces two weeks later to a jubilant reception arranged by the girls. The celebration had just ended when Joey said it was time to let him get some rest. But he was feeling fine. Joey scooted everyone outside and disappeared for almost five minutes.

She returned and quietly entered toting the two *used* articles of armor Rico and Jennifer had worn.

She sure doesn't look very happy I'm here. What'd I do? Maybe they told her I wouldn't walk again, or that I'm gonna die, he pondered. *But…I feel as healthy as ever!*

"I guess there was chink in this armor," Joey said, a solemnness in her voice he hadn't heard in a long time. She held Jennifer's armor shirt for him to see.

Is that a chastisement for putting Jennifer in danger's way? "And…mine?" he asked.

She sat on the bed and stayed silent. Her eyes were dilated. She twirled her hair on her finger. Rico figured she wasn't as composed as she would like him to believe.

"Michelle doesn't seem to think so, and…"

"And you?" His heart ached just having to ask for clarification again, since…forever.

"And the girls think you're still that knight I…"

His sullen look interrupted her; she looked deep into the eyes of the man she loved and couldn't lie to.

Here was another miscommunication—Rico didn't know that she didn't know that he had tried to get out of the protection deal before she had even asked, and then again after. By the time she *had* asked him to, he had nearly resorted to groveling to the feds to release him, almost to the point of looking cowardly. To her, he had in the truest, Latino male, egoistical, *machoistic* fashion, ignored her plea.

She *had* to answer him. "I'm afraid…a chink in your armor? Yes."

They sat in silence.

Joey finally rose, holding up the damaged armor.

"They kinda worked," he said.

"Retirement?"

"Yea, retire them and…"

"I mean…you…you…ret…" *Lord…Oh, what's the use*, she figured.

"Have Jennifer call the company for some free replacements. They'll…"

"Jacob, I will n…"

"We did a good thing, Joey…at least for those kids. I don't know what the other stuff was about…but that had nothing to do with us. And…"

"The sniper, what did *that*…have to do with us? Or did you secretly hire out?"

He paused to think. "Why in…no, I didn't. I don't have a clue…but he, or more likely, *she*, was a lousy shot."

"Ooooh! If you weren't so wounded I'd whop you good!"

Even with the thought of a highly proficient sniper on her mind, she couldn't resist the charm of his boyish grin. She lay next to him, arms draped over him. In utter exhaustion, both fell asleep and slept through the day and night without rousing.

God put her in a deep sleep and gave her nice dreams about what her husband would accomplish—eventually. She missed her normal evening devotion time. He missed hearing her voice.

Joey woke up feeling years younger. Peace would prevail from that morning on in the Rico household for many weeks. The husband worked on keeping the wife happy; giving in to whims he knew she was making up to test his resolve.

She asked God during that morning's devotions whether she had left anything unresolved. God showed her a few things. Convicted, she was ready to forgive Rico for the many faults she was beginning to see. And she didn't want a temporary while-in-a-good-mood type of thing.

From Rico's point of view, things were perfect; surely Joey had come to recognize his actions for what they were—righteous. It had to be that. She was so radiant again, at least when he got to see her. She wasn't asking for much any more, apparently busying herself doing things.

Within weeks he secretly rebounded; keeping to himself his perfectly good health and milking every last drop of sympathy from the less discerning girls and Jennifer, who knew better, but was willing to play along.

Joey had her own secrets. She resumed her previous ministry schedule, with the exception of Bible studies at home (which she intended putting her foot down about, soon), and still routed all church matters through her cell phone.

Life was back to normal for this very blended family in Las Cruces, New Mexico, this little piece of heaven on earth.

But with Jacob Rico in the mix...

EPILOGUE

WITHIN WEEKS of being out and about Rico quickly grew bored and his mental gears began to grind. What he had been planning before he was sidetracked by the *minor* incident soon drowned all other thoughts, including the more admirable ones. Remembering that the encryption and decryption device still sat in his safe sent the vestiges of his focus on the family to the lower echelons of priority.

The medication he was given for his injuries conveniently offered relief for his head too. That proved a convenient byproduct of the nasty incident, another excuse to have pills around. He had privately asked the doctors in Albuquerque not to disclose whatever they had discovered in his cerebral cavity.

There he was for two days fighting with himself. Hours of mental relief turned into minutes; thoughts jumped around in his head totally unrelated to what he was trying to attend to. Even the fun he was having with the students he tutored at the alternative high school wasn't doing the trick anymore. *I'll wait one more day*, he decided, figuring he could stave off utter insanity for not much longer than that.

The next day became a pivotal day. Concealing the mental gymnastics from Joey and the others was sapping his energy. Puzzled looks about things he blurted out got old quick. And he needed to complete something, *anything*, to feel of value and still the voices.

"Joey…," he called out, "…today you and the girls are going to that… umm…*Bible* study thing, right?"

Joey peered into his office. By her body language and facial expressions alone—no longer an enigma—she perceived he was hiding extreme stress behind the transparent courteous and yet cynical tone.

Deep inside he was begging for her to "demand" that he stop his ongoing planning "or else."

Instead, Joey remained silent. Not that she thought he had shelved them, she knew him too well. Besides, God was in control. Wasn't He?

"Bueno pues, gordo. I'll pray for you," she murmured.

He cringed slightly. *Prayer…begging … begging to a nonexistent, impotent entity. Well, that's really gonna help a lot, Joey…and I'm not fat.*

Perhaps if Joey would lift the restriction she had placed on the doctors from speaking with him about his death experience, he would change his mind about that *prayer* thing. But, until she did, those doctors were bound to drive Jennifer and her crazy with their incessant calls wanting to follow up and see the walking miracle. One of them had asked his Christian neighbor a million questions and had become a believer.

Joey sure is playing the church thing to the hilt? Rico thought. *She's too bright to even entertain such nonsense for real. It must be for resume fodder or something… maybe a story, an exposé. Yea, that's it. But then again…*

He thought she missed his facial slip…she didn't. She considered making light of the matter to alleviate the pang in her stomach, but deception didn't come easily anymore. Her demeanor and absence of a good bye kiss was clear. She refused eye contact and his beckoning hand gesture as she closed the door behind her.

"Sin miedo, mujer," he breathed, sinking into the recliner. *That went well.* "Yea, Jacob…without fear," he mouthed, mocking himself. He took the device from the safe…his hand trembling.

Why the hell am I doing this! His mind raced as he argued back and forth among his inner selves. Another soul privy to the raging thoughts would definitely be directing him for help, if not calling 911. He finally mustered sufficient calmness to make a *rational* decision. The Man of War in him prevailed.

"Joey! Are you guys on the way out?" Rico yelled.

"That's so subtle, Jacob," she hushed through pursed lips from behind the closed door. "Rosangelica is right behind me," she added more loudly.

"Her too?" he mouthed. *They're all out there. Am I, and Jennifer, the only* rational individuals in this household?

He still didn't know that Jennifer was, by then, attending every night she was off duty. The others would agree, if they could read his mind, that he was the only individual there; everyone else was part of a team—God's team. And of course, *rationality* could be colored by one's perspective.

"Bye, Jacob!" Rosangelica chirped loudly in Spanish through the closed door, which would stay that way. Joey held possessively and firmly to the doorknob.

"Bye!" he said wryly. *Why didn't she come in?*

He became more annoyed.

"Why not joi ... ouch!" Rosangelica exclaimed, reacting to Joey's pinch. "Para que era eso, Mom?" Rosangelica switched to Spanish as the two walked down the stairs and out the front door.

Their arguing voices trailed away until there was a dead, eerie silence. Rico was at first glad. But, after several minutes, the silence thundered in his ears. The aloneness made him shiver. Dejavu for the millionth time. A tissue dripped with sweat as he wiped his forehead. His eyes glazed over, staring at a quivering hand holding the tissue. It had to belong to someone else, it didn't feel like his hand. An uncontrollable fit of nerves and waking flashbacks rolled over him.

He couldn't think. The gun in the safe became an option for ending the turmoil. A split second of sane thought brought an image to mind; a trustworthy person that had helped him through the two previous times he had almost lost it completely. That was besides some fast acting medication that he hadn't needed since that forgettable phase.

"Jennifer," Rico called over the two-way radio feature on the cell phone.

Of course he was calling *her* because she was on duty on roving vehicle patrol; Sarge was posted at a safe house. At least that was his newest self-deceptive excuse. He would have called her for help if she was in China. He knew himself well enough that maybe, just maybe, his nerves would get the better of him permanently. Even now, married to a saint, he could only get himself to trust Jennifer to see and forget the bizarre battle that might ensue, like before. That trust should have been Joey's domain by now. If she were to find out, he might have another kind of crisis to deal with.

"Yes," she said moments later.

He was a little calmer now. "I have an assignment."

"Wait one, sweetheart, gotta say bye to my friend," she said without concern about making personal cell phone calls on duty.

Joey would describe her as having no guile—Rico as fanatically truthful. He had given her permission anyway, remembering the monotony of the work.

"Say hi for me," he said, solemnly.

The absence of a ribbing comment gave her a hint that something was up.

"He says hi back," she announced. "OK! What's up boss, another deranged ex-partner on the prowl?"

"No, not tonight...at least not so far," he mumbled.

Rico flipped the chunky, dorky-looking, homemade device with his fingers. It looked like one of those memory sticks, but on steroids and round, like a goliath beetle. He mused about what to say, wanting to give Jennifer instructions without raising red flags. The wild eyes he had seen in the mirror moments before were gone.

"Then what's up? See, I tell you, can't be without me!"

That *was* true. "I'll need you to post yourself in front of our office," Rico said flatly. "Across the street, back up quietly into the vacant house's driveway, low visibility."

"Confirm, full ballistic attire," he instructed, almost pleading. "Are you done yet?"

It just so happened that this was the first time she had forgotten to wear it. His fatherly insistence offered another hint. Red flags waved in Jennifer's head.

Rico thought she missed the crack in his voice; no doubt her thoughts were preoccupied with a recent romance. He continually forgot whom he had hired and why; she was a world class pro, rust or no rust.

"Other parameters, Rico?" she retorted, slipping into her command voice.

So much for missing it, she always called him by his last name when she got uptight, serious or otherwise meant business. The "love," "sweetheart," "Sarge" and other pet names were for teasing and business as usual.

"No, just standard video coverage in rear. Persons of interest would include government types, possibly hired guns, spooks, etcetera. That's all."

Even though he felt secure with his back and mind covered, he gave it more thought and disliked more and more the fact that he was putting her in physical danger, *again*. He made an effort at thinking rationally about the decision to have her so close…just for his comfort.

Dang, what a selfish son of a…! he admonished himself. After a few minutes of grilling and chastising himself some more, he called her up again.

"Jenny."

"Go," she said, short of breath. She was a tangle of arms struggling to put on the armor. She stood behind a bush wearing only the shiny-white, striped, liquid-cooled compression undershirt for the minute it took to slip on the "BS," as she called it. It was an accident waiting to happen with cars passing by and a healthy silhouette more exposed than she knew. Not that she was taking her time on purpose. Her nasty shoulder wound was really tender and taking its sweet time healing, at least compared to Rico's wounds, which she asked God about and had no answer yet; was she lacking faith?

"New instructions…go back on roving…or whatever young lady. Dial your friend up again and enjoy," he said.

Her stomach tensed. *Not again, Jacob!* The twinge of tremble in his voice wouldn't have been perceptible to anyone else, even Joey.

To Jennifer it was engrained from the one time during the last combat engagement together, in that same voice he had said, "Bye, Jenny, go back with the team, I'm sorry…" seconds before he plowed forward against an onslaught of enemy fire. She had frozen in place—and still felt tinges of guilt—before rushing behind him and knocking him to the ground just as incoming friendly air cover strafed the ground all around him. Rico cursed himself to no end when he had to tend to shrapnel she caught in the belly.

As she rubbed the skin just right of her belly button, she remembered Joey saying she had asked Rico about retiring, because she sensed something big coming. Bigger than what they endured weeks before even? She had wondered at the time. But right now she didn't feel a sense of foreboding, so she ignored the warning. Instead, she almost blurted over the radio that maybe a company trip to the Bahamas was due, forgetting they were hardly a paradise these days.

"Negative, I'm right where I want to be … Jacob," she insisted, in a tone closer to what one would use to comfort a scared child.

His nerves settled down. Never mind that she was obviously blowing smoke. It was both comforting and discomforting all at the same time—and just plain eerie to him—how she could get into his mind.

He didn't answer for almost a minute.

"Thanks buddy!" he finally whispered.

That brought half a smile to Jennifer's face. She knew she had called it right…as usual, but…

Minutes later she was on alert, wearing the gear *father* Jacob insisted on.

"Active," she whispered back into her radio.

She monitored things via Internet surveillance software. The laptop screen next to her showed the rotating views transmitted by the various cameras, motion sensors showed no activity outside either. All was clear, so far.

Rico gave her a thumbs-up through the window.

Ten tense minutes later he finally logged on. The device still sat on the desk, already thirty plus minutes since Joey had left and twenty-five minutes that Jennifer had arrived. He made a final decision to again enter the slippery slope of the cyber space realm; really deep this time. He did not like the absence of dimensions or intuition it presented—identity only an illusion that came and went with whims without recourse to the deceived.

Rico also knew good and well that in that realm every activity was subject to exposure to the real world at will…and often with destructive consequences. He was making himself a sitting duck to government types bent on control. Not to mention other forces equally dangerous to liberty…and life.

He got online after disconnecting the camera and had until the device was inserted and engaged to bail out. As he half-heartedly chatted with others online, the hint came rather bluntly.

"Now," read a line totally out of context.

Gingerly handling the device and banishing from his mind the last ounce of doubt, he inserted it into one of the four front-mounted USB ports.

"Watch this be a sick joke at my expense!" he whined to himself.

If Joey had been there, or Jennifer, they would've chimed in, *Hush up! Stop your whining*! He followed their imagined command. The five LED's haphazardly placed inside the clear plastic device did a little blinking dance.

His screen went black. "Crap!" he hollered. "I can't believe it!" He was about to let out a stream of choice phrases, in English and Spanish, when text appeared on the screen with a beep.

"This is White Dog," was all it said.

"This is Jacob Rico," he typed in response.

"Use a moniker, just in case you've got something serious on your mind and through some breech of protocol we get pin-pointed. Odds are real slim for that. Not even the NSA can get through my encryption and into our space. You'd have to be Prime Terrorist Number One for them to tap your PC and grab the key from the little device I gave you. For that they'd be spending thousands and thousands a day to monitor you; and you're squeaky clean."

That still wasn't reassuring to Rico. *Why'd he have say NSA? At least nothing comes up.*

"Where is that space?" Rico inquired, thinking he had a bragging loony.

"Everywhere…and nowhere…at the same time. Freaky huh?"

The twenty-eight year-old prodigy had been tossed out of three Ivy League universities because of supposed delusional problems. Years before, he had managed to construct a working quantum computer. When the government heard the rumors they attempted to confiscate it for reasons of national security. Fearing for his life he managed to destroy it and the technical papers.

A well concocted ruse with a phony device led the authorities to publicly declare the whole matter a hoax. It got him off the hook, but the cost was enormous. The ridicule was immediate and drove him into the shadows of laboratories, moving about like a nomad, until that also was taken away.

This was something Rico wouldn't discover for a while. Just then he wasn't exactly in the mood for enlightenment about quantum matters—not that he would understand one iota. Rico pecked away at the keys with two proficient fingers.

"About that girl. She said she was with you voluntarily. I gotta tell you, a sweet person like that can be overwhelmed by a...let's say, 'different' person like *you* sound to me. If I find out you're using her like a toy...I must warn you...I'll find you...and...snuff you out."

He was about to remove the less than probable threat, but his finger tapped the enter key accidentally. *Oops!* he thought. *How the heck would I find him anyway?*

"You just gave me motive. I'll have our conversation and that threat recorded for timed delay, which I'll reset every day, in case I go missing. My question...is there any other reason that would prompt you to do such a nasty thing to me?"

"Yes."

"What?"

"Demonstrate that you are a danger to my family and friends." This he meant.

"Any others? You didn't mention being a danger to you."

"Threat to me...alone...no."

"Why?" typed the puzzled stranger.

"Simple ... I'm irrelevant."

After what seemed a long time he read, "And *you* call *me* different! Pleeeease! Expect hard contact soon. P.S. I took the liberty of installing a stealth spy program on your PC to keep tabs on your contact with any government agency or another cyber-hack besides me. That's why we chatted so long. We won't next time.

"BYE! P.S.S. This green-eyed girl says you're quite handsome, for an old guy, and not irrelevant to *her*."

That's a positive—something to build on maybe, but, for what? Old?

The screen went blank. The whole exchange had taken place in a span of less than four minutes. Rico felt totally drained even though the last "P.S.S." had raised his spirits a little. He figured it was an equitable trade, him threatening to kill the potentially nice guy and the guy monitoring him.

Fair is fair! he thought. *Of course he has the upper hand.* Rico wondered if the person he had just communicated with was the rather hulky fellow who had passed him the device in Roswell. *Why can't geeks look like geeks? Life used to be so simple.*

Rico strolled over to the front office as he mulled things over and sat on the futon sofa. He would wait and see if the communiqué had been intercepted—connecting him to who could just as well have been an international terrorist. And then maybe he could be an over zealous government type on a cyber-drag-net trying to make a name for himself by just now alerting a supervisor and strike team.

It never occurred to him that the "Minority Report" scenario was as improbable as improbable can be; he hadn't discussed anything relevant. Besides that, his mind wasn't contemplating a homicide—and what he *was* contemplating wasn't clear even to him. As yet it was just a hazy delusion he would still try to expel from a foggy mind.

Nevertheless, ideas of how long he would languish in jail even with insufficient evidence danced around his head. That would have been the best scenario as far as he was concerned. Others that crossed his increasingly paranoid mind were slightly more graphic. He figured with the multitude of permits he had been requesting from the security section, he had probably already tripped numerous intelligence surveillance flags. A misunderstanding could cascade into a cascade of other misunderstandings…and so forth. The Homeland Security Act, rooted in the former Patriot Act, had such a circular nature to it. He was playing with fire, and had nary a fire extinguisher handy; a reasonable cover story didn't seem feasible.

Maybe if he felt a warning touch from the long arm of the law, Jacob Rico would stop the tsunami he threatened to cause.

Then again…there was destiny.

THE PRESIDENT rubbed his forehead, reaching up under the helmet. Perspiration saturated his armpits. A tap on the clear bullet-proof plastic partition made him look up. Joey was signaling him to pray. He figured that was a real good idea, remembering that God never promised to check with him or give an explanation about circumstances in his life.

Meanwhile, Rico tried managing his own tension as he monitored the arriving government strike team. A backup, concealed, stationary camera gave him enough intel on when to activate the electric net. The flying camera had been shot down. The deployed government force was lined up, ready to blow the front roll-up door to smithereens with a rocket.

With a push of the remote button the huge one hundred foot net Rico had concealed in the ground flew up in the air as the rocket-assisted, spring loaded launcher released. The net flew almost fifty feet up in the air, sweeping some seventy five feet from left to right, landing atop most of the G-men and two of the three vehicles they were on. The third vehicle only had its hood under the net. An electrical charge flowed through the mostly metallic net and overloaded the circuits on one of the vehicles. The other vehicles couldn't move because of the entangling net. The majority of troops in the vehicles and on foot were writhing.

The delay tactic worked perfectly. Rico sat in his Smart Truck with Joey and their special *protectee*. It was time to make a run for it. He raised the small rear entry door, pushed through the strategically placed boulders and recently planted tree in front of the opening, and calmly drove off.

After a few minutes they arrived at Sarge's location.

"Joey, change of plans for you...this is where you get off this wild ride."

"Changed to what?"

"Get home...and enjoy your family and your life."

"Yea…while you get life," she said. Her voice sounded flat. Maybe the voice masking device made it sound like that. But it worked well in continuing the ruse to conceal her gender.

And maybe POTUS missed the slip that even she didn't realize had occurred.

Where'd that *come from*, Rico wondered. Glare on his clear face shield helped conceal from the President the cringing face he made. Had Joey figured out he never intended to *rescue* the President? And if she did, was she trying to clue him in?

"The deal was that if it got dangerous we would abort. Right now I can't exactly abort with you here, can I? Those folks back there aim to get their man back. Once I'm sure they're for real, they can have him…and me…dead or alive."

"Leave that choice to me all right!"

That sounded a little too emotional for Jacob's liking. It seemed to him that she was done with the acting.

"You can choose, but not me! You brought me on this mission for a reason!"

That could go either way in the President's analysis, Rico was thinking. But he had to silence her quickly.

"You know very well why not! Besides I'm already a dead man. The doc gave me two to three," Rico said as flatly as he could muster. He could picture Joey's hurt. Only later would he realize that she already knew. The only thing she didn't know was how long he had.

From under her dark face-shield she looked at him with a look of anger and betrayal. "Years, right?" It wasn't that it mattered any more, but she did want to find out for how long she had been made a fool of.

"Yea. But that was four years ago."

"With today's technology there's nothing they can't do, remember…?" Never mind spiritual things just then.

Rico was trying desperately to raise the Sarge on the radio and end the dialogue that he knew was giving his *guest* way too much information.

"Never mind that. Sure, with a matching donor and two mil or so."

"But…the bank!"

"It's not my money! Remember, it's the government's money…once this man here tells me how to return it to the coffers."

The President cocked his ears.

Meanwhile, Rico blabbed on, "And besides...finding a matching donor is really tricky. I'm really unique you know."

"You are one arrogant son of a..." the President interjected.

He didn't like Rico's icy stare and stopped mid-sentence—a rarity of self control for the too often brash politician. He felt the subtle conviction of the Holy Spirit, and decided he needed to get this world revered character trait in line with Biblical teaching.

"Drop the subject mister and follow orders. Friends or not...I'm in charge!" he said, again facing Joey. "Remember to follow the checklist to the tee, tell Sarge get those guys paid for the month...maybe a little bonus for medical coverage for their families...and some beer, lots of beer! Get a hold of my newly acquired lawyer and tell him I'm indisposed. He will be transferring the company over to Sarge if my wife agrees. If he goes to jail, an option is available for Jennifer or Tom to take over."

Rico was again in full control of his faculties and spoke with little emotion. That annoyed Joey even more.

"I hope this is all in writing somewhere!" she muttered, seething through clenched teeth.

The tone was not discernable to the president, but resonated unequivocally in *his* ears.

"You know me!"

"Yea." She got her notebook and scribbled.

"Tell my wife she can keep the corporation going or close it out. Otherwise the lawyer will liquidate and donate the cash to a certain charity. I'd hate to leave those kids hanging. I don't know whether I was making a difference" His voice faded away as they approached Sarge's location. "But I have a feeling she really has made a dent with a lot of the folks we worked with. Please write that down and let her know that's how I felt."

"Sounds like a eulogy," she mumbled

Jacob shrugged. "Could be."

For two minutes of crazy driving, no one spoke again.

"Mr. President, don't try jumping out. There he is! Wait right there, Sarge. Our new teammate I told you about, Joey, will take the Hummer now. He'll have to take cover in the brush because they're almost here."

Rico told Sarge over the radio to remain still and cover the front. In reality he didn't want Sarge to recognize Joey's gait. Sarge had been prepped to believe that a former partner of Rico's had been called in for this very dangerous mission. Even though he had acted as if he accepted being upended as the right hand man, Rico wasn't sure. When the man was described to Sarge, and told that his name was also Joey, Rico nor Joey knew whether he just didn't care, because he never asked to be introduced.

He stopped short of where the Sarge was waiting. Jacob stopped the truck about 50 feet away. Jacob hurriedly asked Joey, "Do you think they have switched satellite tracking to infra-red yet?"

"Probably using visible imaging for another fifteen before they do," Joey said, after gathering her bearing.

The grim realization that they were, really, really in over their heads lead her to reminisce; to think of all that she was about to leave behind—like the girls…and her newly discovered twin sister. She barely heard Rico give the next command as she weighed the matter and the matter weighed on her even more. Rico was a big boy and had gotten into this mess himself. She determined, for now, that she would be returning to her kids in one piece, not a body bag—or perhaps disappeared, never to be heard from again.

"Good, then we have a chance. On my mark, you hurry, get to cover under that brush, and don't move until you think they moved the tracking sector."

As Rico activated the countermeasure, the entire vehicle was engulfed in thick smoke and wind blew some to the bush Joey was headed for.

"Go!" was his final word to send his wife on her own—presumably to safety.

"Hey Sarge, you're driving, Rico directed as he dove through the partition after coming to an abrupt stop in front of the waiting man. Smoke engulfed him also, and he felt his way into the driver's seat.

Rico situated himself in the seat, retrieved a throw away phone from the many in a bag, and tossed it to the president. "Please contact who you have to and find out who's trying to meet so *amiably* with us."

The President quickly flipped through his day planner, after a nerve-racked, frenzied search for it, and quickly dialed a number.

"Hello, John?"

Mister…President?" answered the former Vice-president's secretary; silence followed. "Is this some kind of sick joke?"

"Not at all. Listen, I need the NSA Director, and make it quick. My secretary is nowhere to be found right now! Patch me through!"

Rico called his hacker and comm guy on the other line. "I have a little problem. I'm gonna transmit a picture any time now that's probably gonna be blurry. Fix it, get a plate number, and run it through. Maybe I can get a face or something. Stay ready because it'll happen quickly." Rico eyed the President, leaning to hear through the helmet's insulation.

"Yes, sir," the secretary said to the President. A second later the line rang and was picked up.

"Yes, Robert, this is the President."

"Mr. President, are you all right?" the voice asked on the other end, this time instead of reserved elation the other person had expressed at hearing his voice, a tinge of shock and horror bled over the line.

The President paused in thought. "Yes, Robert, I need to know immediately if you have a strike team engaging a target somewhere in West Virginia.

Well, sir I need to call the command center real quick, what is your exact location so I can send over protection immediately."

"We are…" before thinking, Rico tapped the President's arm and shook his head. "I can't exactly tell you that, now do it…I believe I'll hold."

Rico took the hint when POTUS stared at his fingers indicating he was treading a fine line. The glare gave him the impression he may get whacked if he didn't remove them; so he did.

The NSA Director had already signaled the pursuing force.

A moment later, came "No, Mister President, we are on high alert, but no units are deployed." Robert began asking questions. The sharp-minded president picked up on the stalling tactic and cut him off.

"OK, Robert, keep it that way until I call back."

The President looked at Rico and shook his head. He looked sad at having been betrayed.

The NSA Director knew his small tactical team was going to need more firepower…airpower. But aircraft attracted too much attention. Then again, the secret would be out any second if he didn't exterminate it.

"Sarge, get us to DC, please…and hurry," Rico said.

"Yes, boss anything you say," Sarge said. "Who's the client?"

"Someone muy importante."

"That tells me a lot."

"It's for your own good, young man."

"Behind us, boss. Is that one of the vehicles you were talking about?"

"Yes. Slow down for one split second so I can get the plates."

"I don't think that'll be a problem!"

The vehicle only managed to kiss the back bumper before Sarge floored the accelerator pedal.

"I take it they don't want to be friends? Rico, I see gun barrels sticking out!"

"Computer, prepare electronics disrupter, target vehicle directly behind," Rico ordered, nervously.

If this wasn't provocation, what was?

"Target acquired," the computer responded.

"Fire!"

It was obvious that the trailing vehicle suffered no ill effects; it drew even closer with the small device visibly imbedded in the grill emitting electronic pulses as designed.

"White Dog, who are these people…friend or foe?"

Rico was pitting one lone, and unwitting, hacker against a small army of some of the world's best. He needed to disconnect quickly to minimize the government tracking the signal to the poor guy. Thoughts of the man's girlfriend wailing entered his mind. She would never forgive Rico for sure if he got hurt.

"I'm working on it…what's that pinging noise?"

"Hail."

"Must be pretty big."

"Yep! I'm waiting!"

"The plates have mud on them, but my guess is they're government plates, my hunch is either ISS or NSA. Hey check it out, I got a pretty picture of some ugly mugs!"

"Do you recognize any of these people?" Rico handed prints from the Wi-Fi equipped printer to the President. He studied the digitally enhanced, cleaned up prints that White Dog had run through his special software.

"No." *That was fast! Who's working with this guy?*

"Hey, boss!" Sarge said. "It's about time you tell me who our client is."

The divider window started going down.

"Not right now, Sarge. Focus on driving for heaven's sake!"

Rico whispered to the President. "Promise me you will grant him amnesty if he testifies against me, Mr. President. He doesn't know anything … about anything." Rico remembered the plausible cover that had presented itself with the earlier surprise attack by as yet unknown persons and probable agencies. But he thought the President had figured things out any way. "If he stops this vehicle, I think we're all dead men."

The President nodded in earnest, his wide eyes offering the only hint he really wasn't as in control as he wanted to be in.

"On my honor, I will grant him amnesty."

Before Jacob opened the partition, bigger caliber bullets started banging the back of the vehicle, direct hits penetrated through the outer armor.

"Now, Sarge, if you will get these people off our butts, you can…"

"Hang on!" Sarge yelled. The vehicle swerved erratically.

"I can't believe it! Rico, one whacko on the turret is trying to aim a…a, looks like an old Soviet RPG of all things! This is bizarre! Hold on to your britches, here it…"